Everybody Loves Alexis Hall!

"Hall is a dizzyingly talented writer, one likely to spur envy in anyone who's ever picked up a pen."

—*Entertainment Weekly*

"Alexis Hall is the undisputed master of romantic comedy."
—Jenny Holiday, *USA Today* bestselling author

"Everyone needs to read this. Brilliance on every single page. Hilarious, witty, tender, and stunning. I love this book."
—Christina Lauren, *New York Times* bestselling author, on *Boyfriend Material*

"Every once in a while you read a book that you want to SCREAM FROM ROOFTOPS about. I'm screaming, people!"
—Sonali Dev, *USA Today* best author, on *rial*

Also by Alexis Hall

ARDEN ST. IVES SERIES

Rosaline Palmer Takes the Cake

Alexis Hall

FOREVER
New York Boston

Copyright © 2021 by Alexis Hall

Cover design and illustrations throughout by Lila Selle. Cover copyright © 2021 by Hachette Book Group, Inc.

Forever
Hachette Book Group
1290 Avenue of the Americas, New York, NY 10104
read-forever.com
twitter.com/readforeverpub

First Edition: First trade paperback edition May 2021

Forever is an imprint of Grand Central Publishing. The Forever name and logo are trademarks of Hachette Book Group, Inc.

The publisher is not responsible for websites (or their content) that are not owned by the publisher.

The Hachette Speakers Bureau provides a wide range of authors for speaking events. To find out more, go to www.hachettespeakersbureau.com or call (866) 376-6591.

Library of Congress Cataloging-in-Publication Data
Names: Hall, Alexis J., author.
Title: Rosaline Palmer takes the cake / Alexis Hall.
Description: First trade paperback edition. | New York, NY : Forever, 2021.
Identifiers: LCCN 2020054048 | ISBN 9781538703328 (trade paperback) | ISBN 9781538703304 (ebook)
Classification: LCC PR6108.A453 R67 2021 | DDC 823/.92--dc23
LC record available at https://lccn.loc.gov/2020054048

ISBNs: trade paperback (978-1-5387-0332-8); ebook (978-1-5387-0330-4)

Printed in the United States of America

LSC-C

Printing 1, 2021

Acknowledgments

All my gratitude to far too many people. Including but not limited to: my wonderful US editor, Amy Pierpont whose insight and wisdom remain surpassed only by her patience; her fabulous assistant, Sam Brody, who is responsible for most of the baking puns and several title suggestions far better than anything I could come up with; and to my UK editor, Anna Boatman; in British humour solidarity and for actually publishing my book in a country I live in. Also Jodi Rosoff, who I'm technically thanking pre-emptively but I'm sure will have earned this acknowledgment a thousand times over in the months between now and publication. And the amazing teams at Forever and Piatkus for everything they've done to make this book be, well, a book.

Finally, thanks to my brilliant agent, Courtney Miller-Callihan, for literally everything. Seriously. Literally everything.

Author's Note

This story includes a (non-graphic) scene of attempted sexual assault. For further content warnings, please see the author's website.

Week One

Chocolate

Friday

"MOST OF THE bakers have opted for a traditional sponge mix, consisting of, like, eggs and flour and shit," narrated Lauren helpfully or—from a different and more correct perspective—unhelpfully. "Single MILF Rosaline, however…"

Rosaline looked up from her food processor, whose capacity for raw beetroot she had wildly overestimated. "The BBC are not going to describe me as a single MILF."

"Maybe not, but"—and here Lauren fluttered her eyelashes outrageously—"it's how I think of you."

"And what," asked Rosaline, laughing, "does your wife have to say about that?"

"Allison thinks you're a MILF too."

"You know it's still objectification if you're a lesbian."

"Actually, I think you'll find it's empowering."

"No, it isn't." Rosaline grabbed a wooden spoon and tried to scrape the worst of the purple gunk out of her coarse grater attachment. "And besides, I bet Allison's never used the word 'MILF' in her life."

"Well, nobody's perfect." Scooting her stool closer to the bench, Lauren dipped her finger into the molten chocolate that Rosaline had set aside to cool. "Look, why *are* you putting beetroot in this otherwise perfectly good cake?"

"It's a beetroot cake. It wouldn't be a beetroot cake without beetroot in it."

"Most of the bakers"—Lauren went back to her narrator voice—"have chosen to make something a human being might want to eat. Kitchen temptress Rosaline, however, has decided to add beetroot for no fucking reason."

This was just Lauren being Lauren. And normally Rosaline was fine with Lauren being Lauren. But right now, it was the last thing she needed. "It's not for no fucking reason. It's for a very good fucking reason, which is I want to stand out and not get sent home immediately because my cake was too ordinary."

"They don't send people home in week one for being ordinary," said Lauren cheerfully. "Ordinary gets you to at least week four."

Rosaline combined her ingredients in a sufficiently jabby way that she was sure she'd knocked the air out of her egg whites. "I don't want to get to week four. I want to win. And I have to win because otherwise I'm spending the rest of my life working shit minimum wage jobs to support my daughter while my parents shake their heads sadly and occasionally make me beg them for money."

"I...understand where you're coming from." This was about as close to gentle as Lauren could get. "But honestly, going on a reality TV show feels like a bit of a Hail Mary."

"I mean, yes," Rosaline admitted. "But I have actually thought this through. Best-case scenario, I win, pay my parents back with the prize money, and get a slightly better job. Worst-case scenario, I get eliminated, and what have I lost?" She stared into the bowl of brownish-purple cake batter that was supposed to be velvety and was definitely not. "Apart from my time. And my pride. And any sense of privacy. And all hope for the future. And what little remains of my family's respect. Fuck me, you're right. This is a terrible idea."

"It's not terrible. It's..." There was a pause while Lauren, who was a professional word-finder and should have been able to do it more quickly, searched for a word. "Bold. And that's good. It's good to be bold."

"The last bold thing I did was decide I was keeping the baby, and while I'm glad I did, as decisions go it's not exactly been without consequences."

"Ah, yes. I believe that's what they call *life*."

Rosaline glanced at the clock, then at the oven, then at the clock again. "Well, today's consequences are that I had to go directly from taking Amelie to school to an extra shift at work to make up for the time I'm taking off, and I got back late because the bus was late, and now I can't finish my practice cake before we have to go and pick Amelie up again, so I can say goodbye to her before running off to spend a weekend—"

"Gallivanting around a stately home showing off your buns?" asked Lauren.

"You know"—Rosaline made an unmistakable gesture with the nearest utensil—"I'm this close to stabbing you in the eye with a spatula."

"Stabbing me in the eye with a spatula will make it very hard for me to either drive you to the station or spend my free time looking after your daughter."

"Oh, well fished. Of course, your altruism is somewhat marred by the fact Allison is going to be in Glasgow for the week and you blatantly have nothing better to do."

"That," retorted Lauren with great dignity, "is only *partially* true."

"You're right. I'm sorry. You're a wonderful person and I'm very grateful." With a melancholy *schlorp*, Rosaline returned the spatula to the batter. "Slightly concerned that you'll kill my child, but grateful."

"Hey, I've never killed her before."

"But it's a whole weekend." A plaintive tone crept into Rosaline's voice. "I've never been away from Amelie for a whole weekend."

Lauren shrugged. "So you should be glad to have a break from each other. Besides, your mum's taking over on Sunday, so how much damage can I do?"

"Knowing you, quite a lot. Although, honestly, not quite as much as my mum."

"Cordelia will do *fine*." Lauren put a consoling hand on Rosaline's shoulder. "Amelie actually likes her because children are hopeless judges of character. And anyway, terrible parents make incredible grandparents. It's their final way of twisting the knife."

"Thanks. You really know how to make me feel better."

"It's my calling. Now come on, let's go nab the moppet."

Twenty minutes later, Rosaline was standing in an emptying playground, resolutely moppetless. She was briefly clutched by the nebulous certainty that there'd been a terrible disaster—possibly involving sharks, a runaway combine harvester, or the child catcher from *Chitty Chitty Bang Bang*. But then Miss Wooding, Amelie's teacher, appeared in the entryway and made an unmistakable beckoning motion.

That was never good.

Because it could only mean that your child had done something bad or that something bad had been done to your child.

Steeling herself and feeling far too much like she was about to be given detention, Rosaline hurried over.

"Is everything all right?" she asked, hoping to sound maternally concerned, rather than preemptively guilty.

Miss Wooding, who, as far as Rosaline could tell, was made

entirely from marshmallows and pixie dust, gave an insipid smile. "If you wouldn't mind coming with me, I'd just like to have a little word with you about Amelie's behaviour."

Well, at least her daughter wasn't unconscious or on fire. Murmuring her general assent, Rosaline let Miss Wooding lead her into the building, past hip-high coat pegs and colourful finger-painted displays about road safety and recycling.

Amelie's classroom was a pleasant, airy space, decorated with number lines and misspelled poems about summer. Amelie herself was squirming under the watchful eye of a teaching assistant.

"Mrs. Palmer," began Miss Wooding, and Rosaline decided not to correct her, "I've been feeling for a while that we should have a conversation about the kind of language Amelie uses in class."

Oh dear. She and Lauren swore in front of Amelie a lot, but she thought she'd done a pretty good job of explaining that there were some things you could say at home that you couldn't say outside.

"I use good language." Amelie folded her arms, radiating outrage as only a wronged eight-year-old can. "I use 'extemporaneous.' And 'soporific.' And all the other words Auntie Lauren teaches me." She looked momentarily proud. "I'm sesquipedalian."

Miss Wooding glided past this with the ease of a lifelong primary school teacher. "It's true that Amelie has an extensive vocabulary. But she needs to learn that some topics are inappropriate for a classroom."

"Like what?" asked Rosaline warily. There were a lot of ways this could go, most of them wrong.

"Well, in English today we were learning that it can be easier to remember how to spell a word if you know what the different parts of that word mean. So, for example, with the word 'bicycle,' it can help to know that the *bi* part means 'two' and the *cycle* part means 'wheel,' so a bicycle has two wheels."

Okay. Way of going wrong identified.

"Like a binary star," offered Amelie, "because there's two stars. Or a biped which has two legs. Or bifocals which have two...focals. Or bicarbonate of soda which um..."

"Yes"—and here Miss Wooding gave Amelie a look of gentle disappointment—"but you didn't say any of that in class, did you?"

"I *would've*. You told me to be quiet."

Miss Wooding's attention shifted effortlessly back to Rosaline. "The example she gave in class was 'My mummy is bisexual.'"

"Well you *are*," protested Amelie, gazing imploringly at Rosaline.

"She's right," Rosaline agreed. "I am."

Always one to take agreement as encouragement, Amelie launched into the rest of the speech. "And that means she likes men and women which is two—which is what you were saying. But Auntie Lauren says that some people think that you shouldn't say bisexual because that means there's only two types of people and some people think there are more types of people. And other people think that it *is* okay because it means same and different and different can mean lots of types of people. Which still means two again. Which is what you were *saying*."

If Miss Wooding had followed any of this, Rosaline couldn't be sure. Either way, she didn't seem to think it was relevant. "The issue, Mrs. Palmer, is that children shouldn't be talking about sex in class."

"And she wasn't." Rosaline really did not need an argument right now, but long experience had taught her that she was probably about to have one. "She was talking about her family."

Miss Wooding turned the nervous shade of pink that Rosaline found people often turned when her sexuality went from an idea they could support to a reality they had to confront. "I appreciate this is a sensitive topic and one that different people have different beliefs about. Which is why I have to be guided by the policies of our academy trust, and they make it quite clear that learners shouldn't be taught about LGBTQ until year six."

"Oh do they?" asked Rosaline, doing her best to remember that Miss Wooding was probably a very nice person and not just a fuzzy cardigan draped over some regressive social values. "Because Amelie's in year four and she manages to cope with my existence nearly every day."

Having concluded this was going to be one of those long grown-up conversations, Amelie had taken her Panda pencil case out of her bag and was diligently rearranging the contents. "I do," she said. "I'm very good."

Miss Wooding actually wrung her hands. "Yes, but the other children—"

"Are allowed to talk about their families as much as they like."

"Yes, but—"

"Which," Rosaline went on mercilessly, "when you think about it, is the definition of discrimination."

Amelie looked up again. "Discrimination is bad. We learned that in year three."

The d-word made Miss Wooding visibly flinch. "Now Mrs. Palmer—"

"*Ms.* Palmer."

"I'm sure this is a misunderstanding."

"I'm sure it is." Taking advantage of the fact that Miss Wooding had been temporarily pacified by the spectre of the Equality Act, Rosaline tried to strike a balance between defending her identity and catching her train. "I get that you have a weird professional duty to respect the wishes of people who want their kids to stay homophobic for as long as possible. But hopefully you get why that isn't my problem. And if you ever try to make it Amelie's problem again, I will lodge a formal complaint with the governors."

Miss Wooding de-flinched slightly. "As long as she doesn't—"

"No 'as long as she doesn't.' You're not teaching my daughter to be ashamed of me."

There was a long pause. Then Miss Wooding sighed. "Perhaps it's best that we draw a line under this and say no more about it."

In Rosaline's experience this was what victory over institutional prejudice looked like: nobody actually apologising or admitting they'd done anything wrong, but the institution in question generously offering to pretend that nothing had happened. So—win?

"That's probably wise," she said, hoping she'd at least taught Amelie a valuable lesson about standing up for yourself, or compromise, or . . . or . . . something?

"What happened to you?" asked Lauren as they got settled in the car.

Rosaline clicked her seat belt into place and checked over her shoulder to make sure Amelie had done the same. "Don't even."

"I got into trouble," said Amelie, "for saying Mummy is bisexual, which is silly because she *is*. So then Mummy told Miss Wooding that was discrimination and then Miss Wooding got really upset and then we got to come home."

"Fuck me," muttered Lauren. "What a pile of reprehensible bullshit."

Taking way more care than she usually did now there was a child in the vehicle, she eased the car away from the kerb. And, on the one hand, that was good because they wouldn't crash and kill Amelie. On the other hand: train, running late, argh.

" 'Reprehensible' means 'very bad,' " offered Amelie.

"Just to check"—Rosaline twisted round in her seat—"of the words in that sentence, which are you allowed to say in school?"

"Me. What. A. Of. Reprehensible. And pile." Amelie paused a moment. "But not fuck or bullshit because some people think those words are bad. Which is silly because they're only words."

Oh God. This felt like a parenting moment. "Sometimes," said Rosaline slowly, "there are things that seem silly to you that are important to other people. Just like sometimes things that are important to you seem silly to other people. And that's why it's important to think about what you're saying and doing."

Amelie digested this. "Like the way Miss Wooding thinks it's silly to have a bisexual mummy?"

Lauren gave an unhelpful snort of laughter.

"A bit." As so often happened, what had begun as an opportunity to pass on positive values and hard-earned wisdom to her daughter had sharply derailed into not having a fucking clue what she was talking about. "But we've agreed to pay more attention to each other's feelings in future."

There was exactly enough silence to lull Rosaline into a false sense of security.

"Auntie Lauren?" piped up Amelie. "Why did you stop going out with Mummy? Did you think it was silly she's bisexual?"

"No." Lauren kept her eyes firmly on the road. "I'm not the sort of lesbian who thinks bisexuals are letting the side down. I'm more of a vagina half-full kind of homosexual."

"Oh." The advantage of having a sesquipedalian eight-year-old was that Amelie didn't like to admit that she hadn't understood things she probably shouldn't. "So what happened?"

"She dumped me. Because I'd been seeing another girl without telling her."

"Oh," said Amelie again. She seemed to be giving this serious consideration, and Rosaline tried to develop a sudden interest in passing licence plates. "Did you like the other girl better?"

"Not for long, but by then the damage was done. And she

wasn't even a natural redhead." She shot a nostalgic look at Rosaline. "What might have been, eh?"

Might have been wasn't something Rosaline liked thinking about too often. *Might have been* too easily turned into *should have been*. After all, if she'd stayed with Lauren she wouldn't have rebounded with Tom, wouldn't have decided it was probably fine to skip the condom one "just this once" too many, and would have lived the life she'd always assumed she was meant to. But then she wouldn't have had Amelie and that was unthinkable in a whole different way.

"So"—Amelie fiddled with her seat belt in precisely the way Rosaline kept telling her not to—"would you have been my other mummy now, if Mummy hadn't left you?"

"Not *exactly*." Lauren really needed to learn when to bail on a conversation. Especially with Amelie.

"If I'd never left Auntie Lauren," Rosaline interrupted, "you'd never have been born."

Once again, Rosaline could practically hear the cogs whirring in her daughter's head. Every parent, she suspected, thought their kid was clever, but she liked to think that Amelie actually was, at least a bit. "Thank you for making Mummy dump you, Auntie Lauren."

There was a little pause, and, glancing over, Rosaline was slightly surprised to realise that Lauren genuinely didn't have a reply. Sincerity had never been her forte.

"Do you have homework for the weekend?" Rosaline asked, turning to look at her daughter.

Amelie shook her head.

"Remember, I know you were doing spelling today. And that you have spelling every week. So, I'm going to ask you again: Do you have any homework for the weekend, and is it spelling?"

Amelie nodded.

"Then learn your words when you get home, before you do

anything else. And Auntie Lauren will test you tomorrow, won't you, Auntie Lauren?"

"I will," Lauren agreed, "although my spelling is *terrible*."

"You write for a living, Loz. How bad can it be?"

Lauren raised an eyebrow. "You see, they've got these fancy new machines now that *check* your spelling *for* you. Also I'm a bit offended that you think the most important skill in my job is *spelling words right*."

They pulled into the station car park and Rosaline concluded that she could still make her train as long as she was very brusque in leaving her only child and only friend and as long as Great Western Railway was staying true to form and running at least six minutes late.

"Well." Lauren turned off the engine. "This is it. Time to go be moderately famous."

Rosaline dragged her bag out of the footwell. "I don't want to be famous. I just want…enough money to pay for some things and enough people to think I'm good at baking that I might be able to get a slightly better job."

"Truly. Yours is a hubris of Homeric proportions."

"*I* think you're good at baking, Mummy," said Amelie. "What's hubris?"

"It's when you think you're so brilliant," explained Lauren, "that you fuck up horrendously and then the gods punish you."

"I'm sorry." Rosaline scrambled out of the car, feeling like a terrible person. "I love you both, and you're being really encouraging and lovely and stuff, but I've got to run. You"—she pointed at Lauren—"don't start teaching my daughter Catullus. And you"—she glanced at Amelie—"I'm going to miss you, but be good for Grandma Cordelia and don't take advantage of Auntie Lauren because I know what you're like when she's babysitting."

"You shouldn't call it babysitting," Amelie protested, "because

I'm not a baby. I'm a *child*. Then I'll be a *tween*. Then a *teen*. Then a *grown-up*. Then I'll be *old*. And then I'll be *dead*."

Lauren laughed. "Hardly seems worth the effort, does it?"

It was not an auspicious note on which to start Lauren's custody of an impressionable young mind. But there wasn't time to address it now. Flinging her bag over her shoulder, and wishing she'd been able to finish that last fucking practice cake, Rosaline plunged into the rush-hour crowds.

The train was not, as it turned out, six minutes late. It wasn't even four minutes late, which meant Rosaline had exactly enough time to watch it pulling out of the station without her. Rationally, she knew that Miss Wooding hadn't intentionally timed her casual biphobia to have the largest and most negative impact possible on Rosaline's life, but fuck if it didn't feel that way. Having trudged all the way back over the footbridge to the information desk, she then spent an unhelpfully long time extracting from a bored station employee the precise combination of trains, short walks, and replacement bus services that would allegedly get her to Patchley House where the show was being filmed.

The first leg—by train to the middle of nowhere—was at least relatively short. The second—by juddering coach to a subtly different middle of nowhere—took rather longer. Then came the third—and theoretically final—stage of the journey, which was on one of those incredibly slow trains that should probably have been retired in the 1970s and stopped at every tiny station in every tiny village between Upper Whereinthehell and Who-Cares-on-the-Wold. Rosaline's original plan had been to use the journey to relax and centre herself or ground herself or do whatever you were supposed to do to get into the right headspace to come across well on reality TV. Instead of, say, the headspace of a stressed-out single mum whose parents—to whom she owed a nontrivial sum of money—would not have been at all surprised to learn she'd failed to get on a train properly.

Then the train stopped.

And didn't start again for forty fucking minutes.

"Uh"—the antiquated speaker system crackled into life—"hello. This is your driver speaking. And this is an announcement for all passengers on the eighteen twenty-three service from Mopley-on-Pond to Tapworth. Owing to a fault, this train will now terminate at Fondle Backwater."

That did not bode well. Bodewise, things were honestly looking pretty rough. And they looked, if anything, rougher, as the train heaved itself alongside the mid-length slab of concrete that passed for Fondle Backwater station. Not sure what else to do, Rosaline grabbed her bag and disembarked. There was only one other passenger disembarking with her. A man, who—in skinny chinos and a blue shirt casually rolled up at the elbows—looked worryingly like he might have had actual style. He also definitely didn't belong here. But, unlike Rosaline, he seemed to be okay with that, surveying the surroundings with an air of composure rather than confusion-trending-towards-panic.

What he could possibly be surveying Rosaline wasn't certain, because the view consisted of sky, fields, and eight sheep, one of whom was regarding her with an expression she chose to read as pity.

"So I'm guessing," remarked the stranger, who'd walked over while Rosaline was busy being judged by livestock, "that Fondle Backwater wasn't your intended destination?"

Now that he was closer, Rosaline was having to contend with the fact that, as well as stylish, he was also disconcertingly good-looking. In that tall, cheekbony slightly haughty English way that would get you the male lead in a BBC costume drama about a rakish aristocrat who has a tumultuous affair with a coal miner's daughter.

And appears shirtless on a horse at least once a season.

Typical. The first time an attractive person of any gender had spoken to her in months and she felt very much like someone who'd spent their day failing to finish a cake, fighting with a primary school teacher, and being dragged all over the southeast by a barely functional railway company. *Quick, Rosaline, be charming.* "What do you mean? I woke up this morning and I thought, *You know what I want? An evening at a train station with a mildly suggestive name.*"

"Ah, then you should have gone to Much-Tupping-in-the-Weir." He offered an easy smile, brackets forming at the corners of his generous mouth. "It's even milder."

"I hear Lower Bumgrope is nice this time of year."

"Which is ironic, because Upper Bumgrope is an absolute dump."

Rosaline laughed, partly amused, but partly just relieved. Because, in retrospect, bumgrope had been a risky gambit, especially as the second thing you said to someone.

"But seriously," he went on, "as much as I'd love to stay here, exchanging rural innuendos with a delightful stranger, I need to be in Tapworth"—he paused to check an imaginary watch—"about an hour ago."

There was, as far as Rosaline was concerned, only one reason to go to Tapworth. Well, unless you lived there, but then you probably wouldn't get lost a couple of miles down the road. Which meant that she was fraternising with the competition. The well-spoken, well-dressed, well . . . well competition. "What a coincidence. I also need to be in Tapworth an hour ago."

"Ah. Contestant or crew?"

"If I was crew," she asked, "wouldn't I know what I was doing?"

"You could be new." Another smile. This one with the faintest edge of wickedness. "Or horrible at your job."

"You got me. I'm a key grip, but I don't know how to grip anything."

He twitched an eyebrow at her. "That must cause a variety of problems."

Oh dear. That hadn't quite come out the way she'd intended. And perhaps it was Lauren's influence, or not having to set an example for an eight-year-old, but Rosaline decided to double down. "Yes," she said sadly, "it makes it very hard to give hand jobs."

There was a moment of silence. She was worried it was a shocked silence.

Then he laughed. "I see we've progressed from innuendo to outuendo. But in any case, it's nice to meet you. I'm Alain. Alain Pope."

He offered her his hand, which Rosaline took with all the suavity of a woman who'd just been talking about wanking. "Rosaline, um, Palmer?"

"Well, Rosaline-um-Palmer"—his very, frankly *very*, blue eyes gleamed at her through the twilight—"whatever are we going to do?"

"About my...Look, I'm not really a key grip with subpar job skills."

"No, I'd taken that as read. I meant, what are we going to do about the fact that we're trapped at an unfamiliar station when we need to be at a stately home somewhere else."

Oh. That. "When is the next train?"

Alain consulted his phone. "Tomorrow morning." He kept consulting. "And there doesn't appear to be a taxi service, any hotels other than the one we're trying to get to, and the nearest bus is two villages away, goes in the wrong direction, and stopped running an hour ago."

Oh God. They were fucked. "Hot-air balloon?"

"Didn't bring mine with me. You?"

"No, but I do have this"—she dug around in the front of her bag—"tin of travel mints I don't remember buying?"

"Ah, then we're saved. We can use these to . . . to . . ."

"Fashion a makeshift boat and sail up the river? Barter for transportation with a passing circus. Construct a distress flare with the aid of a bottle of Diet Coke."

"Do you *have* a bottle of Diet Coke?" he asked.

"Damn. I left it in the hot-air balloon."

"Don't worry." He tucked his phone away. "Worst comes to absolute worst, I'm sure the production company can send someone for us. Of course then we'd be the people who made them send a rescue team out the day before filming even started, and while they *probably* wouldn't hold it against us, I'm not entirely inclined to take the chance."

If there was one impulse Rosaline would always understand, it was the impulse to avoid doing things that people in a position of influence might resent and hold over you. In her experience, they usually did. "Yeah." She tried not to audibly wince. "I think if we can get in under our own steam, we probably should."

"At the very least, it'll be an adventure." He smiled his leave-your-mining-village smile. "So what do you say, Rosaline-um-Palmer. Do you want to come on an adventure with me?"

All in all, Rosaline told herself, it could have been a lot worse. The day was fading into a soft English evening, complete with pastel sky and mellow sunlight. It would have been an enjoyable walk if she'd been able to ignore the smell of silage and the fact she was late for the reality TV show that she wasn't exactly staking her whole future on. But was also not *not* staking her whole future on. And if nothing else, at least she had company—the sort of company that, if she was being honest, she might have appreciated even if she hadn't been dumped at a backwater station by a privatised rail company.

"I do hope," said Alain as they tromped down a country lane that had about a thirty percent chance of leading directly to nowhere, "that you're impressed by my bold and manly decisiveness. Rather than thinking to yourself, *Oh no, he's one of those clichés who won't ask for directions.*"

Rosaline gave a laugh which she hoped communicated "I am mildly amused" rather than "I am trying too hard." "Who are you going to ask? That tree? The sheep?"

"I'm afraid I only took Sheep to GCSE, and the only phrase I can remember is 'Where is the bathroom?'"

"Okay." She had to ask. "What's Sheep for 'Where is the bathroom?'"

He had the grace to look...not to put too fine a point on it...sheepish. "I think it's 'Where is the baaathroom?'"

"You are really lucky I'm secretly into dad jokes."

There was a measuring pause. "Hi, Secretly into Dad Jokes. I'm Alain."

"Okay," Rosaline told him, "I might have put too much emphasis on the *into* and not enough emphasis on the *secretly.*"

"Don't worry. Jokes aside, I'm not ready to go full dad quite yet."

This time Rosaline's laugh was ever so slightly more forced. She was kind of used to most people her age, or even a little bit older, talking about parenthood like it was part of this unimaginable future you'd get around to once you got careers and relationships and your own dreams figured out. Which made it slightly awkward to come back with "Actually, I've been doing that for nearly a decade."

Their country lane took them across a cattle grid and onto a subtly different country lane, which led onto another. And it was across a field from country lane number three that they finally spotted signs of human habitation. Well, apart from all of the things that were *technically* signs of human habitation but were so countryish that they barely counted, like the hedgerows, the little stiles over rickety fences, and the acres upon acres of grass.

Alain shaded his eyes against the gleam of the setting sun. "Is that a farmhouse? Tell me that's a farmhouse."

"Or a secret military base, and either way there'll be someone we can ask for directions."

"If it's a secret base, won't they just shoot us?"

She shrugged. "They might do that if it's a farm."

"I actually live in the countryside and I've been shot by farmers far less often than you might imagine. Shall we go and say hello?"

"Okay, but if I wind up full of buckshot, you're picking the pellets out."

"And if I wind up full of buckshot?"

"Then I'm using you as a diversion and running for the road."

He gave her an arch look. "You're a cold woman, Rosaline-um-Palmer."

"Not half as cold as I'd be if I was shot dead by an irate landowner."

Since the alternative was wandering aimlessly or admitting to people who'd be making important decisions about their future they were a gigantic liability, they decided to risk approaching the farmhouse-slash-military-base. This, as it turned out, took longer than they'd anticipated because fields were like the Tardis: much bigger once you got into them.

"You know," remarked Alain, "I'm very glad you're here. This would have been incredibly dull on my own."

"So you're saying I'm better company than literally nobody?"

His mouth turned up wryly. "If it helps, I can think of some people who would be worse company than literally nobody. I went to a university friend's wedding last year, and honestly, I'd have been surprised if the bride's family had read a book between them. I got stuck talking to one of their many peripheral cousins, and I swear, the man thought grammar was a nickname for an elderly relative."

It surprised a laugh out of Rosaline—one of the conspiratorial, slightly guilty laughs that you were pretty sure was at somebody's expense but were also pretty sure was at the expense of somebody you didn't like. And who, perhaps more to the point, wouldn't like you either. "Weddings are the worst. Unless two of your friends are getting married, half the people in the room are people you'd never choose to hang out with. And half the rest just happen to be related to someone you would."

"In defence of matrimony, I have been to some lovely weddings. I think the problem with this one wasn't the institution. It was the company." He gave a heavy sigh. "No sooner had I got rid of Cretin A when the bride's father grabbed hold of me and spent ten minutes trying to engage me in conversation about which of the waitresses he or I would like to, and I quote, 'give one.'"

"Urgh"—Rosaline gave an involuntary shudder—"I can't stand men like that."

"Neither can most reasonable people. Then again—and I hate to say this—I think they do sometimes get quite a lot of encouragement. The bride herself was very much"—Alain paused, as if unable to find words to express the horrors he was trying to describe—"let's say that between the fake tan, the fake breasts, and the fake nails I wasn't entirely sure if my friend was marrying a person he'd met at work or something he'd run off on a 3-D printer."

Again, she shouldn't have laughed. Again, she sort of did. And again, she felt guilty for it. Lauren had serious—and honestly, correct—opinions about the way society had gone from judging women for failing to live up to unrealistic beauty standards to judging them for both failing *and succeeding*. Except, in that moment, it seemed harmlessly liberating to share someone else's judgement of a stranger instead of being judged herself.

They turned through a gap in the hedgerow and made their way up a dirt track towards a sprawling but well-maintained farmhouse. In the yard at the front, a woman with a flat cap was doing something incomprehensible to a tractor.

"Well then," Alain whispered. "Let's see if we get shot."

They did not, in fact, get shot. Instead, the farmer confirmed that there was no reasonable way to get to Tapworth that evening, offering to put them up for the night and run them along to Patchley House in the morning. Spending a night in the middle of nowhere with a man she'd just met wasn't something that Rosaline was exactly wild about, but assuming the BBC had vetted Alain as closely as it had vetted her, there was a better than reasonable chance he wasn't a serial killer.

"Of course I'll take the floor," he was saying. "Or if it would make you more comfortable, I can ask our host if she wouldn't mind me using her sofa instead."

Rosaline was sitting on the edge of a crisply made double bed in the little room beneath the eaves that had been all the farmer had available. She'd fired off a quick text to Lauren to explain about the train drama and that she wouldn't be able to call until tomorrow, and she was now waiting to see if she had enough reception for the message to actually send. When it finally did, she looked up. "Wouldn't *you* be more comfortable on the sofa?"

"Not really." He gave a slightly self-deprecating smile. "My feet would probably hang off the end."

So they split the generous supply of pillows and blankets, Rosaline rolling up on one side of the bed, and Alain constructing a makeshift mattress on the floor.

"What a strange day," offered Alain after a predicably awkward pause.

"Just a bit," she agreed. "Are you sure you're okay down there?"

"Actually, I'm quite comfortable. It reminds me of backpacking on my gap year. Although since I went with a schoolfriend, who, on prolonged exposure, turned out to be the most flatulent person I've ever met, I will say you're a better companion."

"So, you're telling me I rate better than nobody, some arsehole at a wedding, and a farting teenager? You really know how to make a girl feel special."

He gave a soft laugh. "You have quite a talent for turning a compliment into an insult."

"Thanks, I put a lot of work into it." There was a long silence. And Rosaline tried to figure out if it was the comfortable silence of people settling down to sleep. Or the uncomfortable silence of a conversation that, like the trains, had come to an unexpected stop in the middle of nowhere.

"I'm beginning to suspect," said Alain, "that I might have skipped the chapter in life's instruction manual that covered the etiquette for being required to share a room with an intriguing stranger with whom you have inadvertently become trapped on your way to a televised baking competition."

Rosaline had skipped a lot of chapters in life's instruction manual. So many that she often felt like she'd dropped her copy in a puddle at the age of nineteen. "It's been a while since I checked, but when it comes to basically all social interaction, the advice boils down to 'Stare straight ahead and say nothing.' Y'know, the Tube principle."

"Now you mention it, that does sound familiar." He paused, making Rosaline wonder if she'd accidentally encouraged someone she was enjoying talking to not to talk to her anymore. "But how about we act like rebels and actually get to know each other?"

And that would have been great in principle. But Rosaline knew how this went. One minute, you were having a nice, normal, maybe slightly flirty conversation, and the next you were having to explain how you'd gone from medicine at Cambridge to a temp job and the school run, and from there it was either "Poor you, what a disaster" or "Gosh, I didn't think you were the type." And you knew that the person you were talking to had stopped thinking *Hey, she seems all right; maybe I should ask her out* and started thinking *Hey, she seems like she's got a lot of baggage; I hope she doesn't ask me to babysit.*

"But," she tried, "won't the space-time continuum collapse if two British people talk about something that isn't the weather or the buses?"

"You know, Rosaline-um-Palmer"—she somehow knew he was smiling—"I'm willing to risk it."

Fuck. Oh fuck. *Okay, Rosaline, take control of the situation.* "So what do you do then?"

There was another long silence.

Once it had progressed from a long silence to a long, long silence, Rosaline—convinced she'd somehow messed up—broke it in a panic: "Um, are you okay?"

"Oh yes, fine. Just waiting to see if the universe falls down around us. But I think we're safe. I'm a landscape architect."

She had no idea what that was, or rather how it differed from a regular architect, but it sounded like it would be arty enough to be satisfying but lucrative enough that your, say, parents couldn't object. "Is that an architect lying on his side?"

"Is it what? No, it's like the— Oh." He broke off and gave a deep chuckle. "Well, as it happens I *am* lying on my side, so I suppose at the moment I'm both. But more generally, it's landscape as opposed to residential or commercial, rather than landscape as opposed to portrait."

"How do you architect a landscape?" she asked. "It's not like you can be all, *Hey, put another mountain over there* or *Can we take the sky down a couple of inches?*"

"You might be surprised. I had a lake moved once."

"How?"

"No idea. That's for the hydrological engineers to sort out. I just pointed at it, and said, 'I think this is blocking access to the deer park.'"

"I can't tell if that makes you cool and powerful or...a bit of a middle manager?"

"Honestly," he told her with a ruefulness she found endearing, "neither can I."

Rosaline rolled back towards the edge of the bed and looked down. She could make out the shape of him—leaning on one side like a statue of a reclining emperor and looking up at her, his face a mystery of shadows in the starlight. "But do you enjoy it?"

"I do." She couldn't make out his eyes, but there was an intensity in his voice that reminded her of the late-night conversations she'd had at university. "It's like baking in a way. You have to balance the technical with the creative. I mean, there's no point putting a path in a park that isn't wide enough for two people to walk their dogs past each other."

"Well, you could be setting up meet-cutes?"

"I'm sorry. You've lost me."

"Okay, stop me if this getting too technical for you, but it's when two people *meet* in a *cute* way."

"Does that happen a lot?" he asked. "You're making me feel like I'm meeting people wrong."

"Clearly you are." She grinned to herself in the darkness. "Because when you're out walking your dog, what happens all the time is that someone will be coming the other way—down the path in the park that's too narrow—and your leads will get tangled up and then, depending on what movie you're in, either you'll say, 'Oh gosh, I'm terribly sorry,' and she'll say, 'Oh no, not at all,' but everyone will know you secretly want to bang. Or else you'll say, 'Hey, watch it, lady' and she'll say, 'Move it, mister,' and everyone will know you secretly want to bang."

He laughed again, and Rosaline permitted herself a small bask in a glowy feeling. You didn't make somebody laugh this much unless you were acing it in the wit department, they liked you a lot, or some combination of the two. "What if I don't have a dog?"

"Then you're in the wrong kind of movie."

"Or," he suggested, "designing the wrong kind of park."

"Yes, you should think about that next time."

"Oh should I?" he asked. "Anything else I should bear in mind?"

"Lots of things. Revolving doors to get your coat caught in. Those fountains that are completely flat to the ground and just spurt up out of the concrete unexpectedly. And if you could design all your staircases to be really hard to go down in heels without either breaking one or falling over, that'd be perfect."

"Are you suggesting"—it was the sort of half-playful, half-dry tone that needed an eyebrow raise—"I deliberately design spaces to be more difficult for women to navigate?"

"Well, how else are we supposed to meet people?"

"I don't know. I suppose you could always wait until you get stranded at a disused train station. That or Tinder."

"I think I'll take the train station. Nobody's pretending to be ten years younger than they are, and you get fewer creepy messages. But," she went on quickly, partly from genuine interest and partly to delay the inevitable questions about herself, "what brought you from architecture to *Bake Expectations*?"

She heard him flump onto his back and then utter a soft, slightly self-mocking groan. "You'll think I'm such a cliché."

"Yes, because I know so many landscape architects who also make cakes on TV."

"Honestly, it's appallingly first world problems of me. I just—" He broke off and then tried again. "I find my job very fulfilling, and—I'm afraid I don't know how to say this without sounding boastful—I've achieved quite a lot of what I expected to achieve in my life. But sometimes I find myself wondering if there isn't something…something else. Something I'm missing out on."

This was all very familiar to Rosaline, albeit for very different reasons. "I don't think that's a cliché. I think that's normal. I mean, I hope it's normal because I feel like that all the time."

"I'm sure you shouldn't," he offered reassuringly. "In fact, *I* probably shouldn't. But I think it's a—well, I suppose it's a hazard of education. It teaches you how large the world can be, but you can never quite encompass all of it. Certainly it's not a feeling I can imagine the guests at that wedding knowing much about. *They* were perfectly content with season tickets to Manchester United, large-screen televisions, and the occasional opportunity to harass a woman from the top of a building site."

"Oh, don't. Once when I was about eighteen, somebody yelled at me like that. And I'd had enough so I stopped and turned around and said, 'All right then, you and me, right here.' And he got really offended, and said, 'Steady on, love; I'm married.' Like I was the one out of line." She huffed out an aggrieved sigh a decade in the making. "You can't fucking win."

"It sounds to me like you won." In the dark, his voice was rich with approval. "He tried to make you feel small and you turned it back on him."

At the time, it had felt like he'd set out to make her feel small, she tried to stop him, and he'd made her feel small anyway. And even now, she was pretty sure that once she'd walked away, the builder and his mates had laughed about what a desperate slag she was. But she liked Alain's version a lot better.

Unfortunately, contemplating the sociological implications of their gendered reactions to an anecdote about a building site had distracted Rosaline for just long enough that Alain was able to say: "It feels like we've been talking about me forever, which, while I'm not shouting at you from a building site, I'm uncomfortably aware is still quite rude and a little bit sexist."

"No, no, it's fine." It was about to happen, wasn't it? "I'm interested."

And here it came, as inevitable as climate change. "Tell me about you, Rosaline-um-Palmer."

"What about me?"

"Well, we could start with what you do when you're not getting stranded at railway stations and work our way up from there."

Rosaline opened her mouth and closed it again. The thought of saying anything close to the truth suddenly seemed impossible. Because here was someone sharp and confident, with experiences and opinions and an exciting career he was passionate about. And he seemed to think Rosaline was like him. That she belonged in his world of feeling you'd achieved everything you set out to achieve and having lakes moved at your command and still finding time to bake at a nationally competitive level. How was she supposed to tell someone like that that she'd got pregnant at nineteen, dropped out of university, and worked part-time as a sales assistant while doing an at best adequate job of parenting an eight-year-old? And what the fuck did that say about her? She wouldn't have traded Amelie for all the degrees and opportunities in the world, but just in that moment, she couldn't quite bring herself to admit her daughter existed.

"I'm a student," she told him.

A worrying pause. "Gosh. I . . . I wasn't expecting that."

"A mature student," she clarified, detecting at once the *Shit, I've hit on a teenager* tone in his voice.

"Oh, thank God." He let out a nervous breath. "I think sharing a room with a woman you've barely met is one thing. But sharing a room with a woman you've barely met who's fresh out of a school gets you on page three of the *Daily Mail*."

"I think," said Rosaline helpfully, "that's usually reserved for pictures of scantily clad women. As a sex pest you'd probably be on page four."

"Good to know. That's exactly the detail I was concerned with." He paused. "I should also say, in my delight at discovering you're not a teenager, I didn't mean to imply that you look old. Would you mind if I just asked what you're studying, and we can pretend the earlier part of this conversation never happened?"

"Medicine?" It was...only half a lie.

"And here I am talking about architecture like it's important when you're learning to save lives."

This was...this was bad. The sensible thing to do was come clean now. Right now. "I don't know, no point saving people's lives if they can't go to a park afterwards."

He gave a soft laugh. "You're very sweet. But that's clearly nonsense. You've worked hard and been successful, and you should be proud of that."

"Thank you," she said, feeling more than a little nauseous.

"Did you not want to go into it straight from school?"

Okay. Get out of the lie hole, Rosaline. Because if you don't, it's lies all the way down. "Oh...I...took a gap year?"

There was a silence like he was waiting for more.

Which was when Rosaline realised that a single year probably didn't explain the difference between the age he assumed she was and the age of the average undergraduate. "To Malawi," she continued.

"To Malawi?" he repeated, in a devastatingly interested voice.

"Yes? And I...liked it so much I stayed out there for a while. Working on...irrigation." *Stop Rosaline stop Rosaline stop Rosaline.* "But then I looked at some studies, which suggested that Western tourists going to less economically developed countries and doing what is essentially unskilled labour might do more harm than good. So, I came home. And reapplied to university."

"Good Lord," he said, "you *have* lived a fascinating life. I confess, I just thought you might have decided to retrain or something."

Fuck. That would have been way more plausible and raised far fewer questions. "Yeah. No. Um, I guess a lot of people do that, don't they?"

There was a rustle of bedclothes in the darkness—the sort of sound you might make as you settled in to hear a remarkable and well-travelled woman tell you her life story. "I've always wondered—" he began.

"You know"—Rosaline cut him off urgently—"we're probably going to have to get up really early tomorrow morning, and I'm sure neither of us want to screw up week one because we stayed up all night talking."

There was a glow from the floor as Alain checked his phone. "You're right. I didn't realise how late it was."

"Yeah, I kind of lost track of time as well."

"But I hope we'll have plenty more opportunities to talk in the future?"

Rosaline winced at the ceiling beams. "I'm sure we will."

Saturday

BETWEEN WORRYING ABOUT the competition and worrying about having told a man she thought she might like a story about her past that was both false and needlessly specific, Rosaline was only just about nodding off to sleep when she had to get up again to scramble into a trailer full of hay. Which turned out to be far less comfortable than costume dramas and historical novels had led her to believe.

Alain, meanwhile, had sprung out of bed with the verve of a Disney prince. And now he was sitting next to her, one wrist balanced on a drawn-up knee, the early morning sunlight threading gold through his hair. "I tell you what," he said, "I'll take this over Southern Rail any day. Faster, more reliable, far less likely to get stuck opposite some prick from Basildon wanking under a copy of the *Metro*."

"Sitting on straw?"

He smiled. "Nature's futon."

Rosaline was about to explain that, being a city girl, she wasn't particularly used to thinking of dead grass as anything other than garden waste, but then she remembered she was supposed to have spent several years doing manual labour in Malawi. So she gave a vaguely assenting grunt instead.

Which made Alain laugh. "Not a morning person, are you, Rosaline-um-Palmer?"

"This isn't morning. This is yesterday."

"Well, that's country life for you." He gently plucked a stalk of hay from her hair. "How are you feeling about the show?"

"Surprisingly calm. I think being stuck in the middle of nowhere took my mind off it. Of course, now we're not stuck in the middle of nowhere. Which means I'll probably start freaking out in about ten minutes."

"There's no need to freak out," he said soothingly. "The trick to going a long way in the competition is to bring something unique to it, and you must be able to draw on your experiences in Malawi."

Fuck. No, it was okay. You couldn't do the *thing from my background* gimmick more than once or twice before the judges got bored, so she could pretend she was saving it until at least week three, by which point probably one of them would have gone home. "I was just hoping to have a bit more time to prepare."

"I can tell you're a medical student. You're clearly very committed to doing homework."

Oh God. Not again.

"But," he went on, "I'm honestly not sure how much preparation you planned to do in a hotel with no equipment."

Relieved that this was about neither Malawi nor medicine, Rosaline jumped on it hard. "Actually, I brought two of the judges' cookbooks with me. For the last couple of seasons the early blind bakes have been from published recipes, and I was hoping to get at least a hint."

"Rosaline-um-Palmer"—his eyes widened—"you cunning little devil."

She blushed slightly. "I mean, it probably won't help. They've written so many books between them."

"Don't sell yourself short. It's still a very clever idea. Which did you bring?"

Reaching inside her bag, Rosaline retrieved her copies of Wilfred Honey's *Cakes from the Mills* and Marianne Wolvercote's *Science of Patisserie.* "We know it's cakes, so that narrows it down quite a bit. And they tend to go homey in the first week, so that means we're looking for something fairly simple."

"And obviously they won't repeat anything," Alain added, taking *Cakes from the Mills* and flipping it open, "so we can rule out Victoria sponge, Battenberg, or—oh, what was it last year?"

"Coffee and walnut, I think?"

His head was close to hers as they pored over the book. His smile private and confiding, like it was just for her. And despite having spent the night on the floor, he somehow smelled of fresh soap and basil—and straw, of course, but in a good way. "Dodged a bullet there, didn't we?"

"Not a fan?"

"I'm sure they can be elevated, but if there was ever a cake that screamed 'third prize at a school fete,' it's coffee and walnut."

Rosaline had, actually, once made a coffee and walnut cake for a school fete. At the time she'd thought it had gone down quite well. "What about angel food?" she suggested. "They sometimes like to do something a bit unexpected."

"Certainly a possibility."

"Or Dundee?"

"Doesn't that have to rest overnight?"

"It's best if it does. But I think they magic-of-television around that kind of thing."

"Well, let's add it to the long list and then we'll revise down like the Booker Committee."

Although Rosaline knew that it was a competition, it was nice to feel even briefly like part of a team. In fact, it was just nice to be able to talk about baking with someone. Amelie was enthusiastic but not terribly insightful, and Lauren—while broadly supportive—reserved the bulk of her enthusiasm and insight for her twin loves of satire and sapphism.

As the trailer rattled slowly down the winding roads of wherever they actually were, Rosaline stole a sideways glance at Alain. His eyes had caught some of the blue of the sky and there was a faint flush on his cheeks, his long, artistic fingers running the length of the pages as he pondered the various recipes.

It would have been one of those unexpectedly perfect moments with an unexpectedly perfect guy. Had it not been for the tiny, tiny detail that she'd lied to him about literally everything.

***

Patchley House and Park turned out to be a lot more park than house—at least initially. The grounds were weirdly familiar because the show always opened with a panning shot of the British countryside, which, as it turned out, was actually a panning shot of what used to be a rich person's garden. The driveway curved smoothly around a green velvet hillside, eventually gifting visitors with their first glimpse of the manor itself. This, too, was familiar, so familiar that Rosaline half expected to see the words "Bake Expectations" emblazoned across it like Sacher across a torte.

As they followed a series of Contestants This Way signs, they were intercepted by a slight, twitchy man with an earpiece and a clipboard.

"Thank God you're here," he said. "You're cutting it very fine. Also, you're covered in straw. Why are you covered in straw? Jennifer is going to be livid if you're covered in straw on-camera."

Alain casually brushed hay from his sleeve. "There was a train-related snafu and we had to get a lift in from a farmer. But it's all under control and if you'll just show us to our rooms, we'll get cleaned up and be with you in no time."

"Um," Rosaline added. "Sorry."

"We're serving breakfast in ten minutes." The twitchy man twitched further. "So please hurry or I don't know *what* will happen."

"We'll be slightly late for breakfast?" suggested Alain.

"Jennifer doesn't like slightly late."

"Then"—Alain plucked two room keys from the stranger's un-resisting hands—"you probably shouldn't be keeping us talking."

The man, who eventually introduced himself as Colin Thrimp, assistant to the producer, Jennifer Hallet, resolutely led them away from the beautiful eighteenth-century manor house to a set of squat, 1940s-looking outbuildings tucked discreetly behind a copse of trees.

"This is the Lodge," Colin Thrimp explained, with the speed of someone who really, really needed to be somewhere else. "You'll all be staying here. Room numbers on the keys. Breakfast on the terrace in—oh, oh gosh, about six minutes. So please do hurry. Filming starts in an hour."

"Well"—Rosaline watched Colin Thrimp scurrying away—"there go my hopes of staying in a swanky hotel for a couple of weekends."

Alain raised an eyebrow. "On a BBC budget?"

"Girl can dream."

He leaned in and brushed a kiss over her cheek in that effortless, vaguely continental way that the real Rosaline always screwed up but international traveller Rosaline should probably have been totally used to. "Good luck today. I'll see you on-set."

While Alain had seemed pretty nonchalant about the possi-bility of being late to breakfast, Rosaline had a deeply ingrained fear of being late that her recent experiences had done very little to alleviate. So she hurried to her room, had the fastest possible shower, and only slowed down to make sure that when she got changed she didn't put anything on back to front or inside out.

As she emerged into the corridor, a door opened a little farther down, revealing someone she assumed was another contestant. There was a moment of mutual faff as the pair of them wrestled with their keys and then the other woman gave Rosaline an enthusiastic wave.

"Hi," she called out. "I'm Anvita. Are you going fooding?"

"Yes. And, um, Rosaline."

They fell into step together. Her companion seemed to be a few years younger than Rosaline and was wearing an aggressively pink T-shirt that she was somehow managing to carry off. Her hair was pulled back in a no-nonsense ponytail and she sported a pair of those oversized glasses, which shouldn't have been cool but apparently were. The light occasionally glinted off a tiny diamond nose-stud that Rosaline couldn't help finding a little bit sexy.

"So." Anvita cast her a glance at once teasing and speculative. "Are you an *I'll just be happy to get through week one* or an *I'm going to win this whole thing*?"

"Aren't we all supposed to be just happy to get through week one? This isn't *The Apprentice*."

"Speak for yourself. I'm going to make it to week five, and the judges are going to love my bold flavours, but then they're going to ask me to make a traditional suet gobbins, which everyone else will remember from their childhood, and I'll have no idea what it is, and then I'll fuck it up, and get booted."

Rosaline laughed. "Okay, I think I'll get all the way to week six by being consistently mediocre and then people will finally remember I'm there and I'll have to leave."

"Aim high, girlfriend." It was mildly impressive how much irony Anvita could pack into three words.

There was a brief pause, and it wasn't totally uncomfortable.

"I think," Anvita went on, "I'm socially mandated to ask what you do. I'm training to be an optician, which is less boring than it sounds, but not by much."

This is it, Rosaline. Tell the pretty young woman you aren't doing anything cool or interesting with your life. Don't make up an elaborate personal history again. Stop pretending your child, who you love, doesn't exist, because that's fucked up. "I'm...a single mum and I work in a shop."

"Which shop?"

"Chain stationery store. Living the dream."

"How old's the kid-slash-kids?"

"Kid. And she's eight."

"Oh, that's the good age." Anvita seemed to have at least a vague idea where she was going, leading Rosaline confidently out of the Lodge and towards the main house. "Old enough they're fun to talk to, but young enough they're not a complete prick. I've got a nephew who's seven. He's the best."

"Yeah, Amelie's amazing, but I have no idea what I'm going to do when she's a teenager."

"Wait until she's stopped being a teenager?"

It wasn't the worst parenting advice Rosaline had ever encountered. As they tramped up the hill together, they passed a small village of vans, temporary gazebos, and bits of scaffolding that had taken over a far corner of the grounds—somewhere that would be artfully invisible from the house to maintain the illusion of unspoiled pastoral beauty.

"Yikes." Anvita was also staring at the tangle of crap from which televisual magic would apparently be wrought. "This is actually happening, isn't it?"

"Well, I'm not naked, so I'm pretty sure it's not an anxiety dream."

"Have you had a chance to scope out the competition yet?" asked Anvita, with an air partway between playful and ruthless.

"Not exactly. I met one guy yesterday. But I more got stranded with him than *scoped* him."

"You got stranded?"

"There was a whole big train thing and we wound up having to crash at a farmhouse overnight."

This earned her a look of mock reproach. "You spent the night with the guy and you know nothing about him?"

"I didn't realise I was supposed to be doing intelligence gathering."

"Fine." Anvita sighed heavily. "I'll share my secret stash of opposition research with you out of pure pity."

"Good thing I have no pride or I might object to that."

Leaning in close, Anvita dropped her voice to an urgent whisper. "Okay. So. Most importantly, there are two stone-cold hotties."

"I mean, good to know? But how relevant is that from the perspective of a baking show we'll both just be happy to get through the first round of, but secretly want to win?"

"It's very relevant from the perspective of me enjoying myself. Don't get me wrong, I've got a boyfriend and I love him to bits, but a girl likes to window-shop."

There was, as far as Rosaline could tell, no real reason not to go with this. "Okay, tell me what's on sale."

"So, there's Ricky. He's a student at Southampton—something something material science something. Bit young, but tall, locs, good cheekbones, great smile. He plays football or whatever and you can tell. He'll look great when he's whisking."

"I feel like I know him already."

"Then there's Harry. I haven't been able to get much out of him, but I think he fixes things. With his hands. His strong, manly hands. I hope he makes it to bread week."

"Have you spoken to anyone who wasn't an attractive man?" As questions went, Rosaline knew this was slightly hypocritical.

"Yes. I've spoken to Nora, who's a gran, so I bet she's going to win. And I've spoken to Florian, who I'm sure is attractive to some people, but I think he's about fifty and really quite gay.

There's also Claudia, who's this terrifying lawyer lady; and Josie, who I've heard owns over four hundred cookbooks."

"I couldn't fit four hundred cookbooks in my house."

"I wouldn't want to. I've got the internet and a phone. Like a normal person."

Breakfast, as it turned out, was a kind of self-service arrangement on the veranda: long, shallow metal trays filled with rapidly cooling offerings of eggs, bacon, hash browns, and other staples of the English breakfast. Vegetarians, Rosaline assumed, would have to make do with mushrooms and toast.

"I'm trying to weigh up," said Anvita, "whether it looks worse to get one enormous plate of everything or to go back about thirty times. Because I am fucking starving. And even if I wasn't, it's a free breakfast buffet and the point of a free breakfast buffet is to eat enough that you don't need another meal until the next free breakfast buffet."

Between the nerves and the...actually, probably just the nerves, Rosaline had lost her appetite. "I might start with corn-flakes and go from there."

Anvita shook her head despairingly. "Weaksauce."

They briefly parted ways to take on the slightly soggy bounty. Grabbing a bowl of off-brand corn cereal and a glass of punishingly tart grapefruit juice, Rosaline glanced around for somewhere to sit. Then she realised she was looking for Alain and kicked herself for not focusing on the competition.

In any case, he wasn't there and the rest of the contestants had mostly separated themselves over two picnic tables, apparently by age. Which made things a little bit difficult for Rosaline because she felt slightly too young for Group A, which consisted of an elderly lady, an older gentleman in a floral shirt, and two middle-aged women. But Group B—Anvita and two guys of university age—seemed far too young, cool, and not-child-having. In the end, she went B, on the assumption that in

Anvita's world "weaksauce" constituted a standing invitation to eat food together.

"So this is Rosaline," announced Anvita as Rosaline perched herself on the end of the table and tried to cornflake. "Rosaline, this is Ricky and Dave."

"All right?" Ricky waved a spoon cheerfully. Anvita had not oversold him, although Rosaline was fast getting to the age where nineteen-year-olds were losing their appeal.

Dave, a skinny man with a goatee, wearing a llama-print shirt, and an item of headwear that Rosaline feared was a fedora, nodded a silent hi. "We were just talking," he said, "about what made us apply for the show."

"I hate to be that girl"— Anvita pushed her glasses back up her nose—"but I'm mostly doing this for my nan. She taught me how to bake and all that shit. And I'm blatantly going to be crying about it at some point."

"Better to cry about your nan," Rosaline told her, "than about a flat scone or collapsed meringue."

This was clearly too much emotions talk for Dave and he turned to Ricky. "What about you, mate?"

Ricky somehow indicated with his whole body that he was far too cool to worry about a little thing like a nationally televised test of his baking skills. "Thought it'd be a laugh. I didn't expect to get in, to be honest. But we'll see."

Not seeming to notice or care that Rosaline hadn't replied yet, Dave plonked his elbows on the table and launched into what felt like a pre-prepared speech. "I applied because I felt I had a really different take on the whole concept of"—he did actual air quotes—"'baking.' Like, Marianne and Wilfred are great, but they're both very traditional in their outlook, and I wanted to show people that they don't have to live their lives the way they're expected to."

In the silence that followed, Anvita, Rosaline, and Ricky

signalled to each other, without speaking or moving, that none of them had a fucking clue what to do with that.

"And," Rosaline tried, "you're going to show them this by...making cakes?"

"Well, what are"—air quotes again—"'cakes'?"

After breakfast, they were hurried through to the ballroom of the main house for a series of briefings. From some angles, everything looked exactly like it did on TV. Those angles, of course, being the ones the cameras were pointing along, where it was all rainbow-coloured workstations set against incongruous baroque grandeur. From a less flattering direction, everything was wires and booms and people in black T-shirts making incomprehensible hand gestures. It was also, Rosaline was rapidly coming to realise, a terrible cooking environment, being vast and echoing and designed for people to dance in two hundred and forty years ago. Right now, it was unpleasantly cold. But given the ten mini-kitchens and the lighting rig, it would probably be uncomfortably hot by about half past ten. And ruinously hot by noon.

No wonder that guy had burst into tears over his sorbet that one time.

Finally, they were permitted access to a row of stools, where they arranged themselves tentatively and awaited further instructions. Their final briefing came from the show's producer. Jennifer Hallet turned out to be a tall woman in her thirties, with long, sandy-brown hair and a general vibe that said she didn't take shit.

"Right," she told them. "Just some things to remember while we're filming." She began to count off on her fingers. "There'll be cameras around: try to ignore them unless somebody actually asks you a question. If they do ask you a question, try to answer it as if you're not answering a question. Sometimes we'll ask you to do something again—you'll find this annoying, but suck it up, buttercups; that's television."

She paused for the smallest of breaths. "And finally, remember that this is a family show so get all the fucks, shits, and bastards out of your system before we turn the cameras on because you *will* lose me footage, and if there is one thing I fucking shitting bastarding hate it's when people lose me footage. Fourteen hours seems like a long time but let's be real, shitbags, this is a dozen people making cakes in a fancy house and ninety-five percent of what happens is *boring as arse*, so if some complete dog's scrotum ruins our only good shot of a wobbly pie or a smashed trifle by dropping a fuck on it, I will personally feed their tits and/or bollocks into a Magimix."

Running her gaze over the line of contestants, she pointedly made eye contact with each one of them to emphasise that she was deadly serious. "That's all I can think of right now. But let me remind you that my entire *pissing* job depends on the great British public finding you lot *completely adorable*, so shy smiles and vapid anecdotes about your families are gold, and for fuck's sake keep your opinions about God and the Prime Minister to yourselves. Good luck, have fun, and nobody speak to me unless they're on fire."

With that, she stalked away, leaving Rosaline slightly uncertain whether she should have been finding her scary or hot. At which point Jennifer's assistant, the still-anxious Colin Thrimp, took over and they were half coaxed, half bullied into an appropriately telegenic formation before the famous people came in.

The two judges were accompanied by the show's longtime host, Grace Forsythe, whose job, as far as Rosaline had been able to tell from watching the series, was to bring a mix of old-world erudition and basic smut to the proceedings. She was one of those performers who got away with a lot of shit you wouldn't normally get away with by dint of being a national treasure—which was to say, she looked like your great-aunt in drag, and she liked to brag about the time she took cocaine in Buckingham Palace.

"Tallyho and pip-pip." She beamed at the contestants like they were the scholarship class at an exclusive girls' boarding school. "And welcome one and all to the warm, yeasty embrace of a new series of *Bake Expectations*. Over the next eight weeks you'll be competing to dazzle our judges with your culinary skills in pursuit of a—may I say—rather vulgar cash prize of ten thousand pounds. And more importantly, the honour of getting to take home an engraved cake slice that says you won a thing."

There was definitely a camera pointing in Rosaline's direction and she hoped she was looking appropriately happy to be there. As opposed to tired, confused, overwhelmed, and wondering if she hadn't made a mistake with those cornflakes.

"As always," Grace Forsythe went on, "you'll be judged by the nation's grandfather, the edibly talented Wilfred Honey. And by the splendid Marianne Wolvercote, who has conquered the nation with her cake shops."

"The term is 'patisseries,'" drawled Marianne Wolvercote. She was the type of woman who could drawl pretty much anything, even words with no long vowels, and whose every gesture looked like it should have been made while clutching a cigarette holder.

"It's still cake, darling, even if you say it in French." Having dutifully bantered, Grace Forsythe clapped her hands like a games mistress. "Now our first round, as always, is the blind bake. You'll be testing your—fuck, sorry, darlings, fucking fucked the fucking line." There was a moment while everybody reset. "Now our first round, as always, is the blind bake. We'll be testing your culinary credentials today with a classic delectable that legend has it was first created for Mary, Queen of Scots. But which was actually probably invented by a marmalade company from Dundee."

Oh, it couldn't be. There was no way Rosaline was getting that lucky. She looked round for Alain, who, being tall, was sat towards the back, and they shared a moment of hopeful conspiracy.

"That's right." Grace Forsythe nodded. "We'll be asking you to produce a perfect, classic, fruit-laden, almond-topped, jes bonny wi' a wee dram o' whisky"—this last part she said in an affected Scottish accent, which Rosaline thought might have been pushing it—"Dundee cake."

Yes. They'd looked at that this morning. It had been in *Cakes from the Mills*.

"And it's my recipe," added Wilfred Honey, "so I hope you'll all take extra special care, because if it comes out right, I promise, it'll be *gradely*."

"Blanch the almonds," said the first line of the haiku that passed for instructions.

And suddenly, a huge wave of unreality swept over Rosaline. What the actual fuck was she actually doing? Somehow, she'd manoeuvred herself into a position where she'd imagined that baking a Dundee cake in front of some cameras would fix her life. And now, staring at a kettle and a bowl of nuts, she was becoming viscerally aware that it wouldn't.

A little under a decade ago, she'd been studying at one of the most prestigious universities in the world. If she'd stuck with it, she'd be about three years away from being a fully qualified neurologist or cardiologist or some other impressive kind of ologist who saved lives or advanced the boundaries of human knowledge. And had more important things to worry about than whether blanching almonds took two minutes or five.

Did blanching almonds take two minutes or five? Did it even fucking matter?

The worst of it was, she'd done this to herself. She'd had

every conceivable advantage. Excellent schools. Affluent parents. Good teeth and twenty-twenty vision. But none of it had quite compensated for her ability to make genuinely atrocious decisions.

After all, she could have responded to Lauren cheating on her by being mature and forgiving, instead of rebounding onto a guy she was only vaguely into. She could have been more careful about condoms. Even after she decided to keep the baby, she could have let her parents step in—like they'd wanted to—and gone back to university. But oh, no, she'd insisted on raising Amelie herself. Being in her daughter's life. Giving her the sort of childhood Rosaline had never had. Except, fast-forward a bit, and here she was, unable to give her daughter half of what she deserved and trying to compensate for that by going on a reality TV competition that was famous primarily for that one time somebody sat on somebody else's trifle.

"What are you doing?" Colin Thrimp was right there, as well as a camera, a camera operator, a sound technician, and a boom mic.

"Doubting the wisdom of every choice I've ever made." Well, balls. She'd said that aloud, hadn't she?

Colin Thrimp smiled his limpest smile. "That's lovely. But can we have it again as if you weren't answering a question."

"I'm not sure I want to say 'I'm doubting the wisdom of every choice I've ever made' on national television."

"Don't worry. Contestants say lines like that all the time. It makes them look relatable."

Rosaline hesitated, trying to figure out if it was worse that she'd committed to doing this objectively pointless thing or that she was now trying to get out of the objectively pointless thing that she'd committed to do.

"So at the moment," she said, trying to sound at least a little bit like she was joking, "I'm trying to work out how long to blanch my almonds for and doubting the wisdom of every choice I've ever made."

They broke for a late lunch so the crew could take glamour shots of the bakes, which, in some cases, were not looking all that glamorous. Rosaline had intended to catch up with Alain, but he and Anvita and a couple of other contestants had been shepherded off for interviews. Which left Rosaline feeling distinctly first-day-of-school as she tried to navigate the curly sandwiches and soggy wraps on her own.

Clutching a sad-looking cheese and pickle in one hand, she approached the tea trolley and found herself standing next to someone who had to be Anvita's second stone-cold hottie— the guy with the manly hands whose tight T-shirt Rosaline felt distinctly regressive for enjoying.

"Do you want a cuppa, love?" he asked.

Oh God, he was one of *those*. And yes, he had arms that said *I have earned these through honest toil* and eyelashes like a baby deer. And yes, his jeans were clinging in places nice girls weren't supposed to notice jeans clinging. But this was going to end one of two ways: either she was going to tell him to stop calling her love and he was going to get defensive and make her feel shitty about herself, or else she wouldn't and she'd feel shitty about herself all on her own.

Opting for the flavour of shittiness where she at least didn't make a scene, she gritted her teeth. "Yes. Thank you."

"Right you are." He picked up one of the large silver jug things that someone had helpfully labelled "Tea" and upended it over the first of two cups. Nothing happened. He put it back down and pushed on the top experimentally. Nothing happened. "Aw, bollocks."

"Sometimes there's a button on the handle," Rosaline offered.

He peered more closely at the jug. "What I don't get is why they can't make them so they all work the same."

"Perhaps they want to make life more interesting for us."

"If I want something interesting, I'll listen to the radio. Right now, I just want some bloody tea."

"You could take the lid off maybe?"

"Knowing my luck, I'd break it. And then I'd have to go up to that Colin bloke and be, *Mate, I broke your thing, I'm really sorry.* And he'd be, *Oh, this is awful, Jennifer will be upset.* And I'll be like, *Mate, it's not my fault. They should make them so they all work the same and they don't.*"

Rosaline blinked, caught off guard by the magnitude of this beverage-based catastrophising. "Okay. Alternative plan. *I* take the lid off."

Stepping back, he put his hands in the air like he was being held at gunpoint. "Be my guest, love."

It was at this juncture that Rosaline realised she couldn't pour tea for a man who kept talking to her like, well, like pouring tea was one of a very limited set of things she was good for. "Sorry, I don't mean to be weird about this, but…can you not call me love?"

He looked briefly surprised, then shrugged. "Yeah, all right. I don't mean nothing by it."

The part of Rosaline that, despite all her efforts, was still her father's daughter itched to correct his grammar. Of course, Lauren would have argued that dialect was an important feature of identity, and the rules about double negatives were made up by a bunch of insecure pricks in the seventeenth century who thought English should either work like maths or Latin. But Rosaline had been raised to believe that there were rights and wrongs about this kind of thing, and you didn't drop your g's or your h's or permit a glottal stop to replace a perfectly functional t.

"I'm sure it's not personal," she said instead. "But you wouldn't call me that if I was a man."

He seemed to be thinking about this. As far as Rosaline was concerned, it wasn't a difficult concept, but at least he wasn't shouting at her. "If you was a bloke, I'd probably call you *mate*."

"You know"—she ended up sounding sharper than she meant to—"you could always use my name."

"What's your name then?" He offered her a slow smile. Not the sort of smile she would have expected from someone who looked like him or talked like him. Shy almost and oddly genuine. "I'm Harry, by the way. Not that you asked."

"Oh. Sorry. Um, Rosaline."

"You what?" he asked. "*Rosaline*?"

"Yes. Like in *Romeo and Juliet*."

"Look, I know I didn't do that well in school, but"—he eyed her nervously—"isn't the girl in *Romeo and Juliet* called . . . Juliet?"

It had been ages since she'd had this conversation. And frankly, she could have done without it now. "Rosaline's the woman Romeo is in love with at the beginning. Then he forgets about her when he sees Juliet."

"Your mum and dad named you after a bird what gets dumped in a play?"

"She doesn't get dumped. She's sworn a vow of chastity, so Romeo never has a chance with her."

"They named you after a *nun* in a play."

This was sounding bad. She'd never really thought about it before. Most people accepted that it was a slightly obscure Shakespeare reference and moved on. "She's not technically *in* the play. She's only mentioned in a few scenes."

"They named you after a nun in a play *what isn't even in the play*?"

"It's not that weird." She was starting to worry it was, in fact, that weird. "I think they just liked the name."

He winced. "Sorry, don't get me wrong. It's a very pretty name and you're a very pretty girl. I don't meet many *Rosalines* is all."

And it had come so close to going well. "I don't want to push my luck, but can you also ease up on the girl and the pretty? I'm here to bake and when you focus on my appearance, I find that a bit demeaning."

Which she knew was the teennsiest-tiniest bit hypocritical, given how very aware of *his* appearance she was, but it wasn't as if she'd greeted him with *Hey sexy, like the arse.* Although— gender dynamics being what they were—he might have been okay with that.

"Bloody hell." He pulled a slightly horrified face. "Made a right mess of this, haven't I?"

"It's fine. It's just we're not in the pub and you're not trying to pull me." At least she hoped he wasn't. At least she mostly hoped he wasn't.

"I don't think we go to the same sort of pubs, mate."

In the brief but intensely awkward silence that followed, Rosaline thought it best to fix the entirety of her attention on making the tea dispenser dispense tea. She twisted something, pushed it, and—with a disproportionate sense of triumph—was rewarded with a hot stream of tea that flowed neatly into her cup.

Then kept flowing.

Then kept flowing.

Harry calmly pushed his own cup under the spout. "Nice one. Now how do you stop it?"

"I . . . I thought the button would come up again by itself."

It was not coming up by itself. And tea was already beginning to spill into Harry's saucer. Slapping a hand over the top of the dispenser, Rosaline tried Canute-like to turn back the tides of brown liquid she had inadvertently summoned. It went about as well for her as it had for him.

"Do you want to pass me another mug?" asked Harry.

Rosaline passed him another mug. They watched it fill slowly.

"Do you want to pass me another...another mug?" asked Harry.

Rosaline passed him another another mug. "I think we should probably be looking for a more permanent solution."

"It's got to run out eventually. It's not that big."

They watched the tea creep steadily up the sides of the third mug like the world's slowest and most civilised disaster movie. Unprompted, Rosaline retrieved a fourth mug from a rapidly dwindling pile.

With no comment beyond a faint mumble that might have been "Cheers," Dave reached past them, grabbed the cup Rosaline had poured for herself, and a carton of UHT milk to go with it, and walked away.

Harry danced his fingers clear of the splash zone. "So any news on that permanent solution?"

"I've got an idea. We make a run for it and pretend it wasn't us."

"I don't think I'm going to make it." He slid a fifth mug into place. "But you go. Save yourself. Tell my mum and dad I went down fighting."

"I can't leave you," wailed Rosaline, not entirely sure if they were joking or not. "This is my fault."

"What's your fault?" Colin Thrimp popped up like a piece of underdone toast. Then he caught sight of the endless tea stream. "Oh my. How did this happen? Jennifer will be livid."

Rosaline stared at him for a long moment. "I'm sorry. But they should make them all the same way and they don't."

When she'd applied for *Bake Expectations*, Rosaline had told herself it was a low-risk, high-reward plan. If it worked, she'd get a decent-ish cash prize and, if the experiences of former contestants were anything to go by, a bunch of career opportunities she couldn't get any other way. And if it didn't work, she'd just end up back where she'd started: owing money to her parents, worrying about Amelie's future, and feeling like a failure. Except, normally, she felt like a failure in a vague, directionless, *oh what might have been* sort of way. And now she was giving a bunch of celebrities permission to make her feel like a failure for specific reasons repeatedly on national television.

Which her parents would also see.

Which her parents' friends would also see.

Which her parents would *tell her* their friends had seen. And then they would ask her, very earnestly, why she had thought going on that baking program—they'd never use the actual title, you could always tell whether Cordelia and St. John Palmer disapproved of something by their refusal to use its proper name—and she would have to shrug and say, *I'm sorry, I don't know; I thought it would help somehow, but it clearly didn't.*

And that was where Rosaline's head was stuck as she sat with the rest of the contestants, trying to do her best poker face while Marianne Wolvercote and Wilfred Honey picked the bakes apart one by one and finally declared which was the best and, more significantly for your future in the competition, the worst. And again Rosaline was struck by the triviality of it all. Her father had probably saved at least three people's lives that week and millions were definitely benefitting every day from her mother's research, and what had Rosaline achieved? If she was very, very lucky, she'd got some nuts to a nice texture.

The critiques mostly passed in a blur, not helped by the fact that the contestants were, to Rosaline, also a bit of a blur. Dave— who was still wearing his fedora—had done notably poorly, having left his cake in the oven far too long. And Alain, either because he was a genuinely brilliant cook or because she'd shown him the fucking recipe that fucking morning, had smashed it.

When they came to Rosaline's offering, Marianne Wolvercote pronounced the bake good and the distribution of fruit excellently even. Then she pried an almond from the top, placed it carefully between her teeth, and bit down.

"Underblanched."

Rosaline almost cried.

She wasn't sure how she got through her end-of-day interview. Mostly she nodded and smiled and tried to think of different ways to say, "Well, I thought that went okay, but it could also probably have gone better." Her sense of reality was still on the wibble. Maybe it was just because what they were doing was so artificial anyway, but filming involved so much stopping and starting and waiting to be told what to do that nothing felt connected to anything else.

Her mind kept drifting to what she'd be doing if she were home. If she'd really A-plussed her mothering, she'd already have convinced Amelie to do her spelling, and if she'd really A-plussed her life, she'd have done the laundry on Friday and would have managed to put off visiting her parents until Sunday, so Saturday—assuming she didn't have a shift at work—could be officially declared an Our Day. That meant they each got to choose something they wanted to do—or, in practice, Amelie got to choose something she wanted to do and Rosaline chose something she secretly knew Amelie wanted to do. Sometimes they'd go to the park, or the swimming pool, and sometimes, Amelie would want to go to space and they'd have to improvise a rocket out of two armchairs and a vacuum cleaner. Quite often, they'd bake. And admittedly, Amelie's help tended to make the final product a bit more, as the judges might have said it, "rustic." But—crammed into the tiny kitchen with her daughter, covered in a range of ingredients Rosaline would swear they hadn't been using—it was also one of the few things that made her believe everything was going to be okay. That maybe they were okay already.

Of course for the next eight weeks every Saturday would consist of Amelie waiting at home with whoever Rosaline could beg to babysit for her while Rosaline herself missed out on yet another sliver of the too-short window in which her daughter would enjoy spending time with her. And how was that worth it? She'd spent hours on a train and a night in a farmer's attic just so she could put in a mediocre performance in a baking competition.

She should have called home, but with the baking and the judging and the underblanched almonds and the increasing sense of having made yet another terrible decision, she wasn't totally sure she'd be able to keep it together. And while Amelie probably wouldn't have *minded* if she didn't keep it together, it wasn't exactly parent-of-the-year behaviour to ring up your kid and have an existential crisis at them.

Maybe she could go and find Anvita and have an existential crisis at *her*. That was the kind of thing you could do with someone you'd met once, right? But then, as she was crossing the lawn she caught sight of Alain finishing up his own post-victory interview. The long day was just beginning to catch up with him, although that only meant his artfully tousled hair was looking slightly less artful and slightly more tousled. It suited him, in a way, that faint hint that his composure could be gently unravelled given the right circumstances. Or the right unraveller.

"Well, obviously I'm very pleased," he was saying, with a little half-smile that Rosaline was certain several key demographics would go nuts for. "I do think I got a bit lucky, but...yes. I'll take it. And as for tomorrow, well, let's say I've got a little something up my sleeve." He paused, his eyes darting to the camera operator. "How was that? Do you have everything you need?"

They did, as it happened, have everything they needed, and Alain stepped away from the tangle of lights and mics and booms to join Rosaline. Who had been lingering, unable to decide whether talking to someone she might be interested in was exactly what she wanted right now. Or very much not.

"Well, that went well," he said. It was a sentence Rosaline hardly ever heard nonsarcastically, but from the way Alain was smiling he seemed to mean it. "And thank you so much for letting me look at your books this morning—I don't think I'd have won if you hadn't."

She shrugged. "Don't worry about it. Looking at the recipe didn't do much for me."

"Nonsense. You did far better than a lot of people."

He might have been right. Or he might have just been trying to be nice. It was hard to tell because it was the sort of show where only the top and the bottom mattered and everyone else was in the middle. "Honestly, I'm starting to wonder what I'm even doing here."

"Rosaline, Rosaline." He gazed down at her, his eyes alight with warmth. And then took both her hands. "Come and sit down."

She let him lead her over to a log that seemed to have been literally designed for people to sit on in the evening and have intimate conversations as the moon rose over the duck pond. Oh God. Oh help. He was doing kindness at her. Rosaline couldn't cope with people doing kindness at her. It made her feel like she'd shoplifted a lipstick. Except the lipstick was made of time and emotional energy.

"I'm being silly." She waved what she hoped was a dismissive hand. "Honestly. I'm fine."

Turning his body slightly towards her, he reestablished his look of compassionate understanding. "It's all right. Everyone has moments of uncertainty. I suppose you're worried this is taking time away from your studies."

What studies? Fuck. *Those* studies. The ones she'd pretended she was doing so she'd look cool or worthwhile or just…better. Like someone Alain might be interested in. It was time to come clean. She had to come clean. She couldn't keep taking advantage of him like this. "Um," she heard herself say. "A bit?"

He was silent a moment, giving real thought to her imaginary problem. "The way I see it, yes, this is time that you could be spending on your course. And you'd probably achieve a higher class of degree if you stayed home every night and studied—but that would be the case whether you were on the show or not. And I'm sure most of your classmates will use the time you're using to bake to do Jägerbombs in the student union and, from what I've heard about medical students, leave severed heads in each other's bedrooms."

This would have been an amazing pep talk if she'd actually been at university. "Yeah, but…what if the show distracts me too much and I end up, like hypothetically, not becoming a doctor at all?"

"That won't happen, Rosaline. It's only eight weeks, mostly over the summer. You've already accomplished so much and your whole life is waiting for you, and even if you get eliminated before the semifinal—which I really don't think you will—it'll be another string to your bow when you move on."

Once again. He'd nailed it. For a different person. Because Rosaline's problem was she didn't have a bow. And so coming on this show was just giving her a useless pile of string.

"I mean," he went on, "you're not like—oh, what's her name. Josie? The…Are we saying plus-sized these days?"

Rosaline gave him a slightly confused look. "I think we're not judging people by body type?"

"Are we not?" He gave her a conspiratorial smile. "Or are we just politely pretending not to?"

She wasn't sure what to say to that. Because she wanted the

answer to be *No, certainly not*, but she was pretty sure for a lot of people it was *Yeah, kinda*. And she wasn't sure if being honest about it was courageous or unhelpful.

Before she could make up her mind, Alain had circled back to his point. "Anyway, for someone like Josie, a vicar's wife whose entire job is to arrange flowers and keep the Victoria sponge flowing at parish meetings, this competition is basically *it*. This will be the high point of what passes for her career. For you, me, and Claudia, this is a challenge but a strictly optional one."

Okay. So not the moment to tell him that she was a university dropout. And the closest she'd got to Malawi was when her parents had taken her on holiday to Florence.

"And then you've got Ricky"—his eyes glinted mischievously—"who I'm convinced thought he was applying for *Love Island*."

In spite of everything, Rosaline laughed. "You're kind of shady, you know that?"

"Yes, but don't tell anybody. I'm only this way with people I like."

She gave him a wicked little smile of her own. "Well, aren't you full of secrets?"

"Aren't I? You'll have to find some creative way to coax them out of me."

"All right then." Remarkably, she was feeling slightly better. Because while she hadn't been totally honest with him about her life, what they had right now, when they were talking, that connection was…real? Wasn't it? "How about we start with you telling me what you've got tucked up your sleeve for tomorrow."

"I'm not sure that's coaxing. It feels more like asking."

"You'd be amazed how far I can get with the direct approach. So come on. Spoil the big reveal for me."

"When you put it like that, I'm afraid I might have oversold it."

"Have you cast your own cake tin?"

He laughed. "No, and I'm not sure how that would help."

"Are you using a weird flour? Is it made from powdered bees and repurposed deck chairs?"

"Actually, it's made from ground unicorn horn and children's wishes."

"Now I happen to know for a fact that you can't get ground unicorn horn over here because of the 1979 Sale of Goods Act. What are you *really* doing?"

"Alas." He adopted a tone of mock exasperation. "You caught me. I'm using ordinary flour like an ordinary person. And I'm worried you're pushing this closer and closer to an anticlimax."

Rosaline drew a little nearer and grinned up at him teasingly. "Then you should have told me straightaway, shouldn't you? Have you trained a marmoset to make French meringues?"

"I think *that* would violate the 1973 Endangered Species Act." He looked down at her and Rosaline wasn't certain, but she thought he might have been blushing. "Actually I . . . I foraged my own mint. Which, now I say it aloud sounds less like a trick up my sleeve and more like some herbs I picked in a woodland?"

"Oh, you're right. That *is* a bit of a letdown."

"And whose fault is that?" he asked, smiling at her through the dapple of fading sunlight.

"Do you want me to try and guess that too?"

He leaned towards her. "I think I'd rather—"

"Drinks in the bar!" yelled Anvita, from a distance that didn't really require yelling. "Are you two coming?"

"I don't know?" Rosaline looked up at Alain. "Are we?"

"I would," he said, "but that 4:00 a.m. start is rather taking its toll. Will you think I'm terribly dull if I have an early night?"

"Will you stay up if I say yes?"

"I would try, but then I'd fall asleep on your shoulder and you'd think I was terribly dull anyway." He gave her another of his effortless cheek kisses. "I'll see you tomorrow, Rosaline-um-Palmer. Enjoy your evening."

She watched him stride off towards the Lodge. He was doing the sensible, mature thing and Rosaline should probably have done the same. Unfortunately, she'd reached the stage of tiredness that felt like restlessness, and she didn't especially want to lie in bed, worrying pointlessly about tomorrow.

"Are you coming?" yelled Anvita, still from the same yell-unnecessary distance.

"Give me ten minutes. I just need to——" Rosaline had been about to say "Call my daughter," but Alain was still in earshot, and while she did need to tell him the truth at some point— probably very soon—shouting to somebody else across a big garden wasn't the right way to do it.

Feeling far more duplicitous than she would have liked, she hurried over to Anvita. Who was still assessing Alain's retreat. "Is that the guy you got stuck with last night?"

"Um, yes," said Rosaline modestly. As if getting stranded at a railway station with Alain had been in any way a reflection of her taste in people to get stranded at railway stations with.

"Win."

"Thank you." Of course, it was less of a win, given that he still thought she was a sexy globe-trotting medical student.

"I mean, I wouldn't call him a *stone-cold* hottie," Anvita went on. "But he's definitely chilly."

"I'm a full-time mum. Chilly is probably all I can keep up with."

"Don't sell yourself short. You can have hotties of whatever temperature you want. It's one of the perks of being a modern independent woman."

Frankly, Rosaline could have done with feeling a bit more modern and independent. Between child support from Amelie's father, the insultingly small amount of welfare she was entitled to, and semiregular handouts from her parents, she was painfully reliant on other people. While also, perversely, being completely on her own when it came to the things that mattered. "Well, I mostly want to be a modern independent woman who wins a baking show."

"Can't you be a modern independent woman who wins a baking show and also gets together with a delicious mansnack?" asked Anvita.

She gave Anvita a look. "I'm not sure I'd call Alain a delicious mansnack."

"Maybe not. He's got a keeper air, which I guess makes him...mandinner?"

"How long do you think dinner lasts?"

"In my family? A very long time."

Rosaline laughed. "Speaking of families, I really need to go ring my kid."

"No problem. What should I order for you?"

"Uh..." It had been way too long since a cute girl had offered to buy Rosaline a drink. This was obviously a platonic drink, but she was still temporarily stumped. "Wine, I guess?"

"Do you want cheap red or cheap white?"

"When you put it like that, it doesn't matter."

Anvita vanished through the main doors of the hotel and Rosaline settled herself under a tree with her phone. It was about half an hour after Amelie's bedtime, which made it the perfect time to ring home and see how she was.

"Roz darling." Lauren only called her *Roz darling* when she was taking the piss or trying to cover something up. "How are things? Amelie's upstairs and sleeping like a baby."

"Just put her on."

"I don't know *what* you're implying."

"*Lauren.*"

There was a scuffling at the other end of the phone, then Amelie's voice. "Hello, Mummy."

"You're meant to be in bed."

"Auntie Lauren said I could stay up until you called."

Reasonable. Also a transparent lie. "Have you had a nice day?"

"Yes. We played games and ate cake and watched television and Auntie Lauren tested me on my spelling except she isn't very good at spelling so it didn't help very much."

"Don't be mean about Auntie Lauren."

Rosaline could practically *hear* Amelie's expression of indignation. "I'm not being mean. I'm telling the truth. We are always meant to tell the truth."

"Not when it's mean. Now you know it's past your bedtime so you should say good night to Auntie Lauren and go to bed right now."

"I'm not sleepy."

"Well, lie down and close your eyes and you soon will be." This was bullshit. Rosaline knew full well that when you weren't tired lying down and trying to *be* tired didn't help. But children needed routines, and so you said what you had to.

"I don't think that works. I try it every night and it takes *ages* and sometimes I don't remember going to sleep at all but I think I probably do because I don't remember being awake either."

"It's *past your bedtime*, Amelie. Go to bed."

There was a ten-second window in which it seemed very likely that Amelie was about to protest. "Okay," she said instead. "Love you to the moon and back."

"Love you to the moon and back too. Put Auntie Lauren on."

Another scuffling, and Lauren was at the end of the line again.

"If I find out she didn't actually go to bed...," said Rosaline in her best parental voice.

"She will, she will. I'm not completely hopeless."

Rosaline stretched out her legs, feeling the grass cool underneath her. "I never said you were hopeless, but you've also never met a rule you didn't want to break."

"I'm just teaching your daughter a healthy disrespect for authority."

"You realise you're going to *be* the authority until my mother shows up?"

"Fuck. I hadn't thought of that." Never one to dwell on a thought she found unpleasant, Lauren swiftly changed the subject. "So what's it like? Do you feel all showbiz?"

"Not really. There's a lot of standing around and answering the same question twenty times. And all I've succeeded in doing is making a mediocre Dundee cake and digging myself into a massive hole with one of the other contestants."

Lauren, of course, latched onto this immediately. "That sounds like a tale hangs thereby."

"Not a very good one."

"Please. I've been watching children's television all evening and while some of it has a delightfully surreal quality, I've been very starved for human drama. Tell me *exactly* what shape hole you're in and precisely how dirty you'll get trying to climb out."

"Fine." Rosaline sighed. "So you know how last night I told you I got stuck crashing at a random farmhouse? Well, someone else from the show got stuck there with me and we got talking and he was hot and interesting and an architect and he's travelled and all this stuff."

"That doesn't sound like a hole, Rosaline. That sounds like a perfectly ordinary conversation."

"I'm getting to the hole. The hole is imminent and now I've said the word 'hole' so many times it sounds weird. Anyway, the point of the hole—"

"Holes can't have points, darling," drawled Lauren. "That's rather definitional."

"Oh, go learn to spell. The point of the hole is that when we got to the bit where he politely asked me what I did, I panicked. And instead of saying 'I'm a single mum who works in a shop,' I said, 'I'm a medical student who spent several years in Malawi.' Which means I have to pretend to know about Malawi. Forever."

At least Lauren had the decency not to laugh, but that was about her limit. "Three out of ten, Roz. All setup, no payoff."

"I hate you. You know that, right?"

"To the moon and back?"

"To the fucking *sun* and back. And don't take the piss out of my and Amelie's thing. That's our thing and it's sweet and she'll probably stop doing it in a couple of years and I'll be a lonely old woman who nobody cares about longing for the days when I had a kid who actually liked me."

"Oh please"—Lauren snorted—"in a couple of years you'll barely be thirty. You'll still be young enough to play a teenager on American television."

"Yeah, somehow I don't think that's going to be a career option for me."

Lauren was silent a moment. Then, "I can't believe you'd told some man you were in Malawi. Why Malawi of all places?"

"I don't know. I think Amelie's dad went there once."

More silence. In Rosaline's experience that meant Lauren was building up to something.

"What is it, Loz?" she asked, resigned to whatever mockery was coming her way.

"Hmm? Oh, I was just trying to work out if it makes you *more* or *less* of a racist that your culturally appropriative journey of self-discovery only took place in your head."

"To the *sun and back*," Rosaline repeated. "I feel awful enough as it is without having to worry about that as well."

"Why do you even care what this random train man thinks about anything?"

"I don't know. Maybe I've been brainwashed by the patriarchy."

"You were into him, weren't you?"

"I mean. Yes. I think?" Rosaline flumped against the trunk of the tree. "It's a bit hard to tell because my only points of reference these days are primary school teachers, parents, and you."

"I flatter myself that I set a high bar."

"Well, he's not married, and he's never cheated on me. Which puts him ahead of you in at least two areas."

"Ah, yes. A love story for the ages. She was a young woman trying to find her place in a world that had wronged her. He...wasn't married."

Rosaline gritted her teeth. "Look, he's a charming, successful, good-looking guy who clearly has his shit together and who, if I'm not completely terrible at this, might like me. And it's a little bit hard to know what I have to offer someone like that. So I freaked out and tried to offer him Malawi."

"Just tell him the truth. If he's not an utter prick, he'll be fine about it. And if he is, the problem rather solves itself."

She was right. She was right. Being right was one of Lauren's worst qualities. "I will. But maybe not exactly this second. Because I'm going to the bar to have a drink. With grown-ups. Who I've met. In my life that I've got."

"Good for you. Now I really need to call Allison, so bugger off and enjoy your evening."

They exchanged hasty goodbyes, the phone clicked. And off Rosaline buggered.

Inside the bar, Rosaline found several of the other contestants huddled around a circular table, nursing an array of beverages and swapping tales of woe from the day's baking.

"I'll be honest," Josie was saying, "when Marianne looked at my cake like that, I thought I was going to poop my knickers."

Florian rolled his eyes theatrically. "Darling, you have nothing to complain about. She said my almonds were limp. I've never been limp in my life."

"It happens." Ricky squidged over to make room for Rosaline

in front of what looked like the promised glass of cheap wine. "Wait half an hour. Try again."

"It's Rosaline, isn't it?" Josie—a posh, comfortable woman in her mid-forties—extended a hand over the table. "Don't think we've actually met."

Rosaline gave what she hoped was a respectable handshake. "Yeah. I was delayed. I got stuck with Alain at a train station and we had to spend the night with a farmer."

"Oooh"—Josie lifted her brows salaciously—"how'd you explain that one to the husband?"

Wait. What? "I don't have one. So…quite easily? Or, from a different perspective, with great difficulty."

"Well, willy bum piddle." Josie actually covered her mouth with her hands. "Sorry. Anvita said you had a daughter so I assumed…Is he not in the picture or are you being terribly modern?"

"He's …on the edge of the picture. Like, he's in Amelie's life, but we're not together or anything."

"My word. What a prize scuzzbucket. You think he'd at least have done the decent thing." Josie sighed with a world-weariness that Rosaline suspected she had in no way earned. "But that's men for you. Only after one thing and the moment they've got it—*poof!*"

Just once Rosaline would have liked to be able to talk about this aspect of her life without people treating her like a fallen woman in a nineteenth-century novel. Which was to say either a terrible victim of the cruelties of the world or a giant slut. "Can you not call my kid's dad a scuzzbucket? Tom's actually a really nice guy, but we were both very young and I don't think getting married would have been right for either of us."

"Yes, but"—Josie wasn't letting this go, was she?—"he's every bit as responsible as you are. Why should you be the one left carrying the can?"

"I suppose," said Rosaline, trying not to lose either her temper or her self-respect, and fearing she might only be able to hang on to one, "I don't think of Amelie as a can."

Josie patted her gently on the arm. "No, no, of course not. I just know what it's like. I've got three of my own and it's hard enough with two of us. You must be terribly brave."

It was *technically* better, Rosaline supposed, than thinking that she was some wanton strumpet determined to sponge off the state, but at least when people looked down on her she could cleanly dislike them. It was when they pushed the "such a hero" narrative that it got difficult because they clearly expected her to approve. "I've got quite a lot of support. My parents are...Well, they're always there if I need them. And my ex and her wife are"—what was Lauren exactly?—"a lot more helpful than I have any right to expect them to be."

"Sorry." Josie blinked rapidly. "Probably being a bit provincial, but did you say your ex and—"

"I'm really rather weary," cut in Florian so abruptly that Rosaline was sure it was a deliberate rescue, "of everyone assuming marriage is the default end state of the human condition. I've been with Scott for twenty years and, ever since it was legalised, our friends keep asking us when we're getting married, and we keep saying *never* and they don't believe us."

It was probably wrong for Rosaline to feel relieved that Josie's attention swung to Florian. But she did. "I'm sure you didn't mean to," said Josie in the sort of tone you reserved for four-year-olds, "but you just interrupted me and that's a little bit rude."

Florian gave a slightly catlike smile. "Oh no, I fully meant to. Perhaps I shouldn't be presuming, but I'd rather we didn't treat each other's sexualities as topics of interrogation."

"I'm not interrogating. I'm taking an interest."

"No." Florian sounded like a man who had several distinct flavours of no he reserved for different occasions. "Taking an interest is when you ask somebody how their runner beans are doing. When you persistently ask someone to explain why their life experiences don't exactly match yours, that's an interrogation."

For someone in a floral blouse, Josie could bristle quite impressively. "I was expressing sympathy. You wouldn't understand because you don't have children."

Rosaline felt a bit like she'd blundered into quicksand and, when Florian tried to help her, dragged him in afterwards. "Why do you think he wouldn't have children?" she asked.

"Well, because—"

"To save you finishing that thought, dear," said Florian quickly, "I don't. But that's because I'm a misanthropist, not because I'm a homosexual."

There was a long silence.

Then Ricky started dramatically, "Is that marmalade? Have I got marmalade on my shoulder? How long have I been going around with marmalade on my shoulder?"

"Probably since you dropped that jar of marmalade?" suggested Anvita.

"But how'd it get up there? I dropped it on the floor."

"I'm not a man of science"—Florian took a sip of his rosé—"but experience suggests that splashback is a bitch."

The conversation, having been resolutely steered from the state of Rosaline's life to the state of Ricky's clothes, should have felt safer. But it didn't. And so Rosaline was left sitting there feeling small, and slightly naked, and like she was probably overreacting, except she didn't know how to not. Because, for fuck's sake, this was a stranger she'd need to see ten times at most. Why did she care what Josie—or, indeed, anyone else—thought of her.

The problem was, she did. She really, really did.

Sunday

BREAKING FOR LUNCH was worse on the second day because instead of walking past a row of very similar-looking Dundee cakes, running a spectrum from "kind of okay" to "kind of rubbish," you were walking past a row of very different-looking cakes, several of which blew yours out of the fucking water. When planning the recipe, Rosaline had thought decorating her chocolate beetroot cake with a simple drizzle of melted chocolate would make it look classy and elegant. Unfortunately, it just made it look...dull. As if the girl from the start of the movie had never taken off her glasses or let down her hair.

Which sort of summed up how she felt about the whole weekend. She hadn't expected to come on and be instantly amazing. Except, well, maybe deep down, she had a little tiny bit? Because Cordelia and St. John had raised her to be amazing, and she'd been amazing at school and, once you adjusted for Cambridge standards, amazing at university. She was even amazing at work, although mostly because the job sucked and most of her coworkers were teenagers. And obviously, parenting had been kicking her arse solidly for eight years. But that wasn't the kind of thing where you got marks out of ten at the end.

Her one consolation was that—for the most part—chocolate cakes were all some variant of brown, so while hers was dull, at least it was dull in company. Of course, that made Anvita's, with its vivid pattern of crushed red chillies, stand out even more. To say nothing of Alain's gorgeous spring morning of a creation, smoothly enveloped in pale green buttercream and crowned with basil leaves.

Having fallen afoul of the tea decanters the day before, Rosaline nervously poured herself a cup and grabbed a wrap she probably wouldn't be able to stomach. She'd just found a quiet spot on the lawn to nurse her encroaching sense of inadequacy when she spotted Alain coming towards her, looking—as Miss Wooding so often did—not angry but disappointed.

Oh God. He knew. He definitely knew.

"Rosaline," he said. "I don't quite know how to put this, but—"

"Okay. Yes. Um, I should—"

"Can you please let me finish?"

She would have preferred to say no and come clean before he could lay her bad behaviour before her like a piece of unfinished homework. But since she was supposed to be apologising and not conducting a hard-hitting interview, she couldn't. "Sorry. Yes. Of course."

"Several people have mentioned in passing that you have a daughter. And I feel, honestly, a bit strange being the only person you haven't told about her. And I confess"—here Alain ran a hand through his hair—"I'm a little confused about how your whole life story fits together. Did you, ah, meet someone in Malawi?"

There had been never been a scenario in which this didn't go badly. Yet, somehow, she hadn't quite been prepared for the crushing humiliation of being confronted with her own terrible behaviour. She hung her head. "No. There's no Malawi. I mean, there is a Malawi, but I've never been there. And I'm not a medical student, I'm a...nothing, really."

"But you *do* have a daughter?"

"Yes. Her name's Amelie. She's eight. She's wonderful."

"I'm sure she is," he told her. "I just...I don't understand why you lied to me. And I certainly don't understand why you *only* lied to me."

She risked an apologetic smile. "I guess I'm a bad liar and didn't think it through?"

"Rosaline." He looked if not devastated then at least lightly pillaged. "You've fucked me about here. You can't cute your way out of it."

"Sorry. Sorry. I didn't mean to...cute. And I didn't mean to lie either. I...I panicked." This was awful. This was unbelievably awful. "Because...we met the way we did and you were clever and funny and successful and I thought we...maybe clicked maybe?"

He blinked, his eyes grey and wounded. "Well, we might have. But how can I tell when I don't even know who you are?"

"You're right. I fucked up. I'm sorry. I just liked you and I didn't want you to...oh God...think *things* about me."

"What do you mean, 'things'?" he asked impatiently.

"You know"—she stared at her sandwich, which was the only object in a ten-foot radius she could trust not to have strong opinions about her life choices—"that I'm whatever sort of person you think the sort of person who gets pregnant at university is."

"I...I don't understand."

"I just..." The words fell pathetically out of her like socks out of a laundry basket. "I just didn't want you to think less of me."

He gave her a look that was colder than any look she'd thought he was capable of giving. "I'm not sure that makes it better. Because not only did you lie to me, but you also apparently think I'm the kind of man who'd judge you for a mistake you made when you were still a teenager."

It was nothing she hadn't heard before. But there was something about the word "mistake" that always made her feel queasy. *I never planned for this to happen* was too close to *This should never have happened*, and then it stopped being about Rosaline's past and started being about Amelie's future. And the thing was, she couldn't say any of that. Because, right here and right now, Alain wasn't wrong. By every standard she'd ever been taught, she'd messed up her life. She'd had everything going for her, and she'd thrown it away on a careless night with a guy she wasn't even that into. Worse, she'd been ashamed of herself for so long that here she was projecting her own mess onto someone who would probably have been fine if she'd had the courage to trust him.

"I'm sorry," she said. "I'm really sorry."

Alain's mouth, with its generous curve and its tantalising brackets, was particularly expressive when he was upset. "So you keep saying. But what exactly am I supposed to do with that? Or with you?"

She'd ruined it. She'd completely ruined it. "I don't know. Can we...can we start again? I mean, I'm still me. I just haven't been to Malawi."

"You sat next to me last night and let me reassure you that being on this show wouldn't get in the way of your fake medical degree. Are you really so desperate for...for I don't even know what...that you have to gaslight people into telling you things are okay?"

Oh God. Had she done that? She hadn't meant to, but did that make a difference? If this had been the kind of movie where their leads got tangled up in a dog park, then being insecure enough to tell someone she fancied a pack of lies would be quirky and amusing and forgiven with a kiss in the pouring rain. But now she'd accidentally behaved that way, it was...it was hurtful.

"I'm sorry," she said again. "I don't know what to say."

He gave a sharp laugh. "Whatever you said, would it even be true?"

"Alain, I..."

"I'm sorry. I'm not doing this." He turned and walked away into the mellow afternoon sunlight.

And Rosaline had no choice but to follow him because the technical crew were hurrying them back to the ballroom.

Selfish and self-defeating though it seemed, Rosaline wasn't in a fit state to pay much attention to the judging. It mostly boiled down to people having done a little bit either side of fine. Dave, however, had skewed far enough into not-fine that Rosaline was at least slightly more confident about her chances of surviving week one.

Despite serving up two tiers of what was clearly intended to be a three-tiered cake, he somehow managed to look at once defiant and defeated, as if his whole body was saying *I dare you to admit this is as shit as we all know it is.*

"So you had a bit of an accident wi' one o't layers," began Wilfred Honey, smiling his most grandfatherly smile, which, for a man so grandfatherly it was like his whole body was made of Werther's Originals was very grandfatherly indeed. "But that doesn't matter as long as the taste is right."

They cut into it, and Marianne Wolvercote nibbled a delicate forkful. "The taste isn't right."

Dave rocked back on his heels a moment, nodded, and then said, "Well, fuck you both very much."

The whole set had gone quiet, like everybody knew there was a wasp in the room and nobody knew where it was. It was just that in this case the wasp was named Jennifer Hallet, and there was very little ambiguity about who was going to get stung.

"David," she said in a voice that could have split cake batter and set meringues, "a word."

The judging proceeded as normal after that, only slightly

interrupted by occasional half-caught phrases like "contractual obligation," "caustic piss-storm," and "faster than your first shit after a salmonella pasty" drifting in from outside.

Once Jennifer Hallet had finished politely explaining to Dave why his conduct had been unprofessional and might have negative repercussions, she brought him back inside, pointed at the spot in front of the judges' table, and said: "From Marianne's last line. Thanks."

"The taste isn't right," Marianne Wolvercote repeated, with exactly the same intonation as the first time. "Rosewater is a delicate flavour that's easy to overdo, and you have *most definitely* overdone it."

There was a really long silence.

Dave picked up his two-thirds of a cake. "Mmhm. Thanks."

And so it went on. Anvita did well, and Rosaline was just focused enough to be happy for her. Then her own turn came around and with a kind of detached relief, she realised that she was too emotionally battered to be nervous.

Marianne Wolvercote peered at her offering with the eye of a connoisseur, which, when Rosaline thought about it, she was. "Now this looks good, but it *is* quite simple, and so I'm not totally certain *good* will be enough."

Rosaline's shoulders hunched slightly. She knew that already. As long as she didn't actively tell the judges to fuck off she would probably get through, but "Good enough isn't good enough" was the Palmers' unofficial family motto. And here she was demonstrating her not-good-enoughness all over again.

The judges sliced into her cake and Marianne Wolvercote poked it with a knife in a way that Rosaline, already raw from the process and Alain and everything, found weirdly invasive.

"Nice lightness," said Wilfred Honey, still chewing enthusiastically. "Tasty and with a really smooth, moist texture to it."

Setting her fork down, Marianne Wolvercote looked grave. "But sadly that's about all there is. If this had been *perfect*, it could have been the best bake of the day, but it's a touch uneven here"—she indicated a line along the base of the cake where the mixture had settled a little, leaving it slightly denser—"and I think you left it in the oven a *shade* too long."

"Also," added Wilfred Honey, "I think it might have looked nicer if you'd made a lovely ganache. Or maybe a buttercream, just to lift it up a bit."

Oh, of course. Put that on the list of many, many things she could have done differently in her life.

"Mmhm," she said. "Thanks."

As she slunk back to her workstation, she crossed paths with Alain, who was striding confidently forward, cradling a tray full of magic. He didn't look at her, but then why would he?

He laid his creation delicately in front of the judges. "This is a chocolate cake with basil buttercream, served with a mint ice-cream." Then, after a small pause and with a self-deprecating half-smile: "The basil's from my garden and I, ah, foraged the mint."

They cut into it with appreciative ceremony, exposing the perfectly even layers of dark sponge and pale cream, and then sampled it with gusto.

"This is rather delightful," purred Marianne Wolvercote. "I was concerned about the basil, but it works surprisingly well against the richness of the chocolate."

Wilfred Honey scooped up another forkful. "By 'eck, it's gorgeous."

A ripple of gasps moved through the hall. This was an informal catchphrase of Wilfred Honey's, and he usually didn't break it out until episode three or four. Clearly, Alain—as well as being the type of person who'd never lie about his personal history—

was also a big deal in the kitchen. And Rosaline had thrown all of that away by being an insecure, disappointing mess of a human being.

So Alain won. Obviously. And Dave went out. Obviously. And Rosaline was safe and unremarkable and desperate to get home. See her daughter. Have a glass of wine. Come to terms with the fact that the thing she normally did to make herself feel better—to wit, baking—was now the third-largest source of stress in her life.

Well done, Rosaline. Nailed it as usual.

Unfortunately, before she could to do any of that she had to wait. In the car park. For her father to pick her up. Like she was sixteen and had gone to the wrong sort of party. It was one of the problems of filming in a picturesque rural setting: no trains out of Tapworth on a Sunday. Which, in practice, meant another favour Rosaline would owe her parents.

It was probably going to be a long wait. Mr. St. John Palmer—a man so successful in the medical profession he'd gone through Dr. and out the other side—tended to arrive late on the grounds of his being so very busy and important. And that would have been…what it was. Except Alain, who Rosaline should have realised would be in a similar situation, seemed to be depending on someone equally unreliable.

For a few minutes they stood in miserable silence.

"Well done on the win," Rosaline tried.

"Thank you."

Well, at least he'd answered? "Sorry again for the…all the, y'know, lying."

"Rosaline…" His mouth curled into a wry half-smile. "If this hadn't happened to me, I'd think it was hilarious. But it did, so it's going to take me a little longer than usual to see the funny side."

"I think you can probably get really good mileage out of the 'girl who liked me so much she invented a life in Malawi' story?"

He laughed, somewhat reluctantly. "I should have suspected something when you were so reticent. I know a few people who've done that kind of thing and none of them will shut the fuck up about it."

This was...better, wasn't it? He seemed amused rather than actively disgusted with her.

And of course, Mr. St. John Palmer chose exactly that moment to pull up in front of them. Emerging from the driver's side, he released the boot to allow Rosaline to stow her bag.

"I got here as quickly as I could," he told her. "I was stuck behind some cretin with a caravan on the motorway and then all the roads round here are full of bloody sheep." It was at about this point that he noticed Alain and, whether for reasons of proximity, gender, or general demeanour, decided he was probably important. "Terribly sorry. Where are my manners? St. John Palmer. I'm Rosaline's father."

As Rosaline tried to apologise with her eyes, Alain was left with no choice but to accept one of her father's extremely forceful handshakes. "Alain Pope. I'm one of Rosaline's cocontestants."

"Oh. I'd assumed you were the producer."

"No, I'm an architect."

"Worked on anything I might know?"

"Possibly. When were you last in Dubai?"

"Not for a year or two."

Alain smiled the kind of smile you were supposed to use in job interviews. "Then you wouldn't be familiar with my most recent project. If you've visited Coombecamden Manor, I've done some work there as well?"

Rosaline had seen her father do this to a lot of people. The game was to keep tacitly implying he thought you were a loser until you gave up and admitted it. And unusually, Alain seemed perilously close to actually *winning*.

"You *do* keep busy," conceded St. John Palmer. "How the hell did you wind up baking?"

"Ah, well. When I was refitting my house a few years back I had an AGA put in, and I thought I should probably learn to use it properly."

"Something for the wife, was it?"

"No. I'm not married." By way of illustration Alain raised his left hand to display his entirely absent wedding ring.

To Rosaline's absolute horror, St. John Palmer clapped Alain on the back and, with one hand between his shoulder blades, guided him towards the rear of the car where she had just dumped her bag. "Rosaline," he called out, "was I interrupting something between you and this young man here?"

"What?" She had no idea how to respond to this. "No. Nothing. I mean—"

"Rosaline's been very sweet." Alain shot her a look that could almost have been conspiratorial. "But the competition has kept us both extremely busy. Still, I'm sure we'll get to know each other better as the weeks go on." A car horn beeped from the other side of the car park and Alain glanced over in recognition. "And *that* will be my friend Liv. A pleasure to meet you, Mr. Palmer." He shook her father's hand again and seemed to be giving as good as he got. "I'll see you next week, Rosaline."

There was just enough time for Rosaline to mouth a very quick, very silent *Thank you* to Alain for not dropping her totally in the shit with her dad before he hurried over to his ride. There he hugged a brief hello to an intimidatingly attractive blond woman, and the two of them sped away.

St. John Palmer got back into his car and Rosaline got in

beside him. She'd barely finished fastening her seat belt when it started.

"Your mother was expecting you to call."

"I've only just left the set."

"You seem to have found plenty of time to socialise."

She had, in a way, but he had no actual evidence of it. "You mean Alain? We were just both waiting in the same car park."

"It looked like you were talking." The rules of the road meant that her father was legally obliged to keep staring straight ahead while he spoke to her. But Rosaline was pretty sure he would have even if they hadn't.

"Just being polite. I think he's...nice, though?"

"*Nice.*" Her father held a lot of things in contempt, but for some reason seemed to reserve his most particular ire for a small selection of words that Rosaline had always felt was wholly arbitrary. "You used to have such a good vocabulary."

"He seems very diligent, capable, intelligent, and"—somehow she thought her father wouldn't accept *hot*—"sesquipedalian."

"Don't be facetious, Rosaline. It's beneath you. Or at least it should be."

She sighed. "Sorry."

There was one of those "lulling her into a false sense of security" pauses.

"Honestly," St. John Palmer continued, "I'm a little surprised a man like that is appearing on a show like—what's it called?"

He knew what it was called. He just liked making her say it. "*Bake Expectations.*"

"Still, I suppose once your career's established you can mess around with whatever hobbies you like. No different from golfing really, is it?"

Her father wasn't a golfer, but it was one of the few pastimes he didn't look down on. Which would have been the closest he'd come in a long time to supporting her choices, had it not been so painfully obvious that his approval of Alain's participation was grounded in the fact he didn't actually need anything from the show. Whereas Rosaline, who desperately did, was wasting her time and embarrassing her family. "No," she said. "It's basically just golf with more raisins."

St. John Palmer didn't reply. Perhaps he was punishing Rosaline for her continued facetiousness.

And after a moment or two, he turned on Radio 4 in time to catch the end of the shipping forecast.

Week Two

Pie

Friday

IN SOME WAYS, returning for week two was even stranger than arriving for week one. As soon as Rosaline had left, Patchley House and everything in it started to feel like a bizarrely specific dream. But now she was back, her time at home—taking Amelie to school, going to her job, making endless mini chicken pies— was heading the same way. Which meant there was nothing to distract her from her performance in week one. A performance that had involved freaking out over the inherent futility of what she was doing. Then making a mediocre cake in front of the nation and a complete fool of herself in front of someone she was maybe interested in. *C-minus, Rosaline. Must try harder. See me after class.*

Having successfully navigated public transport and dumped her bag in her room, she went for a restless wander through the grounds. Short of building a time machine out of hot water crust pastry and the chocolate ganache she should have made last week, there was nothing she could do about Malawigate. But she *could* do something about her attitude. Because, even though winning *Bake Expectations* wouldn't magically transform her into a qualified heart surgeon, Cordelia and St. John Palmer hadn't raised a quitter.

And while they would never approve of her being on reality

TV, they'd probably disown her completely if she went on reality TV and then half-arsed it.

So she had to focus. Do the work. Push herself as hard as she could. Not get distracted by boys. Produce the kind of baketactular that would make viewers at home go "Ooh, that's quite impressive for week two."

And as she meandered through the little woodland that ran alongside the Lodge, Rosaline felt she was doing a pretty good job of psyching herself up to be a deadly, single-minded baking machine. Until she saw Alain coming the other way.

Fuck fuck fuck.

Unfortunately, there was nowhere to hide. Well, technically there were loads of places to hide because she could have run up a tree or jumped into a pile of leaves, but if her aim was to avoid another embarrassing situation, then fleeing like an alarmed squirrel probably wasn't going to help her cause.

"Um," she said, "hi?"

He gave her one of his half-smiles. "Rosaline."

They eyed each other across the bracken. And she was once again struck by how quietly stylish Alain was with his shirts and his chinos and, today, a light jacket that seemed to be part of an outfit rather than a concession to the evening breeze. It was like that bit at the end of a game show where they open door number three to show what you could have won if you weren't a lying sack of shit.

She wondered if she should apologise again. Or if that would just be annoying. So she opened her mouth to say goodbye and found herself apologising for something else. "Sorry about my dad."

"Not at all." He flicked back a lock of hair that had escaped its assigned position in the artful whole. "He's clearly very protective of you."

"Protective" wasn't the word Rosaline would have used. But

better he thought that than realised how much of a letdown she actually was to her father. "Yeah. He's, um, yeah."

Another long pause.

"How about we take a walk?" asked Alain.

Okay. That was good, right? Not that she'd been expecting it. Or hoping for it. Well, not very much. "Are you...are you sure?"

He arched a slightly self-mocking brow. "Not at all, Rosaline-um-Palmer. Shall we do it anyway?"

"Maybe it can be another adventure."

"With the real you this time?"

This felt like a life branch or an olive raft. "I promise."

"Come on then. The river's this way."

She risked a smile. "You're not planning on pushing me in, are you?"

"I'm annoyed, Rosaline. I'm not fucking twelve."

They'd strolled a little way down the hill—surrounded by the soft purples of an English country evening—before Rosaline plucked up the courage to say, "So I'm taking you not wanting to push me into a river as a good sign."

He glanced down at her, his eyes gleaming wickedly. "I didn't say I don't want to. I said I was too mature to."

"You know what's really mature? Calling yourself mature."

"You know what's even more mature? Pretending you went to Malawi when you actually didn't."

It still made her wince. But at least he was teasing her instead of calling her a liar. "Does the fact you're taking the piss out of me mean you're getting over it?"

"Perhaps. I'll tell you when we've got to know each other a bit better."

Rosaline wasn't quite prepared for the sheer relief that rolled over her. She wasn't sure she deserved a second chance, but she was sure as hell going to take it. And yes—as she'd just reminded herself—her priority was baking, not boys. But wasn't

Anvita right? Wasn't it okay to want both? She'd been taught to aim high, and while her parents weren't super sold on where she was currently aiming, if she could come out of it with ten grand, a book deal, a new career, and *an architect*, those were all pretty strong ticks in the "life back on track" column.

Only one problem, though. "There's not a lot to get to know," she admitted.

"Really? It seems to me you've had quite an eventful time of it."

"Eventful" was a kinder way to put it than many she'd heard. "Have I?"

"Well, haven't you? I know what they say about making assumptions, but I can't quite believe getting pregnant at, what, nineteen or twenty was your original plan."

"Not exactly. I was going to be a doctor."

He smiled a little. "So you went dangerously close to the truth on what you were studying and needlessly far from it on where you'd been?"

"I did say I panicked."

"And you did say you were a bad liar."

"Yes," she agreed, laughing. "And I wasn't lying."

There was a silence. It wasn't comfortable. But it wasn't wipe-your-eyes-with-chili-on-your-fingers awful either.

"So." Alain paused delicately. It was a pause Rosaline had heard—or not heard—before. "You don't have to tell me anything you don't want to, but what actually happened?"

She shrugged. "No big drama. No big mystery. The girl I was seeing cheated on me, and I sort of rebounded on this guy who'd always had a bit of a crush. We were together for a while, but we were careless a couple of times, then lucky a couple of times, then less lucky. And...yeah."

"And he just left you?"

"No, I'm not Fantine. He was very 'do the right thing' about it, but neither of us wanted to get married, and it didn't feel like we should still have to."

"I wasn't necessarily suggesting your father should have gone full shotgun. Just—I mean, there's finances to consider."

"I get child support." She shrugged again. "He's a hydrological engineer now, so it's pretty generous."

Alain thought about it for a moment before offering gently, "Seems a bit unfair that he got to follow his dreams and you didn't get to follow yours."

Wow. There was really no way to have this conversation without feeling terrible. Worse, it kept finding new and different ways to terrible at her. To be fair, *Alas, your dreams are as dust* was only a variant on *Oh poor you, your life is ruined.* But with Alain it was genuinely about her, and who she could have been. Instead of the general principle that nice middle-class girls left university to have careers, not babies.

Something of...whatever she was feeling...must have shown on her face because he stopped and turned her gently. "I'm sorry, Rosaline," he said. "I didn't mean to stir up anything painful."

It was too complicated. Because, yes, it was painful. It was just that she didn't quite know where the pain was coming from. She took a deep breath. "No, it's fine. I made my choices and I love my daughter and...and...that's all there is to it."

"And I understand that. But"—he gazed down at her searchingly—"you must have had...options?"

She knew what "options" was a euphemism for. "Do you mean, why didn't I get an abortion?"

His eyes flashed in sudden surprise. He probably hadn't expected her to say it. Most people didn't. "Well, I suppose so?"

"I didn't want to. It's not a big political statement, I'm not religious. It was the right thing for me at the time to...not. So I didn't."

"And your parents couldn't"—he made a slightly abstract gesture—"arrange something?"

In spite of herself she laughed. "Arrange something? That sounds like you're suggesting they have a guy called Joey Nine Fingers give me a concrete overcoat."

"I more meant they could look after her while you went back to university."

Of course they'd had that conversation too. "You've met my dad. Would you leave the person you love most in the world with him?"

"You seem to have turned out all right."

Apart from the whole dead-end job, barely paying her bills, nebulous conviction that she was fucking everything up, pinning all her hopes on a TV baking show thing...sure. "'All right' is very much what I shoot for."

His mouth had that jump-into-my-curricle curve. "You're better than all right. And you know it."

It was just what you said. Obviously, it was just what you said. But she was secretly glad he saw her that way. "Thanks. You're...pretty okay too."

"Steady on. Flattery like that will turn a boy's head."

She laughed a little self-consciously. "Silver-tongued devil. That's me."

And he laughed, too, less self-consciously.

Which was, of course, when Rosaline—overwhelmingly relieved that they seemed to have to have got their... *thing* back, whatever it was—panicked and tried to ruin it again. "So, um, are we, um. Are we good? Does this mean we're... good?"

"Rosaline-um-Palmer"—now his eyes were saying *Jump out of my curricle to somewhere more interesting*—"where's the fun in *good*?"

Her stomach—legit, no lie—fluttered. And she did that maybe-kiss-me-now signal where you angle your face a bit and hope.

But Alain only gleamed down at her for a moment before

stepping away. "Come on. If we don't get to the river soon, all the best ripples will be taken."

They walked on. And this time, the silence was comfortable. Or as comfortable as you could get when you were trying to think of something delightful to say to someone.

"Tell me something else about you," suggested Alain. "It feels like we've talked about a lot of the things you don't normally talk about and very few of the things you do."

Okay. She knew this one. The trick was: *don't panic and invent an entire history to cover your boringness.* "Well. Um. I like baking, obviously. I've got a daughter. Her name's Amelie. I work in a high-street stationery shop, which is very exciting. I tried to take up knitting, because I thought it would be cool to be someone who could knit, but I never quite found the time to knit anything."

"Yes, I can see that being a drawback."

"It's part of being a mum. Your kid's hobbies become your hobbies. So I know quite a lot about sharks, ballet, and astronauts at the moment."

He gave an amused hum. "What about in your pre-mum years?"

"Oh God. I just studied all the time. And learned the violin to make my personal statement look more well-rounded."

"It clearly worked. You got in for medicine. Where were you, by the way?"

She grimaced. "Cambridge."

"Well, aren't you the overachiever?"

"It's not as big a deal as it sounds. It's just like school but more famous."

"Still, you can't have been all work no play." There was the briefest of pauses. "You mentioned a girlfriend."

Had she? She'd been too busy self-recriminating to remember. "What? Lauren? She's still around. And married now—not to the girl she cheated on me with. She's actually looking after Amelie for me this weekend."

He nodded approvingly. "I'm a big fan of keeping in touch with your exes. They're like friends with the added bonus that you know what they look like naked."

They stepped onto a bridge across the curl of the river, the newly risen moon shedding a gleam of silver across the water.

Alain paused. He was the kind of man who looked especially good in monochrome with his height and his faint air of haughtiness and the sharp edge of his cheekbones. "I can't help but notice," he said with studied nonchalance, "that you've mentioned an ex-girlfriend and ex-boyfriend. Which I'm taking to mean you're interested in...well...I suppose a variety of people?"

As a general rule, Rosaline wasn't a huge fan of being asked about her sexuality. Especially by guys, since it was often followed up by "Wow, that's hot; and I bet you find that observation extremely flattering and not at all fetishistic," or "Cool, my girlfriend and I have wanted to try a threesome for ages." But Alain had approached the topic with enough caution that she felt comfortable teasing him about it.

"Oh yes. A huge variety. I've dated playwrights, engineers, a bass guitarist, a lawyer, a florist..."

His mouth twitched. "You know that's not what I meant."

"Brunettes, blondes, redheads..."

"All right." He lifted his hands in surrender. "I just thought it was polite to make sure I wasn't making advances on a lesbian."

It had been a *long* time since anybody had made advances even vaguely in Rosaline's direction. "I'm bisexual."

"So you are, in fact, open to being advanced upon?"

Quick, Rosaline. Sound undesperate. "I could be."

She half turned towards him. The night was kind to them, transforming their little piece of the world—the bridge, and the river, and the star-heavy sky—into a scene from a black-and-white movie. One of those Sunday afternoon stories where he's strong and she's spirited, and everything ends the way it's supposed to.

"I'm very glad to hear it," Alain murmured.

And then his hand was against her cheek and he was tilting her face gently to his, and his mouth was soft and warm and knowing against hers. It was a flawlessly executed first kiss, careful but with the promise of passion.

Saturday

"FOR THIS WEEK'S blind bake," Grace Forsythe was saying, "you'll be working with oranges and lemons, are unlikely to grow rich, but may—if it goes wrong—get your head chopped off." She paused while the contestants exchanged bemused looks, which would doubtless be turned into reaction shots by the editors and gifs by the internet. "Today's challenge is a British twist on an American classic: a St. Clement's pie."

That sounded made up. Like some harried assistant had been told lemon meringue pie was too predictable—and, indeed, Rosaline had half predicted it when she'd been plumbing the depths of Wilfred Honey's *Humble Pies* in preparation for week two—and so had tossed some oranges into the recipe and claimed it was a whole different thing.

Grace Forsythe clapped her hands excitedly. "You've only got ninety minutes for this one, so get ready. Your time begins on three. Three, darlings."

"Prepare the base," began the recipe gnomically.

That was easy. Rosaline had made biscuit bases hundreds of times. She put a generous wodge of butter into a pan to melt and...

She'd kissed Alain last night.

No. That wasn't what she needed to be thinking about. She

emptied a pack of digestives into a food bag and picked up the rolling pin...

She'd kissed Alain last night.

Fuck no. She was not being that person. Not after psyching herself up to go full Palmer on the competition. Never mind whatever Alain had done with his lips in the moonlight; she'd bumbled through week one and she was damned if she was going to bumble again. It was time to stand out from the crowd. Show the judges what she was made of. Rip baking a new arsehole.

Okay. That felt over the line.

Maybe she should stick to making a nice pie.

She smashed the biscuits.

"Do you think," Anvita asked at lunch through a mouthful of slightly stale wrap, "that Harry's okay?"

Rosaline already had no idea where this was going. "Okay in what way?"

"He just doesn't seem to talk to anyone. I mean, I like the strong, silent type, but he's close to being *too* strong and *too* silent."

"Nah, he's sound," offered Ricky. "He's a Spurs fan, but you can't hold that against him."

"You know"—Anvita gave him a disappointed look—"I thought that thing about men only communicating in terms of football was a myth."

"I've met him twice. What else was I going to talk about? My feelings?"

"Baking?" suggested Rosaline. "You're both on a baking show."

Ricky shrugged. "And we're sick to the back teeth of talking about it."

"Anyway." Anvita pivoted towards Rosaline like a cannon on a warship. "You should go ask him to join us."

Her eyes widened. "Why me? I don't even know what the offside rule is."

"He spoke to you, though, last week. Voluntarily. And for more than ten seconds."

Yes, but most of that had been trying to stem a seemingly infinite tide of tea. "Is this because you're actually worried about him? Or because you fancy him?"

"Can you blame me?" With a distinct lack of subtlety, Anvita cast a forlorn glance over her shoulder to where Harry was sitting. "He's so sad and...and...fit."

"I don't think he's sad. I think he's just eating a wrap."

"To be fair," Ricky put in, "I had one of those wraps and it made me pretty sad."

"For the record"—it was Rosaline's firmest voice, which, admittedly, wasn't especially firm—"I'm not entirely comfortable asking a man to come and join us so you can ogle him from a more convenient distance."

Anvita looked aghast. "That's not fair. I want you to ask him to come and join us so that we can *both* ogle him from a more convenient distance."

"I have no interest in ogling Harry," insisted Rosaline. It wasn't *totally* a lie.

"If this was me and him talking about one of you"—Ricky had that "I'm not sure if I'm being sexist" expression men sometimes got when they had to talk about gender—"it would not be okay."

Pushing her shoulders back, Anvita resettled her glasses—pink cat-eyes this week. "Hey, you can ogle me anytime. In fact, I demand it. Ogle me."

"My mum would have my knackers."

"Well, my mum," Anvita retorted, "would say I'm making an

important postfeminist statement and owning my sexuality. So it's important that Rosaline and I be able to talk about what a juicy studbucket Harry is."

The low-key bickering had been gently washing over Rosaline, but that got her attention. "Okay, two things. One, 'juicy studbucket' sounds actively gross. Like it's a sponge a vet would use to artificially inseminate horses. And two, I don't think Harry's the sort of man it's a good idea to encourage. Because I'm pretty sure his mum would *not* have his knackers for ogling you."

There was a pause. "Was he that bad when you talked to him?" asked Anvita.

"Not...not exactly. But when half the words out of a guy's mouth are 'love,' 'bird,' and 'girl' you have a good idea what you're getting."

"Why are the hot ones always such a problem?" Anvita gave a heavy sigh.

"Because they're hot, they don't have to try."

"Hey," protested Ricky. "I'm hot and I try."

Rosaline was, by this point, feeling slightly guilty. She hadn't meant to paint Harry as a complete monster. Just as...well...someone from a certain background with a certain set of values. And given how gossipy the set was, there was a good chance she'd accidentally started a rumour that he was some kind of sexual predator and nobody would talk to him for the rest of the series. "I've...I've probably been unfair. I'm sure Harry's a perfectly nice guy. And I'll go see if he wants to sit with us."

In the short walk across the lawn, Rosaline took the opportunity to scope out the other contestants in—if she was being honest with herself—a slightly Alain-focused way. She spotted him on a bench next to Josie, in the middle of what seemed to be an animated conversation. Which was fine. It was definitely fine. She had no claim on his time or attention, and it wasn't like she'd gone out of her way to speak to him either.

But why hadn't he? Come over. Said hello. Done *something*.

Yes, she was slightly out of practice. Still, it had been...nice? It had been nice, right?

And also, outside the moment, a bad idea. They were competitors in a TV baking show with a bunch of other people who'd probably be really annoyed if they found out they had a thing. If they *did* have a thing.

Maybe all they had was a kiss.

Or Alain was being considerate and trying not to start gossip.

Or Rosaline's lips had accidentally communicated the idea that she wanted him to fuck off and never speak to her again.

"You all right, mate?" said Harry, making Rosaline realise that she'd been standing over him for longer than she'd intended.

"What? Yes. I mean..." She felt suddenly like she was in secondary school again, telling a boy she had a friend who liked him and hoping he wouldn't think that "friend" meant "her." "Um..."

He visibly winced. As well he might. "Look, I've been meaning to ask, I didn't upset you the other day, did I?"

"Upset me?" she repeated, slightly taken aback.

"Yeah. About the name thing. And the love thing. And the girl thing. And the pretty thing." She thought he might actually have been blushing. "I just didn't want you to think I was a dick."

If she was being honest, she wasn't used to thinking about guys like Harry at all. "No? Not really."

"Great. Just, you know, checking." He let out a breath that, to Rosaline's surprise, said *I am relieved*, not *That'll cost you*. "Because," he went on, "sometimes I'll say something and then I'll think *Christ, Harry, you utter ballsack*, and it'll be buzzing around my head forever."

She gave him a slightly curious look. It felt natural for her to be constantly paralysed by the possibility of other people's disapproval. But what did Harry have to worry about? He was a good-looking bloke who lived in a world of mates and pubs and women who didn't mind being called "love." "I think maybe everyone gets that. Although possibly with less ballsack."

"Okay. Good." He was silent a moment, possibly dwelling on the ballsack, and wasn't that a strange mental image. "Thanks, mate."

Rosaline suspected she'd regret asking this but couldn't quite help herself. "Why am I *mate* all of a sudden?"

"You said I wouldn't call you 'love' if you was a bloke. And I thought about it and you had a point. And it was this or start calling all my mates 'love,' and I reckon they'd look at me a bit funny if I tried it."

She couldn't tell if she'd won that one or lost it. "Fair enough, I suppose."

"Well done last week, by the way. You done all right."

"Thank you. You did..."

"Kind of average," he offered ruefully. "My chocolate didn't temper and my decorations melted. It's always something, init?"

"Well, it's still early days."

He nodded. "Yeah, and I'm looking forward to tomorrow. I like a good pie. Except once we're in the ballroom, some bloke with a camera'll come round and be all, *What you doing, Harry?*, and I'll be all, *I'm making a pie, ain't I?* And then he'll say, *Can you say that again like you're not answering a question.* It's a bit daft really."

This surprised a laugh out of her. Because it was, when you got right down to it, a bit daft really.

"Anyway." He gave her one of his unexpected smiles. "I should let you go, mate."

"Actually..." Oh, why had she agreed to this? It was stupid, and terrible, and a bit patronising. "Anvita was wondering if you were okay? Sort of by yourself. Over here. Like you are. And I mean, me as well. Unless you're annoyed by that, in which case it was totally her idea. Which it was."

He gazed up at her, his eyes big and brown and confused. "I'm good, thanks. Just having my lunch. Wondering how badly I ballsed up my filling."

"I think we're all ballsed and wondering." Words kept coming out of Rosaline and she wished they wouldn't. "We noticed you tended to keep to yourself. And we weren't sure if that was because it was a personal choice, or because you hated us, or because you thought we hated you, or because you're allergic to picnic benches, or...some other reason."

"I don't think it's any of those." His air of confusion was not abating. "I figured you lot had your own thing and didn't want to push in."

"It's not really a thing. It's more a...table."

He glanced between her and the table in question, brow crinkling anxiously. "Trouble is, I'm not brilliant at lots of people all at once."

"Is anyone?"

"Well. Yeah. My mate Terry's always dragging me out to stuff and he's always like, *Hey Harry, what are you doing there in the corner not talking to anyone. This is Jim and Brenda what I've just met.* I don't know how he does it."

"Okay, but this is Ricky, Anvita, and me, who you've already met."

"Not all at once, though."

"Oh come on." She held out her hand, and after a moment of obvious reluctance, he took it, letting her guide him to his feet. His palm was warm and calloused, and realising she kind of appreciated that made her feel like Lady Chatterley. "It'll be fine. You don't have to say anything if you don't want to."

"Except that's the problem, init? Because you get that voice in your head going *Why aren't you saying anything, why aren't you saying anything, why aren't you saying anything, why'd you say* that?"

She squinted at him. "I think you're blowing this out of proportion."

"Yeah. Probably."

They drifted back to the group, Harry dragging his feet slightly like a prisoner going to the guillotine or a child at the dentist's.

"'Lo," said Rosaline, with a small flourish. "I have returned bearing Harry."

He sat down next to Ricky. "All right, Gooner?"

There was a long silence.

"Sorry." Anvita gave Harry an appalled look. "Is that a racist slur?"

Harry seemed genuinely shocked. "What? No. Gooner? Woolwich? Scumbag?"

"Arsenal fan," explained Ricky. "What can I say? I like teams that win."

"There's more important things than winning, mate." There was an unusual conviction in Harry's voice.

"In a competitive sport?"

Harry shrugged. "It's about loyalty. Being part of something."

"I'm very attracted," Anvita interrupted, "by this boring conversation about a sport I don't play or watch or care about."

"Sorry, love—er—mate—err, Anvita." Harry reached for a pint that wasn't there, and then hastily folded his hands on the table. "So, err, how's your nan?"

"Pleased I'm on the show. Having real trouble not telling her friends about it."

"Yeah, mine too. I've been like, 'No, Gran. I've signed a thing. You can't tell anyone. Not even Sheila from Bingo.'"

Ricky crumpled his napkin on top of his paper plate and balanced his half-empty water bottle on top of that to stop everything from blowing away. "My mum knows me too well.

She's very supportive, but she's pretty sure I'm going out in week three."

It was at this moment that Rosaline realised she was the only one who hadn't contributed. "My parents aren't huge fans of reality television. But Amelie's thrilled. Of course, she's eight and I'm her mother so she still gets excited to see me on a cctv camera in a shop."

The dangerous, interested look had snuck back into Anvita's eyes. "But your parents don't care at all?"

The answer to that was complicated, and Rosaline wasn't sure she could articulate it, let alone share it. "Oh, they *care*. Just not in a good way."

"I know what you mean," said Harry. "I haven't even told my mates about this. They'd take the fucking piss. They will anyway, mind, but at least this way I'll only get it once."

"Pro tip"—Ricky nudged him—"tell them baking gets girls."

"Not where I come from it don't."

"You're trying the wrong crowd, mate. Come down the SU with me. They'll think you're sensitive."

"I've changed my mind." That was Anvita, a little sharply. "Please go back to talking about football."

While the pattern of filming, and waiting, and filming, and waiting, was already becoming second nature, Rosaline wasn't sure she'd ever get used to the judging.

"This is perfectly adequate," announced Marianne Wolvercote, dissecting Rosaline's pie with the merciless enthusiasm of a doctor in a Hammer Horror. "But nothing special."

Yay. Saved by mediocrity.

Again.

At this rate, it was looking like baking was going to rip *her* a new arsehole.

Anvita and Alain had also done something in the region of fine. Florian, however, hadn't allowed the filling to cool before putting it on the base, so the whole thing had come out as a dribbly mess. And—surprising no one more than himself—Ricky had somehow produced the perfect incarnation of a pie he knew nothing about.

"I have no idea what happened," he said in his interview afterwards. "I've never heard of that pie, I've never seen that pie, I've never eaten that pie. Didn't have a clue what I was doing. But I guess it paid off. Because I won."

By contrast, Florian seemed a little down. "Well, it was a simple mistake, albeit one with profound consequences. In fact, I'm taking it rather poorly. I'm not at all used to being on the bottom. Oh my, can I say that on television?"

Rosaline's own interview involved muttering "I think it went okay" about six different ways and trying not to sound too deflated because she really had no reason to. Assuming she didn't totally screw up tomorrow, or Florian didn't utterly nail it, she was pretty sure she wasn't in danger, but all she'd managed to prove so far was that she wasn't bad enough to get eliminated immediately. Which wasn't even a little bit the same as being good enough to win.

"You all right, mate?" asked Harry, who'd also just finished saying he thought things went okay, but had, at least, got to say it in front of a rhododendron.

She sighed. "Yeah. I shouldn't be complaining, but I hoped I'd done better."

"Well, you didn't win. But you didn't lose either." Tucking his hands into his pockets, he hunched his shoulders slightly. "Consistency like that gets you into the semifinals."

"But only as the boring one who they never quite got around to kicking out."

He gave her that ridiculously sweet and perfect grin. "Hey, that's my strategy you're having a go at."

"For what it's worth," Rosaline told him, laughing, "I don't think you're going to be remembered as the boring one."

"Why? What one do you think I'm going to be?"

There was no good answer to that. Because while she'd been happy to playfully imply he'd be remembered as "the hot one," there was no way she could say it to his face. "Ask Anvita."

He looked comically dismayed. "I'm not sure I want to know now."

"No, it's—" At that moment she caught sight of Alain coming up from the Lodge, and for the first time that day, he was looking at something other than his workstation. He was, in fact, looking at her. "No, it's good," she finished absently.

Alain lifted his hand in greeting. "Rosaline. Hi."

"Hi." She tried to sound casual and collected, like they were both totally the sort of person who could kiss somebody and then go a whole day without speaking to them.

Harry gave one of those man-to-man nods. "All right, mate? Well done last week."

"Oh yes, thank you." Alain's brows arched their shadiest arch. "Your praise means the world to me."

There was a slightly weird lull in the conversation because Rosaline had a bunch of things she really wanted to say— such as, *Are you ignoring me?* and *Am I a terrible kisser?*— but couldn't with Harry standing right there. And Harry himself was either incapable of recognising sarcasm or unwilling to rise to it.

"Got something else fancy planned for tomorrow?" he asked finally.

Alain laughed. "I like that you think basil is a fancy ingredient. But I actually wanted to see if Rosaline felt like coming for a walk. Of course if you're"—his eyes flicked between the two of them—"busy, then I can see you later."

Busy? What kind of evening did he think she was likely to have planned with an electrician whose primary interests seemed to be Spurs and long silences? Rosaline took a sharp step away from Harry, hoping she hadn't given anyone the wrong impression. "Oh no, we'd just finished our interviews and got chatting. A walk would be lovely."

"Have a nice evening, mate." Harry also did the "no wrong impressions" backstep. "You too, Alain."

Rosaline followed Alain across the lawn, away from the main house. They seemed to be taking a different route from last time, down a slightly overgrown path towards a little knot of trees and a mound of stones piled up in an arch. And it was another balmy summer's evening, with the sky swirled into a perfect watercolour and the air heavy with the scent of pollen and meadow flowers. She'd say this for Alain, he certainly knew how to take a girl for a walk.

"What I find fascinating about these old houses," Alain remarked, "is the way they accumulate the trends and fashions of centuries."

It wasn't something she'd ever considered before. But then she hadn't been around a stately home since her parents had stopped dragging her to them when she was a kid. "Oh yes. I suppose they do."

"The thing with people"—Alain sounded unexpectedly sincere—"is that you only ever see them as they're presenting themselves, and their context always has to be the world you find them in. But buildings are different. They reflect every self they've ever been."

"Do you think so?" she asked.

"Well, take this house."

"What about it?"

There was, Rosaline thought, something captivating in hearing somebody talk about their passions—it felt intimate, like they were giving you access to some slightly tender part of themselves.

Of course, with Lauren it had always been pussy and words, so architecture was a nice change of pace.

"In the late eighteen hundreds," Alain told her, "it was fashionable to have a hermit living on your property. Unfortunately, people who wanted one were confronted by the tiny detail that there weren't actually any hermits anymore. So what they'd do was build something they could call a hermitage, and if anyone asked, they'd say the hermit wasn't in at the moment."

Rosaline considered this. "Hang on a second. A person who lives on their own but regularly goes out to get stuff or do things isn't a hermit. They're just single."

"Which would probably have been a point of contention had the hermit existed."

"It should have been a point of contention anyway. Because people would go, *Hey, where's your hermit?*, and you'd say *Oh, he's nipped down the shops*, and they'd say, *Well, he's not a hermit then is he?*"

"I think," said Alain, laughing, "that's more or less what happened. So landowners took to hiring people to live in their hermitages and pretend to be hermits."

Rosaline slanted a smile at him. "Honestly, I've had worse jobs." They stepped into what appeared to be an actual grotto—a slightly crumbling archway, twined about with ivy, the rocks velveted with moss.

"You say that, except"—Alain gestured around them—"you'd have had to live somewhere like this."

It was rather pretty at the moment, with the dappled light and the warm breeze, but it was small enough to really put her kitchen into perspective. "Okay, maybe I *haven't* had worse jobs."

"You see what I mean, though?" Alain's voice had softened in the green-shaded gloom. "About the way history accretes to places like this?"

It was quite a change to go from talking with a man who said "ain't" to a man who said "accretes." "Doesn't it accrete to people, too, though? After all, I might not still wear the leather pencil skirt I had when I was sixteen, but I wouldn't be who I am now if I hadn't been who I was then."

He chuckled. "Intrigued as I am by this leather pencil skirt, it's not the same. Your past is your past. It's not something someone else can see and touch."

Rosaline had never read any of those books about how to get a man, partly because she was at least as interested in women and partly because they were clearly awful. But she was sure they'd all agree that going to a secluded grotto with a guy and then arguing with him about the romantic things he tried to say was spectacularly missing the point. On the other hand, she also kind of thought she was right on this one. "I got a tattoo when I was sixteen," she told him. "You can see and touch that. I mean, not right now, obviously."

"You've got a tattoo?" He sounded...not shocked exactly. But the positive sort of surprised. It was a good way for him to sound.

"Yep."

He eyed her, one eyebrow slightly raised, and asked teasingly, "Is it a butterfly?"

"Actually, it's several butterflies."

"Several butterflies?"

"Down my spine."

The wide, expressive mouth that had kissed her so artfully turned up at the corners. "You don't do things by halves, do you?"

"Well, then you'd only have half a thing."

There was a longish pause that seemed more intense than it should have been in the narrow space and the hazy light.

"Are you going to show me?"

She blinked. "Now?"

"Only if you're comfortable," he said quickly. "There's no one around of course, but I'd never want to put any pressure on you. Although I will admit I'm rather..." He paused and cleared his throat. "Let's say I'm even more intrigued about the butterflies than I am about the skirt."

He seemed on the edge of flustered—and maybe she just had a powerful imp of the perverse, but she suspected she'd enjoy flustering him further. It could have been because he was slightly older and had his shit so much more together than she did, or simply the contrast to his usual self-assurance. Either way, these hints of something like vulnerability made her feel bold and exciting in a way she hadn't for a long time.

She turned and pulled up her shirt. Heard his soft intake of breath.

"That's... that's rather artistic," he whispered. "Quite the wild child, weren't you?"

"I wasn't trying to be. I just knew what I wanted."

"May I," he murmured, "may I touch them?"

Her back prickled with possibility. "Um, okay."

"Didn't it hurt?"

Why did people always ask that? What were they expecting her to say? *No, I love having needles jammed into my epidermis.* "Like a bastard."

She felt the warmth of his fingertips following the familiar curve of wings across her spine. His touch was like his kiss: certain yet delicate, hinting at pleasure rather than pushing it upon her. After a moment or two, he turned her and drew her close.

"I hope you don't think I was avoiding you today."

She definitely had, but there was no way she was admitting that to him. "I was mostly just making a pie."

"I thought it was best not to do anything that might start people talking."

It was embarrassing how relieved she was. "That makes sense. Thank you."

"Obviously, we're both here for the competition. But I... well...I wasn't expecting to meet someone like you."

"What? A single mum who works in a shop?"

"You must know you're more than that, Rosaline." He gazed down at her, his eyes tinted grey in the growing darkness. "You went to Cambridge, for fuck's sake. You're fearless and adventurous and, I suspect, a little wicked."

The truth was that Rosaline felt like hardly any of those hardly any of the time. But she liked that he saw her that way. So she slid a hand behind his neck and pulled him down into a kiss.

Sunday

"AND WELCOME," BOOMED Grace Forsythe, "to the second baketacular of the season. Today we're asking you to blow our socks off with not one, not two, not three, but *twenty-four* miniature pies. There should be a dozen sweet and a dozen savoury, but apart from that they can be shortcrust, rough-puff, hot water crust, pumpkin, pork or paneer, chicken, chorizo, or cherry. You have three hours, and that includes making the pastry and setting up your delightful displays of deliciousness. Your time begins on the count of three. *Three*, darlings."

And they were off.

And Rosaline had barely begun sifting out the flour for her shortcrust when Colin Thrimp *and* Grace Forsythe *and* the judges descended on her station all at once.

"Tell us about your pies, pet," said Wilfred Honey, twinkling soothingly at her while Marianne Wolvercote picked through her ingredients.

Rosaline tried very hard to look at Wilfred Honey and not at the camera that was being thrust directly into her face. "Well, I felt I'd played it too safe last week. So this time I'm trying to push the boat out a bit, and I'm doing…"

Oh help, what *was* she doing?

"Um, sorry, I've completely forgotten what I'm making."

Wilfred Honey's eyes flicked to Colin Thrimp. "Do we need that one again, Colin?"

There was a pause while Colin took instructions from his earpiece. "It's fine. It'll come across as endearing. In your own time, Rosaline."

"I'd rather not," said Rosaline, "come across as not having a clue what I'm doing."

Grace Forsythe put a hand on her shoulder. "Lambkin, I've been making it up as I go along for forty years and nobody's tumbled me yet. It's rather the British way, you know."

"You've got chicken, sherry"—Marianne Wolvercote picked up the sherry and peered at the label with an air of profound interest—"and tarragon here. I'm going to go out on a limb and suggest you might be making chicken, sherry, and tarragon."

"Now, interestingly," added Wilfred Honey, "young Alain's also doing chicken and tarragon."

Rosaline froze. "Oh fu—f—fancy that."

"No sherry, mind." Marianne Wolvercote seemed genuinely disappointed by this. "Which might give you the edge."

"He grew his own tarragon, though, didn't he?" asked Rosaline.

Grace Forsythe threw a look to camera. "That's competitive baking for you. Here today. Tarra-gone tomorrow."

"So that's the savoury taken care of." Wilfred Honey was still twinkling at her. As far as Rosaline could tell, he'd been twinkling solidly for the best part of a century. "What about your sweet?"

Thankfully, her brain did not re-fart. "I'm doing toffee apple pies with dulce de leche."

Marianne Wolvercote got that *You have made a terrible mistake* look in her eyes that Rosaline saw every season on the show and wondered why competitors didn't notice. "And you think you can manage that in the time?"

"If I work really fast, don't make any mistakes, and don't get interrupted—oh God, I didn't mean, I just...at home my daughter sometimes comes in and time works differently for eight-year-olds."

"No, no, we understand." Grace Forsythe threw her hands in the air. "Marianne, Wilfred, we have been given our marching orders. Thus must we march."

They didn't so much march as stop to get a couple more establishing shots and do a short to-camera bit about what a big risk she was taking well within earshot. But eventually, they were gone and Rosaline could confront the fact that her dulce was probably writing cheques that her leche wouldn't be able to cash.

Within an hour, she was forced to conclude that her leche not only wasn't cashing cheques but was having the bailiffs come round for the furniture.

In theory—in bloody theory—it could have worked. It had mostly worked at home. There was enough time to make pastry, make fillings, fill pie cases, and spend an hour and a half continuously stirring a pot of milk until it magically transformed into a smooth, velvety caramel. Except what she'd wound up with, now she was on the show and it was critical, was pies not quite ready to go into the oven and a pan of brownish liquid that might have been slightly sweet-tasting.

And yes, her blind bake had been broadly fine, and yes, there was only one element that was going wrong, but it was going *very* wrong, and it was the element that was supposed to show she could really do this, apart from the bit where she obviously couldn't really do this, and she didn't even pick her own tarragon, and what had she been thinking signing up to show off her cooking on television when all she'd ever done was make biscuits for eight-year-olds, who weren't exactly discerning critics, and shit shit shit shit shit.

"What are you doing now?" asked a random production assistant.

Being about to cry was what she was doing now. "Um," she said. "I…just…I'm stirring this…it's meant to…but it's…"

To her horror, she was actually crying.

And the next thing she knew, Grace Forsythe was gently removing the spoon from her hands. "Fuck shit piss wank bollocks drink Coca-Cola buy Smeg ovens legalise cannabis abolish the monarchy. Oh sorry, did I ruin the segment? What a shame. Maybe go film someone else for a bit."

The producer and camera operator dutifully departed.

Rosaline drew in a shaky breath and wiped her eyes. "God, thank you."

"Part of the job, darling. They're a lovely bunch, the crew, but they're a bit overzealous about capturing their"—she made flamboyant air quotes—"*emotional beats*. Now, stiffen the sinews, summon up the blood, and best of luck with your brown sludge."

The brown sludge simmered at her mockingly.

Home felt suddenly very far away. As did her little kitchen with the eggshell-blue cabinets she'd painted herself, and the hob with one broken ring, and the window where the sun crept through in the early afternoon. The table that barely fit where Amelie would sit and do—or more accurately not do—her homework while Rosaline made dinner or whipped up a batch of cupcakes.

Baking was supposed to be the thing that made her feel better. It was supposed to be hers. It was supposed to be family and togetherness and everything being okay in the end.

But here she was fucking it all up.

Fucking it up all up on national TV.

And fucking crying about it.

She was going home, wasn't she? She'd spent the first week and a half dancing on the edge of not quite good enough, and then been so desperate to prove herself that she'd flown too close to the sun. And by sun, she meant dulce de leche. And by flown too close, she meant tried to make. The problem was, Rosaline had watched enough of the show to know she needed an arc. But she also knew that some arcs were very, very short. And the shortest was always "was mediocre, fucked up, went out." And then you added another item to the long list of failures your parents would never let you forget.

The judges, at least, were fairly kind to her, but in some ways, that made it worse because it was the sort of kindness that said *This has gone so badly that the best thing for everyone is if we pretend it didn't happen.* Her chicken and tarragon, at least, had been passable—although Rosaline was convinced that Marianne Wolvercote liked it only because of the sherry—but the dulce de leche was not dulce de leche. It was a kind of milky sauce drizzled over pies that, thanks to the amount of time she'd spent crying and stirring, were almost inedibly undercooked.

Which left Rosaline to trudge back to her seat and face the depressing reality that her survival now depended entirely on someone messing up even worse than she had.

Alain, needless to say, had not messed up at all, presenting his own chicken and tarragon pies, with their wild gooseberry and custard companions, on a hand-carved wooden display stand. And nearly everybody else had produced some version of fine, with Harry's take on a traditional minced beef pie, mash and liquor being praised for its unexpectedly delicate take on a working-class staple. That just left Anvita and Florian, neither of whom Rosaline wanted to go home either.

Florian had made miniature rainbow pies in an attempt to redeem himself from his disastrous blind bake. Unfortunately, when Marianne sliced one deftly in two, they proved to be less rainbow and more a blob of vegetables in a pastry case.

"Oh my," he observed as an undifferentiated splodgy mass of spinach and peppers oozed onto the plate, "that hasn't worked at all, has it?"

Wilfred Honey sorted through the mess looking for something to praise. "Your crust is okay."

"And the principle was commendable," added Marianne Wolvercote. Before turning to his sweet offering with a frown. "Unfortunately, these jam tarts are, as the name suggests, tarts rather than pies."

Wilfred Honey helped himself to a mouthful. "They're right tasty, though. And who doesn't love a jam tart?"

"I don't," returned Marianne Wolvercote, "on a pie challenge."

They didn't quite play the funeral march as Florian carried his oozy rainbow pies and disqualified tarts back to his workstation, but they may as well have. And Rosaline sat there, stewing in a mess of guilt, hope, and anxiety about as well mixed as her dulce de leche.

Next came Anvita, with her palak paneer savoury and spiced apple sweet.

"Now that," declared Marianne Wolvercote, "is what I call a pie: rich, flaky pastry, just the right thickness, wonderful South Asian flavours, and a fine balance of textures. It's very easy for spinach to become soggy and unappealing, and this is neither. Very well done."

"As for the sweet," continued Wilfred Honey, "you really get all the spices coming through, and it goes beautifully with that sharp green apple. Lovely."

Anvita beamed. "Thank you. Thank you so much." And half skipped back to her workstation.

From there followed the usual period of sitting around, feeling restless and useless, while the judges decided who lived to bake another day and who was cast by the culinary wayside. This week, there was actually some uncertainty to it. For a start, no one had told Marianne Wolvercote and Wilfred Honey to go fuck themselves, so it was a lot less clear-cut who was going home. Florian seemed to be most obviously in danger, but after her disaster de leche, Rosaline felt like she was standing out for all the wrong reasons.

After what could have been forever, but probably wasn't more than an hour or so, the judges returned, the contestants were arranged in the semicircle of fate, and Grace Forsythe stepped forward.

"So, my little pastry protégés, it is time for the moment of truth. And we begin, as always, by celebrating the achievements of this week's winner. It's someone whose St. Clement's pie still owes us five farthings, but whose sweet pie was the apple of our eye and whose spectacular spicing stole the show. I speak, of course, of Anvita."

Anvita made the obligatory face of surprise and delight. And she was radiating such sincere joy that it was hard for Rosaline to be jealous. Hard, but not impossible.

"And now," continued Grace Forsythe, once reactions had been shot, "to the sorrowful moment wherein we say farewell to one of our valiant baketeers. This person has brought joy and levity to the ballroom, but, unfortunately, when he tried to bring colour, it melted all over the plate. We're sad to lose you, Florian, but I'm afraid you've come to the end of your rainbow."

This time the hugs felt a lot more authentic and a lot more earned. A couple of people actually cried. And Rosaline, remembering the way Florian had come to her defence last week, couldn't help but feel she was losing an ally she hadn't quite deserved.

In one of life's small mercies, Allison was busy for the whole weekend, which left Lauren free to take over picking-up-Rosaline duty. She arrived, as Rosaline had expected, slightly late but looking nowhere near as tired or frustrated as she could have done. And after a brief hello, she opened the back door of her car to release a child-shaped missile that barrelled into Rosaline with a force that she should have anticipated but didn't.

"Missed you times a million." Amelie beamed up at her not, if Rosaline was honest, looking hugely like she'd missed her times very much at all. "I had a lovely weekend with Auntie Lauren and we played games and watched television and made sandwiches and"—she cast Lauren a conspiratorial glance—"I always went to bed on time and ate very healthily."

Bending down to put her arms around her daughter, relieved to be back with her family, where she belonged and made sense and it was only her parents making her feel like a failure instead of the whole nation, Rosaline detected a certain stickiness. "Were they, by any chance, *jam* sandwiches?"

Amelie nodded.

"I got the worst of it," Lauren observed, still leaning against the car bonnet. "Remind me to wear a cheaper jacket next time."

"It'll wash out."

"It'll have to *dry-clean* out."

Folding her arms in mock indignation, Rosaline smiled. "Well, if you will let her play with fruit preserves..."

"I was encouraging creativity."

Before Rosaline could devise a suitably devastating reply, she heard an "'Allo there" from a little way across the car park. She, Amelie, and Lauren turned together to see Harry wandering towards them carrying a sports bag that seemed to contain far more...stuff...than any reasonable person would actually need for a weekend stay in a fully equipped hotel.

Is this him? Lauren mouthed hastily at her. *Him* here was doing a lot of work for a single syllable since it needed to convey *Is this the guy you spent the night with in a strange farmhouse, fraudulently told you'd lived in Malawi, and with whom the status of your relationship is the textbook definition of "it's complicated."* Rosaline shook her head as subtly and efficiently as possible.

With a swift smile in Rosaline's direction, Harry squatted down to get on Amelie's eye-line. "Is this your mummy?" he asked.

Amelie looked up for reassurance, and Rosaline made a brief *It's okay* gesture.

"Yes she is," Amelie announced proudly. "She's going to be on television because she makes the best cakes."

"I know she does," he said with a smile. "I'm going to be on television with her."

This seemed to confuse Amelie. "Do you make cakes too? You don't look like you make cakes."

"Amelie," Rosaline cautioned, "be nice."

Harry looked up. "It's okay, I know she don't mean nothing by it. 'Sides, asking questions is how they learn." He turned back to Amelie without missing a beat. "What *do* I look like?"

"Footballer?" Rosaline could see Amelie running through her quite short mental list of jobs she knew about. "Soldier? Fireman? You look like you'd be strong, so maybe you could be a miner or a Viking."

"I was *going* to be a Viking," Harry explained, "but I went up the job centre and they didn't have nothing, so I thought I'd go into electrics instead."

There was a long pause, then Amelie said, "You should have gone back the next day."

"Oh, blow it." Harry made an exaggerated *silly me* gesture. "You're right, I should've." Carefully, he stood up and produced a piece of cardboard from his back pocket. "So"—he waved it vaguely at Rosaline and she took it almost by instinct—"I was just thinking. Do you want my number?"

Rosaline gave him a cautious look. Maybe he thought that once he stopped calling her "love" she'd be suddenly up for it. "Why would that be a thing I might want?"

"I wasn't, like"—he'd gone pink to the ears—"trying anything. But like I told Amelie, I'm in electrics, and I'm pretty handy, and I know it can be rough for a single mum."

This caught Amelie's interest. It was, perhaps, the worst thing that could have caught her interest. "Why is it rough for Mummy?"

Harry squatted back down. "'Cos she's got a lot to do. She can't work a job and take you to school and do her baking and fix the boiler all the same time."

"I could fix the boiler if we learned it in school," Amelie mused. "But we have to do spelling instead."

"Spelling's important. If you can't spell proper, people'll think you're a knob." He started and glanced back up at Rosaline. "Sorry, mate. Just slipped out."

Lauren made a languid gesture. "It's fine. She gets worse from me every fucking day."

His head whipped around. "Sorry, lov—sorry, haven't introduced myself. I'm Harry, I'm on the show with Rosaline."

Before Lauren could introduce herself back, Amelie intervened. "That's Auntie Lauren. She used to go out with Mummy, but then she left her for another girl who didn't even really have red hair. She's been looking after me."

Rosaline inwardly face-palmed. She was very open about her sexuality, but she also liked to control when she was open about it and who she was open about it to. And she genuinely wasn't sure how Harry would take it.

"Oh, right." He seemed to be processing. And also seemed to be close enough to Amelie to notice the stickiness. "Are you the one what got her covered in jam then?"

"It *builds creativity*."

Harry shook his head. "It don't, mate. It just attracts wasps. Anyway, got to go. My nan's expecting me. Give us a bell if you need anything."

Looking only a little flustered, Harry ambled away leaving Rosaline, Lauren, and Amelie alone. They piled into Lauren's car—Amelie stubbornly insisting in the face of all the evidence that she had put her seat belt on perfectly well and didn't need any help with it—and set off back home.

"So," Lauren said as they pulled out of the absurdly overlong driveway onto winding country lanes, "that's not the guy?"

Rosaline leaned back against the headrest, trying to let go of everything that had gone wrong that weekend. And to hold on to the few things that had gone right. "I know they all look the same to you, but no. I mean, he seems nice, and looks…and you'll have to take my word for this…*very nice*. He's just a whole world of not my type."

"I think," offered Amelie helpfully, "it would have been better if he was a Viking. Then he'd have a long boat that could go up rivers because of its flat bottom. And he'd have a helmet but it wouldn't have horns because Miss Wooding said that was a common misconception. Which means made up."

Her eyes at least mostly on the road, Lauren grinned. "I doubt he'll be showing your mummy his helmet anytime soon."

"Definitely not." Exhaustion was creeping slowly over Rosaline again. "I mean, can you imagine my dad's face if I came home with an electrician?"

Exhaustion was not a feature of Amelie's world. "Would Granddad have been upset even if he was a Viking?"

"Probably," Rosaline admitted. "Granddad only approves of doctors."

There was a very slight pause. "Does that mean I have to be a doctor?"

"You can be whatever you want to be."

A slighter longer pause. "Can I be a Viking?"

"Absolutely." Lauren swooped in while Rosaline was still working out the least harmful way to contradict herself. "Only nowadays they call it 'historical reenactment.'"

I enjoyed spending time with you this weekend. The text came in not long after Rosaline had persuaded Amelie to go, if not to sleep, then at least to bed. *And I'd very much like to spend more. Perhaps you're free to visit some time? I'd love to show you my garden.* A pause. Three little dots. Then: *Not a euphemism.*

"That's your I've-received-a-flirty-text look," observed Lauren over her second glass of wine. "I know because it's the look you used to get when I sneak-messaged you in maths."

"Excuse me, I got an A* in maths."

"Yes, and you also got a lot of pussy."

"Not *in* maths. And mostly just yours."

Lauren grinned. "Mine's more than enough for anybody, darling."

"It's the guy from the show," said Rosaline, mainly to steer the conversation away from comparative pussiology. "He wants to show me his garden."

"As a professional playwright I'm far too sophisticated to fall back on 'Is that what they're calling it these days,' so I'll say, 'No, he doesn't; he wants you to touch his penis.'"

Shrugging, Rosaline refilled her glass. "Well, maybe I want to touch his penis."

"Oh, Roz"—Lauren gave a deep shudder—"heterosexual sex sounds excruciatingly dull."

"I'm just pointing out that I'm not a debutante in a Victorian novel. It's quite possible we're two mature adults who want to get laid."

"You know you're not the fuckgirl sort. You never have been."

"I could be," Rosaline protested. "I've had casual sex."

"Name three times."

She did actually have to think about it. "Um. Tom?"

"You dated Tom for eight months and literally had his baby."

"Yes, but my original plan was for it to be casual."

"Original plans don't count." Lauren finished her wine with gusto. "Hitler's original plan was to be a painter. It's not what he's most famous for."

"Ignoring the fact that you just Godwin's Lawed my love life, what about Carolyn? I hooked up with her at your wedding, and you can't get more casual than that."

"Didn't you also nearly buy a dog together?"

"Very casually."

"All I'm saying," Lauren went on, "is that you should be honest with yourselves and each other. There's nothing wrong with being fuckbuddies, and there's nothing wrong with holding out for the love of your life, but you need to be clear about which one you're offering and which one you're looking for."

Rosaline sighed. "It doesn't really work that way in straight people land. At least, not very often."

"That seems like a significant flaw in the system."

"It's not...it's...it's complicated. Even if we're both only in it for the sex, he has to pretend otherwise so he doesn't come across as a predator. And I have to pretend otherwise so I don't come across as a slut."

Lauren's eyes narrowed. "Did you just slut-shame *yourself*?"

"No. We've had a long discussion about how not-a-slut I am despite my best efforts to be one. But I still have to navigate a world where that's a thing."

"And you can't both decide to...make it not a thing?"

"How?" asked Rosaline. "Do I text him back and say *Sure, but can we also step outside the social paradigm into which we've both been inculcated from birth?*"

"Well, *I'd* certainly find that hot."

"This may surprise you, Loz"—Rosaline gave her a wry look—"but I suspect you and Alain are quite different people."

"His loss. And, indeed, yours."

"Anyway." Deep breath. Gulp of wine. "I've already kissed him. Twice."

"Is this a course of action you want me to encourage you in or discourage you from?"

Alain was a tall, good-looking man with an impressive career, a caustic sense of humour, and a garden he wanted to show her. He was, by any objective standard, perfect. "Encourage me, I think?"

"You think? Couldn't have been much of a kiss, then."

"What? No. It was fine."

Lauren gave her a flat stare.

"I mean, it was nice. Good. B-plus. Solid seven out of ten."

"Darling," said Lauren, "you've never been satisfied with a B-plus in your life."

"It was a first kiss. Some things take a while to build."

"It's sex. Not Lego."

"Look." She hadn't quite meant to slam her wineglass down with that much force. "I'm staring down the barrel of thirty. I've got a kid. I think I'm a little bit past the idea that true romance is a horny snog behind a bike shed."

"You know I just want you to be happy. And"—Lauren drained yet another glass—"if this mysterious baking man greases your cake tin, then I'm all for him. Now, if you'll excuse me, I have to pass out. Your daughter made me take her swimming this morning and it made me use muscles I've been happily ignoring for years."

They hugged, Rosaline inadequately trying to thank Lauren for adding another weekend to eight years of unfailing support. And then Lauren vanished into Rosaline's bedroom, leaving Rosaline to make up the sofa for herself. She could really have done with a night in her own bed, but when somebody offered you three months of free childcare, five-hundred-pound gorilla rules applied and they got to sleep where they liked.

Once she was snuggled under the spare duvet, Rosaline fished out her phone and thought about replying to Alain's text. In many ways, the conversation she'd had with Lauren was academic because it would be impossible for her to get away this week—either for garden-visiting or penis-touching, depending on what was actually on the table.

Sorry, she typed. *I'd love to, but I don't think I can get a baby-sitter at such short notice.*

A brief pause. Then *Another time, perhaps?*

Yes, definitely.

A longer pause. Followed by an image slowly downloading: a somewhat hastily composed shot of a bright orange butterfly perched on a phlox flower.

That's beautiful, she told him, oddly touched.

So are you.

Week Three

Bread

Friday

ROSALINE WOULD HAVE been more cut up about her abysmal weepy performance on *Bake Expectations* except she was having A Week. It had started—as Weeks often did—on Monday when the electricity had inexplicably cut off. She'd flipped the circuit breaker, which had fixed the problem only for exactly the same thing to happen on Tuesday. Worse, on both occasions it had ruined one of her practice loaves. Then on Wednesday, she'd finally got someone to come over about the funny noise the boiler was making—and he'd poked it unhelpfully, blown into a tube, told her it needed a full service, which wasn't what she'd booked for, and charged her a hundred and twenty quid. The funny noise returned later that evening. And although she managed to get through Thursday with no disasters, by the time Friday rolled round she was feeling somewhere between frazzled and abject.

"Awoogaloo," said Amelie from her spot at the kitchen table.

Oh dear. "Has Auntie Lauren been teaching you words again?"

"No." Amelie shook her head. "I'm talking to the boiler. It just said 'balurguhluh.' So I said 'awoogaloo' to be polite. Miss Wooding says it's important to be polite."

"Was she including heating systems in that?"

"Well, she also said it's important to talk to people who are different from us and I was watching the television and it said that if aliens tried to talk to us we wouldn't always know they were trying to talk to us because they might not talk like we did. So I thought it was best to be safe."

Rosaline was trying hard not to laugh. "Aliens are probably not trying to talk to us through our boiler."

"We'd think that. But we're not aliens."

Blagugmaguh, offered the boiler.

"See," said Amelie in her vindicated voice. "Glughalughle."

"How do you know we're not accidentally insulting the aliens in the boiler?"

Amelie thought for a moment. "They aren't *in* the boiler. The lady on the television said they beam messages thousands of miles through space and when they get to us they just sound like noise."

"So our boiler is some kind of alien transponder device?"

"Maybe. Or maybe it's broken."

Was there a parenting moment to be had here? No. No, there definitely wasn't. And even if there had been, at that moment the doorbell rang and Amelie jumped off her stool and ran into the hall, shouting, "Grandma and Granddad are here."

It wasn't one of those occasions when Rosaline felt a hundred percent ready to deal with her parents—not that there were many such occasions—but since they were here to take care of her daughter for her, she had only herself to blame.

She followed Amelie into the hall and got there in time to hear her announce: "We've got aliens in our boiler." This provoked an "Aliens, is it?" from St. John Palmer, who was far more indulgent with Amelie than he'd ever been with Rosaline, while Cordelia mouthed something that looked a lot like *What have you been teaching her?*

Rosaline's mother, like her father, was a doctor and, like her father, had progressed far enough in the profession that the title stopped mattering. An oncologist by training, she had personally contributed to research that had led to a significant increase in five-year survival rates for several types of ovarian cancer, which made even Rosaline's most-perfectly-turned-out cupcakes seem a little trivial by comparison. She was tall, rail-thin, and only ever smiled at her granddaughter.

"And today," Amelie continued, "at school we learned that the Mayans lived in a place called Mesoamerica and they had a city called Yax Mutal. And they had a temple that had a big jaguar on it but it's not there anymore."

Say what you would about the Palmers, they went all in on the Grandparenting. "You *have* been studying hard." St. John lowered himself to eight-year-old height. "You're just like your mother when she was your age. Why's the temple not there anymore?"

"Because it's very very old. And very very old things fall down. Also because of the Spanish."

"If I'd known you were interested in Mayans now," said Cordelia, "I'd have got you a different present. Maybe I'd better take this back?"

Amelie's eyes widened in outrage. "No. I can be interested in more than one thing. I'm polyamorous."

"I don't think that's the word you mean," put in Rosaline quickly.

"Yes it is. It means loving lots of things." Her daughter's expression of misplaced pride was, at once, adorable and unhelpful. "I worked it out like we were taught to in school with prefixes. Poly means many and amor means love in French and is also from Latin."

Oh God. Now Rosaline was going to have to tell her daughter what polyamory was in front of her parents, who probably also didn't know what polyamory was. At least not on any level beyond the etymological. "It more sort of means loving lots of people."

"Well I do love lots of people. I love you and Granddad and Grandma and Auntie Lauren."

"Maybe it's better to say"—Rosaline could feel St. John Palmer's eyes burning into her—"it means being *in love* with lots of people."

"Oh." Amelie considered this. "Then I'm not polyamorous. I'm polylikesthingsareus. Can I have my present now?"

The present turned out to be a book called *Real Life Monsters: Creatures of the Deep*, which was filled with pictures of supremely ugly fish. Amelie loved it. And two minutes later she was happily curled up on the sofa, looking at goblin sharks, while Rosaline tried to make her parents a cup of tea that said *I am aware that your actions have created an obligation, but I would very much like this interaction to be over quickly.*

"So what's this about the boiler?" asked her father, prowling into the kitchen while Rosaline desperately washed the mugs she should have washed that morning.

She cringed into the sink. "It's just being a bit weird. I got someone out to come and take a look at it and he said it needs a service."

"And how much did he charge you for telling you your boiler needed a service?"

The problem with being a perfect daughter until the age of nineteen was that Rosaline had never learned the skill of lying to her parents. "A hundred and twenty pounds."

St. John Palmer shook his head in what it did not feel melodramatic to describe as despair. "Saw you coming a mile away, didn't he?"

"What was I supposed to do? Say, *Sorry, strange man with whom I'm alone in my house, I, a small woman armed only with a cheese grater, demand that you leave without the money you're asking for.*"

"You're not funny, Rosaline. What kind of example are you setting for Amelie if you keep letting people take advantage of you?"

Rosaline turned the kettle on with a vengeance. "Sorry. It just happened. I'll try and do better next time."

"Try *to* do better. And do you even have a hundred and twenty pounds to waste on tradesmen who do nothing?"

"Clearly yes," she told the tea bags, "because I did."

"So you won't need any help with your mortgage this month?"

It was about that point that she decided she would sell her hair and her teeth on the streets of Montreuil-sur-Mer before taking another penny from her father. Well, not for a while anyway. "I'll be fine. Now, can you take this through for Mum?"

He collected two of the mugs and left without further commentary. Rosaline picked up her own mug, realised her hands were shaking, and put it down again quickly. For fuck's sake, she was twenty-seven. She wasn't going to cry in her own kitchen because she'd disappointed her father. Again.

A few minutes later, she made it into the living room. Amelie was still on the sofa, a Grandparent on either side of her, all three poring over *Real Life Monsters* in a scene you could have fucking framed.

"That's a moray eel," Amelie was saying. "It says here it's thirteen feet long."

Cordelia Palmer followed her granddaughter's finger across the page. "That *is* big. Do you know how many Amelies that is?"

"Probably not many. Mummy hasn't measured me for a month and I'm much bigger than I used to be."

"I don't think you're quite thirteen feet yet," said St. John Palmer, laughing.

"I might be. I could be having a growth spurt."

"Well, I would guess," Cordelia Palmer told her, "that you're about four feet tall. So how many Amelies is thirteen feet?"

Amelie screwed up her face. "One Amelie is four. So two Amelies are eight. And three Amelies are twelve and four Amelies are sixteen. So more than three and less than four. So three Amelies and a leg."

St. John Palmer smiled at Amelie the way he'd once smiled at Rosaline. "Very good, Amelie. What a clever girl you are."

"I am," Amelie agreed. "I'm very clever. Auntie Lauren says I'm precocious."

"You do know"—Cordelia Palmer gave a delicate cough—"that woman isn't really your aunt."

"Yes she is. I call her Auntie Lauren so that makes her my aunt."

"No." It was Cordelia Palmer's most gentle and least yielding voice. "Words have meanings. And aunt means the sister of one of your parents."

This was not going to go well. And her father had yet to touch his tea.

"I," began Rosaline, "um...the train...I don't want to be—"

"Auntie Lauren doesn't think words have meanings." Amelie swung her legs in happy indifference. "She says they're meaningless signifiers. And she should know. She's a playwright."

Cordelia did not look impressed. "Let's talk about this later. Grandma has to drive Mummy to the station."

Putting the book down, Amelie ran across the room to give her mother a hug that Rosaline sorely needed. "Are you going to win this week, Mummy?"

Probably not. Probably not at all. "I'm going to try."

"And trying your best is what matters," said St. John Palmer, who had never believed that in his life.

Rosaline and her mother both kissed Amelie goodbye, and with that they were out and on the way to the station.

"You know we'd happily drive you down," said Cordelia after a minute or two.

They'd certainly have driven her down. But they'd also have brought it up every opportunity they'd got. "It's fine. I don't want to be a bother."

"You're not a bother. You're our daughter. And Amelie's our granddaughter. And honestly, your father and I are a little concerned by how involved in her life your friend seems to be."

Not this again. "Lauren's my *best* friend. And she's been there for me when no one else was." The moment the words were out of her mouth, Rosaline knew it was the wrong thing to say.

Her mother got that distant look that suggested she'd been wounded but was too decent to show it. "*We've* been there for you. We've *always* been there for you."

"I know. I'm sorry. I didn't mean it like that."

Except, in a way, she had. Because her parents' way of being there—desperately dependent on it though she was—was beginning to feel more and more disconnected from anything she might have chosen or wanted.

"I just think," Cordelia was saying, "that having that woman around all the time must be very confusing for Amelie. I mean, how do you explain something like that to a child?"

"Explain what exactly?"

"You know what I mean. Children need stability and family, not strange women who have nothing to do with them filling their heads with ideas."

"Lauren's not a strange woman." At least not in that sense. "And as you keep on pointing out, Amelie's a very clever girl. She understands that Mummy used to go out with Auntie Lauren and that they're friends now."

"And you think that's appropriate?" Cordelia's mouth had grown thin and tight. "Are you going to keep introducing her to an ever-expanding legion of *aunties* and *uncles* depending on who you happen to be *friends with* at the time?"

Rosaline really wanted to smash something or leave, but since she was trapped in a car, she couldn't do either. "My sex life is none of your business, Mother. But for your information, I haven't been with anyone in a very long time, and when I do I'm extremely careful and you know that."

"Actually, darling, if there's one thing I know about your sex life it's that 'careful' is not a word that characterises it."

There was nothing to say to this. There had never been anything to say to this. They fell into a familiar, uneasy silence.

Until Cordelia said finally, "Your father mentioned that there was a very pleasant gentleman with you when he picked you up the other week."

"Alain?" asked Rosaline warily. Her parents' approval came so rarely these days that she didn't quite trust it when it emerged. "Yes, he's a contestant."

"Well, he made a good first impression."

This was beginning to smell like a trap. "You do remember it's a baking show, not a dating show."

"Well, I know that. But you so seldom get a chance to meet anyone suitable, and you might as well get *something* out of this ... whatever it is that you're doing."

At this rate, her mum was perilously close to putting her off a guy she actually liked. "Yes. Winning is what I'm going to get out of it. Didn't you always tell me to prioritise my career over my personal life?"

"Being on reality television is not a career. A career requires work and qualifications."

"Oh, you mean because I didn't go to university I should give up and pimp myself out to the first man with a decent job who looks my way?"

"You're being unfair," said Cordelia. "And a little childish. Your father and I just want you to be *happy*, darling, and while of *course* we would have been overjoyed if you'd gone back to university and become a doctor like you wanted, you chose not to and"—for a moment Cordelia was silent, as if the topic was more painful for her than it was for Rosaline—"we're only trying to support you as best we know how. That's all we've ever done."

Rosaline knew better than to argue the point. "I'm sorry. It's been a stressful week and I really appreciate you taking care of Amelie for me."

"Don't be silly, we love spending time with Amelie. She's our granddaughter. But you could be a little kinder to your father. He's worked very hard for you his whole life, and he sometimes feels like you barely acknowledge it."

There wasn't much more she could say. Give a conversation with either of the Palmers long enough, and it would eventually deteriorate into a laundry list of grievances. The only way out was to nod, say she was sorry, and promise to do better next time. While privately knowing there was no way she could.

Her mother dropped her off at the station where they exchanged a formulaic back-and-forth of I-love-you-toos, and then Rosaline tucked herself away in a seat on a second-class carriage and tried, for as long as she could, to think about nothing.

"Welcome back, my little Chelsea buns," said Grace Forsythe. "I'm afraid this is the one you've been dreading because it's the week you'll be battling with bloomers, fighting with focaccia, wrestling with rolls, and if you're very lucky, larking about with a loaf or two. That's right, it's bread week. And we're throwing you immediately into our most challenging blind bake yet."

A pause for reaction shots. Rosaline, at least, found it quite easy to look traumatised, mainly because she felt traumatised. She hadn't been looking forward to bread week to begin with—she loved baking from scratch, but she really couldn't justify spending six hours making something she could buy for ninety-five pence from Sainsbury's—and being met at the gates by a harried technician who'd confiscated her luggage and her phone before rushing her into the ballroom for a surprise filming session had been the hell raisins in her batch of doom scones.

Wilfred Honey stepped forward. "What we'd like you to make this week is a traditional sourdough. And it's extra specially important because it's my mam's recipe. We've given you all a little pot of starter that comes out of my own kitchen in Armley from a culture I've kept going continuously for forty years."

Another round of reaction shots. Everyone else seemed to be doing a decent job of conveying how simultaneously intimidated and moved they were. But Rosaline's face was as tired as the rest of her so most of her effort went into keeping her eyes open.

"Because this bread takes such a long time to rise," Grace Forsythe continued, "you'll be making your dough now and finishing your loaves tomorrow. You have one hour for this part of the challenge starting on three. Three, darlings."

Normally this was everyone's cue to start frantically baking, but this time the cameras stopped rolling and Jennifer Hallet materialised like the Wicked Witch of the West with further instructions. "Now we've got our bombshell shots for the *next week on*, here's how this is actually going to work. So pay attention, you bucket of pigs' cocks, because if any one of you fucks this up for me, I'll come down on you so hard that Satan himself will take a break from roasting the arses of sinners in the fires of hell and say, *Are you all right there, Jenny? I think you're being a bit harsh.*"

The rules, as it happened, were fairly straightforward. Because they were filming over two days, and it was supposed to be a blind challenge, they were effectively on blackout until the end of Saturday.

Normally this wouldn't have been a problem—Rosaline tried to call home as much as she could, and when she couldn't, she felt comfortable relying on Lauren to smooth things over with Amelie. But while she knew St. John and Cordelia Palmer wouldn't let her have a massive freak-out, not that Amelie was really the freaking-out sort, they'd also see it as yet more evidence that Rosaline, having failed as a daughter, was now failing as a mother as well.

"Uh, Jennifer," she said.

But Jennifer Hallet was already signalling to the camera operators. "Did any part of that suggest I was taking questions?"

It hadn't, and she wasn't, and they were filming.

And the clock was ticking

And oh God. The instructions literally just said "Make the dough."

Rosaline was going home. She was definitely going home.

"I make this about once a week." Josie's voice floated cheerfully across the ballroom as Colin Thrimp and a camera wielder assembled at her station. "It's actually one of the oldest leavened breads in the world."

Come on, Rosaline. If your neolithic ancestors could do this, you can do this. Although, by that logic, she should also be able to make a flint arrowhead and shoot a mammoth with it.

Right. One thing at a time. Stop worrying about the phone. Wake the fuck up. Think this through.

They had an hour, which meant it had to be fairly straightforward and Rosaline knew dough usually needed to rest anywhere from fifteen to ninety minutes.

Half an hour? That seemed…right? Safe? And in-the-middle enough that even if it was wrong it couldn't be too far wrong. But it did mean she had to start right the hell now.

She whisked water and a little oil into the starter, then gradually added the dry ingredients. The problem was, she couldn't remember if this was a work-the-shit-out-of-it bread or a barely-touch-it bread. From the way Ricky's arms were going—and wasn't the internet going to love that—he'd definitely taken the work-the-shit-out-of-it route.

"What are you doing?" asked Colin Thrimp.

Rosaline looked at the ball of dough between her hands. "So this is a technical process that we bakers call *squishing*. I want to make sure the dough's absorbed the flour. And after that, I'm probably going to leave it alone for a bit."

Normally, at this point Rosaline would be fretting about her bake, but there wasn't a huge amount to fret about yet—unless, of course, she'd fucked it up so hard and so immediately that when she came back tomorrow she'd find her dough, instead of rising, had rearranged itself into the words "you suck." So, instead, she fretted about everything else.

About the aliens in the boiler.

About whatever the fuck was going on with the electricity.

About how she could probably afford to have one of those things fixed but not both.

About how whichever she chose it might not get fixed anyway, because the guy she hired to fix it would just stand there making concerned noises, tell her she needed someone else, and charge her for the privilege.

About how she should have spent more time getting her shit together and being a proper mum instead of throwing her every spare moment at a TV cooking show like she was having a midlife crisis at twenty-seven.

Once the half hour she'd arbitrarily chosen had elapsed, Rosaline stared into her bowl for a minute or two and then—taking a deep breath—worked her dough into a rough ball as quickly as she could.

There. Done. Committed.

"Well," Ricky was telling Colin Thrimp, "having no clue came through for me last time so here we are again. The one thing I know about bread is that you can't be afraid to get your hands in it. So I'm giving it a good hard pounding and hoping for the best."

Grace Forsythe patted him on the shoulder. "Man after my own heart."

When the hour was finally up they were dismissed a little informally, probably because this section would involve one of Grace Forsythe's plummy voice-overs and a clever edit linking it into a continuous sequence with the next. Rosaline hurried out of the ballroom and retrieved her luggage from one of the assistants.

"Look," she said, "I know this is against the rules, but I need my phone for a bit."

The assistant shrugged apathetically. "Sorry. It's like Jennifer said: you're still in the blind bake, so there's no phones, no books, no electronic devices."

"But I need to call my daughter."

"You can call her tomorrow after the challenge."

She'd sort of expected this, but that really didn't help. "She's eight and she's expecting to hear from me."

"Not my rules. Nothing I can do."

Rosaline opened her mouth to protest but could see no world in which that wasn't futile. She wasn't going to get her phone back, she wasn't going to be able to call Amelie, and then five years from now, her dad would be a dick about something and she'd make a very gentle attempt to call him on it and he'd come back with *Well, what about that time you went away for the weekend and couldn't be bothered to ring your daughter?*

"You okay?" Harry, sports bag thrown casually over his shoulder, wandered over from the luggage retrieval pile.

Rosaline did not have time for this. "No. I'm not fucking okay. They won't give me my phone and I said I'd call Amelie, but they don't get it or don't care, and I probably need to talk to

Colin Fucking Thrimp, who I know will be useless except what else can I do?"

"Want me to come with you?" he asked, with that quiet steadiness he had that, right now, when she was anything but steady, Rosaline found quite annoying.

"Why would I want that?"

"Moral support?" he suggested. "Might be easier if you've got someone backing you up."

Great. Now a random electrician thought she was incompetent as well as her parents, the boiler guy, and everybody else she knew. "I'm perfectly capable of sorting this out myself."

He shrugged. "Didn't say you weren't. But there's nothing wrong with getting help sometimes, especially when it's something important."

She stared at him for a long moment. Until then, she hadn't realised how much she'd needed someone to understand that while she might not have been saving lives or making a TV show, her shit still mattered. "Okay. Fine."

They set off in search of Colin Thrimp—and it did feel just that little bit better to have company. In some ways Harry was the perfect person because, given his reluctance to talk to people in general, she was kind of hoping he would mostly stand behind her and look...if not intimidating, then at least more intimidating than, say, her.

Colin Thrimp was semi-hiding in the shadow of a trailer and trying, somewhat unsuccessfully, to eat a hot dog. Onions were slipping onto his shoes.

"Oh gosh." The dog itself followed its toppings to freedom. "Oh no. Rosaline, Harry. Can I...do you...?"

"I want my phone back," said Rosaline.

Colin Thrimp took a sad bite of ketchupy bread. "Ah, well. You see, we have to preserve the integrity of the round. There's actually quite stringent broadcasting standards regulations."

"I need to call my daughter."

"I'm sorry. Is she ill?"

"No." The truth was out before it had occurred to Rosaline how much more useful it could have been to lie. "But I said I'd ring her, and I don't want to be breaking promises to my child."

"That's very sweet." Colin Thrimp nodded with an infuriatingly unhelpful helpfulness. "But you did sign a contract, allowing the company to restrict your communications if necessary during filming."

"Oh come on, mate," muttered Harry. "She's not going to get sourdough tips from a primary school kid."

Colin Thrimp eyed Harry nervously. "I don't make the rules. The production company makes the rules."

"Does that mean," asked Rosaline, "Jennifer makes the rules?"

Dropping what was left of his bun, Colin Thrimp clasped his hands together, half-imploring, half-frustrated. "You cannot go to Jennifer with this."

Aha. Rosaline knew how this worked. "I want to go to Jennifer."

"She's reviewing the footage. She'll be furious."

"*I'm* furious. Get me a phone or get me Jennifer."

Colin Thrimp got the fleeting calculating look of a yes-man not certain who to say yes to. "I...I really can't. You can phone your daughter tomorrow. It'll be fine."

"It's not fine. I promised I'd call tonight."

A door creaked open on the other side of the car park. "Colin," barked Jennifer Hallett. "Get me another six coffees. It's going to be an unlubed arsefuck of an evening to whisk this chunky diarrhoea you call footage into something approaching watchable television."

"Please don't," whispered Colin Thrimp.

No chance. Rosaline strode across the gravel towards Jennifer Hallett. "I need to talk to my daughter."

Jennifer Hallet paused, an unbranded brown cup denting in

her hand. "Am I your daughter? Do I look like your daughter? Then why the fuck are you bothering me about it?"

"You've confiscated my phone like you've caught me texting in assembly."

"You're under a pissing embargo. Either you live with it, or we've got no shortage of ovens for you to stick your head in."

Rosaline sighed. This was getting circular. Like a saw. And she should probably have stopped pressing her face against it. "Look, she's eight, I'm a single mother—"

"Yes," interrupted Jennifer Hallett, "and you're twenty-seven. Born in Kensington. And now you live in some shitty commuter town. You work at WHSmith's and look good in a pinny. I know everything I need to know about you, sunshine."

Oh God. All this time Rosaline had been worried she was the boring one and it turned out she was the pretty one. The one who would get through to week six and who everyone would say was only still on the show because one of the judges fancied her. That didn't say good things about her career prospects, but maybe she could make it work for her now. "And how good do you think I'll look in my pinny if I've spent the whole night stressing about my child?"

There was a cut-the-red-wire pause.

"Colin, give the woman her phone."

"But...but," protested Colin, "they're all locked up."

"Then give her yours, put her on speaker, and stay with her. Never let this happen again."

The trailer door slammed closed before anyone could say anything else.

"Wow, mate," said Harry. "You was a force of nature."

Rosaline had just received an impromptu lecture on the sarcastic fringehead—which Amelie had described as "an angry fish with a sad face and a big mouth that defends its territory by making its head huge." And, from context, was taking this to mean her daughter hadn't been scarred for life by having to wait twenty minutes to talk to her mother. "Look, thanks for coming with me. I'm sorry I was kind of rude earlier."

"I get it. Had to call your kid, didn't you?"

"Except now I feel like I was being neurotic. Because I made an enormous fuss and she was fine. Incredibly fine."

Colin Thrimp had given her a deeply put-out look when she'd handed him his phone back.

Harry shrugged. "You got to keep your promises. Especially to kids." He was silent for a moment, frowning very slightly—something was clearly going on in his head, but she had no idea what. "My sister's ex is a bit flaky with it. Good bloke, mind. Loves 'em to pieces. Except he's a bit of a lad, you know?"

It wasn't anything Rosaline had personally experienced—none of her exes could easily have been described as lads, even the men. All the same, she thought she knew what he was driving at.

"Like," Harry went on slowly, "he'll say he'll be somewhere or do something, and he'll forget. Not always but sometimes. And he don't mean nothing by it, and he makes it up to 'em, but you can see it has an effect."

"I didn't know you had a sister." She wasn't sure why this had surprised her—because he obviously hadn't emerged from a rock like Mithras.

"Got three, mate."

And this was why she didn't talk to him more. It wasn't so much—as she'd first thought—that he never said anything. It was that he kept expecting you to say things back, and Rosaline was a lot more comfortable when people would obligingly fill the silences with themselves. "That's . . . a lot of sisters."

"Tell me about it. Meant the bathroom was really clean, but hard to get into."

"And one of them's a single mum, like me?" Wait. Was that why he'd given her his number last week? Not as a clumsy come-on, but because she'd reminded him of his sister. Was that worse? Or did it just mean he ... understood?

"Not much like you, Rosaline," he said, with an almost playful look. "Her name don't come out a play, for starters."

She laughed. "She could be in a play. What's she called?"

"Sam. Short for Samantha, but she gets well lairy if you call her that."

"What about the others?"

"Nah. None of them are in plays either."

It was probably a bit late in the day to be taking an interest in Harry and his life, but she was beginning to feel slightly uncomfortable about how quietly decent he'd been to her the last couple of weeks and how little she'd noticed or cared. Between his looks and the "loves," it had been far easier to write him off as some kind of Cockney fuckboy. When actually he was ... maybe not that? Maybe not that at all. And what would it mean to her if he was or he wasn't? "What are they like?"

"Family's family, init?" He shrugged. "Heather's the youngest. She's a nurse. Married a doctor, which my nan was very impressed by. And Ashley—she's in the middle—she's a stay-at-home mum, and a bloody good one. And then there's Sam, who's been through some stuff, but she's doing all right now."

"I'm an only child," Rosaline admitted. "Which I sort of think people can tell."

"I wouldn't say that. You don't act spoiled or nothing."

"So you claim, but I just dragged you all over the set so you could watch me throw tantrums at people."

"It's important to stand up for yourself, mate." Stuffing his hands in his pockets, he drove his toe into the gravel. "Look, now you've rung your kid and told Colin what's what, do you wanna—"

"Ah, there you are." Alain emerged from between two of the trailers. "I've been looking all over for you, Rosaline."

She turned to find him looking tall and elegant and familiar, half smiling in the spill of light from the hotel. And it was pretty much perfect timing because, not only had she recovered from her unflattering mumzilla moment, but it had seemed like Harry was about to ask her for a drink. And that would have been...complicated. Because, honestly, if Rosaline had been a few years younger and hadn't had Amelie to think about, she might have taken a chance on a more-decent-than-he-seemed guy whose guns were better than his grammar. Just because she could.

Except in the real world, there was no way she was going to throw away a burgeoning connection with a someone who could genuinely be right for her over—actually she had no idea what it was even over. A moment of curiosity? A private act of rebellion? The magpie impulse to grab at something shiny.

Or none of the above. And a drink would just have been a drink.

"Sorry," she said to Alain. "I had something I needed to deal with. And now it's dealt with. So...go me."

His eyes darted from her to Harry and back. "Yes, I saw you were busy and didn't want to interrupt."

"Thanks," she said. "I appreciate it."

"Well, if everything's okay now, I was wondering if you felt like another walk?"

She definitely felt like another walk. Highlights of their previous walks had included being forgiven for lying about basically her entire life and kissing on a bridge by moonlight. They were, she felt, pretty good at walking. Besides, she'd spent all week being the harried single-mum version of Rosaline—the one who couldn't get her boiler fixed or her parents to take her seriously. So she was almost embarrassingly grateful for a chance to be a different Rosaline for a while. Someone bold and sexy and adventurous who got to be with a man who even St. John Palmer couldn't find fault with.

She nodded. "Definitely."

Alain glanced briefly at Harry again. "You don't mind if I steal Rosaline, do you?"

"I reckon with people," Harry said, "it's called kidnapping."

"Actually, it's called an idiom." It was Alain's most withering voice, which Rosaline wasn't quite used to hearing directed at people rather than about them. But then he offered his hand to her and smiled. "Shall we?"

They left Harry in the car park and headed out into the grounds. And Rosaline tried to let go of everything that was tugging at her and worrying her and weighing on her—wanting to lose herself instead in the sky, the trees, and the man at her side.

And it was mostly working.

It was just that she also felt the tiniest bit guilty.

"Don't you...," she began, "I mean, wasn't that a bit much back there? With Harry."

He paused. "In what way?"

"Well, he was clearly joking about the kidnapping thing. And I thought you were, I don't know, a bit mean to him about it?"

"Don't worry, I'm sure it went over his head."

"I...I don't think that makes it better."

"Oh come on." He smirked knowingly. "He probably thinks Idiom is an island a couple of miles south of Magaluf."

"You're not funny," Rosaline told him, trying not to laugh. "He's been very nice to me."

"Of course he has. He clearly wants to get his spanner into your fuse box."

"Actually, that might be useful. My fuse box is playing up a bit..."

At this Alain gave her a wary look.

"I mean," she went on quickly, "I mean my actual fuse box. In my actual house. Not, you know, my vagina. Which, I hasten to add, is in full working order."

His brow flicked up. "Good to know."

They were approaching the edge of one of the little woods that dotted the grounds, the evening haze settling in shades of pink and gold on the long grasses and the meadow flowers, and the butterflies that danced among them.

"You know," she said, wishing she hadn't brought up her vagina and its functionality or otherwise quite so explicitly. Or so recently. "I think I've changed my mind. I'm not sure I'm quite in the mood for a walk."

Alain, for the barest of moments, looked disappointed. "Of course. It's been a long day. Shall I take you back to your room?"

It had, in fact, been a long day. And a long week. And...fuck it. Fuck everything. She deserved a break. To feel good. To have something for herself.

"You could. And...if you wanted, you could come into my room?" *Suave, Rosaline. Suave.* "For...um. Sex?" With her functioning vagina.

He no longer looked disappointed. "Well well. Rosaline-um-Palmer. You really are a woman who knows how to get what she wants, aren't you?"

She wasn't. She was winging it incredibly hard.

But it would be nice to pretend for a while.

Reeling him in for a kiss, she left him breathless and tousled. "Shall we go?"

"At the risk of ruining the moment"—Alain had that not-quite bashful expression she saw all too rarely—"I didn't actually come—how can I put this—loaded for bear."

So much for being a wild sexual creature who followed her passions and bought condoms accordingly. "Ah. Neither did I. But there are still things we can"—wow, way to sell the Rosaline Palmer Experience—"...um, do?"

"Don't worry." Alain had switched back to decisive at the drop of a prophylactic. "There's a machine in the hotel toilet. I'll meet you in your room."

And before she could really say anything else, he was sprinting off. Which was flattering. In a way?

Sex with Alain was, well, it was fine. It was good. It kept her out of her head, and it gave her a brief, welcome sense of being in control of something—even if it was just her body. While he was no Harry, Alain had a refined sort of attractiveness, and gave every indication of finding her very hot indeed, running through the full repertoire of sexy attentiveness: kissing his way down her neck, lingering over her boobs, not that they'd ever been a particularly sensitive area for her, and grazing his mouth against the jut of her hip and the crease of her thighs.

Lauren might have teased Rosaline for not being relentlessly promiscuous, but she liked to think she had experience in her way. There were definitely a couple of people—like Lauren and Leo, one of her eight-month one-night stands—she'd had that raw chemistry with. The intense messy hunger that made sex effortlessly explosive. But she'd also been with enough people over enough time to know that sometimes it could take a while to get used to getting each other off. It meant you actually had to get to know someone and, as much she hated to admit Lauren had been right, Rosaline did like getting to know people.

With Alain, she was getting the strong impression it would be worth it. He was eager but didn't rush her—or charge into her like she was a freshly opened till at a supermarket. And the moment their bodies came together, and he was braced on his forearms, gazing down into her face with a kind of wonder, made her feel wanted and special and cared for. Best of all, in being a little older—or perhaps confident he had nothing to prove—he seemed to have got past the stage of expecting sex to work like a movie, and was more than willing to make sure she came when—collapsing beside her—he realised she hadn't yet.

Sliding his hand from between her legs, he gave her one of those smug "I just orgasmed you" grins. "You're quite something, Rosaline-um-Palmer."

"You might be overstating it a bit. But"—she was contentedly boneless and floaty—"I can live with that."

"I say it because it's true." He skated a finger lightly over her breast. "And I'm very glad we did this."

"Me too. I needed something nice to happen today."

"I'm happy I could be that for you."

That made her smirk. "Yeah, you really took one for the team."

"I know you think you're joking. But you need to stop putting yourself down."

She thought she *had* been joking and *wasn't* putting herself down. Still, he'd meant well. "You're right. I'll be more narcissistic in the future."

There was a silence as they afterglowed gently together.

"You know what I don't understand about you?" said Alain, rolling onto his side and propping himself on an elbow so he could look down at her. "You're clearly driven and capable. You have a support network you can rely on. Your daughter's at an age where she no longer needs you around all day. Why haven't you gone back to university?"

Rosaline's afterglow got a whole lot less glow and a whole lot more after. When Amelie was a baby it had been out of the question, whatever her parents might have thought. And from time to time down the years it had occurred to her that she could pick up medicine again. But it had always been a broken tooth of a thought, the kind you didn't poke at too much in case it revealed something you didn't like. "It's been too long," she said. "Surely?"

"Not at all. You're only...what, twenty-seven? Lots of people retrain, and there's a shortage of doctors in this country."

"Yes, but that's retraining. Which implies you've trained in something before and I haven't."

"If someone with a degree in law or literature can do it, you certainly can."

Her heart squeezed like it had on A-level results day. "I guess...I could, couldn't I?"

"You really could." For once there was no mockery in his gaze or laughter in his eyes. "You're far from out of chances."

"I'm not that much of a mess, am I?"

"Of course not," he said gently. "But we both know you're not living the life you would have chosen."

"I suppose, but—" But what could she say? That maybe she couldn't perform a coronary bypass but her biscuits were on point? That she'd never spoken at the Royal Society of Medicine like both her parents, but when Amelie had wanted her bedroom painted green they'd done it together?

"Just think about it." Alain moved on top of her, dispelling the need for Rosaline to think seriously about her future. "You're a remarkable woman, Rosaline-um-Palmer."

She smiled up at him. "Eh, you're not so bad yourself."

His eyes glinted. "I think I might be able to do better than that."

"Oh can you?"

He kissed her slowly and deeply, the taste of his mouth already becoming familiar, and almost comforting. And then his fingers were pressing against her, stirring her to fresh arousal. "Rosaline," he murmured.

There was something in his tone. A nervy excitement. "Yes?"

"Why don't you turn over for me? I'd love to see your butter-flies while I'm inside you."

Saturday

ROSALINE'S SOURDOUGH HAD come out fine. Again. Which was, y'know— Oh for God's sake, she was sick of fine.

It didn't help that tomorrow they'd be tasked with constructing a baketactular bread sculpture and her kitchen—even when the boiler was working and the electricity was staying on—was not the kind of place you could practise building the Taj Mahal out of ciabatta.

No surprises that Josie had done well this round—Rosaline had consciously avoided speaking to her since the first week, but she probably had a wood-fired oven, to go with her wood-fired husband and three wood-fired children—except it was Nora who had come out on top. Which was equally unsurprising because Britain was not ready for a granny who couldn't make bread. Slightly more surprising was that Harry got an honourable mention, which made him blush and rub the back of his neck in a way the camera would probably love. And if she was being honest, Rosaline didn't find totally unadorable either.

This was one of the pitfalls of the show. In an ideal world everyone would be either wrenchingly awful like Dave or misguidedly difficult like Josie so you wouldn't have to feel bad about hoping they failed. Instead everybody seemed so fundamentally nice that when someone like Harry did better than expected it was hard not to be—as he might put it—well made up for him.

After the exit interviews, Rosaline was looking around for Alain, hoping for an opportunity to work out her baking-related frustrations through the medium of horniness when Anvita pounced from the shadow of a gardenia bush and dragged her into the bar.

"So," she said. "Something you want to tell me, Rosaline?"

Rosaline made a thinking face. "You might have put too much water in your starter?"

"Come on, I had a bad round, and I'm probably going to have another bad round tomorrow because I fucking hate bread. Take me to the sexscapades."

"That sounds like you're hitting on me."

"Stop being coy." Anvita claimed a barstool. "I'm right next door. If I have to hear it, I should get to hear about it."

"Oh God, you heard?"

"It wasn't like I was up against the wall with a glass. But you were either reading a very rhythmic book or you were totally doing it."

Sighing, Rosaline flumped onto the next seat. "Look, I get you're bored, and there's nothing to do here except drink and talk, but... suppose I'd slept with you. Would you want me to go around bragging about it the next day?"

"Hell yeah, I'd want you to be telling everyone what a brilliant lay I am."

"I'm not sure"—Rosaline gave her a quizzical look—"but that might just be a you thing."

"I'm not looking for, like, *details*," protested Anvita. "You don't have to tell me how big his dick was or, I don't know, how squishy her boobs were."

"How squishy her boobs were? What do you think lesbians *do*?"

"Honestly, not given it much thought." There was a pause

that, while not quite pregnant, was definitely pissing on a stick. "At least tell me who it was."

"I'm surprised you haven't already worked it out like some kind of bespectacled sex detective."

"If I hadn't spent so long training for my current job, I'd so be thinking about a career change now. But based on the assumption that nobody here would be having an affair on live TV, it could only be Ricky, Harry, Alain, or Claudia. And you think Ricky's too young, and I've never seen you speak to Claudia once—"

"Hey, who said I needed her to talk."

Anvita gasped. "That's . . . is that sexist? That would be sexist if you were a man."

"I'm not sleeping with Claudia."

"Please say it's Harry." Her face fell. "It's not Harry, is it? Oh come on, you should have gone with Harry. You've seen his arms. He's even stopped calling you 'love.' And besides, the quiet ones always go like a train."

"I'm not totally convinced I want a train in my vagina."

"I said *like* a train. Meaning powerful and enduring."

"You don't use public transport much, do you?" asked Rosaline, laughing. "You say train to me, and I think overcrowded, end-lessly delayed, and subject to constant technical failures."

"Look, leave my fantasies out of this. I just don't get why you'd pick Alain over Harry."

"I wasn't aware *picking* was an option."

"Of course it's an option." Anvita nearly knocked her G&T off the bar. "They both blatantly fancy you, and Harry keeps giving you those big soulful eyes. You have noticed the big soulful eyes, right?"

"He does not," lied Rosaline, "have big soulful eyes."

"What are you on? He completely does. They say *I can mend a dripping tap, but if I found a bird with a broken wing, I would tenderly nurse it back to health.*"

"I'm not a bird with a broken wing. And nothing about me is dripping."

"I'm just saying, there are choices here and you went with the man who picks his own mint."

"As opposed to the man who barely talks."

"Hey"—Anvita put her hands in the air, smirking—"I never said I needed him to talk."

Rosaline gave up. "I see what you did there."

"Yeah, I said the thing that you said earlier in the conversation, in a different context. Because I am amazing and hilarious. Boom."

On some level, Rosaline felt she shouldn't need to explain herself to Anvita. But they were sort of friends and it was nice to talk about it. "The truth is, I'm not sure I'm looking for...well...a short ride on a train. I'm not saying it wouldn't be fun. But I think I have a real connection with Alain."

"How?"

That was obvious, wasn't it? Except when Rosaline opened her mouth to reply, it was suddenly very hard to put into words. "I just feel we're...similar people who are coming from similar places and who want similar things."

"Like what?" asked Anvita, with irritating to-the-pointness.

"I don't know. Like he's...he's got a very good career and I could have had a very good career, and he's actually encouraging me to think about going back to it. And, you know, it's nice to have someone who believes in you like that."

"Hey." Anvita gave her outraged eyes behind her horn-rimmed glasses. "I believe in you. I believe in you loads. That's why I'm telling you to go for the hottest guy on the show."

"While not listening to me when I say I'm into a different guy."

"Oh God. I'm a chauvinist. No wonder you won't date me."

"I won't date you because you're taken and straight."

Anvita thought a moment. "Okay, but otherwise let's be clear. You'd be all over this."

"Yes," said Rosaline in her deadest deadpan voice, "in that very specific alternate reality we'd be totally doing it on this bar right now."

"That's what I like to hear." Anvita finished the rest of her drink. "And now I need to go wash the sourdough out of my hair. Before I do, though, I'm going to say a thing. And you might not like the thing, in which case I'm sorry."

"I'm not liking this already."

"Tough. Here it is. From my vast experience in the realm of perving on hot men I'm not going to go out with, I think Alain is one of those guys that you'd feel really good for having got. But who might not be that much fun to actually have."

And Anvita had been right. Rosaline hadn't liked that one little bit. "For the record, I'm having quite a lot of fun having him right now."

"In which case, good for you."

She bounced off and Rosaline decided to order a second drink in quiet celebration of her love life looking up even if her baking was still looking resolutely straight ahead. Sure, her master plan to reboot her life by winning a TV show was stalling out a little, and it felt the tiniest bit regressive to be taking solace in the fact that she'd found a boy who liked her, but she'd long ago got used to taking her victories where she could.

Besides, at the very least, if she didn't get distracted by eyes and arms and an accent she was starting to find oddly comforting and wound up with Alain in the medium-to-long-term, it would be something her parents wouldn't be able to shit on her for. Well, until they broke up, and then it would be *Whatever happened to Alain, he was such a nice respectful young man*, and—oh what was wrong with her, they'd had sex on exactly one occasion and she was already imagining a world where she had to explain their hypothetical future breakup to her parents at hypothetical future family gatherings.

Although maybe at that point, she'd have gone back to university and become a doctor and be the one who went a bit off-book for eight years rather than the one who ruined everything. Which should hypothetically have made the hypothetical gatherings more hypothetically bearable. So why didn't it? Had she just got so used to failure she was incapable of imagining success?

"If I said you had a beautiful body," drawled out Alain, resting his elbows on the bar beside her, "would you file a restraining order?"

Despite her profound case of the existential floops, this drew a laugh from her. "You must be tired. Because you were running round a ballroom all day."

"It's handy I have my library card because I'm a big supporter of state-sponsored literacy programmes."

"For the record," she said, "I can do this all night."

He slanted a half-smile at her. "Is that another terrible pickup line or are you telling me you're sick of exchanging terrible pickup lines?"

"Little from column A, little from column B." She sighed. "Honestly, I kind of maybe think we should go back to one of our rooms and, you know, have the sex?"

A pause. "I'm beginning to think you're only after me for one thing, Rosaline-um-Palmer."

He was joking, wasn't he? He was definitely joking. Still, Rosaline felt a little bad that she'd jumped from zero to bang without so much as a *By the way, how are you?*

"Sorry, am I being too much?"

"No, no, it's refreshing." Reaching out a hand, he tucked a lock of hair behind her ear. "I wish I knew more people like you."

"Um…" This was good, right? "How?"

"I think so many of us get stuck in our ways. We're afraid to step outside ourselves or take a chance or try something new. But you're different, aren't you?"

Okay. On the one hand, she liked hearing how cool and special she was. On the other, this was all setting her up to be a massive disappointment later on. "What if I'm not?"

"Don't be silly. Now come on—use me for my body."

It was better this time. Not that it had been bad before, but she'd learned and he'd learned, and some of the self-consciousness that always accompanied a new partner was beginning to fall away. That was sex for you—it only got really good when you didn't care how undignified the whole business was. When you got sweaty and urgent, and you forgot to worry that your face was doing funny things, and your legs were all over the place, and you were showing someone bits of yourself that you couldn't quite guarantee the attractiveness of.

She tried, but with a kid, a job, and a baking competition, she was ever so slightly busy. On top of which, she hadn't super been expecting to get laid that weekend, which meant Alain was getting more of an unfiltered experience than she would have liked. There was definitely a patch of hair she'd missed on the side of her knee. And her moisturising routine could have been way more rigorous. And probably best she didn't raise her arms too extravagantly above her head because, while she was sure she hadn't completely lost control, there was definite prickle under there.

All of which suggested real person.

Rather than the silken sex goddess vibe she'd ideally have wanted to convey.

Still, she came more easily than last time—once before he did, and once after. And then they lay together in the cooling sheets, her head against his chest, and his fingers playing up and down her spine, tracing the wings of her butterflies.

"Christ"—he gave a long exhale—"I needed that."

"Me too."

"I wanted to catch you earlier, but I took a walk after filming to clear my head."

She craned her neck so she could look up at him. "Are you okay?"

"Yes. I mean, mostly. The blind bake didn't quite go my way." Like her, he'd done okay. And like her, he wasn't the sort to think okay was good enough.

"You'll get through."

"Oh, I know I'll get through. That's not the point. I'd expected to do better, and people pay attention to bread week."

"It's a baking show, Alain. People pay attention to the pretty scenery, the nice cakes, and Grace Forsythe's increasingly blatant innuendo."

She'd intended this to be reassuring, but Alain rolled away, tucking his hands behind his head and frowning at the ceiling. "Bread's never been my thing. It's for old men, housewives, and people who buy a machine, use it twice, and then flood Instagram with stories about how fucking rustic they are. Nobody with anything actually happening in their lives has the time to make their own sourdough. I just...I was relying on other people finding it more of a challenge than I did."

Today had clearly got to him. It had been low-key getting to her as well, but she was probably far more used to feeling like she wasn't doing well enough than he was.

"Well, Nora's a hundred and sixty," she tried, hoping to make him smile. "She probably had to make bread out of sawdust and rubble in the Blitz."

"They liked *Harry's* loaf better than mine. When do you think he last ate a bread that wasn't sold with a plastic sticker saying 'Reduced to Clear'?"

Maybe she'd been infected by Anvita's arm fetish, but Rosaline actually found it pretty easy to imagine Harry making bread on a Sunday afternoon. He'd make it for his sisters, and their husbands, and their kids, and probably his parents, and probably his nan. And they'd be so used to it they'd forget to thank him and he wouldn't mind because he'd be surrounded by the people who loved him.

"Rosaline?" Alain nudged her gently. "Have I worn you out?"

"What?" she said quickly. "No. I'm right here. And you're fine. The blind bake's always a bit random. I'm sure you'll turn it around tomorrow."

"No, you're right." He drew her back into his arms. "I'm in my head and there's no need to be."

"It's okay. The competition's stressful for everyone."

He smiled at that. "It has its compensations."

And then turned her face back to his for a kiss.

Sunday

TWO HOURS INTO a five-hour challenge, Rosaline was starting to feel she would have been better off if the previous night had involved more sleep and fewer orgasms. But she'd found distracting Alain more effective than consoling him, and at the time, it had seemed like a win-win.

"So what are you planning this week, pet?" asked Wilfred Honey, appearing in front of her with Grace Forsythe, Marianne Wolvercote, and a camera operator.

Rosaline paused in her kneading. "Well, I've always been interested in biology, and I thought I'd do a bread heart. I'm going to do sweet-filled loaves for the chambers, cherry and blueberry fillings for the oxygenated and deoxygenated blood, and twisted brioche for the aorta and vena cava."

"That's rather macabre." Marianne Wolvercote was looking more impressed than she had so far this series, at least with Rosaline.

"Yes," added Grace Forsythe, "it does have a bit of a serial killer vibe, I won't lie."

Suddenly Rosaline's concerns about coming across as a tragic single parent with mediocre baking skills seemed misplaced. "I haven't been practising on real ones or anything."

Grace Forsythe's eyebrows shot towards her unapologetically

'80s mullet. "I'm not totally reassured you felt the need to say that explicitly."

"I think it's very imaginative." That was Wilfred Honey, who could usually be relied upon to say something defusingly anodyne. "Just make sure the flavours are right, because that's what it's all about at the end of the day."

Grace Forsythe patted her on the shoulder. "Good luck, Patrick Bate-Mum."

"Oh...poo to it," cried Ricky from across the ballroom, which caused producers, presenters, and cameras to zoom towards his workstation like drama-seeking missiles.

"What's happened?" Colin Thrimp was practically vibrating with eagerness. "For the camera, please."

Ricky slapped a hand to his forehead. "Guess what muppet put his oven on the wrong temperature. So his Chelsea buns have been sitting there, getting a suntan."

An hour or so later, Rosaline's dissected organ was in the oven, and she had a few minutes' breathing space. The advantage of the baketacular over the blind bake was that it was okay to talk to each other during it, and now that the group was a bit more established, it felt more natural to wander around and have the occasional chat.

Anvita and Grace Forsythe were standing together at Anvita's bench, staring at the loaf that had just come out of the oven. As ever, there was a camera operator nearby, but she seemed genuinely uncertain whether this was about to generate usable footage.

"What's it *supposed* to look like?" asked Grace Forsythe, stroking her chin and staring at a tall, proud baked column that definitely resembled something but not the sort of thing you would expect somebody to deliberately make on a family-friendly television show.

Anvita was staring at her creation much as Dr. Frankenstein may once have stared at his. "It's Big Ben, isn't it?"

"Darling, technically, Big Ben is the bell. And technically, that is a bell end."

"Oh f—fu—fellatio." Anvita hung her head.

"You're not allowed to say that on camera either, pumpkin."

"I know. My mind went blank." Turning to Rosaline, Anvita flung her arms in the air. "It's me. I've done it. I've made a penis. I've made an enormous bread penis. Someone always makes a penis. And this year it's me who made the penis. My nan is going to watch me lovingly mould a penis with my bare hands on TV, probably with all her friends."

Grace Forsythe collapsed into unbroadcastable laughter. "It is one of the better ones I've seen. I mean, in the ballroom. Outside, I'm no judge. And, frankly, who would want to be?"

"I think," offered Rosaline, trying to be helpful, "you could carve it?"

Lifting the offending article from the bench, Anvita brandished it in Rosaline's face. "You want me to circumcise the penis?"

"Okay. Bad idea. Why don't you say it's a satirical commentary on the current state of our political system?"

"Because I'm on a baking show, not *Have I Got News for You*."

Grace Forsythe pulled herself upright and wiped tears from the corners of her eyes. "You could always leave it out."

"I'm trying to do the Houses of Parliament. Without the clock tower, the Houses of Parliament is just houses."

"Then," said Grace Forsythe, "you'll have to do what we do every year when someone makes something that looks like a penis."

The light of hope flared in Anvita's eyes. "What? What can I do?"

"Pretend very hard that the thing which obviously looks like a penis does not, in fact, look like a penis."

"But then everyone will think I don't know what a penis looks like."

"Excuse me." Colin Thrimp popped up on the other side of the counter. "I'm terribly sorry. It's just that you're saying the word 'penis' over and over again very loudly, and it's drifting into other people's shots."

"My fault, Colin." Grace Forsythe gave an unrepentant grin. "Penised the whole thing up as usual. You'll be fine, Anvita, they can do wonders with camera angles."

From Ricky's side of the ballroom, there came an ominous crash.

"Welp," said Ricky. He was standing with his hands on his hips, surveying the shrapnel of what must once have been a large, fan-shaped crispbread. "There goes one of the wings. But it's fine. He's got two. I'll show him in profile."

Anvita put down her crusty phallus. "What are you even making?" she called out.

"Great Dragon Smaug. You?"

"Big Dick."

"Nice."

"Please stop shouting," implored Colin Thrimp, "and making references to genitalia. Jennifer will be livid."

"Actually"—Josie glanced up from where she was busily producing more bread than any human being had a right to produce—"I'm starting to think one of my plaits looks a little bit like a vulva."

Eventually the room settled down, despite rather than because of Colin Thrimp's entreaties. And Rosaline got back to her heart, which was browning nicely and not losing its shape too much.

Being in a state of what she hoped was okayness turned out to be a little disorientating. Normally she was too rushed and panicky to pay much attention to what was going on around her, but now she was worryingly open to distractions. There was Josie singing folk music under her breath. The restless *tip-tap* of Claudia's kitchen-inappropriate shoes. Nora cheerfully giving a producer baking tips like she was presenting her own show. And the way Harry's shoulder muscles shifted beneath his T-shirt as he took a baking tray out of the oven.

"What are you doing now?" Colin Thrimp asked him, nearly making him drop his rolls.

"Uhm, taking something out the oven."

"Can you say that like you're not answering a question."

"Oh yeah. Sorry." Harry paused and took a deep breath. "Right now, I'm taking something out the oven."

"Could you tell us"—for a man with no corners, Colin Thrimp could sometimes sound remarkably sharp—"what exactly it is you're taking out the oven."

"Rolls."

"Again. Like you're not answering a question. And maybe tell us what the rolls are for."

"So these are rolls, what I've just taken out the oven. And I'm going to use them as rocks. Because I'm making a rock pool. They're sort of a German rye bread. Because that looks a bit like rocks."

"And why are you doing a rock pool?"

"Because—"

"Like you're not answering a question."

Harry's hands curled and uncurled against the bench. "I thought," he said very slowly, "I'd do a rock pool because in the summer me and my mum and my dad and my sisters go down Southend and we take the kids rock-pooling. I don't know much about it, but they like looking at the crabs and stuff, so I'm going to see if I can make a little crab. And maybe a nice starfish. And I'm doing a pesto flatbread for seaweed."

"Thank you," said Colin Thrimp, with visible relief.

"No problem, mate." Harry's relief was equally visible.

But after Colin had gone, Rosaline noticed Harry was still standing at his workstation, staring blankly at his bread rocks as if a wicked enchantress obsessed with the finer points of rye bread had cursed him to a hundred years of waking sleep. He wasn't her problem—he wasn't even really her friend—but he'd been there when she'd been panicking about her phone. And last night she'd…she'd liked talking to him. Hearing about his family and not feeling she had to defend hers.

Besides, her left ventricle still needed a couple of minutes, so she slipped across the room to his side.

"All right, mate?" she said.

He turned, offering her a wry smile. "I do say that a lot, don't I?"

"Yeah, but it's…it's you, isn't it? Seriously, though. Are you all right?"

"Pretty much." Lifting his forearm to his brow, he pushed his hair back, and left a little streak of flour behind. "Those interviews…they're well hard, ain't they? Because when you're doing something, it's not like you're normally telling people what you're doing at the same time. Like, here I am making a sandwich, and I'm cutting the bread so I'll have bread for the sandwich. And you've got to hold the knife proper so it don't go all wonky and you don't cut your hand off."

At that moment, Nora's voice drifted across the ballroom. "Now you can see," she was telling a producer, who didn't even have a camera, "I've got a nice rise on this. And if you ask me, it's all in the mixing. My mother told me you put the yeast and the salt on the opposite sides of the bowl, and that's what I've always done, and it's always worked."

"Or," Harry went on, "I'm wrong and it's a piece of piss."

Rosaline squeezed his arm. "I think Nora just really likes talking about baking."

"I could probably get used to that, but then they want you to have a feeling about it as well. They're all like, *Does this remind you of your childhood?* And I'm like, *Nah, mate, it's a bun.*"

She laughed and then hoped he'd meant her to. "I'm not a big fan of having feelings on demand either. But there can be something quite emotional about baking—it reminds you of when you baked or who you baked for."

"Yeah, and that's great. But then they say 'Make us two dozen mini pies' and my dad's like, *All you've done is ruin pie and mash*, and I'm like, *I know, but that's what they told me to do*. And I suppose I could say this reminds me of my dad, but it mostly reminds me of my dad wanting a bigger pie."

Harry might not have liked talking, but when he spoke there was something about the way he saw the world—simple and complicated and full of people he cared about—that Rosaline found more appealing than she should have. And she laughed again, imagining an older version of Harry unsatisfied by a bijou pie-ette.

"Oi, mate"—he nudged her—"that's my fucking heritage."

A wail of despair echoed around the room. Ricky was on his knees on the floor. "Oh no. It's only gone and exploded."

In a more rational world—the world that Alain seemed to be living in—they should all have taken that as a timely reminder to focus on their own bakes. But instead, the majority of the contestants gathered around Ricky's oven as the companions of Thorin Oakenshield had gathered around the door to the Lonely Mountain.

Within lay the tragically decapitated remains of the Great Dragon Smaug. Rosaline could see at once what had gone wrong. The fillings had been too moist, which had generated steam, which had created pressure, which had split the beast's mighty flanks and made its head tear open like an overstuffed grocery bag.

Anvita patted Ricky consolingly on the shoulder. "Well. At least it doesn't look like a gargantuan wang."

Culinary glamour shots, interviews, and a disappointing lunch, inevitably served late, had become very much part of the routine. And even sitting on a stool, waiting for the cake slice of Damocles, was losing a little of its edge.

Though only a little.

Claudia was up first with what she claimed was a three-tiered bread wedding cake but which looked a lot to Rosaline, and to the judges, like three loaves on top of each other. Harry's rock pool went down well, as did Alain's poppy and fennel seed rooster, and Josie's harvest basket, although that received some criticism for not strictly being a sculpture except insofar as it was a sculpture of some bread.

Then Anvita slunk forward with her model of the Houses of Parliament. And, to be fair to her, it had mostly worked. Apart from the giant schlong at the end.

Placing a hand over her mouth, Grace Forsythe turned her back to the cameras.

The judges exchanged glances.

"Now this is interesting," said Marianne Wolvercote finally. "I can see what you were going for, and if you'd worked it with a lighter hand, you might have given us something really satisfying. But as it is, it didn't quite come off."

Anvita blinked.

Marianne Wolvercote did not. Not fucking once.

Then she closed her fist over the head of the clock tower and sawed vigorously through it. Wincing, Ricky crossed his legs.

Picking up the bulbous top of what everyone was still determinedly pretending was Big Ben, Wilfred Honey inspected it closely. "Now this," he said, squeezing, "has a nice firmness to it. It feels good in your hand. But of course, what matters is if it's good in the mouth."

Anvita was screaming behind her eyes as the nation's grandfather fondled the glans of her giant bread penis.

"Now this takes me back in a way," Wilfred Honey continued, now chewing, "because when I were a lad you'd only get a loaf like this when the baker's boy came round your house on a bicycle and gave it to you hot. I will say, it's a little crusty for my taste. But I like the flavours. It's subtle, and the salt is definitely coming through."

"Great," said Anvita weakly. "Thanks."

Next came Ricky, who sheepishly lowered the pile of crumbs and filling that passed for his bake onto the judges' table.

"Oh dear." Marianne Wolvercote surveyed the carnage like an insurance investigator at a car crash. "What happened here?"

Ricky sighed with an air of soul-deep exhaustion. "What didn't happen, bruv. It was supposed to be the Great Dragon Smaug on a Chelsea bun horde. But the buns didn't cook properly, I dropped his wing on the floor, and then his head exploded in the oven. So now it's the Great Dragon Smaug after he ran into Bard the Bowman."

"Yes." Grace Forsythe peered sadly at the wreckage of Dread Wyrm. "He does look a little bit like he's crashed into Esgaroth, doesn't he?"

Needless to say, Ricky did not get good feedback. And he was followed by Nora, who presented her frankly spectacular garden scene with the air of someone who knew she'd smashed it. While it felt wrong to wish for the elderly to fail, Rosaline held out a faint hope that it would taste awful. It did not, however, taste awful.

"By 'eck," cried Wilfred Honey. "It's gorgeous."

So that was Nora winning this week, then.

Which meant that Rosaline brought her bake to the front of the room feeling, ironically, disheartened.

"Well, this is very clever," observed Marianne Wolvercote, in a tone of mixed praise and suspicion. "It's not what we were expecting from you, but that's sometimes a good thing."

Wilfred eased the chambers of the heart apart and started slicing into them, spilling red and blue compote over the plate. "I'm afraid it's a little bit Halloween for me. I'm quite a traditional man, and I like my hearts on Valentine's Day or in a nice stew. Not anatomically correct and oozing."

"It's not for everyone," conceded Marianne Wolvercote, which was the closest the judges ever got to disagreeing, "but there's no denying the taste is excellent. And I, at least, enjoyed the concept." She fixed Rosaline with an ice-blue stare. "It's nice to see you coming out of your shell."

"Oh." Rosaline, briefly forgetting she was being filmed, stared at Marianne Wolvercote in astonishment. "Really? Thank you."

She still didn't win. Obviously, she didn't win. Because, while one of the judges had quite liked Rosaline's concept, Nora had created an entire fucking garden—complete with brioche grandchildren and a working swing. Ricky, meanwhile, did not recover from the fall of Smaug and was dispatched with hugs, pats on the back, and genuine tears.

Which left Rosaline as much in the middle as she'd ever been, but it felt different somehow. After all, she'd had a quietly approving look from Marianne Wolvercote, and not many people got those. And for the first time, it seemed almost possible to think of herself as a contender. That whatever Jennifer Hallet might believe, she could do more than look good in a pinny.

She could make a competitively viable sourdough with no warning and barely any recipe.

She could construct an anatomically correct heart out of bread and blueberries.

She could have a flirty friendship with a straight optician and get an electrician to stop calling her "love."

And there was a hot architect who gave every impression of thinking she was pretty great.

So why couldn't she go back to medicine? Be a doctor. Live the life she was always meant to.

She finished her debrief—"feeling very positive, actually. Took a risk, and this time, it paid off"—grabbed her bag from her room, and joined the general throng of people saying goodbye to Ricky. Before heading to the car park to wait for her father and, hopefully, say goodbye to Alain before he got picked up.

"Got something for you, mate." The gravel crunched behind her and there was Harry, bag over his shoulder, Tupperware box in his hand.

"Have you? Um, why? What?"

"Yeah, and I've just realised this was probably a bit weird. Only when you were talking to your girl, she was saying she was into fish now, so I thought she might like this."

He offered the box and she peeked inside. Tucked in a protective layer of kitchen towel was the crab from his rock pool.

"Managed to swipe it before the crew got it." Harry shrugged. "It's a bread roll but, you know, sorta cute, init?"

It was, in fact, sort of cute. As was the gesture. As was he but no. Not going there. People like Rosaline were not interested in people like Harry.

"I mean," he went on, "she'd probably prefer an anglerfish or a goblin shark, but I'm not sure I could make one of them."

Rosaline wasn't quite sure what to say. "Thank you. That's really kind."

"Anyway, I should go. I'm giving Ricky a lift back." He kicked dolefully at the path. "I promised if he went out, I'd let him take me up the Emirates."

"Do what to you?"

"The stadium. We're going to a fucking Arsenal game. I was drunk when I agreed to it, and he was being sad, so don't tell my mates."

She gave him an incredulous look. "Come on, it's just a football game."

"Mate, you do not get it. Better dead than red."

With a Sydney Carton sigh, Harry began trudging back to the house. And nestling the crab safely into her luggage, Rosaline scanned the horizon for any sign of St. John Palmer.

She'd been waiting for ten of what she expected to be at least twenty minutes when her phone buzzed.

We seem to have missed each other, Alain had sent. *I very much enjoyed the weekend.*

If he'd enjoyed it that much, why hadn't he managed to see her before he left? Except it was impossible to ask without sounding needy, passive-aggressive, or shrewish. So, in the end, she went with *me too*. Which, while bland, was impossible to take negatively.

Sorry, I was in a bit of a mood last night.

He had, indeed, been in a bit of a mood. And if his sudden disappearance was anything to go by, was in a bit of a mood today as well. But, once again, she didn't particularly want to confront him with it. She was very out of the loop on dating, but she didn't think "have sex a few times and then start complaining at someone" was a good way to kick off a relationship.

I understand. We all have bad days.

If I haven't put you off, I'd love to see you this week. I've just come to the end of a contract so I've got some free time at the moment.

Could she get babysitting? Lauren was already doing a lot for her, and she couldn't ask her parents twice in a row. But maybe if it was Thursday—Amelie had karate on Thursday, so she'd be out for most of the evening anyway.

There's a lovely little pub in the village. We could have lunch. Go for a walk. Or not go for a walk. Sit in my garden. Practise our bakes. I've recently had the kitchen re-done so you're more than welcome to take advantage. A pause. *Of the kitchen. And anything else that takes your fancy.*

It sounded so exactly what she needed. A little bit romantic, a little bit sexy. Taking the time to be alone with someone who was into her and liked the same things she did. But could she get the day off work? Could she afford to?

That all sounds great, she texted back. *I just need to sort some things out first.*

Absolutely.

Can I let you know Tuesday?

Looking forward to it.

Sticking her phone back in her pocket, Rosaline plonked herself down on a wall and watched the few wisps of cloud drift across the slowly setting sun. She wanted to feel more excited—this was a date, a proper date, not a stress-relieving on-set hookup—but the logistics. God, the logistics.

Immediately her mind began spinning through everything she'd need to put in place: she'd have to ask Lauren to come a day early, ask her manager to move her shift, and move it where? She was already taking weekends off. She'd have to let the community centre know that someone else would be picking Amelie up from karate and, for that matter, let the school know someone else would be picking her up from school. And, of course, she'd have to tell Amelie she'd be away for another day, which Amelie would accept but not like, and, fuck, was she being a bad mother? Running away to be with some guy in his garden instead of looking after her child like she was meant to. Or did worrying about that make her a bad feminist? Was she a bad mother *and* a bad feminist? And would Amelie like Alain? *She* liked him, but she wasn't an eight-year-old girl. And while there were lots of good things to say about Alain, he definitely wasn't an anglerfish. Or a Viking.

On top of which she somehow had to find time, space, and energy to make an awful lot of biscuits.

And all this stress and chaos because a guy she liked had invited her to a pretty village for a baking-themed booty call? Surely there'd been a time in her life when good news hadn't fucked with her head this much.

Week Four

Biscuits

Thursday

ALAIN LIVED IN a chocolate-box English village called Something-on-the-Wold or Whatever-on-the-Water, which was sufficiently hard to get to by train that Rosaline had been forced to choose between travelling at an inconvenient time or for several hours. Having plumped for "inconvenient time," she had arrived at Thingummy-on-the-Thinagammy station at five to ten for a twelve thirty lunch date. Texting Alain to say she was early—two hours early—felt a little bit *Fatal Attraction*, so she decided to make the most of a nice morning in the countryside.

And she tried. She really tried. But as she wandered, doing her best to appreciate the little cottages and the sleepy wend of the river between them—a waterway of such profound local significance that it had apparently inspired the council to brand the village as the Venice of the Cotswolds—her mind kept drifting back to her biscuits, her daughter, and her job. All of which she would, in one way or another, have to make up for lost time with.

Eventually she gave up the attempt to soothe her weary spirit and went to the pub instead.

Of course, Alain had said it was a pub but it was clearly an inn—it called itself an inn, it had rooms, and she wouldn't have been surprised if it had a stable. And inside it was all fireplaces and wood furniture, and a man at the bar who'd clearly been sitting there for the last seventy years. As a general rule, Rosaline tried to avoid drinking before noon, but it was a special occasion of really needing to. She compromised and, despite being more of a local gin person than a local ale person, got herself a beer.

Once it had got to a level of earliness that was at least vaguely socially acceptable, she sent Alain a quick text to say she'd arrived, and he replied with *Just need to take my biscuits out the oven. With you as soon as I can.* And sure enough, he turned up a little after twelve looking, as usual, well-groomed enough to leave Rosaline teetering between attracted and intimidated. Whereas she, conscious she had multiple train journeys in her future and packing primarily for a TV baking show with a strict but bland dress code, had failed to push the boat anywhere resembling out and gone with the comfortable sort of jeans and a slightly-nicer-than-usual blouse. But at least she'd dipped into the sexier end of her underwear drawer and, in her experience, people remembered the finale better than the preamble.

"Have you been waiting long?" asked Alain, sliding in opposite her.

"Not too long." Oh God, she was lying to him again. But this was the kind of polite British lie that was practically mandatory. "I took a bit of a walk around the village. It's beautiful here."

He smiled at her across the table, his eyes brightening as if she'd praised him personally. "I know. I'm rather in love with it. My parents have been wanting me to put down roots for a while—get on the property ladder and all that, although my father's in real estate so I suppose he *would* say that. And I tried looking in London for a while but since I didn't want to pay half a million for a two-room bedsit above a public toilet, I decided to go for something more rural. It makes getting into the city harder, but *where* you live has such an impact on *how* you live, you know?"

To be honest, the primary questions that occupied Rosaline when she'd been looking to turn a timely inheritance from a Grandparent into a deposit on a house had been how much she could afford to pay and how long she could afford to keep paying it. Followed closely by "Are the schools okay?" and "Is there any asbestos?" At the time, though, she'd been pretty pleased with her purchase. It was homey and it was hers—one of the few things that absolutely were. But now, imagining how it might look through Alain's eyes, it felt a lot more like a scruffy two-up, two-down in a crappy commuter town.

"Yes," she said. "It does, doesn't it?"

He nodded. "It's probably very dreary and sincere of me, but I really like that sense of continuous history you get in a village. There's evidence of habitation here going back six thousand years, and some of the historical buildings are fascinating. Take the church—it's mostly seventeenth- and eighteenth-century, but you can still see traces of the original fourteenth-century structure, and even the Norman building before that, and the barest evidence of the Saxon original and the Roman Temple under that."

She wasn't quite sure how to respond. Nothing should have changed—Alain was as charming and engaging as he'd been before, especially when he was talking about something he cared about. But something *was* different. Maybe it was just that the show created its own little universe so someone telling you about art or architecture or Victorian grottoes felt natural. Now it reminded her how far she'd drifted from the life that Alain had and that she'd been meant to have.

Except, as Alain had reminded her, it didn't need to be that way at all. She could trade shortbread and the school run for a life wandering through the Venice of the Cotswolds, showing Amelie the Saxon Church and explaining to her what the difference was between the Saxons and the Vikings and that no, the Saxons didn't have horns on their helmets either. Or would it be a life where she spent the next seven years studying and the decade after that constantly on call?

"I've been thinking about what you said," she blurted out. *Well done, Rosaline. Take a nice conversation about something someone else cares about and sharply derail it into talking about yourself.*

"Oh?" His brows went up.

"You know, about going back to university. Because I could, couldn't I? I mean, I should, shouldn't I?"

"Well, it's your decision obviously. But I'd say it's probably a good time."

She took a sip of her beer, wishing she liked beer more. "It'd make my parents happy."

"I'm sure it would."

"And it'd be better for Amelie in the long run. As career moves go, it's way more sensible than trying to win a baking show."

"I don't think it should be about what's right for your daughter," Alain said carefully. "It needs to be about what's right for you. And after all, you've always wanted to be a doctor."

She laughed. And it sounded far weirder than a laugh had any right to sound. "Who wouldn't? It's a really important thing to do."

"I'm glad you think so because—well..." He picked up the menu and put it down again. "Let me know if this is too much, but I was thinking too, thinking about you, and I did actually wind up doing a little bit of research."

Shit. This had got real fast. "You did?"

"Nothing in-depth. It's not like I have a stack of application forms waiting for you at home. I was just interested to know what it would take."

"Wow, you do have a thing for doctors, don't you?"

"It's the stethoscope," he told her, with a sardonic smile. "But tabling my kinky medical fantasies for the moment—"

"Are you sure? I think I might have a thermometer in my bag."

His laugh was indulgent, but he didn't play along. "*Tabling that*, the point is I do actually care and I do actually think this would be good for you."

He was right. He was clearly right. She should have got her act together years ago. "So what...what do I have to do?"

"Well, if you wanted to go back to Cambridge, although I think it's similar for most Russell Group universities, you do need to have done some academic work within the last two years—"

"Oh dear," said Rosaline cheerfully. "Guess I left it too late then."

"Rosaline, I am aware that this is a little intimidating. But let yourself have it. You know as well as I do that you aren't meant to be working in a stationery shop."

Defeated, she gave a long sigh. "So, what, I take my A-levels again?"

"That's one option. But you'd be better off with an access course or something through the Open University. They're very flexible, so you should be able to schedule around your other commitments."

"You mean"—her voice was slightly sharper than she'd intended—"Amelie? That commitment?"

"I know she's an enormous part of your life, but she doesn't define you."

She shifted uncomfortably, trying to work out if she had, in fact, let Amelie define her. And if letting something define you was different from it being the most important thing in your world. And if it mattered? "I know. It's just I don't like it when people talk about Amelie like she's a burden."

"I never meant to imply that. All I meant was you have responsibilities, and if you did want to take your career in a different direction, you have options that will let you continue to meet those responsibilities."

"Alain. Amelie is not a responsibility. She's a person. She's my favourite person."

"I'm sorry," he said. "I didn't mean to upset you. I only want to make sure you're aware of your choices." A slight pause. "Shall we order?"

That was probably for the best. She hadn't meant to be so defensive. But clearly, in her current state, *think seriously about her future* and *have a nice time with a guy* weren't totally compatible. "Yeah, let's do that."

After lunch, they wound their way back to Alain's house. Or rather his terrifyingly picturesque cottage, which to Rosaline's complete lack of surprise turned out to have been elegantly modernised in a way that allowed twenty-first-century convenience to exist effortlessly alongside exquisite period fittings. It made her even more nervous for the day Alain saw her house—with its tiny rooms and low ceilings, and Amelie's ever-expanding collection of interests marching across every free surface like the Golden Horde.

During the back-and-forth of arranging the visit, Alain had suggested they use some of the afternoon to practise their bakes, and so once Rosaline had dumped her bag and rescued her ingredients from its depths, they set up in his rustic yet state-of-the-art kitchen. And this, Rosaline was delighted to discover, was one of the nicest dates she'd ever been on. There was something so comfortable about baking beside someone, swapping the idle thoughts and ideas that came to you when you were wrist-deep in biscuit dough.

And slowly, as the ovens began to warm and the scent of hopefully-televisual-quality biscuits began to fill the kitchen, she started to feel almost— What was it? Oh yes, *good*. Maybe even *optimistic*. The woods and the churches and the history lessons had taken a bit of getting used to—and her maybe-plan to go back to university was lurking ominously in the back of her mind—but *this*? Sharing a space and a moment and rolling pin with somebody? This came easily. Naturally.

Rosaline didn't want to jinx it, and possibly she was reading too much into one ambiguously encouraging look from Marianne Wolvercote, but she thought she could do okay this week. Possibly even well? After all, she had a strong concept. And the part of her that used to do homework under test conditions was secretly rather glad to get to practise in an unfamiliar kitchen.

Once they were both done, they sat at Alain's reclaimed-wood kitchen table and took turns sampling each other's biscuits.

"These are very good, Rosaline," he said finally.

And she should have known that. But still, a part of her relaxed. "I hope so. I think they're a bit different. I took your advice about having a secret weapon."

"And your secret weapon is booze?"

"Well," she admitted, "we all know what Marianne likes."

He gave her what she thought was one of his teasing looks. "So your plan is to get her drunk, so she'll treat you more favourably?"

"Yes. That's the strategy. Get her totally bladdered on three biscuits and take advantage of her while her judgement is impaired."

"That *would* do wonders for the ratings."

"To be fair, you'd go there, wouldn't you? I mean, not on live television. And not to get ahead on a baking show. And not if she was actually so drunk she didn't know what she was doing."

His eyes had gone wide. "Are you telling me you find Marianne Wolvercote attractive?"

"My God. Who doesn't? Have you seen her?"

"Isn't she . . . well . . . a little old for you?"

"She can't be more than forty-five. And last week she was

wearing those wide-leg silk trousers, which made her look like Lauren Bacall."

"Honestly," he said, frowning, "I don't see the appeal. I think I admire different qualities. And speaking of admiring different qualities, my concern with the biscuits would be that Marianne might go for them but Wilfred definitely won't."

Rosaline actually had considered that. But the lesson she'd taken away from last week was that Marianne and Wilfred were very different judges, and trying to please both of them was a recipe for mediocrity. "I'm hoping he'll appreciate the quality of the bake, even if he's not sold on the idea."

"That seems risky."

"Too late now." Turning her attention to Alain's biscuit selection, she took a bite of one. "Is that lavender?"

He nodded.

"It's delicious. Not too 'old lady's bedroom.'"

"Thank you. As we've established, avoiding old ladies' bedrooms is one of my highest priorities." He gestured at the plate. "Those are honey and thyme, and finally rosemary butter."

"Isn't it weird we've been doing this a month and we've never actually tried each other's cooking."

His mouth quirked up. "I swear the crew carry forks in their back pockets."

"They do. I've seen them."

Picking up a honey and thyme, she snapped it in two and ran her thumb across the break, feeling the texture. "I don't quite know what to say. You're obviously really good at this, and you obviously know you're really good at it because you're doing it on TV."

"Yes, but I'd still like your feedback."

She thought for a moment, flattered that he thought her opinion was worth seeking, and wanting to be useful. "They're delicious and the bake is excellent, but...I guess...if I was looking for something to be concerned about, I'm not totally certain it hits the brief."

There was a small, not totally pleasant silence.

"Well, does yours?" he asked. "They're supposed to be childhood favourites so, unless your childhood was very different from mine, I'm not sure how lashings of alcohol reflect that."

The homey sense of comfort she'd had while they were baking together suddenly felt distant and presumptuous. This was Alain's house. She was a guest. And she'd insulted him, however inadvertently. "I think I was trying to do a twist on a fairly traditional family biscuit tin. But yours are just"— she gestured apologetically at Alain's plate—"don't get me wrong, they're very nice, but they are just sort of…biscuits. Posh biscuits. But not biscuits that evoke fond childhood memories."

"The brief didn't say it had to be biscuits you could buy in Aldi."

"No, but…" She gazed at him warily, feeling like Winnie-the-Pooh in Rabbit's front door, not sure if she should go forward or back, and pretty sure she couldn't do either. "I think they're looking for something with kind of a…nostalgia factor? And I'm not sure what the story is with these."

His eyes were cold. "The story is that they're biscuits."

"Alain, I'm not criticising. I just think in this challenge they want it to be a bit more personal. It's not that you have to change the biscuits, but, I don't know, can you give them more context?"

There was a moment of quiet tension exactly long enough for Rosaline to worry that she'd messed everything up.

"Look," he said at last. "The things that take me back to my childhood aren't…they aren't fucking biscuits. I love my parents, and I'm very close to them, but part of the reason for that is that they've never assumed I couldn't cope with adult things. So yes, I grew up on olives and grissini, not jammy dodgers and chocolate

Hobnobs. And the truth is, I don't enjoy being asked to pander to some antiquated notion of relatability."

Weirdly, Rosaline could relate. At least to bits of it. "My family aren't a biscuit family either. But I'm here to win a competition so, yeah, I pandered."

"And I probably should have as well. I just...wasn't sure how to. I wouldn't know a custard cream if I sat on one."

"Well"—Rosaline offered what she hoped was a disarming smile—"I think identifying biscuits by sitting on them is a pretty niche skill."

He gave a grudging laugh. "Besides, my parents are going to watch the show. I don't want them to feel they raised me badly because they didn't feed me the right kind of biscuits. And I certainly don't think my childhood was impaired because I spent more time at the ballet than the supermarket."

Rosaline's parents had taken her to exactly one ballet and she'd thought it was nonsense. It was one of the few things she and her father had ever agreed about.

"I'm sure," she said, "you'll get through regardless. I mean, unless you set the oven on fire or punch Wilfred Honey in the face."

"I can probably restrain myself from doing either—though *getting through* isn't quite what I'm aiming for."

She thought for a moment. "You know what, you should tell them what you told me. About your family. I think it'll work better if they understand where you're coming from."

"Might it not seem...condescending?"

"Well, maybe leave out the bit about Aldi," she told him, laughing. "Maybe you could say, 'I didn't eat a lot of traditional biscuits growing up, but my parents taught me to appreciate food and cooking and I've tried to use some of the flavours they enjoy.'"

"My mother does like lavender," he agreed.

"And if they're going to watch, that might be a nice moment for them."

He smiled at her then. "Come here." She went there and he pulled her down into his lap and kissed her deeply. And afterwards, stared at her for a while, as if he was trying to work something out. "You're not very good at being in a competition, are you, Rosaline-um-Palmer? It's terribly sweet."

"Hey, I still want to win. I just don't want to win because your parents never bought bourbons."

"As I say, terribly sweet."

He kissed her again.

Saturday

SOMEHOW, ROSALINE HAD done pretty well in the blind bake—a type of street biscuit from Delhi that Anvita had made the fatal mistake of baking to the recipe she'd learned from her Punjabi grandmother instead of the one Marianne had put in front of her. Flush with relative success, Rosaline dragged Alain up to her room immediately after filming. He was more than willing, and the combination of urgency and privacy gave the whole thing an intensity that Rosaline found liberating.

"My God," Alain said afterwards, still slightly breathless. "You're amazing."

She was, as it happened, feeling pretty amazing. "Thanks. You're not bad yourself."

"Clearly you bring out my wild side."

"Yep. That's me. Wildy McWildface."

He laughed and pulled her down so she lay across his chest. They were silent for a few minutes, Rosaline drifting in a sleepy, afterglowy haze.

"Whatever are we going to do," Alain murmured, "when I can't keep up with you."

Was that flattering? Or was he implying she was some kind of insatiable pastry slapper? "You've been doing fine so far."

"I don't mean that. It's just, I know you've been with...a variety of people, and—"

"Hang on. I spent the last eight years raising a child. We're still in single figures here."

"Yes, but you've been with women as well as men. And I suppose I'm wondering if you wouldn't come to feel you were missing out."

Oh, not this again. They always asked eventually. And while Rosaline accepted that it probably came from a good place—a sincere desire to accommodate her needs—she'd never quite worked out how to handle it. "Um. Well, do you?"

"Do I what?"

"Feel you're missing out when you've chosen to be with someone?"

"Of course not—although I think everyone in a monogamous relationship wonders a little about the other grass, as it were. And I can only imagine that would be more pronounced if you were accustomed to a larger garden."

"I don't think," said Rosaline, in her best *I'm going to be patient and not ruin the evening voice*, "it's about what you like in your garden. Some people are into monogamy. Some people aren't. I'm personally a fan. And when I'm with someone I'm not particularly looking for anyone else. No matter what their genitals are like."

"Don't be like that, Rosaline-um-Palmer. I'm not judging. I just wouldn't want you to feel that being with me meant making any sort of compromise."

She didn't like to generalise, but dating men would be a lot easier if they'd admit when they were worried about something. "Oh Alain, being with you isn't a compromise. It's a choice."

"Well"—his fingers traced the butterflies down her spine—"I suppose, unlike me, you've already had your adventures."

"You do remember I lied about going to Malawi."

"You've still done things. Things I'd never have dared to do."

Tilting her head, she gave him an intrigued look. "Is this your way of telling me you're bicurious?"

"Not at all," he said quickly. "Not that there'd be anything— I mean . . ." He stuttered to a halt for a few seconds. "I mean . . . it's like your tattoo. All my friends at university talked about maybe getting one, but nobody ever did and then it became, well, how would you feel about this in ten years, what if you want to run for Parliament one day. Whereas you went all the way with it."

"Yeeeeeesss. But being bisexual isn't quite the same thing as getting a tattoo."

He made a kind of "oof" noise. "I'm sorry, I've said this all wrong. I suppose I'm thinking of my ex, who always thought she might be, you know, bisexual, but never found the opportunity to explore it."

Honestly, Rosaline wasn't quite sure how she felt about Alain suddenly bringing up his ex in what was still very much a post-boink conversation. "I guess for me," she offered, "sexuality is about what you feel more than what you do. Especially when you're bi or pan or something, because people are always going to make assumptions about you based on who you're with."

"I think with my ex it's just we never moved in the right circles."

Turning onto her back, Rosaline stared at the ceiling, trying to figure how to help this person she'd probably never meet. "Look, there'll be LGBTQ people who don't agree with me on this, but my feeling is that, on some level, how you identify is informed by, well, circumstance. I honestly believe that there are people out there who pretty much define as straight who might have gone a different way if they'd met a different person at a different time in their lives. But as long as you're happy, it doesn't really matter."

Alain hummed noncommittally.

"I suppose," Rosaline went on, "and I don't want this to come across like I'm telling your ex how to feel. But your sexuality shouldn't be defined by FOMO."

"I know. But she wonders, sometimes—and I think it might ease her mind if she had a safe way of, well, finding out for certain."

"There are places to meet people, real and virtual. But I can't give any more advice because everyone's different."

He propped himself on his elbow and ran a hand lightly over the curve of her hip. "Don't worry. You've been very kind. I suspect she'd be happier if she could be more like you."

And before she could ask exactly what he meant by that, he suddenly became very, very distracting.

Sunday

SHE DIDN'T WANT to jinx it, but things were going pretty well. Rosaline had made up three different types of biscuit dough, her jam was setting, and Marianne had already remarked approvingly on the quantity of alcohol she was using.

Across the ballroom, Claudia—who remained a total mystery to Rosaline, aside from having a vaguely high-powered career and an uninspired approach to bread sculpture—was having the "No, I haven't had time to practise" / "Do you think that's a good idea?" conversation with Grace Forsythe and the judges.

"No," she was saying, "it's obviously a terrible idea. But it wasn't a deliberate strategic decision. I haven't watched the show and thought to myself, *Ah yes, every time someone tries a bake that they haven't previously practised it goes exceptionally well for them and the judges are hugely impressed.* Unfortunately, I had a busy week and that's sometimes just the way the custard creams."

Rosaline was busy measuring off-brand Irish cream liqueur for what, were they not on the BBC, would have been a Bailey's Buttercream but was instead an Other Varieties of Creamy Alcoholic Beverages Are Available Buttercream.

"So lad." Wilfred Honey landed at Alain's station and Rosaline's head came up in semi-appropriate curiosity. "What have you got planned for us. Is that lavender I can see? It's a tricky thing, is lavender."

Alain paused in his preparations. "I think I might have a slightly unusual take on the brief. You see, I didn't grow up in a big biscuit-eating household, so I'm going for a very simple base but infused with the flavours that remind me of my childhood."

"And what flavours are those?" asked Marianne Wolvercote. "We already know you're an excellent baker, so we have high expectations of you."

"I'm afraid it *is* more herbs." Alain gave the camera a winsome look. "But for this challenge in particular the scents really called out to me—my mother loves lavender, the rosemary reminds me of helping her prepare Sunday dinners as a child, and the honey just conjures up an English country summer for me. You know, those long afternoons when you think the school holidays will never end."

Wilfred Honey was nodding approvingly. "What a lovely story. And I will admit I'm partial to a honey biccy myself."

"Yes," added Marianne Wolvercote. "It's quite a clever interpretation of the brief. Obviously not every challenge we set speaks to everyone in the same way, and it's important to stay true to your culinary voice. Get this perfect, and we could have something very special."

Oh fuck. Alain was going to win again, wasn't he? Maybe he'd been right and Rosaline should have kept more of an eye on the competition. She'd been glad enough to help at the time, and, abstractly, she still thought it was the right thing to do, but what a donkle she was going to feel if she lost *Bake Expectations* because she'd given the man she was sleeping with unsolicited advice the moment he looked a bit vulnerable.

"Blimey, mate," said Harry as he sauntered over from his own station. "Smells like a distillery over 'ere."

"Yeah, I wanted to show the judges something different, so I thought I'd show them some alcohol."

He peered into the bowl where she was mixing her freshly cooled blackberry jam with a generous splash of unspecified Chambord-analogue. "Tell you what, you are some kind of genius, because I would never of thought of putting booze in a jammy dodger."

"One of the many things I learned from Lauren is that you can put booze in anything." Then his words caught up with her and she half blushed, half flinched.

Since her mother, like Aaron Burr's, was an actual genius, it was a term her family had always been slightly protective of and would certainly never have applied to a baked good. "Thanks," she added. "I had a good feeling earlier in the week, but you always end up sort of second-guessing yourself, don't you?"

"All the bloody time." He shrugged. "Got in a right state during the blind bake yesterday. Felt a proper dick afterwards, but it was like, *Do I knead it, do I not knead it, should I put it in for ten minutes, should I put it in for twenty.* It was like I couldn't stop asking myself questions, so I did fuck all 'til the last minute and then served up a bunch of crud. Still. Happens, don't it?"

Slightly perplexed, her eyes slid to his. His willingness to admit uncertainty never ceased to disarm her. It was so unlike everybody else in her entire life. "Well, a bit. But maybe not quite that much?"

"Guess it's just how I am then. Always been a bit of a worrier, to be honest."

As the daughter of two doctors, with about a fifth of a medical degree, Rosaline wasn't sure if being a bit of a worrier was the whole story. But it wasn't something you could ask someone in the middle of *Bake Expectations*.

"Amelie loved her crab, by the way," she said instead, hoping it would cheer him up. "Although she did take a surprising amount of pleasure in pulling its legs off one at a time."

He grinned, the slump leaving his shoulders. "That's kids for you, init. Ashley used to torture her jellybabies. Mum was convinced she was going to grow up to be a serial killer. Turned out all right in the end, though. People usually do."

"You've got the beginning of a really good parenting book there."

"What? People usually turn out okay?"

"It's what I need to hear most days."

"Ah well." He looked thoughtful and then gave one of those slow, heart-melting smiles that Rosaline firmly told herself she did not look forward to seeing. "Come round my oven and I'll tell you then." A beeper went off across the ballroom. "Shit, that's my cookies about to come out. So they'll want to film that in case I drop 'em. And I'm probably gonna drop 'em because I don't want to drop 'em, and then I'll be that bloke what dropped his cookies and cried."

Out of nowhere, Rosaline started to giggle.

"Oi, don't laugh, mate. I'm being all vulnerable here."

"I'm sorry, dropping your cookies sounds like a euphemism."

"Oh thanks. So now I've got that in my head too."

She curled her hands lightly over his forearms, paying absolutely no attention to how absurdly sculpted they were. "Listen, you're going to be fine. What's in your head is just in your head. And your cookies are going to be fantastic. Now go get them."

"Thanks, mate." His eyes were warm and soft as they held hers. "You're a top bloke...bird...person."

And then he ambled back to his workstation, where he successfully retrieved his bake from the oven.

"Are these spare?" Without waiting for a reply, Grace Forsythe plucked one of the freshly made cookies from the tray that Harry had, foolishly, taken his eyes off for ten seconds.

"No, they ain't. They said do three lots of twelve and that's me lot of twelve."

Grace Forsythe pressed a hand to her already be-crumbed lips. "Ooofmugoomf Mmfohsorry."

"Mate, did you eat my twelfth cookie?"

"Oh my God, I did. And I have to tell you, it was delicious."

"That's not helping me. I'm going to go into the judging a man down. It's gonna wreck my formation and there ain't nobody on the subs bench."

"And I feel"— Grace Forsythe struck a tragedian's pose—"truly terrible. I think I was overwhelmed by your gooey succulence and lost all control of my mouth."

Harry made a gesture of surrender. "It's fine. I'm just going to dip my Hobnobs."

"And I," announced Grace Forsythe, "shall retreat to a distance at which I can do no further harm." Something on Josie's bench caught her eye. "Oh I say, is that a Garibaldi?"

Claudia was up first for judging, with a selection of homemade Oreos—or rather Oreo-like biscuits—in different flavours, served with a glass of milk. The judges thought it was too simple because, well, it was. Anvita and Nora had both done better, Anvita, as usual, being praised for her flavours and Nora's rationing-era biscuits admired for their theme.

When Rosaline's turn came up, she found her earlier confidence had evaporated like a splash of water in a stir-fry. She'd been watching the show for a long time and seen far too many people admitting shyly to the camera that they had a good feeling or thought they'd nailed it two seconds before they served up the biggest disaster of the series.

"So, um," she said when she finally reached the front of

the ballroom, "I've made a series of traditional family favourites reinterpreted with, um, booze. So there's brown butter shortbread with Bailey's—"

"Sorry." Colin Thrimp darted briefly forward. "Can we have that without the brand name?"

Rosaline took a deep breath. "So I've got brown butter shortbread with an Irish crème liqueur, which is sort of my take on a custard cream. Then I've got black-currant jammy dodgers with raspberry liqueur. And, finally, cinnamon brandy snaps with triple sec Chantilly cream."

Marianne Wolvercote pounced on a jammy dodger. "I do like that. I like that a lot."

She seemed to have nothing further to add. Which Rosaline took as a good sign.

"I was a bit uncertain," added Wilfred Honey, "because for me a biscuit should feel like home. Not like the pub. But actually you got the balance really nice. And the brandy snaps remind me of my mam."

"Big drinker, was she?" asked Grace Forsythe.

Wilfred Honey twinkled. "Well, who don't like a snifter of an evening?"

They both glanced at Marianne Wolvercote for comment, but she was too busy trying the shortbread.

Josie and Alain followed, Josie's biscuity reimaginings of classic desserts, including a treacle toffee macaron and a key lime digestive, hadn't quite worked but were praised for their ambition; and Alain, having preempted any possible concerns about his narrative, received good comments on his flavours and the quality of his bake. Finally, Harry came forward with his two and eleven-twelfths dozen childhood-memory-inspired biscuits.

"Mea culpa," said Grace Forsythe, literally putting her hands up, "bit of a snafu. Someone, who shall remain nameless, but was me, may have inadvertently eaten one of Harry's cookies."

Wilfred Honey picked up one of the insufficiently numerate biscuits. "Well, we can't hold you accountable for random acts of Forsythe, so what have we got here."

"I thought I'd do"—Harry looked nervously from Wilfred to Marianne to Grace back to Wilfred—"one biscuit for each of my three sisters. So those are Toll House cookies 'cos my sister Ashley had a holiday in America and really liked 'em and now she eats 'em whenever she can. And those are party rings because Sam's got kids so they always have party rings in the house left over from birthdays and stuff. And that one there's a chocolate Hobnob—"

"Chocolate oat biscuit," put in Colin Thrimp.

"It's a bloody Hobnob, mate. Everyone knows it's a Hobnob."

"Because of the unique way the BBC is funded, we aren't allowed to broadcast this unless you say oat biscuit."

Clearly feeling either guilty or like she wanted to annoy the production company, Grace Forsythe offered, "What if I say, other oat biscuits are available?"

"And that one there," said Harry, pointing, "is a chocolate . . . oat biscuit. Because my sister Heather is a nurse and that's pretty much all she can eat on her breaks."

Wilfred Honey gave one of his most grandfatherly smiles. "Well, I think your sisters can be very proud. Because these taste lovely."

It wasn't quite a "by 'eck," but it was still pretty good.

"What impresses me," added Marianne Wolvercote, "is that these are surprisingly refined, given their inspiration."

Harry blinked. "You what?"

"The feathering on the party rings is actually rather neatly done. And your chocolate work is very precise."

He returned to his stool, looking baffled but pleased.

Rosaline's brain was in a bit of a whirl as they were herded outside for another round of interviews. For the first time since week one, she thought she might be in the running and that was dangerous. Emotionally, because she'd never been an "every setback is an opportunity" type of person. And practically, because she didn't want to be all *Yes, I'm amazing and have done amazing* on national television, only to find out she was actually mediocre and had done mediocre. Yet again.

Back in the ballroom, they were once more gathered together like the suspects at the end of a *Poirot*, with Rosaline feeling about as anxious as if she'd murdered her great-aunt with a silverplated poniard and now had a moustachioed Belgian descending upon her.

Harry nudged her with his elbow. "Reckon you got this, mate."

"And now my little ginger nuts," began Grace Forsythe, "it is time to lower the digestive of eternity into the coffee cup of fate. Which is to say, the results are in. And I am delighted to announce that our winner this week is someone whose nankhatai were nankhatastic, whose brandy had exactly the right amount of snap, and who, most importantly, got us all pleasantly tipsy. That's right, it's Rosaline."

Rosaline had backed-and-forthed so many times on whether she'd nailed this week or fucked it that she was genuinely shocked.

There was the usual smattering of polite applause and then Grace Forsythe's face fell. "Of course, it's also my painful duty to reveal the baker whose cookie has sadly crumbled. And this week it's Claudia. We'll be sorry to see you go."

Claudia was not a hugger but this was television, so she didn't get much choice.

"The truth is," she told the cameras afterwards, "I was feeling a little burned out on the career front when I signed up for this show. And I thought that since I love baking so much, I could take a left turn at forty. But I've discovered that a big part of the reason I love baking is that I can do it when I feel like it and not when I don't. So…ah…I'm very much looking forward to going back to that and also back to work. Which I've remembered I also love."

Rosaline had thought interviews were tricky when all you had to say was "Well, I think it could have gone better," but they were way worse when you actually had something to talk about and needed to do it in a way that didn't come across as either false modesty or smugness. "Really pleased," she tried. "I…I'm just really pleased."

"Aren't you going to ring your daughter?" asked Colin Thrimp.

"Well, yes. On the way back."

"Can we get it for the camera?"

She wasn't sure how she felt about putting Amelie, even Amelie's voice, into the public domain when she was too young to know what she was doing. But she was already on thin ice after insisting they let her call home mid-sourdough. Besides, she'd signed a bunch of waivers that meant the production company basically owned her life, so she pulled out her phone and called home.

"Fuck me," cried Lauren immediately. "Your fucking child. She insisted on watching a single episode of *Blue Planet* on a loop for the past five hours. It's the one about the spooky fish in the dark and the dead whale. I'm going to have fucking nightmares, Roz, fucking nightmares."

Rosaline winced. "So you're on-camera."

"Oh, bollocks. Other programmes about squoogly fish are available."

"I think it's more the saying 'fuck' they're likely to object to."

"Yes," put in Colin Thrimp, "if you could both stop saying fuck, that would be helpful."

"Is Amelie around?"

"She's still watching *Blue Planet*."

"You know, you are allowed to say no to her."

"I've tried," sighed Lauren. "It doesn't stick."

"Is that Mummy?" came Amelie's voice.

Between Alain and the show, it had only been three days but suddenly that felt like forever. "Yes, it's me. Guess what—"

"Did you know there are underwater chimneys with worms on them? And crabs that eat the worms. And fish that eat the crabs. And everything is all red and white. And there are fish that go invisible and other fish with big eyes that can see them. And if you want to see the fish you have to go in a special submarine and if you put a cup on the submarine it gets squashed really really small."

"No, I didn't know that. That's nice. So Mummy—"

"And there's an octopus with big ears called Dumbo like the elephant in the film. And there are fish that tie themselves in knots and sharks that eat big holes in dead whales and go chomp chomp chomp."

"Darling, Mummy won the biscuit round."

There was a pause. "With the not-for-Amelie biscuits?"

"Yes."

"Well, I'm glad you won because you're brilliant. But I think everybody should be able to eat biscuits so I think you made discriminatory biscuits and I don't think that should have won. Also there are squids that glow and fish with lasers."

Great. Shamed on TV by her own kid for being a biscuit bigot. "I'll be home soon."

"That's good. Then we can watch the squid programme because Auntie Lauren said she's not going to watch it with me anymore."

"Love you to the moon and back."

"Love you to the bottom of the sea and back, which is closer than the moon, but we know less about it."

Hanging up, Rosaline turned an anxious glance on Colin Thrimp. "Did you get what you needed?"

"I'll be honest, I don't think we'll use absolutely all of that."

Now that she'd discharged her televisual duties, Rosaline was free to leave—or, in practice, wander around looking for Alain. She still wasn't sure what kind of label, if any, their relationship needed, but she'd won a thing and she wanted to celebrate with someone, preferably someone who wasn't more interested in squid.

She found him at last in the car park, where he was waiting for his pickup with his bag at his feet and a slightly brooding look.

"Hi." It wasn't the most original opening, but "I won!" seemed, in that moment, childish. As did the fantasy she was definitely not entertaining of his sweeping her into his arms in congratulations.

"Hi yourself. It was nice having you around this week—and I wondered if you wanted to do it again this Thursday?"

She wanted to. She really wanted to. And she was... "relieved" was too strong and made her feel a bit pathetic. But glad. She was glad she'd given good visit. "I'm not sure I can. It was hard enough getting the afternoon off work and arranging a babysitter this time. I think if I tried to do it again so soon, I might lose my job and all my friends. Well. My one friend."

"That's a shame." He sounded disappointed and his manner was, in general, a bit subdued. "Obviously I'd love to see more of you, but if it's not possible I understand."

"Um..." Was this going to come across as pushy? Pushy was not a good look. "I mean, if you're ever in...striking distance of London, we could strike together?"

"My work does sometimes take me that way. But if I'm consulting, I can be quite busy."

Not quite the answer she was looking for. She tried to stifle her disappointment—after all, it was easy to free up time when you had a shit job no one cared about, but she knew from years of living with doctors that some things would always matter more than her feelings. "Oh. Okay. I'll see what I can do about coming to you, then. But probably not for a while."

He smiled in a making-the-best-of-it sort of way. "At least we can catch each other at the weekends."

It did slightly make her wonder what the plan was when filming ended. But rationally she also knew it was way too early to be wondering that. "See you next week then."

He brushed his lips lightly against her cheek. "Looking forward to it, Rosaline-um-Palmer."

There came the unmistakeable purr of an expensive car engine and the same sapphire blue Jaguar that she'd seen in the first week pulled through the gates.

"Ah," he said. "This is me. And that's Liv, by the way. The friend I told you about."

Not quite sure what else to do, Rosaline waved awkwardly at the barely visible figure behind the wheel. And then went to her usual wall to wait for her father, who, as ever, was too important to be on time.

About ten minutes later, a white van, bearing the legend "Dobson & Son, Electricians: Friendly, Reliable, Local," rattled past and then pulled to a stop just ahead of her.

Harry rolled down the window. "Well done on the win, mate. Stormed it this week. Need a lift?"

"It's fine. My dad's on his way."

"Thought I'd offer since you was there. I could probably run you back to yours next week if you like. Save you bothering your old man?"

"Oh no," protested Rosaline. "I couldn't. You don't have to."

"I know I don't. You ain't hijacking me. But offer's there if you want it."

In some ways it would have solved a lot of problems. Her parents continued to insist that picking her up was *no trouble* but also never failed to remind her after the fact how much trouble they were going to on her behalf. Except getting Harry to run her home instead seemed like it would just be swapping one obligation for another, and at least with her parents it was an obligation she was used to. "Thanks. I'll bear it in mind."

"All right. See you next week."

She watched him go, feeling slightly perplexed. She'd been sure when they first met that she knew exactly what kind of person he was. But she'd somehow got used to him. The way he checked in on her and was there for her. The slow rough-velvet of his voice. The summer-day gleam of his smile. So used to him, in fact, that she almost couldn't imagine what the show would be like without him.

Week Five

Puddings

Tuesday

ROSALINE HAD JUST put her Jaffa-cake-themed self-saucing pudding into the oven when the electricity cut out. It hadn't done this for a while, and so it was with relative confidence that she dragged the sofa away from the little cupboard that housed the trip-switch and tried to flip it up.

It flipped down immediately.

And it wasn't until she'd tried to flip it up three or four more times that she realised if it was still staying down, then it probably needed to be down.

Which meant something bad had happened to her electricity. Possibly something house-catching-fire bad.

She went to her computer to look up the number of an electrician, remembering slightly later than she was comfortable with that it needed electricity to work. As did the oven where her cake was half warming in the remains of the preheat. And the fridge where her ingredients were slowly but inevitably beginning to spoil.

Turning to her still partially charged phone, she googled for electricians in her local area, forced herself through the "How do I know these aren't con men and murderers" window that always accompanied inviting a stranger into your home on the basis of a number on a website, and then began the slow and stressful process of ringing around. As ever, she encountered a range of answering machines, weird bleeps, phones that rang endlessly, quotes with outrageous call-out fees, and people who were booked up through Sunday. Eventually, she found some bloke who said he'd be with her that afternoon and was only going to charge her eighty quid.

The afternoon ticked on. And the guy neither arrived nor called back, and when she attempted to phone him it went straight to voice mail. Which strongly suggested he wasn't coming, either because he couldn't be bothered or because he'd been kidnapped en route.

My electricity's gone out, she texted Alain—not because there was anything he could do about it but because she needed a sympathetic ear. Well, eye.

There was a brief pause, and then: *I'm so sorry to hear that. How are you holding up?*

Okay, I guess. Waiting for someone to come fix it. Bit stressed.

You're welcome back at mine until it's dealt with.

She stared at the message, wondering what on earth to say that didn't come across as needy or presumptuous. There were times when British English really needed a plural "you." *What about Amelie?*

Unfortunately my house isn't particularly child-friendly at the moment. I'm sure she could stay with her grandparents or with your friend maybe?

No. No, she was not leaving her child to go shack up with a hot guy. And yes, she'd done that last week, but that was a holiday. This was a crisis. *Thanks. I'll think about it.*

When it got to about three, still not quite willing to leave the house and risk being forever blackballed by local electricians as a lady who books you then isn't in, she called Lauren.

"Have to talk fast," she said. "I've only about ten percent charge on my phone."

"Then plug it in, dear Liza, dear Liza, plug it in."

"My electricity's gone. I'm waiting for a man. Can you get Amelie for me? I'm sorry, I know you're doing a lot for me at the moment."

Lauren sighed. "I am rather exerting myself on your behalf, but, fortunately, I'm a wonderful person. I'm on my way. I'd say I expect cake, but I presume you haven't been able to cook anything either."

"I know. And this is my practice day. Except now it's my piss-around-in-my-front-room-waiting-for-an-electrician day."

Rosaline hung up and used another precious few percent of her battery to let the school know someone else would be picking Amelie up that evening. And then continued the ritual Doing of the Nothing that was pretty much all you could do when the technology that made your life work had stopped working. She tried reading Marianne's and Wilfred's various cookery books so it felt like she wasn't completely wasting her time, but she couldn't quite concentrate on anything.

This guy wasn't coming, was he? But then what? She'd be back to where she was this morning, and he was the only guy who'd said he could come. Which meant she'd either have to find two hundred quid for an emergency call-out or leave it until next week, and that wasn't really an option where electricity was concerned. If it had been just her, she could have crashed with someone. But you couldn't make your eight-year-old child couch-surf, not even for a few days. That would be a formative memory, and not in a good way.

Of course, she could go to her parents. But no.

And yes, Lauren and Allison had a spare room in their frighteningly chic apartment. But while Rosaline was pretty sure Allison didn't hate her, that status was maintained by an unspoken but meticulous series of compromises, one of which she was fairly sure had to be "don't move into my home."

Also, how much was this going to cost her? Between travel to the show that hadn't been reimbursed yet, travel to Alain's, and previous issues with the boiler, she was already way over budget this month. She wasn't even sure she was going to be able to afford practice ingredients next week. And then there was, y'know, making sure Amelie didn't starve and had clothing and soap and a quality of life so the great nebulous They wouldn't take her away.

Fuck, she was going to have to borrow money from her mum and dad again. After specifically telling her dad she wouldn't. And wasn't he going to love that?

There was a knock at the door—and since the wobbly figure through the glass was wearing a purple coat and dragging a child by the hand, it probably wasn't someone here to fix her electricity.

"One moppet," said Lauren. "Freshly delivered."

Amelie scowled. "I can't be delivered. I'm a person, not a parcel."

"Perhaps I meant 'delivered' in the sense of rescued. Like *deliver us from evil.*"

"I thought deliveries from evil was when evil sends you things like bad luck or getting sick."

This made Lauren laugh. "I agree it would make more sense."

"And why," Amelie went on, clearly in a meditative mood, "is Jesus so worried about trespassers? Is that why they're always being prosecuted?"

"Since Jesus doesn't exist, I'm not sure it's an important question."

"Lauren," interrupted Rosaline, "stop trying to turn my daughter into Richard Dawkins."

Amelie, of course, seized on this. "Who's Richard Dawkins?"

"He's a man some people believe is a blasphemer," explained Lauren, "and others have constructed a religion around."

"Does that mean they're going to crucify him?"

"Only on Twitter."

Rosaline went to help Amelie out of her coat and put her schoolbag in the corner. "So, the reason Auntie Lauren was picking you up today is that we haven't got any electricity."

"Where did it go?"

"Back in the walls, I suppose? But someone is meant to be coming to fix it, and he'll be here today, probably. Which means you're going to have to do your homework early while there's light."

"I don't have any homework," said Amelie firmly.

"Not even maths? You always have maths on a Tuesday."

"Maybe a little bit of maths."

Amelie, dragging her feet like a cartoon mouse, pulled her stool up to the kitchen table and started the homework she apparently didn't have.

"Is this an *I need to go and get candles* situation?" asked Lauren.

Shrugging, Rosaline began to tidy up the self-saucing pudding that wasn't. "I hope not, but my faith in 'be round this afternoon' man is dwindling."

"I'd like to help, but unless you want me to write a satirical play about waiting for an electrician who never comes, and, frankly, I think that's been done, we're reaching the limits of my skill set."

"Honestly, you've been great. And I don't want to keep you from your wife."

"She'll be at work for a couple of hours yet so I might as well hang around, warming your heart with my presence."

Amelie looked up hopefully. "Does this mean I still have to do my homework?"

"Yes," said Rosaline in her best *I have boundaries* voice. "But when you're finished we can...we can..." She suddenly realised that every form of entertainment in the house was electronic. Apart from some books, most of them unsuitable for eight-year-olds, and a battered Monopoly set that she was certain she'd never bought. "Spend quality time with Auntie Lauren."

"But I'm *always* spending time with Auntie Lauren. It used to be exciting but it's not anymore."

"Auntie Lauren," pointed out Lauren, "is right here."

"See. *Always*."

Unable to think of any other alternative, Rosaline climbed slightly dangerously up a bookshelf and hauled down at least five years of dust and the Monopoly board that had spontaneously generated up there. "Come on. I'll make us some sandwiches and then we can play...this. It'll be fun."

Triumphantly underlining the answer to her last maths question, Amelie swung down off her stool. "But I hate Monopoly. It's boring."

"Everyone hates Monopoly." Lauren started clearing the kitchen table. "That's how it brings people together."

An hour and a half later, they'd had to dig the tea lights out of the bottom drawer and were still playing Monopoly and there was still no sign of the man who was supposed to come and fix the electricity.

"I told you Monopoly was boring," said Amelie, with the passionate joy of a vindicated eight-year-old.

Lauren stomped her boot four spaces, landed on Super Tax, and reluctantly returned one hundred pounds to the bank. "You're just saying that because you want to buy Whitehall and I won't let you."

"Mummy, why won't Auntie Lauren let me buy Whitehall? I've got all the other pink ones. I'll give you a blue one for it."

"I don't want a blue one," retorted Lauren. "And if I give you

Whitehall, then you'll be able to start building houses. Which means in about six hours from now you might actually win."

Amelie thought about this. "But if nobody will give anybody the things they need, then nobody will ever have the things they need, and we'll have to play the game forever."

"And that, my darling"—Lauren grinned—"is capitalism."

"I don't like capitalism. Capitalism is stupid."

"And to think when Karl Marx said that he got a whole school of philosophy named after him."

"I don't want a whole school of philosophy," Amelie complained, with an air of impending pout. "I want the pink ones."

"Okay." Rosaline squared up her meagre haul of banknotes, finally accepting that Monopoly was a distraction rather than a solution. "I think we've got a problem."

"Yes," retorted Lauren, "you made us play a shit board game."

"No, I mean the electrician definitely isn't coming. And so I might not be able to use anything in my house for a week."

"Does that mean I don't have to have my hair washed?" asked Amelie.

"No. That's the boiler, which is gas. And you still need to keep clean."

"But maybe the aliens won't like it. Maybe that's why they keep making funny noises."

"Maybe they're trying to encourage you. Maybe they're saying, *Look after your hair, or we'll take you away to our planet.*" The moment it came out of her mouth, Rosaline knew it was the wrong thing to say.

"I'd like to go to an alien planet," said Amelie. "I bet they'd look really oogly like anglerfish, and they wouldn't care about my hair, because they don't have any."

Right. This was definitely a parenting moment. And the parenting moment was "Don't completely lose it at your daughter because you're stressed out of your mind and you've just played nearly two hours of Monopoly." Rosaline took a deep breath. "Why don't we pack this game up and then we need to think about what we're doing over the next couple of days."

There was a silence, filled only by the clattering of playing pieces being dropped somewhat dispiritedly into a red plastic box.

"Look," said Lauren. "If you really need it, then—"

"No. I mean, thank you. But I can't do that to you."

"Thank fuck. I mean, Allison's pretty sure I'm over you, but if I tried to move you and your child into the flat, I couldn't guarantee the longevity of my marriage."

"How would you feel"—Rosaline turned to Amelie in defeat—"about staying with Grandma and Granddad?"

"I *just* stayed with them." Her voice was getting a fretful, teary edge. "Why can't I stay here? Why can't we get the electrics fixed?"

Fuck. Rosaline was failing as a parent. "Because I can't get an electrician right now. But I will be able to get one soon."

Amelie still looked on the verge of an understandable but unhelpful meltdown. "Then why don't you ask the Viking?"

"Who?"

"The Viking cake man who made the crab. He's an electrician. He said so."

Did she mean Harry? Oh God, she did, and she was right. He *was* an electrician. And Rosaline had his card. And he had explicitly told her to call him if she ever needed anything.

She'd forgotten because she'd had no intention of ever calling him ever for any reason. And now they were sort of friends— wait, were they friends?—it somehow felt even worse to be all, *Hi, I've mostly ignored you, except for your arms occasionally, and now and again your big brown eyes, but do you think you could possibly come and fix my shit for me?*

Except if she didn't, she'd be sitting in the dark, eating tins of uncooked beans until Monday while her child started a new, and probably better, life with Cordelia and St. John.

"I really feel like I'm letting the side down," said Lauren, "because while I know a great many fabulous and talented lesbians, none of them are electricians."

Rosaline's phone was at five percent. Which meant, if she was doing this, it would have to be now.

Fuck, she had to, didn't she?

She fished Harry's card out from her bag and hesitantly dialled the number. It was fine. This would be embarrassing, and he'd probably have to fight hard not to start calling her "love" again, but she'd get over it. And besides, he was an electrician—if experience had taught her anything, he wouldn't pick up.

"'Allo," said Harry. "Dobson & Son Electricians. Can I help?"

Shit shit shit. "Um. Hi. It's...Rosaline."

"Oh. You all right, mate?"

"Not really. My electricity's gone off and I can't seem to get anyone out to fix it and you did say I should call you if I needed help. So I guess I'm calling you because I guess I need help?"

"Thank you for my crab," shouted Amelie. "It was very... bready."

"Tell me what happened?"

Rosaline blinked. "Well...she ate it?"

"With the electricity."

"Sorry. That. Um, the trip-switch keeps tripping, and when I untrip it, it goes straight back."

"Probably a short. If you tell me where you are, I'll be right over."

"Are you sure? I mean, it's nearly seven and..."

"Nah, it's fine. I was just trying to self-sauce my pud, but it'll keep."

God, what if he was eliminated because she'd made him do an emergency call-out at an unsociable hour on a Tuesday? "I don't want to interfere with your practice. And I can, you know, pay you."

Assuming he didn't want a couple of hundred quid.

"No need, mate. Us bakers gotta stick together. I reckon I'll be there in about an hour."

"Okay. This is . . . kind of you. I really appreciate it."

He hung up after that, which was fortunate, because Rosaline only had a minute or so left of battery, and vanishing without saying goodbye or thank you after someone had volunteered to do some quite highly skilled labour for free would have wiped out what little remained of her pride.

"Right." She turned to Lauren and Amelie, who had been watching the call with equal curiosity. "He'll be here by eight. So if you want to get back to your wife now, I'll totally understand. And you"—she pointed at her daughter—"need to have a bath, wash your hair, and get ready for bed."

"But I want to see the Viking," said Amelie. "I want to see the Viking fix the electrics."

"I'm not sure there'll be anything to see. He'll probably just want to walk around and poke plug sockets."

"I still want to see. I might want to fix electrics when I'm older. It's important for more girls to fix electrics."

"Well, then I'll buy you a book on it for your birthday."

"I don't want a book for my birthday. I want a bike or a laser or a robot."

"And I want," said Rosaline firmly, "you to go upstairs, have a bath, and put your pyjamas on. If Harry's here when all that's done, then you can say good night to him."

"And I," added Lauren, "should be getting back to Allison. So you can say good night to me now if you're not too bored of my company."

Amelie went to give Lauren a hug. "Good night, Auntie Lauren. Sorry I said I saw you too much. You're very nice to me."

Not being great with affection at the best of times, Lauren patted Amelie awkwardly on the head.

***

Harry arrived at about ten to eight, which meant Amelie did indeed get to see him before bedtime.

"'Allo, princess," he said, kneeling down in front of her and putting his toolbox on the floor.

Amelie thought about this for a moment. "I'm not a princess. Princesses are undemocratic."

"All right." He paused. "'Allo... Prime Minister?"

"I'm Prime Minister of Sloths." Amelie proudly showed him her pyjamas. "Although these say 'so sleepy' and I'm not sleepy so they're lying sloths."

"Maybe the sloths are sleepy."

"Oh. That makes sense."

"All right." Rosaline tried to shepherd her child vaguely bedwards. "You've said hello to Harry. Now go and clean your teeth."

"I've already cleaned my teeth."

Rosaline gave her a look. "Have you?"

"Well, not *tonight*. But I have."

"You have to clean your teeth every night. And every morning. Or all your teeth fall out."

"My teeth are falling out anyway and then a fairy gives me money. So, I shouldn't brush my teeth because then I'll get more money."

Still kneeling on the floor, Harry grinned at them. "The tooth fairy only pays for clean teeth, Prime Minister."

"Okay." Amelie gave a tragic sigh. "I'll go and brush my teeth and go to bed even though I'm not tired and will never go to sleep ever. Night-night, Mummy. Night-night, Mr. Viking."

Now that Amelie was gone, Rosaline was suddenly aware that she and Harry were alone in candlelight. And by candlelight, it was somehow easier to admit how ridiculously...everything he was. Those cheekbones. The trace of stubble along his jaw. The way his face looked so sculpted in repose. But then softened—came alive—when he smiled or laughed or talked. He was so blatantly the sort of man you were supposed to fancy that Rosaline felt deeply uncomfortable about fancying him.

It felt...shallow, somehow. Like she was giving in to social conditioning.

"Well." Harry stood. "Better take a look at the circuit breakers then."

So he took a look at the circuit breakers, while Rosaline hovered somewhat uselessly. One of the many, many bits of etiquette she'd never worked out for having somebody fix your house was whether you were supposed to hang around to show interest, and risk making it look like you were worried they were going to steal the furniture. Or else leave them to it to signal trust, and risk looking like you didn't give a shit. And this was about a billion times worse when it was someone you knew.

"Can I get you," she offered, "a cup of t— Actually, forget that. The kettle won't work."

"I think"—a series of clicking sounds and the lights came back on—"the problem's upstairs."

"How did you...?"

Emerging from the cupboard, he smiled up at her. "Do you really want to know?"

"Are you suggesting it's too complicated for me?"

"Nah, mate. Just a bit boring."

"Boring or not, it would probably be helpful if I didn't have to call you for a problem I could fix by pressing some buttons."

"Ain't fixed yet." He stroked his chin. "What's going on is, you've got a short on one of your rings."

"One of my rings?"

"Yeah. You got your downstairs ring, what's all your plugs downstairs. And your upstairs ring, what's all your plugs upstairs, and your lighting ring, what's your lighting, and some people have others—depends how their house is put together."

"Okay?"

"And the lights are fine, and the downstairs is fine, but if I put the upstairs on"—he reached into the cupboard, flicked a switch, and everything went off again—"that happens."

This sort of made sense. "Then I'm fine as long as I don't want electricity upstairs?"

"In general, when I come round to fix someone's electrics, they take it pretty bad if I say 'Well, don't use the upstairs.' So no, this is step one. Step two is I use one of these"—he pulled out something that looked a lot like the multimeters that Rosaline remembered from her A-levels a lifetime ago—"to find out where the short is and then I replace the socket. And if you did want to make tea, it should work now."

"How do you like it?"

"I reckon you'll look down on me for this, but milk, lots of sugar."

Rosaline squirmed. "I don't . . . look down on you."

"Come off it, mate. You're a nice middle-class girl. I bet you never had a sweet tea in your life. I bet you was raised on caramel macchiatos."

"I was not. My parents don't approve of flavoured coffee."

"I know you're joking, but the fact they had an opinion about it really proves my point."

Feeling nonspecifically guilty, Rosaline went into the kitchen and put the kettle on. Her cake had long since died, so she rather forlornly scraped it into the bin and put the tin into the sink to soak. A quick check of the fridge revealed that most of the contents were okay, though the freezer was sitting in a rapidly expanding pool of icy water that she hastily mopped up while waiting for the kettle to boil. All in all, the situation could have been a lot worse.

Although she'd been a little affronted by Harry's assumptions about her beverage preferences, the fact that her cupboard contained green tea, camomile tea, Earl Grey, and Assam but no English breakfast didn't exactly speak to her status as a woman of the people. She decided that Assam was the closest to regular tea that she had and made two cups of that, one black and slightly less infused, and one full of milk and sugar.

She found Harry sitting at the top of the stairs. "So I've checked the hall sockets," he whispered, "and it's none of them. Which leaves your room and Amelie's room. You want to do yours first? That way we might not have to wake her up."

Rosaline didn't wholly want to invite Harry into her bedroom—but she suspected that said more about her than it did about him. "Can you give me two minutes to...you know. Make it presentable."

"Got three sisters, mate. Ain't nothing I ain't seen before. But go ahead. I'll have my tea."

She slipped inside and hastily stashed away her pants, bras, and vibrators—not that any of these things were particularly visible or shameful, but she felt they were best witnessed by choice, rather than by accident. When she was done, she opened the door and Harry, who'd made surprisingly rapid progress on his tea, came in and had a quick look round.

"We might need to move the bed." He struck the universal tradesman pose of mild consternation. "I'll check the others, but I reckon there's a socket back there."

There was, though Rosaline hadn't thought of it since she'd moved in. But as fate would have it, she needed to think of it now because the other sockets were fine.

"Which end do you want?" asked Harry.

Did it matter? "I'll take the footboard."

"All right. Bend from your knees. Keep your back straight. On three."

Fortunately, the only bed she'd been able to afford was made from MDF and held together with glue and hope so it moved fairly easily. Underneath, of course, was a warren of dust bunnies that appeared to have taken half her socks hostage.

Harry bent down—she wasn't looking, she wasn't looking—and poked his machine into the socket. There was a beep. "This'll be the one."

Pulling a screwdriver from his back pocket, he opened the panel and then, pulling a different screwdriver from a different pocket, did something Rosaline would never have been able to replicate with the tangle of wires.

"Here we go." He stood and passed her the detached plug socket. "That there"—he pointed at a brownish-yellow stain running between two of the terminals on one side—"is where some damp's got in and it's built a connection from the live to the earth. And that's what's setting your switch off. I'll go get another one out the van and we'll be sorted."

It took less than twenty minutes in the end, and that included getting the bed back into position as carefully and quietly as possible. And then they were standing awkwardly in the front hall, Harry holding a mug in one hand and his toolbox in the other.

"Well," he said. "Better be leaving you to it."

That just felt bad. *Hi, drive for an hour at no notice, fix my house, refuse payment and then fuck off immediately.* Although maybe he wanted to go. Maybe he had a hot date to get back to. Or, if nothing else, a self-saucing pudding. "You...you don't have to. If you wanted to hang around and have another cup of tea or something."

They eyed each other uncertainly. Then he shrugged. "Up to you, mate. Don't want to wear out my welcome."

"No, please. It's fine."

"Yeah, but"—his feet shuffled against the threadbare carpet—"it's late and you've probably got stuff in the morning."

"Well, I don't want to make you stay if you've got to rush off. But you've come a long way and done me a favour, so I don't want to chuck you out."

He frowned. "Mate. You don't owe me nothing. I said I'd give you a hand if you needed it and I have. I'm happy to stay if you fancy a natter, but just 'cos I like you and you're pretty—which I know I shouldn't be saying—don't mean you gotta give me the time of day for a plug socket."

"Um," she said.

Truthfully, she wasn't sure how to take this. She'd been raised with a very strong sense of social obligation, and the idea of being given a choice about it was on the edge of disorienting. Besides, she did sort of…actually want Harry to stick around for a bit, although she wasn't overinclined to dwell on the why of it, and having to tell him "Yes, I do want you to stay" felt a lot more revealing than just assuming he had to.

Also, he thought she was pretty.

Which he'd mentioned before. But felt different now.

"Um," she said again. "It would be nice if you…wanted to stay? For a natter?"

He plopped his toolbox back on the floor and followed her through to the kitchen. "All right then."

Thankfully the room was in a reasonable condition—its diminutive size coupled with the edge of fussiness she'd inherited from her father meant Rosaline was a tidy-as-she-went kind of baker, and although the elements of an abandoned pudding were still readily visible, they were arrayed neatly towards the back of the work surface. On top of which, fridge door aside, it was a relatively Amelie-free zone.

"My hospitality's a bit limited, for obvious reasons." The freezer had continued to melt and she hastily remopped, since while she was sure Harry had been sincere about not wanting anything from her, he'd probably have been a bit upset at winding up with a nasty fall and a twisted ankle. "There's more tea. And...well, not much else. Unless you want to help me use up some prematurely defrosted fish fingers."

"You got bread?"

Yanking open the freezer door, she began sorting through the things that could be saved and the things that really couldn't. "Yes, I've got bread. I mean, it's from a shop. I'm not Josie."

"If you're serious, I could murder a fish finger sandwich."

"If you like. They're going in the bin otherwise."

"Tell you what. Sling us a pan. I'll fry 'em up while you put the kettle on."

She slung him a pan. And tried not to stare as he heated a splash of oil and gently extricated the slightly-sorry-for-themselves fish fingers from their soggy cardboard packet.

"What's wrong, mate?" He cast her a suspicious glance. "You're not one of them what grills 'em, are you?"

Her kitchen could just about cope with her and Amelie, and even squeeze in Lauren. But they were all, in their own way, small people—which was one of the many things Lauren had in common with Napoleon. Harry, though, while shorter than Alain, could not be described as small in any meaningful way. This should have made Rosaline feel crowded. Except, somehow, it didn't. It was nice to...share the space. Step around each other. Pass things across the hob.

"I might be," she admitted. "But I was thinking how betrayed Amelie would feel right now. She's convinced grown-ups start having fun the moment she goes to bed. And if I tell her we made fish finger sandwiches at ten o'clock, she'll never sleep again."

"We could have ice-cream sundaes after."

"And then go on the secret adults-only merry-go-round. Oh wait. No. That sounds incredibly wrong."

The fish fingers gave a merry crackle as they hit the pan. "Yeah, my sister had one of them on her hen-do."

Rosaline laughed, remembering abruptly that she was supposed to be making tea rather than watching Harry fry battered cod sticks. It shouldn't have been a particularly attractive thing for a man to be doing, but right then, it struck this incongruous balance between cosy and sexy that she wasn't at all prepared for. Maybe she could blame the fact he'd come to her rescue like a blue-collar knight in denim armour. Or his T-shirts. He really could afford to wear slightly looser-fitting T-shirts.

A kettle, four slices of bread, and a lot of butter later, they were sitting opposite each other at the kitchen table, knees almost touching beneath it—something else that was not a hazard with either Amelie or Lauren.

"They're better with white bread," said Harry.

"I know, but I'm trying to make sure my daughter grows up with a healthy bowel."

Harry gave her a playfully appalled look. "Thanks for talking about bowels while I'm trying to have a sarnie."

"Sorry." She winced. "Between Amelie and Lauren, I'm used to far worse mealtime conversation."

"Just taking the piss, mate. Besides, posh voice like yours, 'bowels' sounds like what you call your chihuahua."

"You do know I'm not that posh."

"Your kid's named Amelie, you eat wholemeal bread, and you ain't got no salad cream in your fridge."

"There's mayonnaise."

"It's not the same thing, and you know it."

She took a sip of tea. "What even *is* salad cream? I mean, I know what it is. But nobody knows what it is."

"Well, it's one of them things like Branston pickle, init? It's made of Branston. You put it on sandwiches."

"And Marmite," she offered in her best academic tone, which, thanks to her mother, was pretty good, "is made of marm."

"Oh, them poor little marms. They're an endangered species now. Bloody shocking."

Giggling, she turned her attention to her food. "I probably shouldn't admit this, but I've never had a fish finger sandwich before."

"Well, since you got no salad cream or white bread, you basically still haven't."

This observation did not help her giggling, which made eating difficult. It wasn't fair. Men who looked like Harry did not have the right to be funny as well. "Um," she heard herself say out of nowhere, "sorry I was such a dick to you that first week."

He gave one of his slow blinks. "Didn't think you were, mate. But now I know you was, I'm a bit offended."

"You don't have to make a joke out of it."

"And you don't have to feel guilty about telling me you didn't like how I was talking to you."

It shouldn't have kept surprising her—Harry's general willingness to...well...care about things because someone else did? But she kept waiting for the bridge too far or the straw that broke the camel's back or the compromise he wasn't willing to make. And the more she let herself relax, the more she let herself enjoy his company, the worse it was going to hurt when it finally happened.

"But I'm really good at feeling guilty," she protested. "I've had a lot of practice. And anyway, it's not what I said, it's...it's sort of...I just think I had you wrong."

"I mean"—he shrugged—"I'm not sure I had you had right

either. Like, I only talked to you because I reckoned you was this pretty posh bird and you wouldn't give me the time of day anyway so if I fucked it up it wouldn't matter. Course I still fucked it up by calling you 'love' and all that. And now I think about it, you probably don't like bird either, do you?"

"Not a huge fan of bird, no."

"See"—he made a defeated gesture—"fucked it up again."

"It's...it's fine. And for what it's worth, Jennifer Hallet thinks I'm just a pretty posh bird too."

He laughed. "I bet she don't after the way you yelled at her in bread week."

"I'm not sure that's better. You can't go around yelling at people."

"Well, it depends on who's doing the yelling and who's getting yelled at. You gotta stand up for yourself, mate."

In Rosaline's experience, people who told her to stand up for herself meant "to everybody except me." So it was an idea she approached warily at best.

"And anyway," Harry went on, "I never said you was *just* a pretty posh bird. I mean, you are still posh. And you look the way you look. But I also know you're not scared to have a go at someone what could kick you off a show, and you brung up a daughter who's well into ugly fish, which means she probably knows you'll love her whatever she does, and that's really important. And when everybody else is pantsing about making flowers out of bread you make an actual heart what bleeds because you're a fucking weirdo. And I also know you're with another bloke so I should probably shut up."

Rosaline opened her mouth and—realising she had absolutely no idea what to say—closed it again. Because she *was* kind of with another bloke. So probably letting stone-cold hotties tell her she was a fucking weirdo was over some hypothetical but very specific line.

Except what if Alain had been right however many weeks ago and she was desperate for...something? Because she didn't actually want Harry to shut up at all. She needed more of—actually, she wasn't quite sure what. If it was the quiet otherworldly feeling of your child being in bed. Or not having to worry about the electricity going off for no reason or about how she'd pay to fix it if it did. Maybe it was because she'd come first on biscuits, and every time she thought about it she had to stop herself bouncing like Tigger. Or maybe it was the company. Being with someone who'd seen her house and met her kid and knew what her life was like. Someone who seemed to care about who she was. Not who she should have been.

Standing, Harry gathered up their plates and then took them over to the sink—where he started to wash up.

"You cooked," she said. "You shouldn't be—"

"I stuck some fish fingers in a frying plan. Marcus Wareing ain't gonna be knocking on my door anytime soon."

"It was a really good fish finger, though. And Marcus Wareing did serve a custard tart to the Queen."

"Can you imagine, though?" He glanced over his shoulder. "If I tried to serve the Queen a fish finger sandwich. They'd hate me worse than they hate Meghan Markle."

"That's not funny," she told him. "And I feel bad for wanting to laugh anyway."

"I know. Poor girl. I mean, poor young woman. Had a terrible time of it. My mum and dad still remember what happened with Princess Di. You think they'd learn, wouldn't you?"

Rosaline pulled a tea towel from the rack—it was a souvenir one from Battle Abbey, which Amelie had picked up on a school trip—and started drying. "Shock horror: monarchy terrible system."

"Eh, someone's got to open things, and it can't always be the Archbishop of Canterbury or someone what came third on *X-Factor*."

There was a pause while they finished up, Rosaline tucking the plates back in the cupboard while Harry rinsed the grease out of the sink with more diligence than Rosaline herself often displayed.

"So," he asked, "why'd you come on the show, then?"

Now *Bake Expectations* was in full swing, it had been a while since she'd had to answer that. "Honestly, I'm kind of...Saying 'desperate' sounds really overdramatic. And, actually, I'm fine. I'm much better off than most people in my situation. It's just I feel...stuck."

He tilted his head in gentle curiosity. "How'd you mean?"

"Oh, it's complicated. And I'm not even sure it makes sense. Because, the thing is, I'm so glad to have Amelie. And if I could go back and do it all over again, I'd do everything the same. But I'm tired of never having quite enough money and never having quite enough time. And I'm tired of feeling like my whole life is an expensive hobby that my parents are bankrolling for me. Sorry, that's"—she slumped down at the kitchen table again—"a lot."

"Is what it is, init? And there's nothing wrong with wanting a bit of extra cash, and you ain't got nothing to lose by going on the telly for it. I mean," he went on, with far more confidence than Rosaline had ever felt, "you're a good baker, and I reckon folk'll like you even if you don't win. Look at her with the teeth from last season—she went out in the semifinal and she's got her own TV series now."

Strangely, talking to Harry about the show had made it feel realer than it ever had before. Like it was actually a plan, not a pipe dream or a detour on the way to something better. "I think maybe I was hoping more for, I don't know, a recipe book or a column in the *Guardian*. Writing for a website. Something I can do from home that pays more than eight pounds seventy-two an hour."

"Go far enough and you can have your pick. And that's what

life's all about at the end of the day. Doing something you're okay with that pays enough that you can take care of the people you want to take care of."

It was a very...a very *un-Palmer* way to think about it. "My parents would say that life was about making the most of your talents and finding a career that challenges you and makes a difference."

"Well, baking's a talent." Harry gave half a smile and half a shrug. "And I reckon you've got enough challenges already. And if what you do makes you happy and makes other people happy, that should be enough of a difference for anybody."

She wished it was that simple. And while she appreciated his, well, all of this, she had to change the subject, or...it was too much to think about. Especially when she was supposed to be looking at access courses and going back to university and turning her life into whatever it was meant to be. "What about you?"

"Well, I'm doing all right. Working for my dad at the moment, but I'll take it over when he retires. I know it's not Harrods, but it's something. It's what we do and I like doing it."

"No, I mean why did you go on the show?"

He blew out a long breath. "Bit daft, if I'm honest. I'm trying to do more things what scare me."

"And going on a baking show scares you?"

"Oh yeah. Gotta be on TV. Gotta talk in front of cameras. Gotta wonder what my mates think. It's all my worst things."

"If your friends are that bad, they're not your friends."

"They ain't. I mean, Terry is. But mostly I just get in my head about what people are going to say. And they never do—well, hardly ever, except Terry—only it keeps going round and round anyway." Joining her at the table, Harry brushed away the last fish finger crumbs. "So I thought, *Fuck it. You like baking, go on the baking thing.* Did not expect to get this far if I'm honest."

"You've done really well," she offered.

"Cheers, mate. I reckon I've got another week in me at least."

Rosaline wasn't quite sure what to say to that. And so she found herself watching him, half enjoying having someone to talk to who wasn't either her child, her ex-girlfriend, or a man she was trying to impress, and half confused because Harry was never quite who she expected him to be. Or maybe he was, but it meant something different than she'd thought it would. "You...you seem to worry about things a lot."

"Yeah. Always have. It's just how I am. My dad's the same."

This wasn't her business. But it wasn't the first time he'd mentioned feeling like this, and ignoring it—especially when he kept doing things for her—felt wrong. "Have you considered maybe seeing your GP?"

"You what?" He laughed. "You want me to go see my doctor and be like, *I get scared sometimes.*"

"Well, I mean—I'm just going by what you've said. But I think there might be...things out there to help you?"

"What you saying? That I need to see a shrink?"

"Would that be so terrible?"

He stood abruptly—and tall people standing abruptly was not Rosaline's favourite thing in the world. "Yeah it would, mate. I'm not mental."

"I don't think you are." She slid her chair backwards slightly. "Look, I know you think my dad's a dick, but what he'd say in this situation is, 'If you had a bad back, you might take up walking or you might go to a chiropractor or you might go to your doctor for a painkiller, and those are all options. And you're already doing things to make this better for yourself, which is great, but it's also okay to ask for help.'"

"Yeah, but I don't need help. I'm fine."

"You told me you went on national television to try and get out of your head. And that's brave. But it's probably not the most effective thing you can do."

Seeming genuinely upset, Harry pushed a hand through his hair. "I'm not having this. I know you think I'm common, and that's fine 'cos I am, and I don't read Shakespeare, I don't forage, and my dad's not a doctor. But I'm not standing here while you tell me you think I'm a nutcase."

"That really wasn't my—"

"I think I'd better go. Thanks for the fish fingers."

From her seat in the kitchen, she heard his footsteps in the hall, the clank of his toolbox, and the soft thud of the door closing behind him.

And that, Rosaline, is how you take something nice and fuck it up beyond all recognition.

Saturday

"I MISSED YOU last night," said Alain, leaning over her shoulder.

"Sorry. I was late getting in. My whole week got thrown off because of the electricity."

"I did say you'd be welcome at mine."

Rosaline—who hadn't slept especially well and was pretty certain she'd fucked up her blind bake—turned sharply. "Still got a kid, Alain."

"I know, but you have to think of yourself as well."

"To a point. But it does eventually become criminal neglect."

"No one"—he gazed at her sincerely—"could deny what a devoted mother you are."

"Thanks. Sorry. I'm just stressed."

He smiled. "Well, perhaps later I can help you unwind."

Honestly? She wasn't sure she needed unwinding in that particular way. At least not right now. She'd been running around like a blue-arsed fly since Tuesday, still felt nebulously guilty about upsetting Harry, and was definitely on track for a low-performing week. Put it all together, and it was the kind of situation where the solution was *Put your feet up and have a cup of tea*, not *Do me hard from behind*. On the other hand, she wanted

Alain to think she was a vivacious sex kitten, not a tired single mum scared of losing her spot on a TV baking show.

"Yeah," she said. "That'd be...great."

She was almost relieved when they were called back in for judging a moment or so later because it meant there wasn't time for him to pick up on her lack of enthusiasm.

The challenge that week had been parkin, which was only debatably a pudding, but also only debatably a cake, so what could you do? Rosaline had struggled from the outset, letting her golden syrup boil when she hadn't intended to and, she felt almost certain, leaving her ambiguous pudding in the oven for too long and at too high a temperature.

Marianne poked at Rosaline's offering with a world-weary air. "It's competent. But we're expecting more than competence at this stage."

It was exactly what she'd been expecting, but it still felt like a rebuke. She hung her head, feeling tears prick the corners of her eyes. And seeing that Josie had done about equivalently and Harry slightly worse wasn't much consolation. Especially when it turned out that Alain had knocked it out of the fucking park and won the round.

"So"—Alain caught up with her as she made a beeline from dinner to the bar—"how about that early night, Rosaline-um-Palmer?"

She told herself that it would be...nice. That it would take her mind off things. That something something endorphins. "Actually," she heard herself say, "can I just have a drink and a sit-down first?"

"We can bring a bottle up. Have a very small bacchanal."

"Look...I really need a few minutes to get myself together."

"I understand." He ran his fingers lightly down her arm—which was probably all the PDA he was willing to risk on-set. "Let me know when you're done mourning your perfectly adequate parkin."

He was right. He was right. "I just...feel like I should be doing better."

"You're doing better than some people. And there's no way they'll send you home while there's weaker bakers still in the competition."

"They'll send home whoever does worst this week. And that could very well be me."

"It's not going to be you. And punishing yourself won't make you do any better tomorrow."

She wasn't sure sitting at the bar and moping into a G&T rather than dashing off to catch the two-for-one special at Poundland was punishing herself exactly. Or maybe it was. Maybe she was so messed up about the competition, her future, and her choices that she thought a mediocre parkin meant she no longer had the right to get laid.

"Tell you what," she said, "I'll have one drink and I'll come and find you."

He smiled. "Looking forward to it. I'll be in my room."

When Rosaline got to the bar, all hope of a quiet, consolatory G&T evaporated because Anvita and Josie were already ensconced in a corner. And by the time she'd seen them they'd definitely seen her, which, by unbreakable social convention, meant they would have to invite her over and she would have to go.

"Oi oi oi," called Anvita. "Lads lads lads."

Although Rosaline knew objectively that Josie wasn't actually evil, the events of week one had put her very low on the list of people Rosaline could be fucked to hang out with. "Um," she said. "Who are the lads?"

"Apparently"—that was Josie—"it's us now."

Sitting down beside them, Rosaline found herself no more illuminated than she had been ten seconds ago. "Why?"

Anvita shrugged. "I don't know. It just looked fun. I thought I'd try it."

"Okay, but if you suggest going for a cheeky Nando's, I'm leaving."

"Don't worry," said Josie. "My cheeky Nando's days are long gone. The best I can manage now is a grumpy Uber Eats."

It was unfair, Rosaline knew, to assume Josie's ever-passing allusions to her lifestyle were a coded way of saying "I'm married and had my kids at a socially acceptable age; what's your excuse?" But it still felt like that. Gritting her teeth, she raised an imaginary glass in Anvita's direction. "Well done on your parkin, by the way."

"Thanks. I totally Rickyed it."

"Oh Ricky." Sighing fondly, Josie topped up her wine. "I can't believe he's gone. I mean, I can. He blew up a dragon's head. But I miss him."

"Me too," Anvita said. "I miss them all. Well, except Dave. He was clearly a cock."

"I know there's only been four of them, but it feels really empty all of a sudden. We'll be half gone by the end of tomorrow." In fact, now Rosaline thought of it, the night they'd all sat around this table and Josie had made her feel like shit and Florian had come to her defence seemed almost to have happened to a different person.

Josie gave a macabre grin. "Unless, of course they decide we're equally rubbish and can us both in a shock twist."

"Or"—Rosaline made a valiant attempt to stay positive—"they'll decide we both have real potential and—"

"Dump Harry?" Anvita finished.

"I was going to say, 'save all of us.' But I suppose that's an option too."

"Don't get me wrong, he's great. But if he goes out"—and here Anvita got slightly misty-eyed—"then when they're doing the interviews in the final, he and Ricky can both be all, *We're rooting for Anvita, she's excellent and sexy.*"

"*Alternatively*," put in Josie cheerfully, "you could have a tremendous disaster and go home to your nan in disgrace."

Anvita's eyes widened. "Wow. Is that what passes for tough love where you come from?"

"I have three kids." Josie's wineglass was emptying rapidly. "All my love is tough."

Nope. It wasn't Josie's fault, but Rosaline...just didn't like her. Didn't want to spend time with her. Didn't want to contemplate going out of the competition while nice normal Josie and her nice normal kids sailed triumphantly through to the final on wings made of niceness and normalcy.

She stood up again. "Anyway, I came here for a drink and, as with so many things this week, I've failed to achieve it. I'm going to the bar. Does anyone want anything?"

"The bartender's cute," suggested Anvita.

"Anything you can put in your mouth—actually, forget I said that."

Since no actual drink orders were forthcoming, Rosaline left them to it and was in the process of securing the planned consolatory G&T when Harry—the man she'd driven from her home with an unsolicited and unqualified mental health diagnosis—claimed the barstool a couple of spaces over.

"All right, mate," he said, with visible discomfort. "I reckon I acted like a bit of a knobhead the other day."

She'd been braced for something a lot worse. "No, it's fine. You were doing me a favour and I shouldn't have...got so personal."

"Your heart was in the right place, though, weren't it? And I shouldn't have got so shirty with you."

"Let's put it behind us, shall we?"

"I mean, yeah. If you want. But"—he picked at a bowl of complimentary peanuts—"we don't have to. Like, you shouldn't have to worry I'll blow up any time you say anything that's not *Hello* or *How are your fish fingers*."

To be honest, she was low-key worried about that with most people. Maybe not in such a specifically fish-fingery way. But she'd tiptoed round her parents for nineteen years until she'd untiptoed in the most dramatic way possible—and that kind of thing was probably more habit-forming than it ought to have been. "I don't really," she said, taking a fortifying sip of her G&T. "Or if I do, it's not on you. It's just blah blah gender socialisation blah blah history."

"You what?"

"Oh, you know. We teach boys to talk about what they want and girls to talk about their feelings. And then you grow up and you realise you've got to do both, and it's all a bit of a shock."

He thought about it for a moment. "Not sure I'm good at either. I mean, if I know how something's gotta be, I can be like, *This is how it's gotta be*, but if I don't, then I'm a bit stuffed."

"I think that's the difference, though. Even if I do know *how it's gotta be*, I'll always end up saying, *Have you considered maybe thinking about it being this way, but I'm sure you know best.*"

"Does that mean," he asked, "I've got to learn to talk about feelings? 'Cos my mates will take the fucking piss. I can't just sit there being, *Guys, we got knocked out the Cup before the quarter finals again. That, like, makes me sad.*"

"You know there are more emotions than happy and sad, and that also you can have them about things that aren't football?"

"I think we've read different rule books, mate."

"Also," Rosaline said, really hoping this wasn't breaking some secret man-law, "you talked to me last night. That was about emotions."

He didn't seem shocked exactly, but there was a definite colouring, and he did that thing he sometimes did where he rubbed the back of his neck and looked away. "Yeah, but, well. Like I want to say it's different on account of how you're a woman and that, but I reckon that's a bit messed up now I think about it."

"A bit, but that's gender socialisation for you."

"Well"—Harry heaved a deep sigh—"if we're talking about stuff what gives you emotions, my parkin was bollocks today."

"Mine wasn't much better. It might not have been bollocks, but it was definitely in the scrotal region."

"I'm not sure I want to talk about parkin in my scrotal region, thanks."

"You brought it up."

"I did not. I did a perfectly normal swear. You had to make it weird."

She giggled. "Sorr— No, wait. Not apologising. Fighting my gender socialisation. Suck it, bitch."

"What?" Harry gave her a fake-startled look. "You can't call me a bitch. That's sexist."

"I'm reappropriating."

"Leave it off, mate. You're worse than my sister-in-law."

Since she'd started seeing Harry as a friend rather than "some bloke with nice arms" she really thought she'd been doing a better job keeping track of his family. "I'm sure you've never mentioned a brother."

"Well, look at you making assumptions." He folded his arms—which were still nice—but his tone was playful. "Heather's married to a girl. Sweet story, actually. Met at school. But Caitlyn was well smart and went off to university, which none of my family ever have. But then she and Heather met up again when they was working at the same hospital. Doctor and nurse, bit *Holby City*, but it works for them."

Okay, Rosaline. Embarrassingly obvious note to self: working-class people can be queer too. "Wow. Sorry. Actually sorry. That was tragically heteronormative of me."

"Yeah. Turns out bisexuals ain't like quinoa. You get 'em round my way too."

"Oh shut up. Or I'll sabotage your pudding."

"You probably won't need to, mate. I'm pretty sure I'm done for."

She didn't want to think about that. "No, you're not. You can always turn it round the second day."

"Honestly, I think it's my time." He took a swig of his beer. "That's the thing with putting yourself out of your comfort zone: once you get there, you're like, *Now I'm uncomfortable, what am I supposed to be doing?* Besides, I'm not sure there's anyone I want to send home."

Rosaline sort of understood and sort of didn't. There was no one she especially wanted to leave, but she sure as hell knew *she* wanted to stay. Besides, once she was out of the competition, she'd have to start the whole go-back-to-university saga. And thinking too hard about that made her feel ever so slightly like she'd drunk a cup of somebody else's vomit.

"I mean," Harry went on, "no two ways about it you're a better baker than me. Josie puts a tonne of work in, even if her bakes are sometimes a bit funny. Anvita's just..."

"Excellent and sexy? If you get knocked out, she wants you to say she's excellent and sexy."

"Yeah." His brow crinkled. "I might not do that. That might make me look like a perv."

"I don't think she'd mind."

"*I'd* mind. Also, her nan watches this. You can't go telling a bird's nan that her granddaughter's excellent and sexy. But either way, she's a good baker and deserves to be in the competition. And so does Alain. And Nora's a granny—and nobody wants to be the one what sent the granny home."

"Yes, but," Rosaline protested, "I don't want you to go home either."

"What? You going to miss my sunny face and sparkling conversation?"

She squirmed. And did not blush. Or maybe she blushed a

bit. "You've been…a really good friend to me. Even though I've been shit sometimes."

"You ain't been shit, mate. It's been good getting to know you, and when I'm sixty I can tell me grandkids about this classy girl— I mean, young woman—I met once what was named after a bird in a Shakespeare play what weren't in a Shakespeare play."

"You think you'll tell your grandchildren about me?" She weirdly liked the idea and couldn't say why.

"I'm going to tell my grandchildren my whole bloody life story. That time Terry broke his leg falling into a hole outside a pub. That time I found a potato looked exactly like Jeremy Corbyn. That time I let a bloke take me up the Arsenal."

"Well, I'm glad I mean as much to you as a humorously shaped vegetable and a man you've told me several times is a knob."

"That's gender socialisation for you." He shrugged. "Can't talk about feelings, so it's all knobheads and funny potatoes."

Rosaline laughed, and then—

"This is a lot less quiet," said Alain, "than I was imagining when you said you were going for a quiet drink."

She wasn't sure how long he'd been there or how much he'd heard—not that they'd been talking about anything he could object to, but she still felt weird about him overhearing. "Shit. Sorry. Lost track of time."

"Yes, I can see that."

Harry threw Rosaline a *Shall I get out of here* glance, to which she half shrugged, half shook her head, not sure what outcome she was hoping for. "Ain't nothing to it, mate." He nudged a barstool in Alain's direction. "Get you a drink?"

"Yes"—Alain's attention was fully and coldly on Harry—"I'll have half a pint of get-the-fuck-away-from-my-girlfriend."

Harry got up, unhurriedly finished his beer, and then stepped away from the bar. "Not trying to start nothing. Have a good evening, Rosaline."

And oh God, this was awkward. Technically she *had* promised to come and see Alain so she could see why he was angry, but this felt really not-about-her in a way that made her, if anything, even more uncomfortable. She made brief "you too" noises at Harry to be polite, then turned back to Alain.

"Look, I didn't mean to mess you about. But it's been a long day—"

"And that's all you needed to say." With a slightly showy gesture, Alain checked his phone. "Perhaps you were right the first time. We'd have all been better off this evening if we'd called it a night."

Which left Rosaline sitting looking up at Alain, still not entirely sure who the arsehole was in this situation. "I promise I didn't mean to—"

"Let's leave it there. Have a good evening, Rosaline."

Honestly, it seemed unlikely she would. "You too."

Sunday

"FOR THIS WEEK'S baketacular," Grace Forsythe was saying, "we have a first for *Bake Expectations*. It's been the bane of many a baker and the shame of many a chef. It's something many cooks have cocked-up." She paused for what would surely be ominous incidental music. "For your final challenge, you'll be making a self-saucing pudding. It can be sumptuously sticky or silkily smooth, as long as when you slide your spoon inside, it drenches itself in a rich, delicious sauce. And to make it that little bit harder, you have to serve it with a homemade ice-cream. You have four hours from the count of three. Three, darlings."

Right. Rosaline surveyed her bench of ingredients.

This was what she was here for. Well, not self-saucing puddings specifically. But baking, rather than feeling fretful, guilty, and messed up because she might have upset the man who only called her his girlfriend as part of a pissing contest with another guy.

The problem was, while the arsehole question was still a little bit up in the air, she was drifting ever closer to the conclusion it was her. It was flat-out rude to say you'd come and meet someone, and then...not do that. And instead, have a drink with someone else. Of course, if she hadn't had a drink with Harry, she would still be feeling fretful, guilty, and messed up because she'd upset *him* on Tuesday. So all she'd really done was put her list of self-recriminations in a slightly different order.

Also, she was increasingly wondering if she hadn't at least partly been using Harry as an excuse to avoid sex. Which was unfair on Harry and on Alain, and on, well, her. Because it had, in fact, been a crappy week. And she should have been able to say, "Sorry, I'm not up for it tonight," and she knew Alain wasn't the kind of guy who'd be pushy. It was just there were few things that made you feel less like a dynamic liberated woman who was in control of her sexuality than not wanting to have sex on one of the rare opportunities you might get to.

Fuck, what was she doing? She made the mistake of looking at the clock. While she'd started making ice-cream in an angsty cooking trance, she could not at all swear she'd done it right. And it didn't help that a glance around the ballroom confirmed that everyone else, even Alain—who was always incredibly meticulous—was way ahead of her.

Oh God. This was her week. This was the week she fucked everything up, and her ice-cream exploded, and her self-saucing pudding didn't self-sauce, and then she'd have to stand in front of the camera and say, *Yeah, I got distracted because I was sad about a boy*. And wasn't that a great message to send to Amelie: Remember, darling, you can do anything you put your mind to. But if you have a minor disagreement with someone you fancy, it'll all go out the window.

"So what have you got planned for us this week, Alain?" Marianne Wolvercote asked from the back of the room.

Rosaline, zesting an orange as if her life, or at least her position in a television baking competition, depended on it, did her best to ignore their conversation.

"Well"—Alain sounded charmingly self-deprecating as always—"as you can see, I've taken a step back from the herb garden."

There came the slight clink of Marianne Wolvercote picking up a bottle. "A step back by way of an eighteen-year matured Highland single malt, I see."

He laughed. "Yes, it would be rather a waste to cook with. But I'm serving a glass of it beside my whisky, caramel, and banana pudding."

"You know," said Grace Forsythe, "it's against the rules to bribe the judges."

"A drink isn't a bribe," drawled out Marianne Wolvercote by way of a reply. "It's a courtesy."

Her orange thoroughly zested, Rosaline juiced it along with two of its companions and began dissolving icing sugar into the mixture. She hadn't exactly patented the idea of exploiting Marianne Wolvercote's notorious fondness for spirits, but it did sting a bit that he'd nicked the move she'd nicked from at least two competitors in every season.

"What are you doing?" asked Colin Thrimp.

What was she doing? "Panicking. Flailing. Running out of time."

He beamed. "I love that. Comes across as really normal and relatable. But as if you're not answering a question."

"Right now," she said, too stressed to do anything other than go along with it, "I'm panicking, flailing, and running out of time."

"Could you tell us why?"

"This ice-cream has taken a bit longer to come together than I thought it would, and I know it takes at least three hours to set. So I might take it out of the freezer and put it in front of the judges and it'll just"—she spread her hands across the table in a way she hoped resembled melting ice-cream—"blululeuuh."

Oh God, she was going to be Blululeuuh Girl now. Was that better or worse than Looks Good in a Pinny Girl? And maybe this was her final day on the show. Maybe blululeuuh would be her legacy.

"And the last thing you want," she heard herself say, "is for your ice-cream to blululeuuh."

They broke for lunch at a slightly awkward point in the baking process because the puddings had to be served hot and the ice-cream would take a long time to freeze. It was kind of the nightmare scenario—having disasters and being British about it was an integral part of the show, but if your biscuit stack collapsed or a layer of cake fell on the floor, you at least had something to put in front of the judges. With ice-cream, you had ice-cream or you didn't, and she could all too clearly picture herself standing in front of Marianne Wolvercote and Wilfred Honey, saying, *Well, I've made you an overcooked pudding served with nothing.*

Which mostly killed her desire to sit on the lawn, eating an egg and cress sandwich and trying to make conversation with people who she needed to fail spectacularly if she was going to have any chance of getting through the week.

"It's all right, mate." Harry—on his way to grab a sandwich of his own—dropped a hand briefly on her shoulder. "You never know what's gonna happen with ice-cream. You just have to stick it in the freezer and hope. It's anyone's game."

She appreciated the thought. But accepting that they were all in danger didn't make her feel much safer.

"I hate to be a *can we talk* person." Alain sat down next to her, clutching an avocado wrap. "But can we talk?"

Honestly, she'd rather have brooded in peace. Except having ducked out of sex, she wasn't sure she should also duck out of a serious conversation about feelings. "I really am sorry about last night," she tried, hoping to get it over with as quickly as possible.

"You know"—Alain's eyes were as cold and grey as a car park in October—"you could have said 'I'm not particularly up for sex this evening.' Instead of making excuses like I was some knuckle-dragging mouth-breather who wouldn't be able to stop himself humping your leg."

She winced. "I was in a bad place and not thinking clearly. I'm sorry."

"So you keep saying." He made a slightly exasperated noise. "Perhaps next time you should just tell me you're going to Malawi."

Fuck. She'd hoped they were past that. "Alain, I think you're being a bit unfair."

"Am I though?" he asked. "Because you seem to have this pattern where you'll make a totally unfounded assumption about me and then use it as an excuse to lie."

"It's not the same thing. I wasn't lying to you, I was lying to myself. Because I was fucked up and didn't know what I wanted." She gave up on her sandwich and hugged her knees. "Which, as you have noticed, is kind of part of the deal with me."

"Is Harry aware that's part of the deal?"

"What? No. I meant . . . with my life. I'm very uncertain about a lot of things right now. Like whether I wanted to have sex yesterday or whether I want to go back to university. Or both. Or neither."

"What's university got to do with any of this?"

He was looking at her like she was talking utter nonsense. And oh God, she was messing everything up. "Sorry, it's just a lot. And I know I'm probably a lot right now as well. But—whatever you might think—you are definitely not one of the things I'm confused or uncertain about."

There was a longish, tense-ish pause.

Then he seemed to relent. "Well, that's good to know, Rosaline-um-Palmer. And if it's any consolation, a lot about this is new for me as well."

"You mean, because of Amelie?"

"You're not the sort of person I've usually been with."

"You mean," she repeated, "because of Amelie?"

His mouth turned up slightly. "Because of a great many things. We're on television together, for a start. But I have been giving some thought to how difficult it must be for you to get to Gloucestershire with your other commitments. And as it happens, I'm going to be in London next week if that's easier for you."

Well, not as easy as, say, her house. Or her town. But definitely better than the Venice of the Cotswolds. If nothing else, the way UK transport infrastructure worked you had to go through London to get basically anywhere from anywhere else. The important thing here was that Alain was trying, and given her own recent behaviour, she more than owed it to him to meet him halfway. "Yes, I'd love to."

"I'm meeting up with a friend so perhaps we can all go to dinner?"

Oh. "That sounds nice."

"It's Liv, who I think I've mentioned a couple of times. You'll really like her. You've got a lot in common."

"We do?"

"Yes, she shares your spirit of adventure." He offered his slightly crooked smile. "Also, she's never been to Malawi either."

"Ha-ha. Am I ever living that down?"

He made a show of thinking about it. "Of course not. You promised me a story I could dine out on, and I intend to dine out on it."

Okay. He was teasing her. That was good, right? It meant they were in a good place again? Unfortunately, she only had about eight seconds to enjoy it because then she was summoned back to the ballroom to finish an unsuccessful pudding and discover the fate of her ice-cream.

"This has just about set," said Wilfred Honey, delicately nudging at Rosaline's ice-cream, "and the flavour of the oranges is nice. I like the way you used the lime to add that edge of bitterness to it."

"But the whole thing," added Marianne Wolvercote, "lacks joy for me."

From the back of the room, Anvita drew in a sharp breath. And Rosaline tried very hard to keep her face ungifable. They'd clearly reached the stage of the competition where the gloves were off. Because joyless pudding was frankly no pudding at all.

Although, to be fair, it hadn't been a particularly joyful week.

Marianne Wolvercote was picking through the rubble of Rosaline's bake like she was looking for survivors. "Chocolate orange is such a classic combination that I was expecting this to have a real celebratory feel to it. But even with the caramelised orange segments, it's a little bit lacking."

"Mmhm," said Rosaline, "thanks."

Okay, she was putting her chances of survival at fifty-fifty. Anvita's coconut and lime pudding with margarita ice-cream had been a big hit, especially with Marianne, as had Nora's sticky toffee with clotted cream ice-cream, especially with Wilfred. Harry's chocolate with vanilla had been described by Marianne Wolvercote as "rather basic," and Rosaline wasn't sure whether joylessness or basicicity was the more unforgivable sin in the gospel according to Wolvercote.

Perching herself back on her stool, Rosaline folded her hands in her lap and did her best not to look devastated. It was bad enough that she might be going home slightly too soon to say she'd done well but slightly too late to pretend she hadn't tried way too hard. And knowing it was probably her or Harry made the whole thing worse.

"So I've made"—Alain placed his tray of delights in front of the judges—"a whisky, caramel, and banana pudding served with cream cheese ice-cream, and a glass of whisky on the side."

"Now this," declared Wilfred Honey as golden-brown sauce flooded luxuriously from the soft interior of Alain's perfect bake, "is a pudding. It's sticky, it's rich, it takes you right back to your childhood, but it's got a touch of sophistication that elevates it."

"And the cream cheese ice-cream," said Marianne Wolvercote, "works surprisingly well. It just takes the edge off a dish that might otherwise have been a little overwhelming."

Wilfred Honey had taken a second helping. "It's a very balanced dish. And the little banana slices on top add a slightly different texture that stops your mouth getting bored."

"This is good work from you, Alain." Marianne Wolvercote gave him an approving nod. "I'm glad to see you getting off the allotment."

"Thank you." Alain was blushing in a way that Rosaline suspected would be very telegenic. "Thank you so much."

Finally, it was Josie. "I thought I'd try something a bit different this week," she said. "This is a fourteenth-century recipe that I've tried to update for the twenty-first century."

The judges exchanged heavy looks. And with a sense of schadenfreude she tried very hard to be ashamed of, Rosaline knew she was back in the game.

Josie's medieval molten pudding—which was apparently called a payne foundewe—had been described as "valiant" by Wilfred Honey and "definitely not a self-saucing pudding" by Marianne Wolvercote. Either of which could have been the kiss of death on its own and together became a double whammy of doom. Sure enough, Josie was eliminated. And once again, Alain took the top spot. Which, as the person who had made the most successful parkin and the best pudding, he clearly deserved. Even if he had, Rosaline thought resentfully, hopped on the booze train to victory station. But then again, so had she.

She was on her way to the car park when Alain himself came bounding over.

"Congratulations," she told him. And was glad to realise that—petty resentment aside—she mostly meant it.

He grinned. "Oh thanks. I'm glad it came together because I was getting visions of people watching the show and saying, *That Alain guy was really good in week one, but what happened to him?*"

"I don't think you were ever going to be that guy."

"Good. Because I was running out of herbs to forage. So"—he gave her a look that hovered in between hopeful and winsome— "have you thought any more about coming to London this week?"

She hadn't, particularly, but fuck it, she'd work it out. "It'll depend on babysitting," she said. "But I think I can probably do it."

"Marvellous. I'll text you the details."

Checking her phone, Rosaline realised that while she wasn't late for getting picked up, she was sufficiently not-early that her mother would consider it late anyway. "I'm so sorry. I need to dash. My mum'll be waiting."

Which, now that she'd said it, sounded way too fourteen to be something you were comfortable saying to someone you were shagging.

"Don't worry. I'll dash with you. Liv has an abstract relationship with time, so you never know when she's going to turn up."

It wasn't really a dash. It was more sort of a brisk walk down the drive. And sure enough, there at the end of it was Cordelia Palmer standing by the bonnet of her Tesla—which she'd somehow managed to park in the most accusing spot possible.

"I'm sorry I'm late," said Rosaline, who was actually neither.

"Don't worry, I'm used to it." Cordelia Palmer's smile said she was joking, her tone didn't. "You must be Alain. Rosaline, of course, has told us *nothing* about you, but St. John says you gave him a run for his money and that's no mean feat."

Alain offered her one of his deft little cheek kisses. "It's good to meet you, Dr. Palmer."

"And you." There was the faintest of pauses, signalling that only Cordelia Palmer's heroic intervention was preventing this from becoming an irredeemable social failure. "I hope the show's treating you well?"

"Well enough. Actually won this week, as it happens."

"Oh did you? That must have taken a lot of work, balanced against your career commitments."

He gave a modest half-shrug. "Candidly, yes. Especially because I had final designs to submit for a railway conversion project I've been involved in. But my parents always told me that a job worth starting was worth seeing through."

"Yes"—one of Cordelia Palmer's famous sighs—"St. John and I tried to teach Rosaline the same thing."

As far as Rosaline was concerned, they had. It was just that what she'd chosen to see through was having a daughter, not attending an eight-hundred-year-old academic institution. But there was no point having that argument again. She toed at the gravel like the unruly teenager her parents would always see her as.

And that, adorably but unfortunately, seemed to make Alain want to come to her defence. "Then you've succeeded. She's still in the competition and she's planning to go back to university."

Cordelia's eyes flashed with sudden interest. "You see. I said she never tells us anything."

"Oh, it's quite a new idea," he said quickly. "We've only talked about it a couple of times."

"Well, I'm glad you're looking out for her. It's about time someone did."

Once again, Rosaline could have mentioned that she had Lauren and, for that matter, herself. But, once again, there were only so many times you could have the exact same conversation.

"Anyway"—Alain took the smallest of steps backwards—"I've put my foot in it quite enough for one day. I should let you go."

Dreading the conversation that would inevitably descend upon her the moment she and her mother were alone, Rosaline fumbled through a polite goodbye and then got into the Tesla with all the enthusiasm of a damned soul being ushered onto Charon's boat.

"So," said Cordelia Palmer two seconds after the engine started.

And Rosaline kind of expected the sentence to continue but it didn't. She sighed, but less famously than her mother. "Nothing's definite. I'm sorry I didn't tell you. It's something I'm thinking about and I didn't want to get your hopes up."

"We'd just have liked to know you were considering it." A slightly different flavour of Cordelia Palmer pause. This was one that said, *I don't want to say the hurtful thing I'm going to say next, but you have driven me to it.* "Especially given how steadfastly you've ignored the same suggestion when it came from your father and me."

Even for her parents, taking offence at the fact she was doing something they liked now because it meant she hadn't done it earlier was a new low. "Amelie was a lot younger then."

"Amelie's age has nothing to do with it. You'll listen to Alain because you're in a relationship with him, and while I tried to raise you not to rely on men to make all your decisions for you, I apparently failed."

"Weren't you on at me to settle down with him a couple of weeks ago?"

"Your father and I want you to do what makes you happy, you know that."

Rosaline took a breath so deep it made her lungs ache. "And what if I said I was happy right now?"

"Then you'd be lying. To me, your father, and yourself."

"Why?" asked Rosaline ill-advisedly. "Why is it so unimaginable I could be happy raising my daughter and baking my cakes and living in my tiny house and working my ordinary job in a shop that sells pencils?"

"Because, darling, you're better than that."

And, after a moment or two, she turned on Radio 4 in time to catch the start of the shipping forecast.

Week Six

Patisserie

Wednesday

ALAIN HAD ARRANGED for Rosaline to meet him and his friend at a cocktail bar in Shoreditch called Some Kind of Cocktail Bar—which she hoped he'd chosen because it was fairly easy to get to from Liverpool Street station, and not because he thought she might be into it. Which, from the name, she definitely wasn't. As a teenager, her social life had generally revolved around places that had a relaxed attitude towards ID and charged less than thirteen pounds a drink. And as a plucky single mother, her social life had revolved around not having one. Either way, she'd very much missed the little-black-dress-let's-do-cocktails stage of adulthood.

Wait. Was this a little black dress occasion? Did she have a little black dress? Was it appropriate to wear a little black dress to meet a woman you weren't dating? Surely if she turned up in a sexy dress—or as sexy as any of her dresses got—she'd just look desperate and threatened. But if she showed up in jeans and a T-shirt, she'd look like she didn't give a fuck, and she might not even be allowed in the front door.

Though, now she thought about it, that might actually be an advantage. *Whoops, sorry. Didn't realise there'd be a dress code. Let's go somewhere not awful instead.*

In desperation she tried googling the place to see if there was anything on its website that might offer a clue re vibe or attire. But all she found was a black page and the words "coming soon" underneath a massive logo.

"Why don't you wear this?" asked Amelie, tugging on the hem of the very pink, very puffy-shouldered dress that a combination of Allison's traditional aesthetic and Lauren's cruel sense of humour had forced the bridesmaids to wear at their wedding. "It's pretty. And it makes you look like a princess."

"I thought princesses were undemocratic?"

"They are. But yesterday when I didn't want to wash my hair you said this family isn't a democracy."

"She's got you there." Lauren was lounging in the doorway, a glass of pre-babysitting wine firmly in hand.

Rosaline led Amelie gently away from the wardrobe. "Please don't gang up on me. I'm trying to get ready."

"Can I choose your lipstick?" Apparently interpreting being led away from the wardrobe as an invitation to retrain as a makeup artist, Amelie started digging through the contents of Rosaline's dressing table. "What about this one?"

The lipstick in question was deep purple and glittery and had been sitting in the back of Rosaline's makeup drawer since before Amelie was born. "Assuming it's survived the last decade, Mummy's no longer interested in looking like a drag queen."

"Why not? Drag queens are pretty."

Lauren shook her head. "No, darling. I remember your mother's glitter phase very well, and while I was madly in love with her at the time, even I have to admit she did look a bit silly."

"It wasn't *my* glitter phase," protested Rosaline. "It was a generalised glitter phase. Lots of people were doing it."

"You did it quite hard."

"Oh come on. I was seventeen. Everyone makes terrible fashion choices when they're seventeen. What about you in your whole…" Rosaline had been about to say "lick my pussy and call me Byron phase," but Amelie was right there and the makeup box wasn't quite that distracting. "...wannabe Oscar Wilde act? You had a crushed velvet frockcoat and everything."

Lauren gave her a withering look. "I think you'll find I'm still doing that act. And I was wearing that coat yesterday. And what Allison was doing while I wore it, I will never tell you."

"Was she," asked Rosaline, "preparing a detailed analysis of her client's recent expenditure?"

"On this occasion, yes. Last week, definitely not."

"I make sensible fashion choices." That was Amelie, deciding the conversation had gone on long enough without her. "I wear my uniform when I'm at school and other things when I'm not at school. I always have pockets because they're useful and I like things that have pictures on them I like."

"Well, I'm going to wear this." Rosaline turned away from the mirror in her wardrobe door, having settled on a nice pair of slim-fit trousers, boots, and an off-the-shoulder top that had been pretty fashionable about three years ago. "I think it's a bit flirty but not pushing it."

"It would be better if you were an anglerfish," offered Amelie.

"I admit"—Lauren peered disappointedly at the dregs of her wine—"straight men aren't my forte, but I suspect Alain wouldn't like your mummy anywhere near as much if she was an anglerfish."

"I don't know. I'd have one of those cute little lights on my head." Putting her hand to her forehead with one finger hooked over in a vague approximation of an anglerfish's bioluminescent appendage, Rosaline pushed her jaw forward and began swimming about her bedroom.

"I meant," explained Amelie patiently, "that if she was an anglerfish..."

"I am an anglerfish," said Rosaline.

"Stop being silly, Mummy. Anyway, if you were an anglerfish

you'd release a pheromone into the water and a boy anglerfish would follow it and then he'd bite onto your tummy and he'd stay there forever which would be very convenient."

Lauren raised an eyebrow. "Well, that does sound better than most heterosexual dating."

"You'd rather"—nudging Amelie aside, Rosaline dug through her makeup for something more sedate than her ancient stick of Electric Plum—"have a man permanently attached to your stomach, than go for drinks with one?"

"From what I've seen, that's what happens anyway. Why not ditch the preamble?"

"You're going to give my daughter very weird ideas about relationships."

Plopping on the edge of Rosaline's bed, Amelie swung her feet gently back and forth. "If you were a puffer fish he'd draw a pattern in the sand, then if you liked it you'd lay your eggs in it."

"But I'm not a puffer fish," pointed out Rosaline, "I'm an anglerfish."

"Mummy, you're not an anglerfish."

"Yes I am." Makeup as done as she could be bothered to make it, Rosaline screwed her mascara closed and swam towards her daughter. "I'm going to lure you into my mouth with my little light and eat you."

"If you eat me, social services will come and take me away."

There weren't many things that Rosaline regretted telling Amelie about but social services was one of them. Despite the spectre of state intervention, Amelie eventually consented to be chased around the house by a variety of pretend sea creatures, pausing occasionally to correct inaccuracies in her mother's performance.

When they'd grown tired of the game, Rosaline kissed her daughter goodbye, and, leaving her in Lauren's louche but ultimately capable hands, made a dash for the train station.

Some Kind of Cocktail Bar turned out to be pretty much what Rosaline had expected—it was all wooden floors and exposed brickwork and leather sofas that were probably supposed to be vintage but had a faint air of the DFS summer sale. The bar itself was a glassy cage in the middle, which had the unfortunate effect of making the bar staff look like penguins in a zoo as they shuffled back and forth shaking their shakers and garnishing glasses with sprigs of lavender.

Alain and his friend already had both a table and a couple of drinks behind them. Rosaline was sure this had just been a question of logistics, but it still made her feel like she was interrupting.

"Um, hi." She gave an awkward wave. "Sorry I'm late."

Rising, Alain kissed her lightly on the cheek—he smelled faintly of cologne, something clean, sharp, and expensive, which was new. As was the business casual look, with the deep blue jacket over the slightly open shirt. "If anything we're early. Rosaline, this is my friend Liv. Liv, this is Rosaline, who I was telling you about."

Another kiss on the cheek, this time from Liv. Who was frankly devastating—tall and effortless, and poured like a twenty-pound cocktail into the sort of sleek black dress that wouldn't have looked out of place on Audrey Hepburn.

They exchanged lovely-to-meet-yous and then everyone settled back down around the table, Liv and Alain still sharing a sofa, Rosaline opposite them as if she was being interviewed for a girl-friend vacancy. In an effort to fit in, which was always the best reason to start drinking, Rosaline picked up the menu. All the drinks had names like The One with Mint and Berries and The One with a Lot of Crushed Ice.

"Oh God," she said. "It's one of those places, isn't it? I

mean, seriously, who calls their cocktail bar Some Kind of Cocktail Bar?"

"Alain. Liv." A man with a hipster beard and his sleeves rolled up his forearms swooped down on them. "Great to see you. And you've brought a friend."

Alain looked up with a smile. "Hey Robb, this is Rosaline. She's on the TV thing we're not allowed to talk about. Rosaline, this is Robb. We went to university together and he owns the place."

Shit. "Wow." She tried to look like she hadn't been insulting his business two seconds ago. "I . . . you . . . Well, this is some kind of cocktail bar."

"Hence"—he lifted his brows behind his black-rimmed glasses—"the name."

"Yes, I see what you did there."

"We apologise for Robb," said Alain. "He used to be in marketing."

Robb leaned slightly invasively over Rosaline's shoulder. "If you'll permit, may I recommend The One with a Bit of Kick?"

"Do you have anything . . . nonkicky?"

"Well, there's The One Which Doesn't Actually Have Any Alcohol in It."

Rosaline wasn't sure she could face the evening ahead of her without *any* alcohol at all. "Some kind of middle ground, maybe?"

"How about The One That's Quite Summery. It's passion-fruit-infused vodka with verjus and sugar syrup, topped off with soda."

"Sounds great."

"Seriously. Don't mind him," Alain murmured the second his friend was out of earshot. "He's an utter wanker."

Liv laughed. "He really is."

This was hard to navigate. On the one hand, it made her feel slightly better for having criticised the bar. But also paranoid that they'd be saying similar things about her the moment her back was turned. As it was, she gave a weak grin. "Good to know."

The silence that followed managed to pack a lot of awkwardness into a small space of time.

"So," she tried. "Liv . . . what's your . . . I mean . . . I don't . . . what do you do?"

"I run a small interior design firm." She draped one immaculate leg over the other. "It's how I met Alain, actually. There was a Georgian country house near Oxford that the owners wanted renovated."

"I was the outside," added Alain, "she was the inside."

Liv nodded, her edged smile reminding Rosaline faintly of Alain. "Which meant I was charged with installing a full range of modern conveniences in a listed building without sacrificing either comfort or the original aesthetic. And Alain put a big pond in the garden."

"As I recall"—Alain's tone perfectly bisected the boundary between teasing and deadly serious—"I reimagined several hectares of eighteenth-century landscaping while you spent the whole time saying 'I think we'll just leave that as it is.'"

"Actually," Liv cut over him, "leaving things as they were was the most difficult part of the job. Because the house was intended for a family, I needed to make sure that whatever original features were maintained formed part of an environment that would speak to a child throughout their development. Inspiration is such an important part of a child's life, don't you agree?"

Rosaline blinked, slightly dazed and uncertain whether this had been the friendly kind of bickering or the kind that led to everyone going home in separate taxis. "Well. Yes. I suppose so. Do you have children, then?"

"Oh heavens no." Liv's horrified laugh echoed off the exposed brickwork of Some Kind of Cocktail Bar. "I was speaking purely professionally."

As far as Rosaline was concerned, speaking about children without having children was speaking very much as an amateur. "To be honest, I think kids can find their own inspiration pretty well. I mean, my daughter is into deep-sea fish at the moment, and before that it was Norse mythology."

There was a pause. "You have a daughter?" asked Liv in that *What went wrong in your life?* voice.

"Did Alain not mention that?"

"He did not." She turned an arch look on Alain. "What else have you been hiding?"

He smirked. "That's for me to know, and for you to find out."

Rosaline glanced between them. "So, what *has* he told you about me?"

"Not very much. You know what he's like. He's not the kiss-and-tell sort."

"Which means," Rosaline pointed out, "he did mention kissing."

"*I* mentioned kissing. *He* demurred. But he did say you went to Cambridge, you're very pretty, and he likes you very much."

Shading his eyes with his hand, Alain shifted uncomfortably. "You're embarrassing me, Liv."

"I'm intending to, Alain. You're rather adorable when you like a girl."

"Ah yes," he said wryly. "Adorable is exactly how an adult man wants an adult woman to see him."

"I'm sorry, darling." Liv did not sound at all repentant. "And Rosaline, you don't have anything to worry about. He's been nothing but uncharacteristically sweet about you. He said you're fun and brave and doing well in the baking competition. In fact, if I didn't know him better, I'd think he was a little bit jealous."

"I'm not jealous," Alain insisted. "I just had one bad week that I now regret telling you about."

Rosaline's cocktail was finally delivered by a penguin on day release, and she took a slightly needy sip. It was fine. Probably not worth the exorbitant cost, but definitely summery. "He's got nothing to be jealous about. He's doing far better than I am."

"I suppose"—Liv reached for her own drink—"it must add at least the tiniest charge to the relationship, being in competition."

Alain rolled his eyes. "We're not in competition, Liv."

"We're both doing our best," Rosaline agreed. "And whatever happens happens."

"Well, that's very magnanimous of you." With one finger, Liv traced the rim of her glass, making it sing. "Especially since we both know Alain is competitive *AF*."

Did Rosaline know that? Looking back, she thought she probably did know it, but maybe didn't know she knew it. Also, who said "AF" in real life?

"I'm not competitive"—Alain was pouting slightly and not wholly playfully—"I just set myself high standards. And I wouldn't have invited Rosaline to meet you if I'd known you were going to gang up on me."

Liv's gaze darted briefly to Rosaline and back again. "Sorry, Alain. Us girls have to stick together."

It was a principle that Rosaline mostly agreed with—although she wasn't quite sure how it applied to two friends snarking at each other over cocktails.

"But anyway." Liv leaned conspiratorially forward. "Enough about us. Tell me something about Rosaline-um-Palmer that'll surprise me."

Okay, so that was cute when Alain said it. At least, she'd assumed it was cute when Alain said it. But it was weird coming from somebody else. "You were surprised I had a kid."

"I was surprised Alain hadn't mentioned you had a kid. It's not quite the same thing."

"I wanted to let her tell you on her own terms," put in Alain. "She's sensitive about it."

"Sensitive" wasn't the word Rosaline would have used. But since, as Alain enjoyed pointing out, she'd concocted a fake trip to Malawi—and did Liv know about that too?—to hide her actual child from him, she was a bit low on legs to stand on.

Liv hmmed thoughtfully. "That makes sense. I suppose some people can be quite judgemental."

"You get used to it." Rosaline shrugged, not wanting to have a repeat of her conversation with Josie. "But I'm not really a very surprising person."

"That's very far from true." Alain was giving her one of his *Think better of yourself, Rosaline* looks. "You've done a lot of things most people only talk about."

"Have I?"

"Well, take Liv here. She's been saying she's going to get a tattoo for years. But does she have one? Does she bollocks."

"It's true," Liv admitted, blushing slightly. "The truth is, there's quite a lot I've been meaning to explore in my life that I've always backed away from at the last minute."

While she appreciated that Alain saw the best in her—well, usually saw the best in her—Rosaline wasn't quite sure if she was okay with him using her to make his friend feel bad about herself. Except making each other feel bad seemed to be kind of their thing. "I think, for me, it's always been that old cliché about how I'd rather regret some of the things I've done, than all the things I've never dared to do."

"But what if it changes who you are? Or people don't understand."

Rosaline didn't consider herself the least neurotic person she'd ever met, but this seemed conservative even by the nice middle-class standards she was accustomed to falling short of. "It's just a tattoo. No one has to know about it."

"I'll know."

"Then it'll remind you of who you were in a different time,

and that can be nice. I mean, it can be sad, too, sometimes. But I like remembering I can be the sort of person who does something because she wants to and does it all the way."

"I think," said Liv softly, "I'm beginning to understand what Alain sees in you."

"Um. Thanks?"

She had a nonspecifically wistful look. "I wish I could be more like that."

This was beginning to make Rosaline feel depressingly hypocritey. Because, while she *could* be like that, she mostly wasn't. After all, being a sexy butterfly who went where the wind took her wouldn't have created an environment she wanted her daughter to grow up in. Or maybe she was still like that, but *like that* looked different now. When she'd been seventeen, she'd wanted to get a tattoo and to get laid, and she'd got both. Now she was twenty-seven, she wanted to provide for her daughter, show the nation she made nice cakes, and, um, get laid. And wasn't she, in her own way, working on all three? It was just that they took a bit longer than a trip to a tattoo parlour or a quickie in Lauren's room before her mum got home.

"It's not magic," Rosaline said, "and I'm not special. If you want to do things, you can do them. And if you don't, that's okay as well. Not everyone needs a tattoo."

There was a thoughtful silence.

"Why don't I"—Alain rose—"get us another round."

Despite the setting and a shaky start, the evening wasn't going as badly as Rosaline had feared. Even so, with Liv's slightly too-interested gaze upon her, she very much welcomed the cushion of another drink.

Saturday

"HELLO," BOOMED GRACE Forsythe, "good morning, and welcome, my fabulous, flaky final five."

A pause so the cameras could gather shots of them looking bashfully pleased to have made it this far and adorably apprehensive of what was to come.

"This time you're in Marianne's hands because we're about to delve into the intricate world of madeleines and meringues, macarons and mille-feuille, pièce montée and Paris-Brest. That's right, it's patisserie week."

Marianne Wolvercote prowled forward, looking especially in need of a cigarette holder. "Today's blind bake is a savoury recipe that requires a delicate touch, a mastery of choux pastry—"

"And a willingness," added Grace Forsythe, "to be just a little bit cheesy."

"I want you," continued Marianne Wolvercote, "to make twenty-eight perfectly formed, identical gougères. They're a personal favourite, so don't disappoint me."

Grace Forsythe bounced on the balls of her feet. "You have one hour. On the count of three. Three, darlings."

Okay, this could have been a lot worse. Rosaline had been worried they'd ask her to make something fiddly with layers, and she'd never done well at fiddly with layers. There were always so many elements that one of them was bound to go wrong—especially with time pressure—and there she'd be with a runny crème pat or fruit in the wrong place and Marianne Wolvercote saying something like, "This lacks both joy *and* finesse."

Anyway. Her joyless pudding was in the past. Her future lay in making twenty-eight cheesy buns from a recipe that she knew, without even looking at it, would start with the line "Make choux pastry."

"Preheat oven to a high temperature," said the recipe.

Dammit.

"Make choux pastry," it continued.

Ha.

Rosaline awarded herself an A-minus for effort. And got on with the choux.

It wasn't anybody's favourite pastry because it was tricky to work with and the bake-verse was filled with weird myths about how you knew it was cooked properly. But she and Amelie had tried to make profiteroles once, and while the bake had gone horrendously badly, they'd had a lot of fun with the piping bags and eaten left-over crème pat straight from the spoon.

Once the dough started pulling away from the sides of the pan, Rosaline plopped it into a bowl and tried to remember what you did with the eggs.

"I'm trying to remember," she told a hovering camera without being prompted, "what you do with the eggs. I think if you put them in while it's too hot, they'll cook and then you're making…scrambled egg buns. When I made choux with my daughter, we squished it until it cooled, but honestly, that might just be because she likes squishing things, and I think that did overagitate the dough. And I definitely don't want my choux to be agitated. I want it to be"—she was doing hand gestures again—"mellow and friendly. The kind of dough you could go for a drink with."

Rosaline prodded tentatively at her choux-to-be. It was not exactly hot but not exactly cool, and she had no idea what that meant, so she decided to wait before chucking eggs in it. And somehow, waiting and trusting her instincts had stopped being the most terrifying thing in the universe.

It seemed impossible, but had she actually got used to the ball-room? It still didn't feel like her own kitchen because it was a giant oak-panelled room in a stately home full of TV cameras, but her workstation had grown familiar to her as the weeks had passed. As had the other contestants: Nora with her incessant narration, Alain with his obsessive focus, Anvita's tendency towards chaos, and Harry's painstaking care that sometimes disintegrated into paralysis.

And in two weeks it would all be over. Or one week. Or, if things went very badly, zero weeks. It was probably a bit late in the game to work out that she'd miss it. The place and the people and even the challenges. Because even when she fucked them up abominably and made a leche that wouldn't dulce or a joyless pudding, she was still baking. And she loved baking and the show made that okay.

Made it into something that millions of people shared and appreciated and celebrated.

Instead of something she did because she couldn't be a doctor.

It had been a fairly speedy challenge and a fairly brisk judging—Rosaline thought the production company might have been going easy on them because the next day's baketacular was prob-ably going to be gruelling. She hadn't won but she hadn't lost—that misfortune having fallen on Anvita, who had definitely put her eggs in too early. Nora and Harry had both done well, Nora just claiming the top spot with a combination of long-honed technical skills and giving no fucks.

"I can't be doing with patisserie," she told Colin Thrimp. "It's just regular baking but smaller. And who wants less of something nice?"

Harry, meanwhile, was left explaining his unexpected success to an un-Thrimped camera crew. "When they said what the challenge was, I hadn't got a"—the pause of someone trying not to fuck all over the BBC—"bloomin' clue. But it turns out, I make 'em all the time. Only in my house, we don't call 'em gougères. We call 'em cheesy bites."

Interviews concluded, they were left milling around on the lawn, everyone aware that it was slightly too early to start drinking and not quite willing to be the first to do it anyway. Detaching herself like the man with no name at the end of a Western, Anvita wandered off and sat down under a tree, staring moodily over the grounds.

"She's having a bit of a time, ain't she?" said Harry.

Nora made the sort of noise your gran makes when you fall over and scrape your knee. "Poor dear. It's tough for you young things. She'll be okay, though. Most people are."

"I'm sure she will," offered Rosaline. "But if the way she's feeling now is anything like I was feeling last week, then it super sucks."

Alain's hands landed gently on Rosaline's shoulders, and she half turned so he could whisper in her ear. "I'm quite disappointed as well. I think I might need to head back to the Lodge and spend some quality time with my recipes."

"Oh." She wasn't entirely sure what Alain had to be disappointed about given that he'd done about as well as her and significantly better than Anvita. "Um, okay?"

"I'll see you later?" Without waiting for a reply, he strode off—his long legs carrying him swiftly across the lawn and away.

"I think," announced Nora, "I'm going to take advantage of this lovely afternoon to sit on a bench with a glass of lemonade and finish my book. The Greek billionaire has just offered the virgin cellist a very saucy proposal, so I think we're about to get to the good bits."

While Rosaline was still processing this, Harry asked, "How many of them books you read, anyway?"

"About one a week for the last fifty years."

Rosaline couldn't quite help doing the maths. "That's two and a half thousand books."

"Yes, my husband's forever making bookshelves. I should probably give them to charity, but it's a collection now."

"Well"—Harry gave an easygoing shrug—"don't let us keep you from your billionaire."

Nora grinned. "Wild horses couldn't. You certainly can't."

That left Harry and Rosaline alone in front of the hotel, watching Anvita being sad at a distance.

"It's a bit weird having all this time, init?" remarked Harry. "I feel like I should do something about Anvita, but I reckon I'll bollocks it up."

"I'm sure she'll be glad to know we care."

"I'd probably say one of them things that's not allowed anymore like, *Cheer up, love, it might never happen.*"

"Why don't we," suggested Rosaline, on the assumption that Harry was probably right and Anvita would prefer a differently phrased encouragement, "ask if she wants to come to the village with us?"

"Yeah. All right. Why don't you do that, and I'll...kinda stand next to you."

She gave him a confused look. "You don't have to come if you don't want to."

"Nah, I'll come. It's just I don't want her to think I'm trying to pull her."

"Well, she won't?"

"I know. I just...I have the worry."

"You mean"—she smiled up at him—"that she'll think you're an utter ballsack?"

"Yeah."

"Fair enough." She set off towards Anvita's Sad Tree of Sadness. "I'll be a ballsack for both of us."

Harry's arm nudged gently against hers. "Mate, the things you say."

"It was your ballsack originally. I just made use of it."

"I really would like us to stop talking about my ballsack if we could."

"Why," asked Anvita, who they suddenly realised was now within earshot, "are you talking about Harry's ballsack?"

Rosaline sat down on the grass next to her. "We were wondering if you wanted to come to the village with us."

"That doesn't answer the ballsack question."

This was probably a sign that Anvita was feeling better. "You'd almost think it was a deliberate choice."

There was a pause. "Is this a 'pity' *let's go to the village*?"

"It's a *We finished a bit early, I thought it might be nice, and you've had a bad day* let's go to the village."

Anvita sighed. "I knew I was going to fuck up patisserie. I mean, who thinks, *I've got some people coming over this weekend. I know what'll be nice, I'll make twenty-eight mille-feuille and a croquembouche*?"

"You've still got tomorrow, though, ain't you?" said Harry. "It's just a big cake with biscuits on it."

Anvita made a visible, though not totally successful, effort to be cheered.

"How about," suggested Rosaline, "we discuss how much we will or won't fuck up tomorrow on the way to the village?"

Climbing to her feet, Anvita dusted the grass off her jeans. "What's with you and the village? Do they have, like, an orgasm museum or something?"

"I think they have, like, a pub? Maybe a nice tearoom?"

"So instead of staying in the hotel having a drink in the bar the way we usually do, your special *make Anvita happy* treat is to walk twenty minutes up the road so we can have a slightly different drink in a slightly different bar."

"Yes," said Rosaline. "Yes it is."

"All right. I'm in."

They set out for the nearest village, which rejoiced in the name of Crinkley Furze. Rosaline wasn't sure, but she suspected its economy had been ever so slightly distorted by the popularity of *Bake Expectations* because there were an *awful* lot of cake shops, although it was late enough in the day that most of them were closed. And even if they hadn't been, cake was not something that any of them were feeling a particular lack of in their lives.

Crinkley Furze had two pubs, one of which—the Duke's Arm's—had that "local pub for local people" vibe that suggested three stray reality TV contestants would be decidedly unwelcome, and the other of which—the Rusty Badger—was the kind of place that put prosciutto on its burgers. They went Badger and found the choice of non-TV-grade food slightly overwhelming.

"What even is ceps?" asked Harry, picking up the menu. "They use it on *MasterChef* all the time, and I've never worked out which bit it is."

Anvita, too, claimed a menu. "Isn't it that long green stuff?"

"Nah. That's samphire. Which I know 'cos they only do it with fish 'cos it's a sea vegetable. And apparently they're all too good for mushy peas."

"When I'm done with the show," said Rosaline, "I'm going to go on *MasterChef* and my signature dish is going to be ceps served five ways, and I'm going to call it Everything You Ever Wanted to Know About Ceps but Were Too Afraid to Ask."

That made Harry laugh. "Bit long-winded for me. I'd probably go with The Joy of Ceps."

"Sounds delicious," added Anvita. "I might go so far as to say I Want Your Ceps."

There was a pause as they menued. But Harry apparently still had ceps on the brain. "It's in a coco bean and ceps soup. So it must be something what goes well with coco. But it's not like marshmallows, is it? It's probably like…another bean? Or a type of pepper maybe?"

"We could google this." Anvita was already pulling out her phone.

But Rosaline firmly covered it with her hand. "No. It's a mystery. I'm not having spoilers. What else is in the soup?"

"Cavolo nero."

"I know that one," said Rosaline. "It's fancy kale."

"Mate, all kale is fancy where I come from. If it's not fancy, it's called greens. And there's also Parmesan in it. So it's gotta be something that goes well with coco, cheese, and greens. I don't think anything goes with coco, cheese, and greens."

Anvita obligingly turned her phone facedown. "Weirdest *Only Connect* round ever. And I think Harry should order the soup and we should bet on what the ceps are."

"Why am I," asked Harry plaintively, "the one what's ordering the mystery soup?"

"It's your punishment for doing better than us in the blind bake."

He sighed. "Fine. I reckon it's a type of bean what isn't a coco bean because they always put more beans than you want in bean soup."

"I don't care what it's been," interjected Rosaline in a moment of weakness, "I care what it is now."

"Mate." Harry shook his head. "I can't believe I thought you was a classy bird."

"I'm still a classy bird. But one of the tragedies of being a single mother is you have to do your own dad jokes. Anyway, I think ceps are… They sound like they'd be a bit like capers."

"What?" cried Anvita. "That would be horrible with kale and coco beans. It'd be all briney and yick."

"I said *like* capers. Sort of little round things that you don't know what they're called or what they're bringing to the dish. Now come on. What's your pick?"

Resting an elbow on the table, Anvita screwed her face up thoughtfully. "Judging by the flavours already in the dish, you'd need something earthy to tie it together. So it's probably some kind of mushroom?"

"You think"—Harry gave her his flattest stare—"it's chocolate mushroom soup?"

"I'm not sure, but I suspect coco beans without an 'a' are different from cocoa beans with an 'a.'"

"Hang on." Rosaline did a *Hold your horses* gesture. "Are you going double or nothing here? Are you committing to the prediction that not only are ceps mushrooms but also that coco beans aren't cocoa beans?"

"Hell to the yes. What do I win?"

There was a silence.

"Our marginally increased respect?" offered Rosaline.

Anvita's lip curled. "You must be really fun at poker night. I'll see your respect and raise you slightly more respect."

"Okay. Losers will buy the winner another drink because this is already quite expensive and I'm not going to let my child starve because Mummy is bad at food trivia."

"Fuck, yeah," shouted Anvita, startling an innocent waiter who had just set down a bowl of mushroom soup in front of Harry.

Rosaline held up a finger. "Hold on. It could be brown because of the cocoa beans."

"There"—the excitement in Anvita's voice was almost adorable—

"that thing on the top. That's definitely a mushroom. And it must be a cep. Because those are Parmesan flakes and that's cavolo nero and I bet there's beans in it and I bet they're not chocolate."

Nervously, Harry dipped in a spoon. "She's right. They ain't."

"Who da...woman? Who's got two thumbs and can correctly identify slightly obscure cooking ingredients." Anvita turned the digits in question towards herself. "This person." She turned them upright. "Suck it. Now buy me a drink. Buy me two drinks. Because you are *losers*."

Trying not to take more than her share, Rosaline spread some of the mackerel pâté she was splitting with Anvita over a piece of toast. "So how are the mysterious ceps?"

Harry shrugged. "It's mushroom soup. It's nice mushroom soup, but I'm not sure I'd pay seven quid for it. I mean, apart from the fact that I will, 'cos otherwise that'd be a crime. But it's not what I'd normally have on a Saturday night."

"What do you normally have on a Saturday night?" asked Anvita. "Is it two lagers and the bird next door?"

"Well, Mrs. Patel is eighty, and she's a nice lady, but I don't think she's into me that way. Sometimes, I'm out with the lads and I'll get a pie from the chippy. And sometimes, I'm at home and I'll make myself..." He paused and thought for a moment. "Actually, I'll usually make myself a pie."

Anvita gazed at him, still slightly perplexed. "I don't know why I'm surprised by this because I see you baking every week."

"Yeah, it's not just something I do on telly. It's how I eat. Like, I sometimes make a little one for tea, or a medium-sized one to last me a couple of days, or a big one if the family's coming round. It's pies, mate, not rocket science."

Their starters finished, the waiter Anvita had scared came back and took away the crockery. Harry had the look of a man resigning himself to having paid way over the odds for a bowl of mushrooms, and Anvita, without the distraction of telling her friends to suck it, was falling back into the doldrums of her poor showing in the blind bake.

"So"—Rosaline attempted to rouse her companions—"what's everyone got planned for tomorrow?"

Harry shrugged. "Like I said. Big cake with biscuits on it."

"No, but"—if Anvita hadn't perked up, she was certainly doing a good impression of it—"you've got to have a theme, right?"

"Well. Um." Harry fidgeted. "It's sort of a...like...it's gonna be a bit blue. And maybe a bit sparkly. Gonna have some fondant on it. Which I might shape and stuff."

If he'd been trying to discourage Anvita's interest, he'd picked exactly the opposite of the right strategy. "Why are you being weird about this? Is it a secret? Are you making a secret cake? Is it going to be decorated with the nuclear launch codes?"

"In sparkly blue fondant," Rosaline added.

"No," he mumbled, "it's a bit...hard to describe."

Anvita plonked her elbows on the table and subjected him to an interrogative glare. "You're embarrassed, aren't you? You do remember this is going to be on television?"

"Yeah, but I'll be braced for it then."

"Blue and sparkly and a bit embarrassing," repeated Anvita. "We must be able to work it out from that. Is it *Magic Mike*–themed? Are you going to be baking with your shirt off?"

"What? On the BBC? At eight o'clock on a Tuesday. Not bloody likely."

"You mean"—Anvita's eyes were sparkling—"you *would* bake with your shirt off after the watershed? Are you aiming for a spin-off called *Dobson After Dark*?"

Harry seemed genuinely appalled. "I know you've had a bad day, but you're going to stop this right now."

"It'd be brilliant, though. You could be the male Nigella Lawson."

Without her telling it to, Rosaline's brain put together a quick mock-up of what a male Nigella Lawson would be like. And to give it credit, it did get to Harry pretty quickly.

"You could be all," Anvita went on, "*What you need to do is knead it firmly, but tenderly, caressing the dough with your thumbs and fingertips.*"

"Mate, that'd make rubbish dough." Harry paused. "Also, if that's what women find sexy, I've been doing it very wrong."

Rosaline grinned. "If it helps, so have I."

To Harry's visible relief, their mains arrived a moment later. True to form, he'd gone for the pie, she'd gone for the cheapest thing on the menu, and Anvita had taken the dish with the coolest name, which in this case had been a pan-fried skate wing.

"I was expecting it to be wingier," admitted Anvita. "But it just looks like a fish triangle." She stuck a fork in it. "It's all right, though. Fishy. How's the tagliatelle?"

Currently, it was dangling from Rosaline's mouth in a thoroughly indecorous manner. "Mmmestly mmwishing—" She managed to partially de-pasta herself. "I'm wishing I'd chosen something less messy."

"Don't worry about it, mate." Harry glanced up from his two-bird pie. "I know there's a bunch of long words in the menu, but at the end of day, it's just a pub, init? Anyway. It's your turn. What you doing tomorrow?"

"How can it be my turn?" protested Rosaline, half convinced she had mascarpone on her chin, but not sure how to wipe away something that might only exist in her imagination. "When you totally wouldn't tell us what you were doing?"

"I did tell you. It's blue and sparkly and a cake. And it's got macaroons on it."

"Is it Elsa from *Frozen*?" asked Rosaline. "I promise, we'll *let it go* if it's Elsa from *Frozen*."

"I did think about doing Elsa, but—oh right. Yeah. I get it. Very funny, mate."

"Is it," Anvita suggested, "unicorn poo?"

Harry's brow crinkled. "Why would unicorn poo be blue?"

"Because they're magical."

"And magical things have blue poo?"

"Or"—something bubbled up from the lake of Rosaline's "was going to be a doctor" factoids—"they've all got porphyria."

"You what?"

"I see that 'you what' and raise you an 'I beg your pardon?'"

"Porphyria," Rosaline explained. "It's the thing George III might have had. It turns your poo blue."

Harry gave a heavy sigh. "Mate, I have to tell my nieces not to talk about poo at the table, but they're all under ten."

Something clicked in Rosaline's brain. "You have nieces. They are under ten. And they're girls. And you're not doing *Frozen*. It's a mermaid, isn't it?"

"Bloody hell." Harry went pink to his ears. "Yeah, all right. I'm doing a mermaid. I thought it'd be nice. I'm doing it diving into the cake so you just see the tail bit. 'Cos that way I don't have to do boobs on telly."

Anvita nodded sagely. "Good call. Because otherwise the judges would come round and say, *What are you doing*, and you'd have to say, *I'm moulding a pair of fondant whammers*."

"I mean"—Harry had yet to return to his original shade—"I wouldn't have said it exactly like that."

Unable to resist, Rosaline asked, "So how would you have said it?"

"I think I'd have gone with . . . 'This is my mermaid. Right now finishing off her bra area.'"

"That's my favourite name for them." Anvita was noticeably giggling. "I love it when my boyfriend tells me, 'Anvita, your bra area looks great in that dress.'"

"I'm not trying to pull the mermaid," muttered Harry. "I'm trying to talk about the mermaid on telly without saying 'tits.'"

To be honest, Rosaline could have carried on teasing Harry about his hypothetical fondant boobies for quite a lot longer. But he had fixed her electricity for free. "I'm doing space," she announced.

Harry slanted her a mischievous look. "Ah, so blue and sparkly as well then?"

"Maybe more purple and sparkly? And with macaron planets."

"Well," said Anvita loftily, "these are nice ideas. But I—I should warn you—am going to smash it. I'm making a three-tiered vanilla-bean sponge with Swiss meringue buttercream icing and macarons cascading luxuriously from top to bottom."

"But what's its theme?" Harry's imitation of Anvita's tone was not especially accurate. "I thought you had to have a theme."

"The theme is Marie Antoinette."

There was a pause. "How is a bunch of macarons like Marie Antoinette?"

"Because"—Anvita tossed her head proudly—"they're fabulous."

In the end, Harry had picked up the bill. Not, as he insisted, because he was the only bloke but because Rosaline was a single mum with a minimum wage job and Anvita was still a trainee.

"When you both get rich and famous," he said as they walked down the main street of the village in the deepening twilight, "you can pay me back."

Anvita eyed him curiously. "If I'd known electricians were this flush, I'd have picked a different career. Though, that said, I do look hot in glasses."

"It's just the family business." Harry gave one of his slightly self-conscious shrugs. "It's what we do."

They strolled on a little farther, the path wending lazily round the hill towards Patchley House and Park. During the day, pretty as the village was, the cars and the road and Tesco Express made it hard to forget that you were in the twenty-first century, a short train ride from London, and about twenty minutes from the filming of a popular television show.

Now, though, the magic of streetlight and shadows made the old stone and the bare fields real in a way they hadn't been before. They'd come out of a mediocre gastropub, but in the pale orange glow from its windows, it looked like it belonged in a fairy tale. Tucking her hands in her pockets, Rosaline gazed up at the sky. The stars were so naked when you weren't in the city. It made the whole world feel different. Newer, somehow.

"Let's take a shortcut," announced Anvita. "It'll be fun."

Harry did not seem to share her faith that this would be a once-in-a-lifetime thrill ride. "It's twenty minutes up the road."

"Okay. So not a shortcut so much as a let's-take-an-exciting-walk-across-some-fields-in-the-dark-cut."

"And you don't think"—Harry still sounded unconvinced—"it'll turn into a let's-fall-in-a-ditch-and-have-to-do-tomorrow's-episode-hopping-cut?"

"It's fine. I was a girl guide. I can do orienteering."

"And I've got my silver Duke of Edinburgh award," added Rosaline. "What can go wrong?"

"Lots of things could go wrong. We could step in cowpats. Get done for trespassing. Or walk for half an hour and then realise we're on the wrong side of the bloody river."

Anvita brandished a finger. "Counterpoint: if we go back now, I have to spend the rest of the evening sat in my room, sobbing over the failure of my gougères."

"Fine, but when we get back to the hotel and you're covered in brambles and mud, don't blame me."

So they took a sharp right turn over a stile, which, according to the little green sign, led to some kind of public footpath. Sceptical as Harry had been, Rosaline was glad for the walk—they'd spent the last five weekends at the same hotel, alternating between extreme stress and mild boredom, and the minimal freedom offered by a short ramble through the countryside was, well, it wasn't much, but by God she'd take it.

"We should sing a song," said Anvita. "Like that one about how you love to go a-wandering."

"You mean...'I love to go a-wandering'?" asked Rosaline, half singing.

"That's the one. 'Something something ack. Something something something something knapsack on my bag.'"

"'Val-deriiiiiiii,'" they both burst out. "'Val-deraaaaaa.'"

Harry pulled on the collar of his polo shirt like he was trying to hide behind it. "Leave it out, people live round here. We're going to be them annoying tourists what walked past their back gardens shouting 'val-deri' at 'em."

"Okay, fine." Anvita paused for zero seconds before coming up with a new idea. "I spy with my little eye...something beginning with 'g.'"

"Grass," suggested Harry.

She scowled. "Right. Give me a second. And watch out because this is going to be hard. I spy with my little eye...something beginning with 't.'"

"Trees," suggested Rosaline. "Or trousers."

"No." Anvita shook her head. "But good one."

"And not trainers or T-shirt or anything else any of us are wearing?"

Anvita managed to project smug through the gloom. "Do you give up?"

"Yeah," Harry sighed. "We give up."

"No we don't." Probably if Rosaline had been going to get hypercompetitive over anything, it should have been the television competition she was on. Not a spontaneous game of I Spy in the dark. But her honour was at stake here. "I can totally get this. Tortoiseshell butterfly. Thistles. Tyre tracks. Somebody's thumb."

Harry put a gentle hand on her arm. "Seriously, mate. You get one more guess and we're cutting you off."

"Toad. Tawny owl. Tannenbaum."

"Um," said Anvita. "It's tractor."

There was no way, Rosaline was certain, she had missed a large piece of agricultural machinery. "What fucking tractor? There's no fucking tractor."

"Well, there was when I said it. It was across the field."

"There was not."

"There so was."

"Show me."

Harry got as far as "Uh, guys," but Rosaline and Anvita had already started backtracking.

"There." Anvita pointed triumphantly at a vague shape in the distance. "Tractor."

Rosaline squinted through the darkness. "I think that's some-one's car."

"Isn't it a combine harvester?" asked Harry.

"Or two bales of hay quite close to each other."

"It's a tractor," insisted Anvita. "Come on. I'll prove it to you."

Swept up in the drama of the moment, they scrambled over a gate and began running towards the ambiguous machine, which was turning out to be much farther away than they thought it was.

Harry cupped his hands to his mouth, calling after them: "That's someone's field. You can't just run into someone's field. That's like a farmer's house."

"It's fine," Anvita called back. "People must do this all the ti—"

The next thing Rosaline knew she was sprinting alone across

the furrows. And it took her a moment to remember that she wasn't going to win anything by leaving Anvita in a heap on the ground. She jogged to a halt.

"Ow," said Anvita. "Ow."

Harry was also bearing down on them. "I'm not saying I told you so. But I am saying I could if I wanted to."

Kneeling, Rosaline checked Anvita for signs of obvious breakage. "Are you okay?"

"My ankle hurts and I've scraped my knee. And I'm going to have to film in this top tomorrow and it's covered in poo. How am I going to bake a cake worthy of Marie Antoinette covered in poo?"

"It's not poo, it's mud."

"Oh, well, that's fine then."

"I'm pretty sure"—Rosaline dredged up her first-aid training from, ironically enough, her Duke of Edinburgh award—"it's just...hurt. It's not broken or fractured, and it's probably not even sprained."

"People are going to think it's poo. My nan's going to watch this and she's going to say, *Anvita, I watched you on the television and I was very proud until I saw you were covered in poo.*"

Hooking an arm under Anvita's shoulders, Rosaline helped her to her feet. "You do realise you could have genuinely injured yourself. A slightly dirty top is very much the least of your problems. Now come on, let's go back to the hotel."

"Fuck no," cried Anvita. "I've been wounded in pursuit of this fucking tractor. I'm showing you the tractor."

Harry put his hands up. "How about we believe you that it's a tractor, and we admit we lost the game of I Spy, and we all go home."

"No. My integrity has been maligned and I'm showing you this tractor."

"I don't need to see the tractor." In some ways, it would have been easy for Rosaline to stop Anvita pressing on with the great tractor quest, but it would have involved letting her fall flat on her face again. So she grudgingly shuffled along beside her. "I'm sorry. You won. I'm a loser. Suck it, me."

After about twice as long as any of them had expected it would take, they arrived in front of a large machine that none of them could identify.

"Is it a harrow, maybe?" asked Rosaline. "Or a tiller?"

Anvita nodded. "I think it's probably a tiller. Tiller begins with 't.'"

"You can't retroactively change your I Spy word to match what the thing you spied turned out to be."

"I'm injured and covered in poo. I can do what I like."

"And I'm supporting you and letting you get poo all over me, so no you can't."

"It's mud," said Harry. "It's just mud. Stick it in to soak for a bit, leave it to dry overnight. You'll be fine."

They contemplated the tiller, tractor, or, at Harry's suggestion, muck spreader a while longer.

"All right," Anvita concluded. "We can go now. Um, which way is it?"

Harry glanced around vaguely. "You're the one what did orienteering in the guides. You tell us."

"Yes, but when I did orienteering I had a compass, a map, and, most importantly, three other girls who knew what they were doing."

"All right." Harry's gaze settled on Rosaline. "It's down to you, Duke of Edinburgh."

This couldn't be that difficult. Fields were square. You had a one in four chance of getting it right. "That way," said Rosaline decisively.

And off they went.

Two fields in, the road had yet to emerge, and Rosaline was

beginning to remember that she'd spent most of her Duke of Edinburgh sneaking off to make out with Lauren.

"Hey, Rosaline," began Anvita.

"Look. If we pick a direction and keep walking, we'll find some people eventually. And then we'll just tell them we're idiots on a baking show and—"

"It's not that." Anvita's tone was unusually careful. "It's more...you see that thing over there, with the four legs and the horns. Is that a bull?"

"Maybe," suggested Harry, "it's a tractor."

Anvita poked him. "Not the time. If that's a bull, we're dead."

"Nah, it's all right. I saw this on a programme once. What you do is, you run towards it, shouting, and that scares it away."

It was hard to see through the heavy darkness that had crept in with the night, but there was definitely something out there. It was a moving blob with a faint aura of horned malice, and Rosaline was sure it was staring at them.

"No," she said quickly. "Don't do that. Because if you're wrong, you're going to get gored by a bull."

"I think," Anvita put in, "you're supposed to grab it by the ring through its nose."

Harry snorted. "While it's running at you? How's that meant to work?"

"I think it's like judo and you sort of...use its own momentum against it."

"How about"—this was Rosaline, whose fear of imminent trampling was not being alleviated by the conversation—"we walk slowly away and don't do anything to provoke it."

A strange and ominous grunting came from the shadows.

"Oh shit," whisper-screamed Anvita, "it's provoked."

"You want me to run at it?" asked Harry.

"No, it will definitely kill you. We need to run away in a zigzag."

"I thought that was crocodiles."

The thing in the dark was moving towards them now, and quickly. Rosaline also tried to pick up the pace, but Anvita's ankle had other ideas.

"I can't go any faster." Anvita gave her a little push. "Leave me. Save yourselves."

"I'm not going to leave you in a field," protested Rosaline.

"You've got a child. Think of your daugh—"

At this moment, Harry swept Anvita off the ground and into his arms. "All right. I've got her. Peg it. Don't look back. You're not supposed to look back."

Rosaline did not, in fact, look back—just raced through the grass, convinced at any moment she was going to hear the thud of hooves behind her and then the grisly crunch of Harry and Anvita getting ground into tapenade by an enraged bull. She hit the fence and, although still concerned for her safety, couldn't help being a little proud of the agility with which she managed to vault over it.

Harry arrived a moment later, bundling Anvita over the top before clambering across himself. They had a few moments to ride the adrenaline wave together, breathless and giggling with relief, before the goat caught up with them.

It gave an aggrieved bleat. Then started nibbling the edge of Harry's shirt.

"Did you see that?" yelled Anvita. "He totally superheroed me out of that field. He literally saved my life."

Harry scratched his jaw awkwardly. "I mean, from a goat."

"It was a bull at the time."

"I'm pretty sure it was always a goat." He tried to get his shirt back, which the goat was not happy about. There was a brief tug-of-war and the bull impersonator managed to tear a strip off the bottom. "Oh bloody hell. Now *that* is gonna show up on TV."

Given their evening's activities had consisted of going to a pub and taking a short walk, they made a disproportionately tragic party as they returned to the hotel, with Anvita limping, Harry's shirt torn, and all of them covered in mud.

"Right," said Anvita the moment they got through the gates. "Bar."

"You don't think"—Rosaline did her best to keep up with Anvita's increasingly enthusiastic hobbling—"maybe see a first-aider?"

"Oh come on. It's fine. You said it wasn't broken and you must know what you're talking about because you nearly did two years of a medical degree."

Somehow, Rosaline felt she wasn't going to win this one. "I said, 'It's not broken.' Not 'Feel free to get drunk and run around on it.'"

"I'm not going to run around. I'm going to have a glass of wine, maybe two, and then see if I can persuade Harry to carry me to my room."

Harry frowned thoughtfully. "I reckon carrying another bloke's bird is all right if you're escaping a bull—"

"It was a goat," Rosaline reminded him.

"—but I think if I was carrying you up to your bedroom, your boyfriend might have a problem with it."

"Don't ruin this for"—Anvita tried to stamp her foot and then yelped—"ow—me. How often do you think I get carried places in my life?"

"How about," said Harry, "we go to the bar, you put your foot up, I stay on the lemonade so I don't get pissed and drop you down the stairs, and we see how you feel?"

"Works for me. How about you, Dr. Rosaline? Want to come along and keep me under observation?"

She did, in a lot of ways. Because honestly she couldn't remember the last time she'd had a night like this—one of going out, being silly, and doing things you'd at least half regret in the morning. But she was also beginning to feel a bit bad for having jaunted off, leaving Alain stuck in his room to brood about meringues. Of course, he had said he'd wanted the time alone, but looking back, that probably hadn't meant *Fuck off to the village and ignore me for several hours.*

"Actually..." She gently disentangled herself from Anvita. "I should probably go check on Alain."

"Check on, eh?" Anvita waggled her eyebrows. "You mean, check on his *penis* with your *vagina*. Sorry, that sounded way better in my head."

Rosaline stared at her. "I don't know how to leave now. Because whatever I say will be weird by association."

"You're right. Let's try again. Have a lovely evening. Say hi from me."

"I will. Thank you. Goodbye. And I really appreciated the way you avoided mentioning anyone's genitals."

Anvita's hand swished through the air like she was swiping left on cosmic Tinder. "Pshaw. Who'd do something like that?"

Somewhat regretfully—not that she should have been regretful—Rosaline trudged down the hill towards the Lodge and then up the uninspiring whitewashed staircase to Alain's room. She knocked on the door more sheepishly than she'd intended.

"Rosaline." Alain was looking a little tousled, which suggested he'd just woken up. A suggestion reinforced by the fact that he was wearing black lounge pants and no shirt. "I didn't think you were coming."

"Sorry," she said instinctively. Though since she hadn't told him to expect her and he plainly didn't she wasn't quite sure what she was feeling guilty about. "We went for dinner. Are you feeling better about tomorrow?"

"I think so. It's going to be one of those 'all about the execution' days, but I've done all I can."

She dithered on the threshold. "Great. So, should I...can I?"

"Of course." He stood aside for her. "If you wouldn't rather be with your friends."

Well, fuck. She'd messed this up. She'd met a hot guy, with his own house and a good job, who liked baking, and it'd been going well, and then she'd gone all mixed-signalsy for no reason and now he didn't know where he stood.

"I'd rather be with you," she said, slightly more decidedly than it really warranted.

And to prove it, she pushed him gently towards the bed, sat him down, and straddled him. Cupping his face between her hands she kissed him deeply.

"Much as I love indulging your wild side"—he drew back slightly—"you're covered in mud."

"Sorry. I went for a walk with Anvita and Harry and she fell over in an I-Spy-related accident—"

He blinked at her. "In a what?"

"Okay, so we were playing I Spy in the dark"—out of nowhere, Rosaline started giggling and couldn't quite stop—"and Anvita said 't' and Harry and I tried everything and then she said it was tractor and we said there wasn't a tractor and she said there'd been a tractor a couple of minutes ago when she'd said it..." Rosaline was still giggling, which made it difficult to weave a coherent word picture.

"I've no idea what you're talking about," Alain told her.

"You see, it was Schroedinger's tractor."

"Are you drunk?"

"I had a glass of wine while we were arguing about ceps."

"Why were you arguing about sex with Anvita and Harry?"

"Not sex. *Ceps.*" Rosaline had just about managed to calm down, but this set her off again. "Because he thought they were a bean and I thought they were a caper—"

"They're a mushroom," interrupted Alain.

"I know. We checked. And also coco beans aren't cocoa beans. And the tractor wasn't a tractor and the bull," she finished triumphantly, "was a goat."

There was a long silence.

"I'm glad," Alain said finally, "you had fun. But that made very little sense and you're still getting mud on me."

"Sorry."

She pulled off her blouse, which she'd intended primarily as a practical gesture rather than an erotic one, but Alain—his eyes darting to her breasts—seemed less concerned by the distinction. They kissed again, and Alain unhooked her bra, and they fell back on the bed together.

And afterwards, Rosaline lay in the dark with her head nestled against Alain's shoulder wondering what the fuck was wrong with her. Because she liked sex. She liked sex *with Alain*. And yet the whole time she'd only been half-there, constantly having to drag her mind back to the room she was in.

Instead of wondering what Harry and Anvita were talking about in the bar. Or remembering how it felt to fly across the field in the dark like there was nothing in the world that could hold her back.

Anvita exulting in her ceps-related triumph.

Harry blushing as he let them tease him about his mermaid cake.

The way he'd moved so carefully around her kitchen, like he didn't want to take up her space. The way he just accepted that Amelie was part of her life. The deep rumble of his voice when he said "All right, mate" as if it was their secret.

How warm his brown eyes could be. His broad shoulders. That slow half-smile that seemed at once so shy and so knowing.

Sunday

"...CANNOT BELIEVE," JENNIFER Hallett was saying, while Harry, Anvita, and Rosaline were lined up in front of her like naughty schoolchildren, "that you pack of maladjusted oven-fuckers are forcing me to negotiate a pissing out-of-court settlement over a traumatised goat."

"Hey now." Anvita was the first to speak up. "If anything, the goat traumatised us."

"I don't give a fuck about your trauma. I give a fuck that you were fucking trespassing. Because, funnily enough, if something happens in the local area when we're filming the show, it comes back on the show. And when I get an angry call from a farmer the same night you three bewildered cockmanglers limp home covered in mud it is not hard for me to work out whose tits and/ or balls I have to nail to the fucking table." Jennifer Hallet started pacing. "*And* if you'd bothered to read your contracts, my little sacks of shit and sunshine, you'd know you're supposed to behave in a way that supports the values of *Bake Expec*-fucking-*tations*. Which means, and I can't believe I'm having to fucking say this, you don't do any fucking *crimes*." She kept pacing. "My job is to make you look like the kind of adorable pieces of flaccid scrotum that my Tory auntie could take to her bridge club, and I can't do that if you're on page three of the *Mail* naked in someone else's field ramming chickens up each other's rectums."

A little shocked, Harry put up his hands. "Wait a minute. We didn't do nothing to no chickens."

"Nor," added Rosaline quickly, "I really want to clarify, to each other's rectums."

Jennifer Hallet stopped pacing. But it was only to glare. "You three had better be on your best fucking behaviour until next fucking season. And if I see so much as a slightly insensitive tweet from any of you, I'll sue you so hard your grandkids will be selling blow jobs to pay your legal fees."

Coming to an unspoken consensus there wasn't much they could say to that, they hurried away to grab something resembling breakfast and then were hustled into the ballroom to start filming for what promised to be a gruelling day of baking.

Although it was a macaron challenge, Rosaline was starting with the cake. Because while macarons were fiddly, you could actually make them fairly quickly, and the last thing she wanted was to be serving up a plate of macarons next to an unfinished pile of sponge pieces.

"The trouble is," she told Colin Thrimp without being asked, "I've somehow reached the stage of the competition where the things I'm being asked to make aren't things that fit in my kitchen. So, while I've practised all the elements, the finished product is a bit theoretical."

"Do you think that's a good idea?" Marianne Wolvercote had clearly scented weakness from the other side of the room. And now she pounced. "This *is* week six, Rosaline."

"I know, but I also couldn't risk doing something"—Rosaline tried to strike a balance between *I'm taking on feedback* and *I'm being passive-aggressive*—"joyless."

Marianne Wolvercote arched a single cold eyebrow. "Very wise."

"So what have you got in store for us?" asked Wilfred Honey.

"Well, I'm doing a simple three-layered chocolate cake with a Swiss meringue buttercream, but the icing is going to have a sort of dark-blue marbled space effect, and I'm going to make macaron planets, and then dust the whole thing with edible glitter so it looks all starry."

Wilfred Honey nodded approvingly. "That sounds very nice, pet."

"And of course," Marianne Wolvercote added, in that tone that made it weirdly hard to tell approval from contempt, "marbled buttercream is very *in* right now."

"Yep, that's me." Rosaline gave a kind of awkward thumbs-up. "Totally on fleek. Um, I meant that ironically. People are going to know I meant that ironically, right?"

Wilfred Honey now just looked confused. "What's a fleek?"

"Nobody knows, darling," drawled out Grace Forsythe. "It's the Voynich manuscript of the modern age."

"I'm not sure I know what that is either," Wilfred Honey admitted.

Grace Forsythe got that *I went to Cambridge, darling* look on her face. "Neither does anybody else. That was rather the joke."

"Well"—Wilfred Honey got that *I'm from Yorkshire, don't fuck with me* look on his face—"my mam always said that if you'd have to explain it to the milkman, it's not funny."

Still bickering, the party moved on, leaving Rosaline to finish her sponge. The atmosphere in the ballroom was pretty tense, but she couldn't tell if it was because it was a big challenge or because they were so close to the semifinal or because sixty percent of the competitors had spent their morning being chewed out by the producer for holding an imaginary goat orgy.

"I think," Alain was saying from his workstation, "that this is going to come down to flavours. I'm guessing most people will do chocolate or vanilla, so I'm hoping I'll stand out because the whole thing is shot through with a hint of matcha. So it's a matcha green tea sponge with a matcha buttercream..."

Grace Forsythe leaned in before he could continue. "Are you not afraid that might be...a little too matcha?"

"Well, I don't think so. It's quite a complex ingredient. My feeling is that using it in different ways will bring different elements of the flavour out."

Grace Forsythe patted him on the shoulder. "Too matcha information, old boy."

Rosaline didn't look up again until her layers were in the oven—everyone was pretty much at the same stage she was, apart from Nora, who seemed to have made three gigantic macarons; and Anvita, whose bench was covered in sandwich tins, mixing bowls, and layer after layer of as yet unovened cake.

"This is fine," she was telling Colin Thrimp. "I know exactly what I'm doing. When it all comes together it's going to—" Her elbow caught a mixing bowl, sending a spray of bright green buttercream up her apron and across the floor. "Still fine. I've got plenty."

Colin put a hand to his headset. "Did we get that? Fabulous. Quick close-up of the spill, then get technical to deal with the slip hazard."

Sensing she had about a three-minute window before she had to start on her macaron, Rosaline nipped over to Anvita's workstation. "Are you...sure you're okay?"

"Definitely," she said, in a definitely-not voice. "This is all part of the plan. I just need to bake...um...seven more layers, two at a time, for about forty minutes each."

"That's three hours twenty minutes, just on the cakes."

"Yep. Yep. Worked that out. As long as I do the macaron quickly, and perfectly, while batches two and three are in the oven, then I'll have time to cool, ice, and decorate everything with"—absently, Anvita tasted the buttercream from her apron—"about thirty seconds to spare."

This was exactly the sort of thing that Alain had told Rosaline not to do. And she went ahead and did it anyway. "Do you want to use my oven? I need a shelf for my third layer, but you can have the other one."

Desperate hope flashed in Anvita's eyes. "Really? Is that allowed?"

They both glanced towards Colin. "Oh no, it's wonderful. Jennifer says the US market loves to see British people being hopelessly noncompetitive."

"Anyone got a spare oven shelf?" Rosaline called out. "Anvita's decided to do all the cake."

Alain seemed absorbed in his matcha buttercream and didn't even look up.

"Yeah, all right," said Harry. "You can have mine in about twenty minutes."

Nora, still waiting for her giant macaron to dry, was perched on her stool, slyly reading a book that appeared to be called *The Playboy Prince's Secret Baby*. "You can have mine now," she offered. "I think I'll need it again in about an hour."

Only slightly hindered by the camera crew, and Colin Thrimp's multiple requests for retakes, Harry, Rosaline, and Anvita dispersed Anvita's many layers across the ballroom. And then Rosaline got back to her macarons. Operation Stop Anvita Imploding had taken slightly more time than she'd budgeted for, but—to quote Anvita herself—it was fine. It was fine.

And it was, as it happened, mostly fine. The cake came together nicely and the marbling pretty much worked—although she'd been a little too heavy-handed with the black colouring so it was quite a dark night sky in the end. Her iridescent macaron planets, though, she was genuinely proud of. At one point, she'd been planning to do them to appropriate scale with an enormous Jupiter and a tiny Mercury, but when she'd tried it at home they'd cooked at different rates so while Earth had been about right, Saturn had been mush and Pluto was basically a bullet. Although that probably served it right for not being technically a planet. Rosaline was adding the popping-candy asteroid belt when she heard a despairing wail from Anvita's direction.

Her cake, which about three seconds ago had been a baroque masterpiece in jewel tones, with a trail of macarons spiralling around it like a feather boa on a particularly delicious drag queen, was now listing heavily as both Anvita and Grace Forsythe did their best to support it without ending up elbow-deep in sponge and icing.

"Oh no," cried Anvita. "This is a caketastrophe."

Grace Forsythe tried to give her a reassuring look from the opposite side of a cake that was rapidly turning into a landslide. "It's fine. I'll just stand here holding it for the rest of my life. You can tell the judges I'm an especially elaborate fondant decoration. Which, now I think about it, is what my ex-girlfriend used to call me."

"Five seconds," called Marianne Wolvercote.

The entire top tier of Anvita's baketacular swan-dived to the floor with a wet little splat.

"And time. Step away from your bakes." Marianne Wolvercote shot a sharp look across the ballroom. "That includes you, Grace."

"I'm not doing anything," protested Grace Forsythe. "I'm resting my hands."

"Please do as she says." That was Colin Thrimp, fingers to his headset as usual. "And don't shoot any messengers, but Jennifer asks me to remind you that it's not too late to replace you with, and I'm sorry, these are Jennifer's words, 'some other cosy-voiced shitstain people vaguely remember from the '90s.'"

Grace Forsythe snorted. "We both know that's an empty threat. All the other cosy-voiced shitstains from the '90s are either off their face on cocaine, in rehab, doing documentaries about getting off their faces on cocaine and going to rehab, or far too busy banging their much younger spouses."

"It's all right," said Anvita. "I'm prepared. Let her die."

"Anvita's cake." Grace Forsythe gazed solemnly at what was left of it. "In the short time we knew you, we loved a lifetime's worth."

She stepped back. And the whole thing slumped sideways like an Old West gunslinger with a bullet in the chest.

"This"—apparently the drama had been sufficient to summon Jennifer herself from wherever she'd been lurking during filming—"is going to get us renewed for another two series at least. I fucking love it."

They arranged for Anvita to go first for judging and kept their comments short and positive. Because there was no need to go into detail when the feedback was "This would have been fine except it all fell on the floor."

Alain was next, with an elegant and very green offering, decorated with dark chocolate, and dark chocolate macarons.

"There's no denying," said Wilfred Honey, having cut a perfect slice out of Alain's perfect cake, "you can bake. You've got three even layers with a good filling of buttercream between them, and the flavours are balanced nicely. But it's very"—and here he made a sad Granddad gesture—"expected. When we set this challenge, we were hoping to see a little more of who you are: and all you've shown us is what you can do."

"I see." Alain was frowning in a way that Rosaline had learned meant he was pissed off and trying not to show it. "Thank you."

"Next week, if you get through," continued Wilfred Honey,

maintaining the polite fiction that Anvita wasn't definitely going home, "try to have some fun wi' it."

"For my part," added Marianne Wolvercote, "I'm just sick to the back teeth of matcha."

And since she seemed to have nothing further to add, Alain was obliged to pick up his cake and return to his seat.

Then it was Rosaline, who, if she said so herself, had done a pretty good job. Assuming the judges weren't sticklers for astronomical accuracy, and it didn't taste like arse, she was hoping that between this and her adequate performance in the blind bake she might be able to go home with the W. And then she felt bad for thinking about the W at all when they were probably losing Anvita.

"Now this," observed Marianne Wolvercote, "is very pretty."

"The marbling's come out well," added Wilfred Honey. "And I like you've told a story with it."

Honestly, the story was mostly "It's space," but Rosaline would take it.

Marianne Wolvercote plucked a macaron planet from the top. "Good, even bake on the macaron." She nibbled it. "Very light, which is what we want. Just the right level of chew."

"And the cake's nice too." Wilfred Honey had cut himself a piece and was running a fork against the sponge to test the texture. "This has been a very good week for you, Rosaline." He took a mouthful. "It's got a nice rich, chocolatey flavour—and not too much buttercream. I think I could have a second piece of that."

It wasn't quite a "By 'eck, it's gorgeous," but it was still high praise.

Glowing but trying not to do it in a smug way, Rosaline went back to her seat, passing Harry on the way.

"So this," said Harry, setting down his creation, "is a mermaid cake what I made for my nieces. Only they're a bit of sick of it now on account of how I made six of 'em."

The cake in question was a rich opalescent blue, with marbling that, Rosaline had to admit, had come out better than hers. The surface was decorated with carefully piped seashells and barnacles, and the top with a treasure trove of macaron oysters, tiny white chocolate pearls gleaming inside them. A fondant mermaid was diving into the top of the cake, leaving only her beautifully sculpted tail visible, and conveniently sparing Harry the embarrassment of having to create beautifully sculpted breasts.

"This is rather charming," said Marianne Wolvercote, with the air of someone who resented being charmed. "I'm not normally a fan of whimsy, but I think it works. And you've shown a real eye for presentation here."

"It looks smashing," declared Wilfred Honey. "And the way you've used the macarons as little seashells is bloody marvellous. Of course, what really matters is what it tastes like."

Rationally, Rosaline knew she should be hoping it was overbaked, or soggy, or close-textured, or the macarons would have air bubbles in them, but she . . . couldn't. Any more than she could have celebrated Anvita's cake falling over.

Wilfred Honey popped a forkful of Harry's vanilla sponge into his mouth. "By 'eck, it's lovely. So light. You've got a delicate touch for a big lad."

"The macarons are exceptional as well," chimed in Marianne Wolvercote. "The traditionalist in me would have preferred them to have a slightly more conventional presentation, but the whole thing has come together so well that I can't hold it against you."

Harry blinked. "Blimey. Cheers."

This left Nora, who, in a slightly different interpretation of the brief, had made one gargantuan macaron, decorated with smaller macarons, along with fresh fruit and cream.

"Golly," said Grace Forsythe, "it's macaronception."

Marianne Wolvercote eyed Nora's offering. "This is actually quite current. You're starting to see these all over the place, and when they work they can be marvellous. But it's not what we were looking for, and I suspect Wilfred will be particularly disappointed to be served a cake with no actual cake in it."

"I am disappointed," agreed Wilfred Honey, cracking the layers of Nora's uncake with a knife. "The macarons themselves look very nice, but the filling's just cream and fruit, isn't it?"

"Which does," added Marianne Wolvercote, "make it very light and give it a refreshing tartness—which I like."

"But it's not," concluded Wilfred Honey, "a cake."

For once, the contestants were allowed to remain in the ballroom while the judges conferred—it had been a long enough day, and the results conclusive enough, that an extra round of interviews would have been gruelling and pointless. Instead, they sat patiently, mostly avoiding each other's gazes until Grace Forsythe and the judges came back in.

"As always," said Grace Forsythe, "we have reached the part of the show where we mix delight and despondency. The delightful part is that I get to name this week's winner, who impressed us with his technically brilliant gougères and then frankly surprised us with his delicate touch, his dainty macarons, and his fondant mermaid. This week, at last, it's Harry."

There was just enough time for the camera to catch everyone's "pleased for you" faces, some of them more natural than others before Grace Forsythe continued.

"But, of course, as with so much in life, our store of pleasures must be sauced with paine. And so it is with genuine heartbreak that, after six weeks of illuminating the ballroom with her rich flavours and seemingly inexhaustible supply of fancy glasses, we say goodbye to Anvita."

Rosaline, to her mild embarrassment, burst into tears.

"I'm going to really miss her," she told Colin Thrimp afterwards, wishing she didn't have to say this on-camera, "because she's...she's...excellent and sexy."

He gave a kind of nervy, ferrety blink. "Why is everyone saying that? I had to tell Nora of all people that it's not appropriate in the time slot. Can you try it again in a way that doesn't suggest you're sexually attracted to the eliminated contestant?"

"Was that a concern with Nora?"

"Please," whimpered Colin Thrimp, "we've all had a very long day. Say something lovely about how lovely Anvita is that we can actually broadcast."

"She was"—Rosaline was misting up again—"a really good friend and if you're watching this, Anvita's nan, I hope you're incredibly proud of her. Because she's...she's...excellent and...excellent."

An interchangeable technician brought her another pack of tissues.

From under a nearby tree, Nora had moved on from Anvita and was mounting a spirited defence of her bake. "They told me to make a macaron cake and so I made a macaron cake. If they wanted me to make a cake with macarons on it, they should have said make a cake with macarons on it. They also said I was current. I've never been current in my life. Even when I was twenty, I wasn't current. I'm slightly vexed."

"Well," Anvita was saying as she sat on the loser wall, swinging her feet, "that was a disaster. But they say go big or go home, and it looks like I'm doing both. And I do feel I stayed true to the spirit of Marie Antoinette. It just all ended up a bit postguillotine."

They reunited outside the Lodge for another round of hugs, goodbyes, and promises to stay in touch.

"I tried telling them you were excellent and sexy," explained Rosaline through a cloud of sniffles. "But Colin told me it was inappropriate to imply I wanted to do you."

Anvita grinned. "Ah, so you *do* want to do me?"

"I mean, if we weren't both seeing someone and you had any interest in women, I'd probably be willing to have a tumultuous fling with you."

"What makes you think it'd be tumultuous?"

"Because I've met you."

Anvita thought for a moment. "Fair."

"I tried to say you were excellent and sexy too," Harry offered. "But they wouldn't let me say it either. And frankly, I'm relieved. I don't want your nan or your boyfriend coming after me."

"Yeah"—Anvita gave him an appraising look—"my boyfriend couldn't take you. But my nan is vicious. Anyway, let's swap numbers because you're not getting rid of me this easily and you should know by now I always get my own way."

There was a brief flurry of phones.

And when they were done, Anvita poked Rosaline firmly on the shoulder. "And you, lady, had better win this for me. Err, no offence, Harry."

He shook his head. "Nah, it's all right. I reckon I've peaked with the mermaid cake."

"And your dainty macarons," added Anvita, in her best Grace Forsythe voice.

"Leave it out. I'm going to get enough of that from Terry."

Anvita wrinkled her nose in genuine bemusement. "I still don't understand why you're friends with this man."

"Ask your boyfriend. It's a bloke thing."

"That's not an answer. That's internalised sexism."

"I think you'll find," he told her in his driest voice, "it's gender socialisation."

Before either of them could reply, Alain sauntered over.

"Ah, Rosaline," he said.

She knew she should have been pleased to see him. And, well, she was. It was just that she knew how seriously he took the competition, and he hadn't done as well as he was probably hoping this week. Plus, he didn't exactly gel with Harry and Anvita.

But to her surprise, he slid an arm round her waist, pulled her close, and kissed her full on the mouth before turning to Anvita with an expression of what seemed to be genuine sympathy. "I'm so sorry you had a bad week, Anvita. I really think you could have gone further."

She shrugged. "Well, I didn't because my cake fell over."

"Anyway"—his attention returned to Rosaline, who he was still holding tightly—"I was wondering if you were free to visit again next week?"

It wasn't super convenient, but then it was never going to be super convenient. Besides, she remembered the afternoon they'd spent baking together—how good it had felt to share that time with him, when they were both doing something they loved. "I can probably get a babysitter."

"How about Thursday?"

"Sure—I'll do my best."

He smiled. "Are you headed for the car park?"

All things being equal, and knowing her father would be late, Rosaline would probably have lingered for a little while with Harry and Anvita. But having accidentally ditched Alain the night before and then tried to make up for it with less-than-enthusiastic sex, she felt that refusing to walk with him to a place she would definitely need to go was crossing the line from distracted to, well, diss. "Give me a moment to grab my things."

She offered a hasty farewell to Harry and Anvita, and by the time she came back with her bag, they'd gone their separate ways. Alain was where she'd left him, staring off into the distance with a slightly frowny, slightly contemplative look.

"Thanks for waiting," she said.

He started. "Not at all."

And so they set off up the hill together, the dreamy early evening somewhat marred by the desperate scurrying and shouting of the technical crew as they dismantled the sprawl of rigging and electric gear that discreetly occupied much of the grounds.

Since Alain still seemed distracted to the point of brooding, Rosaline thought she'd better seize the bull by the horns. Or, at least, the goat by the ears. "Alain, are you okay?"

"Yes. I'm just"—he huffed out an aggrieved sigh—"I'm getting a bit sick of all this *You're not being wibbly-wobbly, airy-fairy, touchy-feely enough*. Frankly, I feel I am showing who I am. Except apparently *who I am* needs to be the sort of person who cries over meringues or has a profound emotional reaction to buttercream."

It wasn't personal. But Rosaline still cringed a bit remembering the time she'd sincerely broken down over dulce de leche. "It's *Bake Expectations*. You have to cry over meringues. And then you have to give a teary interview where you say *I can't believe I'm crying over meringues*. It's what people love about the show. Low stakes that we all care way too much about."

"Perhaps this is another aspect of my upbringing that the BBC finds defective, but when I care about something I try—and stop me if this sounds absurd—to do it well."

If there was anything Rosaline got, it was that. And probably she'd be feeling the same way if she'd been as consistently excellent as Alain. "I think you can probably take it as a compliment?"

"How is *Your personality is wrong* a compliment?"

"Well…" This had the potential to go very badly, and the last thing Rosaline wanted was a repeat of the biscuit argument. "The way I see it, what these shows have to do is find a flaw in you that they can fix. Because otherwise, it's not a story, it's just about someone who's better than the competition. Like in season one there was the young woman who was very good but lacked confidence, and in season two there was the guy who was really brilliant but really erratic and needed to be more disciplined, and in season three there was the slightly older woman who was really good but lacked confidence, the woman who won season four had amazing presentation but her flavours were sometimes off, and—"

"So what you're telling me," Alain cut over her, "is that I need to be a woman who lacks confidence?"

Okay. So this had, in fact, gone very badly. Shame they couldn't just have sex. That usually seemed to fix it. "I think it's more that male contestants usually don't lack confidence because blah blah patriarchy. And so the show needs to give them a different story. And because of blah blah patriarchy redux, *You're very technically skilled but aren't in touch with your feelings* is probably a good arc for them to give a male contestant."

And now she'd articulated it, Rosaline's heart flumped like a soufflé. Because, yeah, that was definitely the story for this season. Which meant Alain was winning and she was the one who looked good in a pinny.

Question was, did she look good enough in a pinny to get through to the final?

Alain was frowning again. "It's a baking show. It should be about how well you bake."

"It's a TV show. It's about how well you TV."

"Aren't we cynical, Rosaline-um-Palmer?"

She put what she hoped was a reassuring hand on his arm. "You know you're an excellent baker. You just need to show a bit more of what you're feeling when you do."

"What I'm mostly feeling is *Oh I'm glad this going to plan* or *Oh I'm concerned this isn't going to plan.*"

"No, but baking in general." She made a nebulous gesture of togethery-joy. "It's an inherently sharey thing to do. You bake for people or because of things or to celebrate or remember or to cheer yourself up."

"Or because you found an interesting recipe and wanted to try it out."

They walked on in silence, at a kind of weird impasse.

But when they reached the car park, Alain turned her gently to face him and kissed her. "It's very sweet that baking means that much to you. But to me, it's a technical skill. It's one I enjoy demonstrating, but I'm not interested in pretending it's more than it is."

Rosaline swallowed. Her heart had gone past collapsed soufflé and into dropped mixing bowl. "You're right. I'm...I'm being silly and sentimental."

"Rosaline"—he gazed down at her with that intense, serious look he sometimes got—"you have far more in your life than baking."

She opened her mouth, not quite sure what she was meant to say or what she would, or if they were going to be the same thing. Because of course she had more in her life than baking. It was just that she wasn't sure if her *more* was the same as his *more*. Thankfully, she was saved from having to answer by the rough screech of tires on gravel as Liv's Jaguar careened to a halt in front of them.

"I should go," said Alain, leaning in to give her one final kiss. "Liv adored you, by the way. See you Thursday."

As the car was pulling away, leaving Rosaline alone again, her phone buzzed. *Your father has been called into work. I can come and collect you but I'll be two hours at least.*

This was so typical it wasn't even hurtful. Besides, you'd have to be a pretty shitty person to be hurt by someone else's medical emergency. *Don't worry*, she sent back. *Take your time. I can wait at the hotel.*

Shouldering her bag, she set off back up the driveway only to meet Harry walking the other way.

"Something happen, mate?" he asked.

"Oh, nothing. Just my dad can't pick me up and it's going to take a while for my mum to get here."

His brows tightened in concern. "Is he all right?"

"He is. Someone else probably isn't. He's a cardiologist, and these days he doesn't get out bed for anything less than a triple bypass with complications."

"Blimey." He seemed to be casting around for a more detailed statement on St. John Palmer's medical career. But apparently gave up. "Look, you don't live that far from where I'm going, and it seems a shame to run your mum all this way. There's space in the van if you don't mind sticking your feet on a toolbox."

Rosaline was about to say "No, it's fine, you don't have to," except he'd offered and the choice was taking Harry twenty minutes out of his way or Cordelia two hours out of hers. "Actually, that'd be really helpful."

"All right, mate. It's over here."

And so, having just pinged away from the car park, Rosaline found herself ponging back, texting her mum awkwardly with one hand as she followed Harry to the Dobson & Son van. He opened the passenger door for her and she clambered in. A few moments after that he joined her, and a few moments after that they were on the road.

There was something unexpectedly intimate in sharing his space with him—especially when the space itself was small, and she was very aware of how close they were. The soft curl of hair over his forearms. The well-cut line of his jaw with its shadow of fresh stubble. Those deep-set eyes of his, and the long, dark lashes more noticeable in profile.

"Harry?" she asked.

"Yeah?"

"Why...why do you like baking?"

He let out one of those tradesmen's *I'm not sure what's wrong with the boiler* breaths. "It's relaxing. And it's nice to have a thing what you know what you're doing with. And everybody knows if they bother you while you're making cakes, they don't get cakes. So it's good if you need to calm down and stuff."

"Amelie hasn't learned that lesson."

"Well it's different when it's kids, init? Two seconds after Ruby and Amber get in the kitchen—that's Sam's kids, by the way— you know nothing's getting done. But that's not the point, is it? It's about, you know, family and that."

She nodded. "I guess so."

"What's brought this on?"

"I don't know. I . . . I put so much into it, I sometimes wonder if I'm wasting my time, maybe?"

"What, 'cos your dad's a cardiologist and you ain't?"

That was the problem with Harry. He didn't look like he was supposed to be perceptive. But he kept . . . getting her? "And my mum's an oncologist."

He thought about this for a second or two. "Bloody hell, you aren't half a bunch of clever bastards, ain't you?"

"They are. I got knocked up and dropped out of university."

"Don't mean you're not clever. Just means you made different choices."

"Maybe." She sighed. "The thing is, though, they feel like *lesser* choices."

"I wouldn't know, mate. Or maybe I want lesser things as well."

"How do you mean?"

He shrugged, eyes firmly on the road. "Well, way I was raised, you got a job that pays the bills, you got people around you care about, that's all you need."

"Is it though?" she wondered aloud. "Can that really be enough?"

"Well "—his gaze flicked to her so quickly she half thought she'd imagined it—"there's a couple of things I'd like what I ain't got. But that's life, init?"

"And you aren't worried there could be, I don't know, more?"

He laughed at that. "Of course there's more. But so what? No one can have everything. You've just got to figure out what matters. And then not let stuff what don't matter get in the way of stuff what does."

It all seemed so simple, so attainable, so...right in front of her when he said it. But she knew the moment she got out of the van she'd be swept straight back into an ocean of coulds and shoulds and other people's expectations.

It didn't stop her from pretending, though. Imagining for a moment she could have a life like Harry's. Where your world was whatever you made of it and whoever you let into it and you were allowed to be happy with that.

Week Seven

Semifinal

Thursday

ROSALINE ARRIVED AT Alain's place a little before eight. To her surprise, the door was opened by Liv, who was wearing another sleek black dress and had a half-empty wineglass clutched in her other hand.

"Rosaline," she exclaimed, hugging her somewhat unsuccessfully on account of the wineglass and Rosaline not having expected to see her, let alone be enveloped by her. "Hi. Come in. Alain's in the kitchen."

Hoping that her feelings of *What the fuck?* hadn't reached her face, Rosaline followed Liv into the living room—where she stood looking dazed while Liv kicked off her Louboutins and curled up catlike on the sofa.

"Isn't it wonderful," she purred, "to be seeing a man who cooks."

"Well, I did meet him on a cooking show, so it'd be weird if he didn't."

Liv waved her wineglass. "Believe me, you still can't take that type of thing for granted. Every man I've been with since Alain has been very much the 'lives off takeaway and fucks his secretary' sort."

What was happening right now? "Maybe you've been unlucky?"

"Oh, I've been very lucky. I've known exactly what I've been getting into." A pause. Then a sigh. "But I have missed Alain.

He was always different." Another pause. "I think it's being an architect: it's just creative enough you can't be totally dry and miserable but not so creative you're obliged to act like a total wanker. And it's just corporate enough that you can't get away with living in sandals but not so corporate that you can get away with anything."

"Have you tried," suggested Rosaline, "dating somebody...not like any of those things?"

Liv gazed at her solemnly. "I admit the thought has crossed my mind."

This had started weird and was showing no signs of de-weirding. "Sorry, am I stepping on your...Is there some kind of..." Rosaline did her best approximation of an *Are you still in love with my boyfriend* gesture. "Are you and Alain...?"

"Not at all, darling. I'll admit we've been a bit on-again, off-again, but I think we're off for the foreseeable."

It seemed a bit rude to say, "So why are you in his house dressed like you're on a date?" but Rosaline really wanted to know why Liv was in his house dressed like she was on a date. Before she could formulate an even halfway-polite version of that question, Alain appeared in the doorway, with—of all things—a tray of savoury macarons.

"You made it, Rosaline," he said, putting the macarons down on a coffee table before brushing his lips across her cheek. "I'm so glad you're here. I can see you've both already made yourselves comfortable."

Which didn't entirely make sense, because while Liv might have been lying around like Cleopatra eyeing up a delivery of ass's milk, Rosaline was standing in the middle of the room with her coat still on and her bag in her hand.

"Let me take these." Alain relieved her of both and replaced the bag with a glass of wine. "And I hope you're not too macarorned-out. I thought it might be nice for us to dine mezze-style tonight."

Rosaline tried to communicate with her eyes that it wasn't the finger food she was confused by.

Catching up a macaron between two exquisitely manicured fingers, Liv popped it into her mouth and crunched. "Alain darling. These are delightful."

He nodded. "If last week's baketacular hadn't involved a cake element, I'd have made these for it. Of course, the judges would still have gone with something full of sugar and feelings, but at least I'd have stood out."

Having spent most of the day at work and the first part of the evening ferrying her child to Lauren and Allison's flat, Rosaline was starving. Mezze-style savoury macaron would not have been her first choice of starter. A burger, a pie, or a big vat of macaroni cheese would have been her first choice of starter. But savoury macaron—much like Liv—was apparently what she was getting. So she sat down and tried to make the best of both of them.

After all, it wasn't that she disliked Liv. It was just that in her experience, a cosy evening in with your boyfriend didn't normally involve a third party.

In any case, the savoury macarons were nice—feta and olive, if Rosaline was any judge. But then they would be, because Alain was good enough at this shit that they'd put him on TV.

"So, uh, Liv," Rosaline tried, "what brings you to…the Cotswolds?"

"I was in the area, working on a farmhouse conversion, and Alain happened to mention that you might be visiting, and so I thought it'd be nice to see you again."

This seemed a bit excessive, considering they'd met once and had nothing in common. "Oh. Um. I guess, it's nice to see you too?"

Alain was opening another bottle of wine— Was he drunk? Were they both drunk? "It's wonderful," he said, "to see my two favourite girls getting on so well."

Okay, so he was drunk then. Or joking in a way that wasn't quite coming across. At least she hoped he was one of those things.

They finished the macarons, and Rosaline would have finished her glass in an effort to take the edge off the evening, except Alain and Liv, in an excess of hospitality, kept topping it up for her. Which made it a little bit difficult for her to keep track of how much she was drinking.

And then Alain vanished into the kitchen to put the finishing touches on the next course, leaving Rosaline with an awkward silence and an interior designer.

"Alain tells me you live with your ex-girlfriend," remarked Liv after a moment or two. "Isn't that a bit...intense?"

"God, I don't actually live with her. She's just around a lot."

"That still sounds intense."

"Well, she's quite an intense person. But she's also happily married, and I think we're better friends than we were girl-friends."

One of Liv's perfect eyebrows formed a perfect arch. "Why's that?"

"Partly because we were seventeen, but"—a more sober Rosaline might have spoken more guardedly—"it was a lot of fucking and screaming, sometimes simultaneously."

"Oh my. I...suppose I always thought things would be, I don't know, I assume two women would understand each other better."

"It's not about understanding. People are messy, relationships are messy, teenagers are very messy, and"—Rosaline took another sip of wine—"Lauren's incredibly messy."

"It must have been exciting, though. All that passion."

"I mean, yes. But again, we were seventeen. You can be passionate about anything at seventeen."

Standing, Liv smoothed her dress down her thighs and went to open yet another bottle. "No, but with a man there's so much...*difference*. It's almost absurd. Their emotions work differently, their brains work differently, their bodies work differently." She threw back almost half her glass. "Take sex. Men get turned on, apply friction, and then they're done. But women...women are *sensuous*. We need time, we need care, we need to be touched, we need to marinate like..."

"Tofu?" offered Rosaline.

"No," she said, pouting.. "Not like tofu. Like...like...a fine wine."

Rosaline was definitely tipsy, but she'd have to be a lot drunker than this to forget basic cooking terminology. "You don't marinate wine. You can marinate things *in* wine."

"You're missing the point." Liv tottered back to the sofa and threw herself down, a lot closer to Rosaline than she had to be. "The point is, if you were with a woman, you'd want the same things. You'd feel the same things. You'd be like...like two orchids. Growing on the same vine."

"I think," said Rosaline carefully, "you might be romanticising things ever so slightly. Bad sex is just bad sex, and I've had plenty of bad sex with women."

"Well." Alain reappeared, holding an even bigger tray. "I *have* missed an interesting conversation."

"You really haven't," replied Rosaline, trying to once again communicate with her eyes, although in this case she was trying to communicate *Your friend is being very strange and drunk.* "Um, is there any water? Liv, do you want some water?"

Alain settled his tray on the coffee table and began unloading dishes. "So what we've got here is a field greens salad with peaches and prosciutto and a fig balsamic vinaigrette, chicken wings with mango-habanero glaze—I know it's a little American, but I thought it might be fun to get sticky; do be careful, though, they've got a kick to them—sugar snap peas with handpicked mint, and stuffed mushrooms with walnut, Gorgonzola dolce, and black pepper."

"Darling"—Liv leaned forward to pluck a mushroom—"you do know how to spoil us."

Rosaline was feeling less spoiled and more sort of underfed. Also, Alain had not been exaggerating when he'd said there was a kick to the chicken wings—one bite and she was reaching for her wine.

"Anyway," Alain began as he lowered himself into an armchair, "what was that about bad sex?"

It was a conversation Rosaline definitely wanted out of. "Just girl talk."

He gave her what she thought was meant to be a playful look. "Keeping secrets from me already, are you?"

"No," said Rosaline at the same time as Liv said, "Wouldn't you like to know?"

Alain held up his hands in a gesture of surrender. "I wouldn't dream of coming between you."

"I was telling Rosaline," went on Liv, regardless, "that I think, and we've had this conversation a hundred times, Alain, that being with a woman makes a lot more sense to me than being with a man."

"And I was telling her," interrupted Rosaline, "that there's nothing special about women. I mean, not in a bad way. Just in a...they're just people, and they can be great or shitty or the best you've ever had or the worst you've ever had. And usually, in my actually quite limited experience, they're kind of in the middle like everyone else."

"Rosaline"—Alain adopted a tone of mostly mock outrage—"is this your way of telling me I'm mediocre in bed?"

"What? No. I'm saying sex is what you make it."

"Oh, Alain." Liv licked chicken glaze from her fingertips. "You've got no cause for concern in that regard. You're easily in my top ten. Probably in my top five. Don't you think, Rosaline?"

Was she the only person who didn't keep a score sheet on

her clitoris? "Well"—she was about to explain that she'd only actually had sex with six people but decided it wasn't worth the conversation—"yes, he's definitely in my top ten."

He smirked. "And her list has twice the competition."

"I'm not sure it works like that."

"Don't take this away from me," he told her, laughing. "You're so much more adventurous than I am, I have to take what I can get."

She put her wineglass down with a clink. "Please stop saying that. If I was as cool as all that, do you think I'd have told you I lived in Malawi?"

"This is the thing about Rosaline," Alain explained to Liv, "she pretends she's this terribly demure, terribly dull, terribly diffident little wallflower. But she's got a secret wicked streak, and when she wants something she goes for it."

"What I'm going for at the moment"—Rosaline really needed this evening to start heading in a radically different direction— "is winning a baking competition on the BBC."

"You see?" Alain and Liv seemed to be exchanging a significant look. "You should show Liv your butterflies."

Okay. This had gone from weird to worrying. Two old friends getting drunk and indiscreet, and wanting to talk about sex like teenagers, she could understand—even if it wasn't what she'd signed up for. And honestly, she liked her tattoos and was usually happy to show them to people if she felt comfortable enough to talk about them. But there was a difference between *I've got tattoos / Can I see them / Yes* and *Take your top off in front of my drunk friend.*

"Do you mind if I don't?" she asked. "We're trying to have dinner."

Liv looked up from her wineglass. "Oh, I don't mind. Alain's told me all about them—he says they're beautiful. And you know I've never had the courage to do anything like that myself."

"Maybe another time?"

"There's no need to be embarrassed," Alain said soothingly. "Nobody's judging. We're all friends here."

"I don't feel judged." Rosaline edged along the sofa away from Liv. "I just don't feel like taking my clothes off."

At which point Liv rose, with what was probably supposed to be graceful fluidity but was more a lurch. "We don't want to do anything to make you feel uncomfortable."

"Oh good."

"I'll go first."

"Wait. What—"

Liv's immaculate black dress was already on the floor, revealing her equally immaculate, equally black lingerie, and everything that went with it. Rosaline glanced wildly at Alain to see how he was taking this. "In his stride" seemed to be the answer. Which was not comforting.

"Err, Liv," said Rosaline, feeling at once too drunk and too sober. "I think you should probably get dressed."

"Just when we're getting to know each other?"

This was what Rosaline imagined defusing a bomb must be like: she didn't want to be here, she had no idea what she was doing, and there was a really good chance it was going to blow up in her face. "Look, I'm sorry if I've given the wrong impression, but I'd be way happier if this stayed a drinking-wine-and-chatting type evening. Rather than a, y'know, getting-naked type evening."

"Oh come on." Alain also stood up, making Rosaline suddenly aware of how difficult it would be to get out of the room. "You must admit she's a beautiful woman. Don't you think she's beautiful, Rosaline?"

"I mean, obviously. But—"

All at once, her lap was full of Liv. And Liv was kissing her. And Alain was watching Liv kiss her and not in an *Oh dear, my drunk friend is embarrassing herself* way. Since she couldn't remove

Liv without throwing her on the floor or putting her hands places that could well be interpreted as encouraging, Rosaline was reduced to turning her face away in a vain attempt to signal she wasn't into this.

"Your mouth is so soft," murmured Liv.

"Can you please get off me?"

"And you taste so sweet."

"No. Really. Get off me."

"Calm down, Rosaline." That was Alain. "It's just a bit of fun."

She glared at him as best she could past Liv's ever-encroaching lips. "It's not a bit of fun. It's a sexual assault."

"Don't be silly. You're both very attractive women. You know me, you trust me, and you like each other. What's wrong with three adults coming together to explore themselves?"

"The bit where I'm not up for it."

Past the point of worrying about mixed signals, she grabbed Liv by her upper arms and attempted to shove her sideways. But then Liv grabbed her back and they fell in a tangle on the sofa, Liv laughing in her ear and trying to kiss her again as Rosaline fought to get free. With a desperate twist, she managed to roll herself onto the floor, cracking her elbow on the coffee table as she went down.

From there she scrambled to her feet, knocking what was left of the chicken wings all over the carpet, and made a dash up the stairs for the bathroom. Slamming the door and locking it behind her, she scrambled to the far side of the room and crouched against the wall, trembling.

After a minute or two, she heard Alain's footsteps outside and saw the door handle twist.

"Rosaline"—his voice drifted through the wood, muffled but definitely exasperated—"you're being very childish."

Oh God, how had she got herself into this mess? Had she given the wrong signals or accidentally said, *Hey, you know what*

I'd really like? For you to hook me up with a bicurious woman I've met exactly twice. "You both tried to have sex with me when I didn't want to have sex with you. I'm not being childish. I just don't feel safe right now."

A sigh. "You know that's not what happened."

"I was there."

Now a pause. Followed by Alain's most reasonable tone, "Clearly this evening hasn't gone the way any of us intended. Why don't you come downstairs and we'll try again?"

"By 'try again,' you mean try to get me into bed with Liv again, don't you?"

"I mean, try to enjoy each other's company and see what happens. You're many things, Rosaline-um-Palmer, but you're not a prude."

It was very much the wrong moment for him to "Rosaline-um-Palmer" her. Cute and, now she thought about it, slightly demeaning nicknames did not go down well when you'd freaked someone out enough that they were hiding *from you* in your bathroom. Because actually she hadn't got herself into this situation. Alain had put her in this situation. Deliberately. "What the absolute fuck? Are you seriously trying to convince me that I should prove that I'm not sexually repressed by screwing your straight ex?"

"Liv isn't certain she's straight and I think it's important to respect that."

"Oh my God. You never stop, do you?"

He rattled the door handle, slightly harder now. "I don't understand what's got into you tonight. You've been very open about the fact you're attracted to women, you've obviously lived rather recklessly, and we've done nothing to make you uncomfortable."

"Not telling me you were inviting your ex made me uncomfortable. Plying us both with alcohol made me uncomfortable.

All your shitty little comments made me uncomfortable." She was running out of breath quicker than she was running out of grievances. "Talking about my body with your friend made me uncomfortable. Watching me get assaulted like it was a late-night film on Channel 5 made me uncomfortable. And standing outside the bathroom where I have locked myself for good reasons acting like you're the one who's been hurt doesn't make me uncomfortable. It makes me fucking furious."

There was a long silence.

"Self-righteousness doesn't suit you, Rosaline," he said finally.

It was really important that she stayed angry so she didn't cry. "I'd like to say this...this...entitled predator deal you've got going on doesn't suit you either. But actually, I'm starting to think it's just who you are."

"I'm going to give you some space now," he told her through the door. His voice wasn't cold exactly, but it was calm—the kind of calm she tried when Amelie was throwing a tantrum and refusing to eat her peas or do her homework. "Perhaps when you've settled down we can have a proper conversation."

This was pointless. This was completely pointless. Worse, it was beginning to feel like arguing with her father. There was that same refusal to acknowledge any reality outside of his own narrow perceptions. "I want to go home," she said.

"That's all very well, but none of us are in a fit state to drive and the trains have stopped running so—when you're ready—you might as well come out of the bathroom, apologise to Liv, and make the best of things."

The idea that he thought Rosaline was the one who should be apologising was enough to make her want to strangle him with the hand towel. But she knew this game. She'd been playing it for years. If she stayed quiet, it meant she was admitting defeat; if she got angry, it meant she was being irrational. All she could do was hang on to what she knew and stop trying to talk to somebody who had clearly never been listening. "I don't trust you. I'm not coming out of the bathroom."

"You can't stay in there the whole night."

"Watch me."

"Fine." Another sigh. "I'll be downstairs with Liv when you come to your senses."

What Alain was missing here was that she'd already come to her senses. Unfortunately, that had left her stuck in a bathroom, in the Venice of the Fucking Cotswolds, three walls and a flight of stairs away from a bicurious drunk woman and an arsehole.

Now Alain had gone, there was nobody for Rosaline to be angry at, and that left a lot more space to be scared. She was pretty sure they wouldn't force her to do anything—not in the directly physical sense—but she was also well aware that alcohol, isolation, and social pressure could get you a long way. Especially when you were convinced you were a good person who was doing nothing wrong.

Which left her with one option and that was to get the fuck out of there. Except when the person you spent most of your time with was eight it really shortened your "in case of emergency" list. Lauren and Allison were a no-go because they were already looking after Amelie, and she didn't want one of her daughter's most abiding childhood memories to be the time she was dragged out of bed at midnight to rescue Mummy from a threesome gone wrong. And her own parents... Well, even if they hadn't been busy that evening, she'd rather fuck Liv.

She stared at her phone. And made the only call she could. After all, they were friends. Basically friends. It would be fine.

"You all right?" said Harry, picking up after a couple of rings. "Your electrics gone out again?"

"No. Not exactly."

"If it's the water, I can get a mate round, but probably not 'til tomorrow."

Okay, that bit where she told herself it was fine? Not fine.

Because her mum had been right for years: being in a situation where you needed a guy to rescue you just fucking sucked. "Harry, I'm sorry to ask. But I'm at Alain's. Can you come and get me?"

"Has something happened?"

"Yes. No. Sort of."

"You safe, mate?"

"I'm...locked in the bathroom."

Mercifully, he didn't ask any further questions. "All right. Stay there. Send me the address. I'll be with you as soon as I can. I'll text you when I'm outside."

Rosaline let out a trembly breath. "Okay. Thanks." She didn't want to hang up. But she couldn't afford to run the battery of her mobile down. "Um. Bye? See you soon."

It was not the best two hours of Rosaline's life. Alain had made another attempt to convince her she was being silly for not wanting to help him live out some fantasy he must have been cooking up in his head since they'd first met. But after the third time she'd told him to fuck off he'd given up. Leaving her to stare at her phone in peace, until she heard the rumble of a van outside and saw a text pop up.

Here, it said.

Which was exactly the word she needed to see right then.

Rosaline heard the doorbell jingle. Then the hum of conversation below. And footsteps in the downstairs hall.

She'd been wanting to leave Alain's bijou sex cottage since, if she was honest, some time before Liv had taken her kit off. But now the moment had come, she was finding it hard to move. Pulling herself up on the towel rack, she got unsteadily to her feet and unlocked the door as quietly as she could.

"—the fuck are you doing?" Alain was saying.

"Come to get Rosaline."

"Rosaline's my guest. I'm not going to let you drag her off in the middle of the night."

"She asked me to come pick her up."

Alain, as far as Rosaline could tell from his back and the tone of his voice, seemed genuinely surprised by this. "Whatever for? We had a bit of a misunderstanding, but we're having a perfectly pleasant evening."

"Not my call, mate."

"Well, I'm sorry you've had a wasted journey, but—"

"I'm here." Rosaline hurried down the stairs. "Let me get my bag and coat."

"Rosaline, darling, you're not leaving?" called Liv plaintively from the living room. "We were just getting started."

So she was still pissed then.

"Don't think I can't see what you're trying to do here." Alain took a step forward, looking down at Harry in a way that made it very clear he was the taller of the two. "You've been after her for weeks."

"Alain, mate. I can see you've had a few. We're all tired. But I'm gonna ask you to take a step back, please."

"Take a step back? It's my own fucking house. And you have no fucking right to be here."

Harry had lifted his hands in the universal symbol of *Chill out*. "I'm not in your house. I'm on your doorstep. And I'm about to leave."

Coat bundled under one arm and bag clutched to her chest, Rosaline squeezed past Alain and out into the night. "Okay, let's go."

"You got it, mate." Harry turned, but Alain seized him by the sleeve of his T-shirt and yanked him back.

"Do you think," he sneered, "I'm going to let you walk away with my fucking girlfriend."

That brought Rosaline up short. "Sorry, do you still think I'm your girlfriend after everything that's happened?"

"I wasn't talking to you, Rosaline." Alain tightened his grip as Harry tried to step away.

"Don't wanna be rude"—although Harry's voice was low, Rosaline thought she could see tension in his neck and shoulders—"but I'm gonna need you to take your hand off me."

Alain grabbed his other sleeve.

"Mate," Harry sighed. "You do not wanna do this."

"Oh, who the fuck do you think you are? You thick Cockney c—"

Anvita, Rosaline reflected, had been right about Harry's arms. And one of them now shot upwards with remarkable speed, driving his knuckles squarely into Alain's jaw. In response, Alain took two paces backwards and fell over.

"You all right, mate?" Harry asked.

"You fucking hit me, you fucking thug."

He shrugged. "I did say to get your hands off me."

"Have I got a concussion?" Alain was still on one knee and clutching his face, like he was doing the world's shittiest proposal. "Did you give me a fucking concussion?"

"Nah. You didn't bash your head or nothing. Just got a bit of whiplash. Put some peas on it, you'll be fine. See you at the weekend."

Alain said some more things after that, but Rosaline wasn't listening, and she didn't think Harry was either.

He took her bag and let her in the passenger side of his van. "Mind the toolbox, mate."

She got herself settled and Harry climbed into the driver's seat, closing the door behind him with a satisfying air of finality.

They drove along in silence for a while, twisting country roads giving way to the flat grey haze of the M40.

"I," said Rosaline, curling over her knees, "am a fucking idiot."

Harry's eyes flicked briefly to her. "Nah you're not. You just went out with a dickhead for a bit. Lots of people do."

"Except this whole time he clearly saw me as some kind of slutty bisexual sex toy, and I don't know, is that who I am? Is that who I appear to be on television? Is that going to be me forever now?"

"Well…no. Like, any of 'em."

"I mean, you spoke to me that first day. So you must have been thinking something."

"I thought you was pretty and that you might want a cup of tea. That's not the same as thinking you're a slutty bisexual sex-whatsit. And even if I did, I know a lot of slutty birds and they're all-right people. Terry's sister, Shirl, she's had more cock than Colonel Sanders, but she ain't hurting no one, and when Sam's fella walked out she was right there for her."

"Sorry"—Rosaline hugged her knees harder—"are you saying you don't think I'm a slut or it's okay if I am?"

"Both. With the baking and the kid, I don't reckon you've got much time for getting yourself some, but if I'm wrong, so what? And as for TV, well it's just TV, init? I've never watched a series of *Bake Expectations* and come away thinking *She's well up for it.* It's not the show's…what's the word. Brand."

She sighed. "I know. It's always in the back of your mind, though, isn't it? The whole stereotype. Except it turned out that was exactly what Alain wanted. So that's fun."

"Yeah, but that's on him, not on you."

"Then why am I the one in your van, feeling shit about myself, while he's probably banging his drunk ex-girlfriend and complaining about what a complete bitch I am?"

"I hit him quite hard. So it's more likely he's sitting on the sofa with peas on his face complaining about what complete bitches we both are."

For some reason that cheered Rosaline up slightly. "I don't condone violence, but he did have it coming."

"It's what you do. Bloke gets in your face. Won't get out of it. You have to get him out of it." A pause as Harry manoeuvred them round a long Eddie Stobart lorry. "So, you want to tell me what happened? You ain't gotta."

Rosaline groaned. "It's fucking embarrassing and a fucking cliché."

"Wanted you to have a threesome, did he?"

The worst thing about it was how fucking obvious it was. Obvious and sordid. "Yes, he did. With his bicurious ex-girlfriend. Who wouldn't take no for an answer."

"Oh, mate. I'm sorry. Like, I've got to admit I've never worked out why people are so into it."

"Porn?" suggested Rosaline. "Bragging rights?"

"No, I get that. And I can see how, at first, you'd think it'd be great. 'Cos it's like having a second helping of pudding. But actually it's really confusing. I mean, you've only got two hands and one dick. Or else they get well into it and you're like, *You know what, shall I just leave you to it?*"

Rosaline slanted a slightly curious look at him. "Are you speaking from experience?"

"I don't spend every Saturday eating pies with Terry."

"Fuuuck." She flopped back against her seat. "I still feel like a complete fucking idiot."

"You've got to stop blaming yourself, mate."

"You know, and this is going to sound unbelievably bad out of context, but I'm starting to think I don't blame myself. I blame my fucking parents."

"Have a lot of threesomes, did they?"

"Very funny. No. But they liked Alain. And I knew they

would. And why am I twenty-seven, with a kid who knows what 'sesquipedalian' means, and still making decisions about my own life based on what I think would please two people who are fundamentally unpleasable?"

He made the same sound that the guy who'd charged her a hundred and something quid to look at her boiler had made when he looked at her boiler. "You might've lost me. The way I see it, if they're your family, either they'll love you no matter what, or fuck 'em."

"Yeah, they don't work like that. They're more, *We're here for you no matter what you choose, as long as you choose what we want you to.* It's sort of the Model T Ford of emotional support."

"That sounds like a fuck 'em situation, then."

"It's not that easy. For a start, I keep taking their money because if I don't my house will fall down and my daughter will starve. And I don't actually want to cut them out of Amelie's life because they're her grandparents and they love her. Also, there's a non-zero chance they might be right and I *have* been fucking up my life since I was nineteen. For no reason."

"I never said it was easy," Harry told her. "Terry and Shirl's dad's a proper arsehole. Messed 'em up real bad and they both know it, but every"—he made another of those *This'll cost you* noises—"two, three years he'll show up again and sometimes they'll tell him to piss off like they should but sometimes they don't 'cos he's still their dad and either way they get through it and try to do better next time."

"Is that why Terry's such a knobhead?"

"Nah, he wouldn't want you to give the old man that. He's a knobhead on his own account."

She laughed. "So, what? I just write off having latched onto a prick because my parents approved of him as a learning experience?"

"Well, it's that or carry on beating yourself up about it."

"I think," she said after a moment, "I'll carry on beating myself up about it."

"Fair enough."

They drove on for a while, the motorway sliding past interminably. And Rosaline, who was nothing if not true to her word, carried on her beating herself up. Now she was out of immediate danger—and was it okay to call it "danger"? It had been scary and uncomfortable, but it wasn't like she'd been storming the beaches at Normandy.

In any case, now she was out of whatever she'd been in, she had plenty of space to catalogue her regrets. To which she could now add having wasted the best part of two months dating a well-spoken wanker who'd clearly never seen her as a person at all. Just a university dropout whose insecurities he could leverage into a threeway. Especially when there was a guy right in front of her who'd twice dropped everything to bail her out of a bad situation.

"There's services up ahead." Harry nodded towards the big blue sign. "Mind if we stop for a coffee?"

"Oh God. This has been a four-hour round-trip for you, hasn't it?"

"Yeah, and I thought it'd be a bit awkward to take a piss at Alain's."

"Let's take a break."

They pulled into a car park sparsely dotted with late-night travellers and made their way beneath the triangular glass awning and into the incongruous brightness of the Welcome Break.

Harry glanced around at the variety of fast-food concessions. "Reckon I'll go Burger King. You always know what you're getting with Burger King. There's a Smith's down that way if you want to get a book."

"Why would I want a book?"

"I dunno. Just thought you might want a book."

"What? You think I'd make you drive all the way out to the Cotswolds to rescue me from my atrocious romantic choices and then ignore you in favour of Marian Keyes?"

"It's up to you, mate. I mean, I'll be honest, if what I wanted was a chat, there'd be easier ways to get it than driving to the Cotswolds. I came to get you 'cos you needed got. You don't owe me nothing."

"I am grateful, though."

"Yeah, I know. You don't have to prove it. Fancy a Whopper?"

She did, in fact, fancy a Whopper. She really fancied a Whopper. "Oh God yes. Not only did Alain try to make me fuck his ex-girlfriend, he tried to make me do it on savoury macaron and pea salad."

"Now that's evil."

They Whoppered up, courtesy of a stoned teenager, and then claimed a space in the mostly empty seating area, on either side of a table that was trying hard to pretend it was made of wood.

"I always liked these places as a kid," remarked Harry. "They felt sorta magic."

This would never have occurred to Rosaline, but it did make sense in a way. "They do have a…detached-from-space-and-time quality."

"Yeah, and sometimes they'd have an arcade or one of them vibrating massage chairs. We used to fight like cats and dogs over 'em. Dunno why, though, 'cos they was shit."

"I'll remember that if I'm in the vicinity of a vibrating massage chair."

"So…" Harry drew a line of ketchup with a fry he didn't seem interested in eating. "Thought you might want to know I went to the doctor's the other day. Apparently I've got an anxiety thing…like you said. And they're trying me out on some pills and I'm on a waiting list for phone therapy. You know, like over the phone. Not, like, with a phone."

Rosaline glanced up from her burger, trying not to look as shocked as she felt. "You went to the doctor's?"

"Yeah. Seemed I probably should to be honest. I know I bit your head off, but then I thought, *Well, Rosaline's pretty smart. Probably knows what she's talking about.*"

"You have way overestimated my competence."

"Don't be daft, mate. I'm just saying you're worth listening to. And well, you was right. Turns out I'm a mental."

"I don't think," she said, "that's the technical term."

"You don't get to do that no more. As a mental, I get to decide what to call myself."

"And 'person with an anxiety disorder' doesn't strike you as more appropriate?"

He flashed her one of his sly smiles. "Bit of a mouthful, init?"

"Okay. But for the record, I want you to know that I don't think of you as mental."

"Thanks, mate." He was still playing with the same fry. "It's weird, though. Like, you know, disorienting. 'Cos it's like a lot of stuff that you thought was just how it was...isn't how it is or doesn't have to be. And that does my head in."

"I think...the...doing your head in is part of the process."

"Maybe. But right now I've gone from *Does everyone think I'm a dick; I hope everyone doesn't think I'm a dick* to *Does everyone think I'm a dick or do I only think everyone thinks I'm a dick 'cos I'm a mental or am I a dick*. And I'm not sure that's helping."

Rosaline rescued the disintegrating fry and tossed it into their designated rubbish bag. "It'll get easier as you get used to it. And the pills might take the edge off, and therapy can give you new strategies for dealing with this kind of thing."

"Yeah, and I do feel better, actually. I mean"—he shrugged— "I thought I was going to get laughed out of the doctor's office, but she was really good about it. Said it was a common thing. Lots of options. Nothing to worry about. Which was a bit of a weird thing to say to someone what you've diagnosed with anxiety."

Despite being in a motorway service station after a disastrously failed threesome, Rosaline smiled. "I'm honestly glad you're getting help with this. I know how hard it is. After all, I'm the last person who should be lecturing other people on confronting their mental health issues."

"'Cos of your parents?"

"Basically." Now it was her turn to pick at her food, folding a stray piece of lettuce into a weird mayonnaisey parcel. "It feels so unbearably middle-class. You know, *Woe is me, my life is fine, but I'm sad because Daddy didn't buy me a pony*."

"I mean, I don't think you're sad. And it's not that your dad didn't buy you a pony, it's that him and your mum was pricks your whole life."

"But even that's just them being unsupportive. It's not like they ever locked me in a cupboard or anything like that."

"It's not a competition, though, is it, mate? And if it was, we'd all be losing, 'cos there's people what've got cancer or got their houses blown up in a war and that."

"I'm not sure that's entirely consoling?"

"I just meant, yeah, there's always someone worse off than you, but you're not helping 'em by ignoring your own problems." He started tidying up the remains of his Whopper meal. "'Cos the thing is, I'm feeling like a bit of a cock for not having got this sorted out years ago. And I guess I couldn't because I didn't have the, like, words to think about it until you sat me down and was like, 'There's something wrong with you, mate'—"

"I did *not* say that."

"In a nice way. Point is, if I had known, I could have done something, spent less time worrying and more, you know, being there for people. Being a better mate and a better brother and a better son and things. It's not selfish to work on your problems.

It's selfish not to. Even if hearing you've got a problem makes you yell at a nice girl what's trying to help you."

Rosaline squirmed, feeling that she didn't deserve quite as much credit as he was giving her. "I . . . I didn't . . . I'm not the one who fixes people's electricity and drives halfway across the country to pick them up from a sex party they hadn't consented to be at."

"Leave it out, mate. It's just different types of things, init. And from where I'm standing, I reckon we're even."

Maybe he was right. Or maybe *even* wasn't the point at all and you didn't have to keep a constant record of who owed what to whom. Because most people, at least most people you wanted in your life, wouldn't be out to use it against you anyway.

It was a strange thought, but a comforting one.

It was close to three by the time they got back to Rosaline's house—which stood at the end of its terrace, with the lights off, and a strange air of emptiness about it.

"You going to be all right, mate?" asked Harry as she hesitated on the doorstep.

"Um. Probably? This is really silly, but I'm not used to sleeping in the house on my own."

"Are Lauren and Amelie not there?"

"No, Lauren's wife was in town, so Amelie's staying with them." She dug her keys out of her bag. "It's probably for the best. I wouldn't particularly want to explain this to, well, anybody."

"I'm sure they'd understand. Well, Lauren would. Amelie's a kid."

"Oh, Lauren would understand, but she'd have opinions about it. And Lauren's one of those people who are sometimes on your side in a very unhelpful way."

He nodded. "Yeah, Terry's like that. Like, I was going out with this girl last year and she had to go to Jersey to be with her sister and so I rang Terry up and I was like, 'Emma's dumped me 'cos she's gotta go to Jersey to be with her sister.' And he's all, 'Aw, mate, how dare she, I never liked her, you're too good for her.' And I'm like, 'Her sister's got cancer, mate.' And he's like, 'She still shouldn't have led you on like that.' And I'm like, 'She didn't know her sister was gonna get cancer.' And so for the next half hour I'm defending Emma from my best mate when all I wanted was for us to go out and have a pint."

"Yeah, and when I tell Lauren about this, because I will inevitably tell Lauren about this, she'll go immediately to, *Roz darling, that's exactly what you get for messing around with straight men.* And then I'll have to defend them as a class to my best friend after one of them has just been a complete wanker to me."

"You know," he went on thoughtfully, "I can't tell if your Lauren and my Terry would get on real well or fucking murder each other."

Rosaline pushed open the door and stared into her shadowy hall. "So...um...you want to come in?"

There was a pause. And then Harry put a hand to the back of his neck. "You've just had one really bad experience with a bloke off the show. I'm probably not the person you want hanging around."

"Why? Are you going to sit on my sofa and suggest a threesome?"

"I wasn't planning on it. I just mean...you still don't know me very well. It's an empty house. I know you don't want to be on your own, but I don't want to make you feel...worse."

Maybe she would. But if there was one thing Rosaline had learned over the past few weeks, it was that second-guessing her own instincts and emotions got her nowhere. "How about we try it and see how it goes?"

"All right. Just making sure it's what you wanted."

"Yes," she said as she put her key in the lock. "It is. I'm going to try this new thing where, if I want something, I'm honest with myself about it."

She flicked on the hall light and led the way into the living room, turning the light on in there as well, and the light in the kitchen. It wasn't like anyone was lurking in her fridge ready to jump out and make her bang an interior designer, but she wasn't in the mood for things to be dark right now.

"Cup of…something?" she asked as Harry lowered himself slightly gingerly onto the sofa. "It's probably a bit late for tea."

"Glass of water'd be fine."

"I think I've got some Horlicks?"

That made him grin. "Go on then. I haven't had it since I was ten."

"Yeah, Amelie's best friend has it before she goes to sleep so Amelie wanted to have it as well. But she tried it once and decided it was horrible and now it's hanging out sadly in my cupboard."

"It is a bit weird, init? Like drinking the inside of a Malteser. Which, now I think about it, makes sense on account of how it's a malt drink."

"What even is malt?" asked Rosaline.

"It's a type of marm, init?"

Laughing, she ducked into the kitchen and put the kettle on. And a couple of minutes later she emerged bearing two mugs of creamy beige liquid that immediately filled the room with the smell of bedtime.

"Thanks, mate." Harry took his drink and blew some of the steam off the top. He waited a moment as Rosaline tucked herself next to him, and then continued, "How you holding up, then?"

"Oh, I'm fine. I'm fine. I'm honestly fine. Maybe even a

little relieved because all the time we were together it was like I was trying to prove something to him, or to myself, or to my parents. And now I don't have to and actually I never had to and that...that's pretty great?"

"I'll drink to that."

They clunked their mugs together clumsily because Horlicks was not a beverage designed for toasting. It also wasn't as calming as the adverts made it sound. In fact, Rosaline was starting to think Amelie might have been onto something when she'd said it tasted like sand and old people.

Silence settled between them. And it should have been a cosy silence, because what was cosier than Horlicks, but Rosaline was...well. She hadn't lied when she'd told Harry she was fine. She *was* fine. She was just...jumbly, as if her whole life was a jigsaw puzzle that had been put away in the wrong box, so she'd been trying to make a picture of a sunset with pieces that were meant to be a cow. And while the prospect of no longer trying to build a skyline out of hooves was enough to make her genuinely giddy—like when she'd been running through some poor farmer's field with Anvita and Harry—she was also on the verge of resentful.

Deeply, deeply resentful.

Not because of Alain. Because of everything. Everything she'd overlooked and ignored and missed out on. Even when it was staring her right in the face.

And what...what if it was already too late?

"Whoa, mate"—Harry was hastily putting his Horlicks on the floor—"what you doing?"

And it was at that point Rosaline realised she'd tried to kiss him.

"Sorry. Sorry." Oh God, was she Liv? "I...I know this a fucked-up situation, but I think you maybe...and I maybe...and so I..."

For a long, long, really long time, Harry said nothing at all.

And then he stood up. "I think I should probably go."

"Shit. Sorry. You don't have— Shit. I've been an utter ballsack, haven't I?"

"You ain't, mate. It's just." He drew in the kind of breath he drew in when Colin Thrimp insisted he have a feeling about his baking. "Look, you know I like...like you and that. But I don't reckon you'd like me very much if I...went along with what you was trying just now. What with everything that happened."

He was right. He was probably right. But she didn't like he was right. "So, what. One bloke tries to get me to have a threesome I don't want and I lose my ability to know my own mind?"

"What? No?" He rubbed the back of his neck in a slightly tormented way. "You've had a drink and a scare and it wouldn't be right."

"You don't get to make that call for me."

"No, but I get to make it for me."

The double whammy of sexual assault and rejection was not doing wonders for Rosaline's self-esteem.

"Look," Harry went on, in that slow, steady way he had when things were important to him. "I'm not trying to tell you what to do or that you can't make your own choices. Thing is, though, I don't want to be the rebound guy. Or the bloke you hook up with to make yourself better because another bloke was shitty to you."

"You're not," she protested. "I know circumstantially it looks like that. But...but I really have always liked you. Well, I've always fancied you. And then I liked you. And then I liked and fancied you. And now I think I've lost you."

"You ain't lost nothing, mate. It's just right here and right now it don't work for me." He took another deep breath. "'Cos if something did happen with you and me, I'd want it to be something what could work out. You know, long-term-like. And when you're trying to win a show, and you just got out of another thing, and you're making all these changes in your life, that ain't how long-term starts."

Okay. So it turned out you couldn't make yourself an entirely new person over the course of a two-hour van ride. Because while she had the right to be free and confident and happy, someone who made impulsive sexual decisions while slightly drunk wasn't the Rosaline she wanted to be. It was the Rosaline Alain had tried to make her into.

"Okay," she said. "I get it. I'm sorry I..."

He made a reassuring *It's nothing* gesture. "Don't worry about it. You've had a day."

"And I haven't... We're still friends, right?"

"Course, mate. I probably should be pushing off, though."

She still didn't want to be alone. But it was time to be. "Thanks again. I'll see you... God. It's Friday. Later today I suppose?"

"I can still run you home on the Sunday if you want?"

"Are you sure that wouldn't be weird?"

"Not if you don't want it to be."

It was a little bit amazing, how straightforward Harry could make things sound and how willing she was to believe he was right. There was power in it, she was starting to realise. Living in a world where you got to choose what mattered. And with time, and work, and perhaps a tiny bit of therapy, maybe she could have that too.

"That'd be great," she told him. "Thank you."

She walked Harry to the front door, slightly surprised when he lingered for a moment on the step.

"So you know." His hand was on the back of his neck again. "So we're clear. If you ever ask me again, I'll probably say yes. But there's no rush."

She wasn't sure what to say to that—because it felt enormous and trusting and slightly magical—but as it turned out, she didn't have to say anything because he just said a quiet "Good night" and walked back to his van.

"—cannot believe," Jennifer Hallet was saying, "what you greasy puddles of anal drippings are putting me through now."

No sooner had Rosaline arrived at Patchley House that afternoon than Colin Thrimp sent her to Jennifer Hallet's trailer for what he had optimistically described as a "quiet word." And a tiny, perhaps delusional, part of her had hoped it would genuinely be a quiet word, at least by Jenifer Hallet's standards, about something relatively minor. Maybe she wasn't looking good enough in her pinny or the goat was still having flashbacks. But no. The moment she stepped inside and saw both Alain and Harry were there already, and mid-chew-out, she knew it was going to be more serious.

A lot more serious. Because while Rosaline had not been looking forward to seeing Alain again that was on the grounds that it would be socially awkward. Not on the grounds that he would make an official complaint to production and ask to have her removed from the show.

"Did you think," Jennifer went on, "that when I said 'Don't do any more crimes' what I really meant was *Immediately go out and commit felony battery against another contestant*? What in the name of Prince Philip's shrivelled bollocks is wrong with you?"

Harry put his hands in the air. "It weren't nothing to do with Rosaline. Me and Alain got into a bit of a disagreement. I thought he was out of line. So I stuck him one."

"Excuse me." Alain looked up from where he was sitting and maybe Rosaline was imagining it, but his jaw still seemed slightly swollen. "You forced your way into my house and punched me in the face."

"I never come inside because you didn't want me to. But I asked you to take your hands off me. Twice. And you don't get a third ask."

"That might be how it works in your world," snapped Alain. "In mine, we don't go around throwing our fists at each other whenever we feel like it."

"Mate, from what I've seen of your world, I don't want nothing to do with it."

"Oh, how will I bear the—"

"Everybody"—Jennifer Hallet's voice cut through Alain like a machete—"shut the fuck up right the fuck now. I don't give a dead rat's limp cock what happened or why or who was to blame. What I care about is making a lovely fucking TV show about lovely fucking people making lovely fucking cakes. And you're ruining it with your goat fiddling and your macho bullshit because you both want to spaff on the same woman's tits."

"Um," said Rosaline. "Can we leave my tits out of this?"

Jennifer dervished round on her. "Your tits are what got us into this, sunshine."

"I want her off the show." That was Alain. "She was drunk and aggressive. To me, and to a close female friend of mine."

"You mean," asked Rosaline, "the close female friend that you deliberately got wasted and were trying to force me into bed with?"

There was a dull thump as Jennifer Hallet beat her fist against the wall. "Fuck me with a rusty egg whisk." She bore down on Alain. "If you've come to me with a sob story because you got smacked in the teeth for being a dirty sex pest, then I might actually have to lose my temper with you."

"That isn't what happened," protested Alain, wilting a little. "I invited Rosaline to stay with me, and I invited a friend to stay with us. We had some drinks and one thing led to another. I'm sorry if she misread the situation."

A silence, mostly occupied by Jennifer staring at Alain through narrowed eyes. "If you think I believe that for the length of a weasel's cumshot, you smug little prick, you really don't know who you're dealing with."

"And who do think the *Daily Mail* will believe?" Alain folded his arms tightly. "Me or the girl who got pregnant at nineteen?"

"I think the *Mail* and the *Mirror* and the fucking *Sport on fucking Sunday* can do what the fuck they like because we're the goose that lays the pissing golden eggs. But if you think you can hurt us more than we can hurt you, you're very welcome to step up and take a crack at it. Though"—Jennifer paused ominously—"I'd advise you to check your contract for the bit that explains what happens if you say a fucking word to the press that we don't want you to say."

"You," said Alain, "are a—"

"Just get the fuck out of my trailer. Go back to your room. Have a nice wank over a picture of your mother. And, in the morning, it'll be like none of this ever happened."

"I'll be—"

"Go."

Comprehensively out of options, he went. And Rosaline let out a deep breath that turned out to be embarrassingly premature.

"And as for you, you pair of second-hand urinal cakes," Jennifer went on, with barely a pause, "do *not* think you're off the hook. You"—she pointed at Harry—"committed an actual crime. Again. And you"—her finger travelled to Rosaline—"are just pissing me off."

Rosaline winced. "It's my fault. Harry wouldn't have been there if I hadn't called him."

"He still stuck his fist in the mouth of one of my contestants."

"He had it coming though," Harry pointed out. "Also it was on the chin."

"Neither of those are legal defences. I am *this close* to sending you home right now and telling the audience that you had to deal with a"—Jennifer's lip curled in actual disgust—"family emergency."

That seemed miserably unfair to Rosaline. "If he goes, I go."

"Don't fucking tempt me, sunshine. I've got contingency plans coming out my fucking urethra. I could still make this show if every single one of you fuckers was killed in a freak blending accident. But"—and here Jennifer cast herself disconsolately into her chair—"I do not like to waste footage. And I've put a lot of work into giving you a beautiful fucking journey, so a beautiful fucking journey you will pissing well have. Now get out of here, both of you, look humble yet grateful, and leave the rest of this objectively faecal situation to me."

They got out of there and were about halfway across the lawn before they realised they weren't sure where they were getting out of there *to*. The bar seemed wrong now Anvita was gone, and the only place they could be certain of not running into Alain again was one of their rooms and that felt way too intense, especially given how things had ended last time they'd been alone together.

"Bloody hell." Harry plunged his hands thoughtfully into his pockets. "I can't believe he tried to get you kicked off the show. I mean, you weren't even the one what smacked him."

"Yeah. I get men don't like being turned down for sex, but that's a level of pettiness I was genuinely not prepared for."

"I reckon it was tactical. I mean, he's obviously narked he didn't get to have a threesome with you, but he also takes the competition way too seriously and I think he saw a chance to get rid of someone what could beat him."

She was about to say something reflexively self-deprecating, but then she changed her mind. "You know, I think I can kick his arse. There's only so many times you can put handpicked lovage in something that doesn't need it."

"I know it's not nice of me," Harry offered. "But I really would like to see his face if he doesn't win."

"He honestly seems to think he's the only person who deserves to." She drove her toe into the grass. "God, I can't believe I dated him."

"To be honest, mate, I can't either."

"Hey." She couldn't tell if they were both working hard to make this feel normal or if it felt normal because they were that comfortable with each other. And probably she should stop fretting about it in case it went away. "That was a complicated low-self-esteem-slash-quarter-life-crisis thing we've discussed at length and you're not allowed to be mean to me about it."

"I'm not being mean. I'm just saying, it never made much sense to me on account of how he's a dick and you're not."

A feature of Rosaline's love life that she'd previously taken for granted was that none of the people she was romantically interested in had ever watched her previous relationship play out in its disastrous entirety. "Aren't you always telling me how your best mate's a dick?"

"No, he's a knobhead. It's a very different thing."

"Is it? Because it sounds like it might be quite similar."

Harry stroked his jaw. "Like, a knobhead usually don't mean nothing by it. But a dick just don't care."

"And a ballsack?"

"Kinda...hangs there, not doing much good to anyone."

"Speaking as someone who wanted to be a doctor," said Rosaline, "I'm pretty sure they do have a useful function."

"Speaking as someone who has to live with one, they don't half get in the way. I mean, sitting on your own balls is, mate, it's like, it hurts, and it's embarrassing, and you shouldn't be able to do that to yourself. Oi, what are you laughing at?"

"Sorry." She made a valiant attempt to control her giggling at Harry's testicular misadventures. "The human body is weird like that. There's a whole bit of your nervous system dedicated to making sure your muscles don't break your bones."

"Tell you what, if there's a God, he's taking the fucking piss."

"I know, right? A girl in my class once dislocated her elbow pointing too vigorously."

"What was she pointing at?"

"Funnily enough," Rosaline told him, giggling again, "that's not the detail I most remember from the incident."

Harry gave a low, answering chuckle. Then abruptly stopped chuckling and glanced over Rosaline's shoulder. Turning, she saw Alain—who she hoped had ignored Jennifer Hallet's advice to masturbate over a picture of his mother—striding away from the Lodge and towards the hotel. He had that very fixed posture that said he knew they were there but was making a point of not looking.

"Oh shit," she whispered. "It's dinner, isn't it?"

"Yeah. I'm not sure I can hack it, to be honest."

"We could go to the pub again, but that didn't end well last time."

"We won't have Anvita, though, so there'll be no one to cheat at I Spy and get us lost in the dark." He paused. "Sort of miss her, mind."

"Me too. It's so strange with the four of us. It feels like you've survived some horrible catastrophe and then you remember everyone else has just gone home and is fine."

Harry nodded. "I had Ricky round to play *FIFA* the other week. Good bloke. Not very good at *FIFA*."

"Did he make it explode in the oven?" asked Rosaline.

"Nah, but he kept getting own goals. I think he was doing it deliberately at the end."

They watched Alain disappear into the hotel.

"Do you fancy..." Harry jerked his thumb backwards. "There's a chippy in one of the villages we went through. We could drive out and grab something."

"Actually, that sounds really nice. As long as we don't punch anyone, trespass anywhere, or upset any livestock."

"I reckon we can give it a go. Come on, mate."

They climbed into Harry's van and wound back through the countryside until they found the chip shop, which was, in fact, called the Old Village Fish and Chip Shop. Once they'd received their newspaper-wrapped parcels of steamy goodness, they decided it was best to get somewhere inconspicuous and unobjectionable in case they got hauled up in front of Jennifer *again*. And so they drove on to a quiet lay-by near a little hill and a copse of trees, where Harry parked and opened the rear doors of the van. The two of them sat side by side in the back, next to Harry's neatly packed shelves of electrical supplies, eating their fish and chips in quiet satisfaction.

It was another beautiful evening—English and golden, and full of hope and birdsong. And for once Rosaline wasn't running late for anything or trying to catch up with anything. Well, she had a certain amount of Jennifer Hallet's goodwill to claw back. But for now this moment was just for her. And she got to share it with...with a friend. With someone who mattered to her.

Maybe it was the quiet and the wide-open sky, but a sense of contentment was settling over her, warm in the summer haze. And the strangest thing about it was that it didn't feel unfamiliar. It felt like a cup of tea at the end of a long day. Like taking Amelie to the park and watching her claim the big tyre swing before anyone else. Like singing along to Mitski while she did the washing-up on a Wednesday afternoon. It was the scent of cupcakes fresh out of the oven. It was Lauren and Amelie bickering over a jigsaw spread across the dining room table. A soft thread of certainty that had always been there.

If only she could allow herself to believe in it.

Sunday

IT WAS A tense weekend of baking. The theme of the week, as tended to be the case in the semifinal, was highly spurious. In this case, Regency. And the blind bake had been, of all things, Turkish delight—which was apparently big back then, and not even Nora had made it before. As far as Rosaline could tell, it involved stirring continuously for a full hour and created a strange glutinous substance that just about stood up and tasted a little bit of roses. She'd come first sort of by default in that hers had been the least awful. But nothing anyone had put forward that round would have tempted an annoying child to sell his siblings to a witch. Probably he'd have taken one look and gone back through the wardrobe.

On top of which, being endearing on camera was borderline impossible with that much resentment seething between three quarters of the cast. Nora, at least, was on good form, grumbling placidly that life was too short to spend this much of it whisking cornflour, and she would know because she'd had most of hers already.

Another night's sleep had helped a little, and today's marathon challenge to produce "three distinct desserts that celebrate the pineapple" was going better than Rosaline had feared it might.

When Colin Thrimp appeared at her workstation she dropped

into narration mode without thinking. "So I'm making the pineapple filling for my pineapple-shaped pineapple biscuits. Which, now I say it out loud, might be too much pineapple even for a pineapple challenge. What I've got here is pineapple juice, sugar, and bits of actual pineapple in a pan. I'll leave those to simmer. And while that's doing its thing, I'm going to put together my brown sugar espuma for my molasses-roasted pineapple with dark brown sugar cream."

"Espuma?" said Grace Forsythe, whose innuendar had, once again, called her to Rosaline's side. "Hardly knew 'er."

She probably shouldn't have taken her eyes off any of the things she was cooking, but Rosaline couldn't help but ask, "Are you allowed to espuma before the watershed?"

"If she's up for it."

Alain glanced up from his apothecary's counter of wholesome-looking ingredients and Rosaline cringed in case he said something. But either he thought better of it or hadn't been paying attention, and quickly returned to work.

Which was typical, wasn't it? She'd spent nearly the whole competition worrying about what other people thought and felt, and he'd spent it going after things he wanted. It was an arsehole way to live your life, but it was definitely a better way to win a baking competition.

When judging rolled round, Rosaline was called up first, and she carefully laid her selection of pineapple-themed desserts on the table at the front of the ballroom.

"Well, these," declared Wilfred Honey, "look lovely."

Marianne Wolvercote subjected Rosaline's offering to flensing scrutiny. "I'm impressed by the espuma. That's quite technical. But the cupcakes"—she took a bite of one—"while nice, aren't really at the level I'd be expecting from you at this stage in the competition."

Oh God. She was going out. She was going out for serving substandard cupcakes to a renowned patissier.

"And the biscuits"—Marianne Wolvercote was still not done—"although I understand the whimsy and the rosemary representing the fronds of the pineapple are an interesting touch, are just a bit too...jam-in-pastry for me."

Rosaline blinked, trying not to cry. Tears on-camera were bad enough. Tears in front of her dickhead ex would be a whole different level of mortifying.

Wilfred Honey folded his arms mulishly. "See, I disagree. Your espuma's lovely and technical. The cupcakes, yes, they're simple but they've got a lot of heart, and they're perfectly baked, and they taste grand. As for the biscuits, they're fun, and I can see your little girl really liking them."

Feeling slightly shaky and not at all sure whether that had been a good judging or a bad judging, Rosaline went back to her stool.

Harry was next. "Right," he said, "I've done a sort of range of pineapple sweets. There's pineapple fudge, piña colada ice lollies, and a yellow velvet cake, which is like a red velvet cake, only it's yellow and it's done with pineapple."

The judges sampled his various delectables.

"I think this is actually quite clever again," said Marianne Wolvercote in the surprised tone she seemed to reserve for the times Harry did something impressive. "You've taken classic favourites, made them fit the brief, and presented them in quite an elegant way. I will say that you got lucky with your ice lollies because"—and here she snapped a corner from one of them—"they've only just frozen."

"Call me a stickler," added Wilfred Honey, "but I don't like ice lollies on *Bake Expectations*. Because it's not baking and, to be honest, it's barely cooking."

Harry nodded. "That's fair."

"I think you're getting away with it here," Wilfred went on, "because the challenge was for a range of desserts. And they do complement the cake and the fudge very nicely. The yellow velvet was a risk because I've not seen a pineapple velvet before, but it has worked and it is very velvety, which is what it's supposed to be."

Although she hadn't been super thrilled with her own feedback, Rosaline still shared a smile with Harry as he returned—blushing slightly—to his place.

"Basic," declared Marianne Wolvercote in response to the three cakes Nora plonked down in front of her. "We wanted a cohesive set of desserts that celebrated the pineapple. And what you've given us are three cakes with pineapple on them."

"There's also pineapple in them," Nora pointed out.

Wilfred Honey sliced into the pineapple cheesecake and gently levered out a slice. "We can't fault you technically. This is nicely tart, well set, and has a lovely sweet base. The Victoria sponge is perfect, and I know how much skill it takes to bake a perfect Victoria sponge. And you've also made a great pineapple upside-down. But Marianne is right that you're not showing a lot of range here, compared to the other contestants."

"Mmhm," said Nora. "Thanks."

Finally, it was Alain—bearing his usual tray of trying too hard.

"So," he announced, "I've prepared coconut panna cotta with spiced pineapple, a pineapple mint sherbet with fresh fruit, and a vanilla bean and pineapple lattice tart."

Oh fuck. It all looked great. Of course it looked great. He was a smug prick, but he was annoyingly good at baking.

"I'm probably going to be a bit prejudiced about this," said Wilfred Honey, "because I do love a tart."

"Don't we all, darling," put in Grace Forsythe from the sidelines.

"You've got a lovely even bake on it," went on Wilfred Honey, "and the vanilla bean really softens the acidity of the pineapple. This is just perfect."

Alain smiled modestly. "Thank you."

"You've outdone yourself, Alain." Marianne Wolvercote was testing the wobble on the panna cotta. "I particularly appreciate that you went for a sherbet, which, of course, is another dessert that was popular in the period. In fact, I like it so much that I'll forgive you for going back to the herb garden for the mint."

"The texture on the panna cotta," went on Wilfred Honey, "is exactly where it needs to be. And I like that for this one you've used the pineapple more as a garnish so that you get it incorporated differently into each dessert."

Marianne Wolvercote nodded. "I absolutely agree. I think the way you've used the flavours across all three dishes shows a real subtlety of touch. Each one gives us a different side of the pineapple, and that's exactly what we're looking for."

So he won. Of course he fucking won.

Grace Forsythe still did the enormous rambling speech where she hinted it might be somebody else, but he fucking won.

"And that," Grace Forsythe went on, "brings us to the sad part of the afternoon. It's always difficult to say goodbye to somebody this close to the end."

Nora was looking crestfallen. The three-cake gambit had clearly not been the right call in this situation.

"But I'm afraid, and you're all wonderful bakers, we have to lose one of you. And this week it's Harry."

Everyone looked shocked. Except Alain, who looked borderline triumphant.

"It's...Harry?" said Nora.

Grace Forsythe cleared her throat. "It was a very close week and the judges felt that the last place in the final had to go to the more consistent performer over the whole competition."

"Makes sense." Harry got off his stool in preparation for the farewell scene. "I'd be first to admit I ballsed up a bunch of times."

Colin Thrimp fluttered into view. "Um, actually, we might want to use some of this footage so if you could keep the balls to a minimum, that would be very helpful."

"Well deserved, Nora," offered Alain with infuriating sincerity.

Harry drew Nora into a hug. "Yeah, well done."

"All in, please," trilled Colin Thrimp. "Show the viewers how much you've bonded."

And they had in a way. With one notable exception.

"This is bullshit," yelled Rosaline, bursting into Jennifer Hallet's trailer. "No one who watches the show is going to believe that Nora stayed in this week because she baked better than Harry."

Jennifer swung her chair round from her wall of screens. "Magic of editing, sunshine. And I'd rather not have had to do it. But let me remind you that your Cockney goatfucker of a boyfriend fucking punched a fucking contestant in the fucking face. And if Jeremy Clarkson can't get away with it, he certainly can't."

"But Alain apparently can."

Leaning back, Jennifer Hallet adopted an expression of mock horror. "Oh no. A middle-class white man might get away with pressuring his girlfriend into doing sex stuff she wasn't into. What an unexpected development. My understanding of the world, it is shaken."

"Don't act like this is out of your control," said Rosaline, pointing in a way that was probably ill-advised. "You're in charge here. You get to decide what happens."

"And is that what you want? For me to kick Mr. Streak of Piss and Lemongrass off the show so he can always be the guy who should have won season six of *Bake Expectations*? You want to send him home? Beat him. Then get on with your life."

Rosaline wasn't much good at righteous indignation at the best of times. And this wasn't the best of times. She drooped. "What about Harry?"

"What about him? The little bit of rough who's there to give forty-five-year-old women something to whack off to and to make everyone else think, *Oh, I'm surprised he bakes.* It's a miracle he made it past week three."

"Is this how you see everyone? Is Nora just the comforting granny and Alain the guy you want your daughter to marry? Am I just the nice girl with the sad life story for the eighteen- to thirty-five demographic?"

Jennifer Hallet threw back her head and unleashed a grating laugh. "Think very carefully about this, sunshine. Do you really want to hear the answer to that question?"

As it turned out, Rosaline did not need to think very carefully. "No. No I don't."

"Fabulous. Now fuck off. Because I've got to make this completely avoidable shitfire look charming and relatable."

In the car park, she found Harry waiting for her.

"Ready to go?" he asked. Followed by, "What's wrong, mate?"

Rosaline was struggling with tears—she hadn't expected yelling at Jennifer Hallet to help, but now she'd done it she'd run out of actions and was stuck with nothing but emotions. "I got you kicked off the show."

"I got kicked off 'cos it'd be unfair for Nora to go out from one bad week and 'cos I lamped Alain one."

"But you only hit him because of me."

"I didn't. I hit him because where I come from, bloke puts his hands on you and you tell him nice to take 'em off and he don't, you hit him." He lifted one shoulder in a shrug. "I didn't like the way he was treating you, mind, but I reckoned you was already dealing with that on account of you leaving. What happened between him and me was between him and me."

That made Rosaline feel slightly better, but only slightly. "I still don't think you should have gone out."

"Yeah, but I did. Just TV, init? So we heading off or what?"

"I guess. We'll need to get Amelie from my parents, though. To add insult to injury, I had to pass my child between two different sets of babysitters this week so I could be pressured into a threesome I didn't want."

"Not a problem, mate. Where do they live?"

"Kensingon."

He chuckled. "Course they do."

Truthfully—after everything that had happened in the last couple of days—Rosaline was not quite ready to face Cordelia and St. John. But it was the only way she could get Amelie back. So she had to.

"Blimey," observed Harry as they pulled up outside Rosaline's parents' house. "Is your dad the bloke from *Mary Poppins*?"

Rosaline gazed somewhat sheepishly at the extremely desirable Earl's Court residence in which she'd grown up. "What? Dick Van Dyke?"

"No, the one with the bowler and the moustache. Did *Bedknobs and Broomsticks* and all."

"Yeah. My parents are kind of…actually incredibly rich now I think about it."

"See." He grinned triumphantly at her. "I said you was posh."

"We're not posh. They've just…both been very successful in their fields."

"You know the two poshest things in the world?"

"Um, the Queen and Victoria Beckham?"

"Saying you ain't posh," he told her. "And saying the words 'very successful in their fields.' My dad's successful in his field.

But because his field's electrics they say, 'That's Ringo Dobson. He's an electrician.'"

There was a pause. "Sorry. Your dad's called Ringo?"

"Yeah, my nan's a big Beatles fan."

"And you think my name is weird."

"To be fair, mate, Ringo Starr is still alive, was actually in the thing he's famous for being in, and ain't a nun. Also, I reckon you're stalling. You know, I can wait in the van if you want."

She was stalling. But not because of Harry. "You don't need to do that. Unless *you* want. Which you might. Because my parents can be...a lot?"

"Nah, you're all right. Be good to stretch my legs."

They stretched their legs—Rosaline's quite reluctantly—up to the front door. Where she knocked and waited.

"Ain't you got a key?" asked Harry in the brief silence that followed.

"If I had one to their house, they'd want one to my house, and that would be a whole big thing." Rosaline hoped he wouldn't ask for any more explanation, and as the mixed luck of the moment would have it, he never got the chance.

The door opened to reveal Cordelia Palmer in her at-home wear, which honestly wasn't that different from her picking-her-daughter-up-from-a-baking-show wear, which wasn't that different from her giving-a-speech-at-a-conference wear. "Rosaline," she said, "who's this?"

As greetings went, it could have been worse. And occasionally had been. "This is Harry. He's from the show."

"Nice to meet you, Mrs. Palmer." Harry offered his hand and Cordelia started at it, like it was literally covered in faeces.

"What happened to Alain?" asked Cordelia.

"You don't want to know."

"I do want to know. You just don't want to tell me."

Rosaline curled her nails into her palms. "You're right. I don't want to tell you. Can I have my daughter back, please."

Sighing, Cordelia stood aside. "She's in the upstairs drawing room with your father and her marbles."

It was hard for Rosaline to meet Harry's eyes after her mother had not only refused to shake his hand but also referenced the drawing room in a way that made it very clear they had more than one. Sliding past Cordelia, she led him up to the largest space in the house, which was now filled with the most complex and elaborate marble run Rosaline had ever seen. The Palmers made little secret of their desire to "get Amelie into STEM," and so, over the years, they'd spent a small fortune on GraviTrax kits that Amelie loved and Rosaline tried not to feel betrayed that Amelie loved.

"Mummy," Amelie called out from across the small forest of towers, ramps, and magnetic catapults. "Look. Look what me and Granddad made."

"Granddad and I," said Granddad, who was sitting on a nearby stool and assembling a flipper.

"Look what Granddad *and I* made. It's a race. For marbles. And there's a blue marble and a red marble and a green marble and they go *whoosh*. And we're going to start the green marble here and the red marble here and the blue marble here and see which one wins because of gravity and momentum."

Harry crouched to get a better look at the track. "That sounds well exciting."

"Hello, Mr. Viking." Amelie looked up from her construction project. "Look what Granddad and I made."

"I heard, Prime Minister. It's a race for marbles."

"Rosaline"—St. John Palmer got his feet—"who's this?"

"He's from the show," explained Cordelia, emerging from the stairwell. "Apparently Alain is out of the picture."

St. John Palmer shook his head regretfully. "Pity. Seemed a good sort. What went wrong this time?"

"I don't want to talk about it," Rosaline told him as firmly as she could.

"Talk about what?" asked Amelie very loudly. "Who's Alain?"

"Alain used to be a friend of Mummy's. But he's not anymore."

"Why?"

"He turned out not to be a very nice person."

Amelie thought about this for a moment. "Why?"

Oh God. "He pretended to be...the sort of person Mummy might like. But actually he was very selfish."

Amelie still had that "why" look on her face, but Cordelia got in first. "He didn't seem that selfish to me. He was encouraging you to make some very positive changes in your life."

"Yes." St. John Palmer chose, as ever, to act on his perennial conviction that what the world really needed was his opinion. "Your mother told me you were going back to university. I've looked into it, and an Open University level-two course is the best place to start. I'll have a word with Edward—he's been working for them since the last recession."

This was rapidly becoming typical. "Dad, don't have a word with Edward. Don't have a word with anybody."

"Rosaline." Cordelia was gazing at her coldly. "I hope you aren't going to abandon your career plans just because things didn't work out with a man."

"They weren't my career plans," Rosaline tried to insist. "They were something I was thinking about."

"Mummy..." And now Amelie was involved again. This felt nastily like it was escalating. "You didn't say you were going back to university. Why didn't you say you were going back to university?"

They didn't often have Rosaline's back, but if there was anything Cordelia and St. John would rush to defend, it was her right to do something they'd been wanting her to do for a decade. "It'll be very good for you," St. John was saying.

"Mummy might be a bit busy for a little while," Cordelia continued, "but after that she'll have a much better job and you can live in a much nicer house—"

"Will I be able to have a dog?" Amelie asked. "Or a hissing cockroach?"

In theory, this was a good time for Rosaline to put her foot down, but that was hard with the Palmers working so much at cross-purposes with her. "We aren't getting a new house."

"Then why are you going back to university?" Amelie was beginning to sound confused, and a confused Amelie was a short step away from a tearful Amelie. "If you get to go back to university, I should get a dog or a cockroach or a house."

Harry, who had been fiddling with one of the loose bits of track in Amelie's marvellous marble monorail, looked up. "Sounds to me like your mum ain't made up her mind yet."

"*Hasn't* made up her mind." That was both the Palmers at once.

"And I think you'll find she has." That was Cordelia.

That was also, at last, enough. "Oh *do you*," Rosaline snapped. "I'm so glad you're here to tell other people when I've made my mind up because I'm *clearly* incapable of doing it myself."

"Well, if we're being honest, darling"—Cordelia clasped her hands like she was delivering painful news and not just being shitty—"you've always been a little indecisive."

"I'm not *indecisive*, Mother, I'm bisexual. There's a difference."

It was the wrong thing to say, because if there was one thing the Palmers excelled at... Well, if there was *one* thing they excelled at, it was pursuing careers in medicine lucrative enough to pay for large houses in central London and a private education for their daughter to waste. But one of the many *other* things they excelled at was plausible deniability. "You're the one who's making this about your lifestyle choices. I'm simply pointing out that your father and I have met two of your gentlemen friends in as many months—"

"We're just mates," Harry offered in a doomed attempt to set the record straight.

All he got for his trouble was a femtosecond of Cordelia's attention. "Nobody's talking to you, Harold dear."

"It ain't Harold, it's Harry. And I don't like to say nothing, but I think you're being a bit rude now."

"The fact that you *don't like to say nothing* is quite self-evident." St. John Palmer looked from Harry to Rosaline. "Are you really going to let this man talk to your mother like that?"

And what the fuck kind of question was that to ask her?

"Sorry, Mrs. Palmer." Harry put his hands in the air almost as if a gun was being pointed at him. As if a gun *were* being pointed at him. "Didn't mean no offence."

"Can't be helped, I'm sure."

Okay, maybe *that* was enough. "Mum, stop being such a condescending—stop being so condescending. Harry, you've got nothing to apologise for, you're right. They *are* being rude. They're not just being rude, they're being..." This wasn't a conversation she wanted to be having in front of her daughter. "Can you take Amelie to the van, please."

At the sound of her name, Amelie flicked back into life like one of those fish you get in a certain sort of pub. "I don't want to go in the van, I want to finish my marbles."

"Let the girl finish her marbles, Rosaline." St. John Palmer had the same commanding tone he'd been using whenever Rosaline disagreed with him for as long as she could remember. "They're educational."

This...this was a deep-breaths situation. "Amelie. Thank Grandma and Granddad for a lovely time. You can finish your marbles when you come back. But for now, I need you to go to the van with Harry."

"Are you really sending our granddaughter to go and sit in a van with a stranger you met on a reality television program?"

Cordelia couldn't have sounded more aghast if she'd taken lessons.

"No. I'm sending *my daughter* to go and sit in the van with *my friend* because she shouldn't have to be here for this."

"What shouldn't I be here for?" asked Amelie. "Why do you always think I can't understand things? I can understand lots of things. I can understand what makes the marbles go fast and the fish with the big eyes that live under the sea and where the energy comes from in the hydrothermal vents even though there isn't any sunlight so they can't do photo…photo…"

"Photosynthesis." St. John's voice shifted from scolding to avuncular so quickly that he almost sounded like he was operating outdated text-to-voice software.

"Amelie. I've asked you twice now. Say goodbye to Grandma and Granddad and go to the van with Harry."

For all that Rosaline spent half her life feeling like the twelfth-worst parent in the world, she very seldom had to tell her daughter to do anything more than three times. Amelie stood up, recited a slightly rote but passably adorable round of thank-you-for-having-mes and went to stand by Harry.

"C'mon, Prime Minister, we can play I Spy while we wait."

The dozen or so seconds that it took for them to get out of earshot were longer by far than the hours Rosaline had spent on the show waiting for the judges to tell her why her baking sucked this week.

"Well?" St. John had actually folded his arms. "What was this thing you wanted to say to us that was so momentous you had to send your daughter away?"

The look in his eyes was defiant enough that for a very, very long moment Rosaline seriously considered retreating into "You know what, forget it." But she'd been doing that for more than eight years and where had it got her? "You…" There was no good way to start this and no not-objectively-terrible way to continue it. "You honestly don't see what you're like, do you?"

Her father blinked. "What I'm *like*?"

"Rosaline"—Cordelia was shifting to her understanding persona, all I-statements and a voice that went up about an eighth of an octave—"I recognise that you've had some disappointments recently, but lashing out at your father—"

"Oh fuck me, Mum, I mean both of you. Don't you—I mean, do you even—I come here to pick up my child and you second-guess my decisions, insult my friend, make constant digs at my entire fucking life, and you do it all *in front of Amelie*."

Had that worked? It seemed to shut them up for a moment at least.

But only a moment. And Cordelia rallied first. "Well, I'm sorry if your...friend felt insulted. But you have to see how confusing this is for your father and me. And for Amelie. Your lifestyle hasn't exactly been stable recently."

"Maybe n—" She'd been about to concede the point but no. That was how this always worked. "Um, actually I'm pretty sure that's bullshit. Like actual, utter bullshit."

"Language, Rosaline." Now that Amelie had left the building, playful St. John had done the same.

"Oh, fuck language. Language is for saying things and what I'm saying now is that what you just said"—she turned to Cordelia, who was looking thoroughly taken aback—"can only be described as *bullshit*. My life has been unbelievably stable for a fucking decade. I've had three jobs, none of which have got in the way of looking after Amelie. I've dated four or five people, most of whom I have made damned sure she didn't meet."

She should probably have stopped there. But she found she couldn't. Or maybe it was that she didn't want to, and maybe that was more important. "I've kept you pair of—you pair of snobbish gaslighting fucks in her life because she apparently loves you, probably because she doesn't actually *know* you; and yes,

I've also kept Lauren in her life because Lauren has actually been there for me this whole time."

The mention of *that woman* drew winces from both Palmers, but Rosaline kept going. "Even while I've been on the show I've picked my daughter up from school every day I wasn't filming and I've not missed one single ballet recital or school fete or parent-teacher evening, which, let's be really fucking clear, is *far* more than I can say for either of you. So no, my life hasn't"—she threw the world's most vicious set of air quotes—"*been unstable recently*. It's just that it hasn't looked the way you've been telling me it has to look since I was fucking *six*."

"We know we weren't perfect parents." Cordelia was speaking slowly now, almost guardedly. "But we thought that with a child of your own you'd understand how difficult it can be."

That was...that wasn't even not the point. It was inventing its own point that was easier to deal with. "I know it's difficult. Of course I know it's fucking difficult."

"Then why are you having a go at your mother for missing your parent-teacher meetings?" There was an almost protective note in St. John's voice that Rosaline hadn't expected.

"Fuck me, is that the only thing you're going to respond to? I've spent my entire life with the spectre of your expectations following me around like Banquo's ghost and you think I'm narked that you missed my year-nine play."

St. John gave her a sour look. "And did you pick up 'narked' from the man with the van or the ex-girlfriend?"

"You mean from Harry or from Lauren? They both have names. And I don't know. Both? Neither? Why does it matter? Why does every tiny detail of every part of my life *matter*?"

At this Cordelia looked almost heartbroken. "You're our daughter, darling, of course you matter."

"That's not..." This was beginning to feel a lot like making Turkish delight. Hot, stressful, taking forever, and producing nothing anybody actually wanted. "Why is it so important to you that I live in the right sort of house, that I have the right sort of job, that I go out with the right sort of man and before you say anything, you clearly do find it easier if I'm going out with a man."

"Only because we want what's best for you," said St. John, as if that wasn't a terrible answer.

"There's such a lot of prejudice around," explained Cordelia, as if that made it better.

The Turkish delight was beginning to crystallise. "Okay. Let me try again. Because I think you've mistaken this for a discussion."

"Well, you've hardly been clear, darling." Cordelia still had the gall to look disapproving.

"Then listen. I am not going back to university. I do not want to go back to university. I do not want to be a doctor, and actually"—she'd never said this out loud before, but now she was forcing herself to, it seemed like the most natural thing in the world—"I'm not sure I *ever* wanted to be a doctor. It's just that until Amelie it never occurred to me that I could want anything else."

It had felt good to say. A feeling that dwindled rapidly as she saw the utterly uncomprehending looks on her parents' faces.

"You're not saying you got pregnant on purpose?" asked Cordelia, who was taking a solid crack at redefining the word "mortified."

"No. But when I did I had to make a choice, and I think the choice I made was—well—it was what I wanted. I like my life. I like being—"

"A single mother who works in a shop?" St. John might have been trying not to sound incredulous, but he wasn't trying very hard.

Rosaline gave half a nod. "I like that I have time for my

daughter. I like that I'm not killing myself studying or working or whatever it is I'd have been doing now if my life had stayed on the track it was meant to be on. And I know I'm supposed to want to have it all, but I...don't? I want what I've got. What I've got is...it's enough. It's everything."

For a moment it seemed like it was over. St. John Palmer nodded in the way he used to do at the end of dinner to signal that it was okay for everybody to leave the table. "Just as long," he said, "as we keep paying your bills."

Rosaline was breathing hard as she threw herself into the double passenger seat of the van alongside Amelie.

"Your kid," said Harry, "cheats at I Spy."

Amelie was at that age where she had a strong sense of fairness when it came to anybody else while also having a strong desire to demonstrate her cleverness by finding as many ways round as many rules as she could. Thankfully, because she was eight, her resources were somewhat limited. "I do not cheat at I Spy. I said 'I spy with my little eye something beginning with a and the answer was—'"

"Atoms?" guessed Rosaline.

"You see. Mummy got it."

Harry made a great show of exasperation. "You can't see atoms, can you?"

"Everything is atoms," explained Amelie. "So if you can see anything you can see atoms."

Having checked their seats were all belted, Harry released the hand brake and eased them carefully out into the road. "Well, then I could say *haitch* for ham sandwich because I had one for lunch and so if you're looking at me, you're looking at a ham sandwich."

Rosaline wasn't sure how well she was hiding her just-had-a-blazing-row face. Given Harry's commitment to distracting Amelie and not asking questions, she assumed the answer was *Well enough for an eight-year-old.*

Amelie drummed her toes impatiently against Harry's toolbox. "That's different."

"Why's it different, Prime Minister?"

"Because you're made of atoms. You're not made of sandwich. Otherwise you'd look like a sandwich."

"I don't look like an atom neither."

"Yes you do because everything looks like atoms because everything's atoms which is what I'm saying."

Secretly Rosaline was a little bit proud that she'd raised her daughter to both fight her corner and know a lot about the structure of matter for a child. Picking her battles, however, was a skill that Amelie had yet to master. "Amelie, be nice to Harry. He took Mummy all the way home from the show and he's been looking after you."

It was the right call parentingwise. But it did have the unfortunate side effect of reminding Amelie that her mother existed. "Mummy, what happened with Grandma and Granddad and why couldn't I finish my marbles?"

Well, fuck. Because while in her current mood Rosaline didn't care whether Cordelia and St. John ever saw their granddaughter or, for that matter, their daughter again, weaponising your children in an argument was one of the shittiest moves it was humanly possible to pull. "Grandma and Granddad," she said slowly, "are upset because I told them I don't want to go back to university and be a doctor."

"Why don't you want to be a doctor? Do you not want us to have a new house and a dog and a cockroach?"

"It's not about the house. Or the dog or the cockroach. It's just...you know how you don't want to do something, and I'll say *When you're a grown-up, you'll get to decide for yourself?* Well, I'm a grown-up, and I've decided for myself that I don't want to be a doctor."

Amelie thought about this for quite a long time. "But if grown-ups get to decide and you're a grown-up why are Grandma and Granddad upset with you?"

Being a good parent, or what she hoped passed for a good parent, always seemed on the edge of impossible. Trying to be a good parent ten minutes after you'd had a shouting match with your own parents about the way they'd parented you was over the edge and plummeting. "Lots of reasons. I think it's hard for people to realise that their children are grown-ups too."

"Yes," agreed Amelie very fervently. "You still think I need to take Mary Shelley to bed even though I'm eight."

"And Grandma and Granddad really do want the best for us. It's just they think that means me being a doctor because they're doctors."

Amelie was thinking again. "Are they racist?"

Weirdly, they weren't very. They tended to reserve their prejudices for people with less money or education than them. "Where did that come from?"

"Miss Wooding says racism is when you don't like someone because they're different from you so I thought Grandma and Granddad might be racist about people who aren't doctors. We're not supposed to be racist. We did a lesson on it."

To be fair to Miss Wooding, England's long history of colonialism and systemic injustice was a complex topic for Key Stage 2. "I think racism is more about"—yep, definitely complex for Key Stage 2—"culture and religion and, um, what someone's skin looks like. I suppose Granddad and Grandma might be a bit…classist?" She shot a guilty look at Harry, whose grammar she'd once found so completely off-putting. "That's when you don't like people who talk a certain way or have certain sorts of jobs."

"Like saying 'ain't'?" asked Amelie, who was sometimes far, *far* too perceptive for comfort. "Or being a man who fixes electrics?"

Rosaline was kind of paralysed. So Harry—with surprising gentleness—answered for her. "Something like that, I reckon."

And once more, Amelie lapsed into a thinky silence. Which was good, wasn't it? It was good to have a daughter who thought for herself. Fucking terrifying, but good.

"Well," announced Amelie finally. "I don't think you should have to be a doctor if you don't want to be a doctor. And I don't mind if we don't have a bigger house or a dog but I would like a cockroach. And fixing electrics is useful because if nobody fixed electrics we wouldn't have any electrics and then nothing would work."

As a summary of centuries of entrenched social stratification and a lifetime of her own personal neuroses, Rosaline had heard worse.

Rosaline was very ready for an early night. Amelie had different ideas, but she was a child so she lost that argument. And Rosaline was just crawling into bed—and thinking how good it would feel to put the last few days firmly behind her—when her fucking phone rang. It was an unknown number, which gave her a totally irrational sense of anxiety in case it was the police, wanting to tell her that Amelie had been eaten by an escaped rhinoceros, or Jennifer Hallet calling to tell her she'd been kicked off the show after all. Though of course, realistically, it was far more likely to be someone trying to get her to change her broadband provider.

"Hello," she said wearily.

"Hi. Rosaline?" It was a woman's voice and not one Rosaline recognised.

"Who is this?"

"Don't hang up"—never an auspicious start—"but it's, um, Liv?"

On the list of things Rosaline needed right now, this might actually have been last. "I think you're going to have to do quite a bit better than 'Don't hang up.'"

"I got your number off Alain's phone. And I wanted to say...Fuck. Can you say sorry for...for...well—"

"Sexually assaulting someone?" Rosaline offered.

Liv made a slightly horrified noise that made Rosaline feel several complicated types of discomfort. "Um. Yeah? That."

"I don't know. Can you?"

"Okay." Unsteady breathing that suggested Liv might actually be crying. "I'm sorry that I...I— Shit. Sexuallyassaultedyou?"

There was a long pause as Rosaline wrestled with a far wider range of feelings than she should be arsed to deal with. "I want to be a good person and say *it's okay*. But—"

"It's not, is it? And I don't think I expected you to say it was. I think I needed you to know I knew it wasn't."

"Well, thank you for saying so. And for knowing that, I guess? I mean, I hope you're taking this as read but don't do it again. Because that shit is still not okay even if you're both women."

"I do realise that," said Liv a little sharply. "I'm not making excuses, but I'd been drinking since three and Alain really did tell me you were attracted to me."

"For the record, I wasn't." Did that sound mean? Did it matter if it sounded mean? "It's not that you aren't...very nice...in the face and things. It's just I wasn't looking to look at you that way."

Another woeful sound from Liv. "I know, I know. I've sort of been...letting men tell me I'm bicurious for years. They like it so fucking much. And get so disappointed if you're not."

It wasn't totally impossible for Rosaline to empathise with

straight women who felt pressured to appropriate her sexuality. But it was pretty fucking difficult. "Yeah. Maybe stop doing that? Because face it, Liv: you, me, and Alain could have wound up in a threesome that only he wanted."

"I'm sorry. I feel...honestly, quite disgusting. And very, very stupid."

Oh God. "Look, it's a bit obnoxious that you're making me reassure you here. The thing is, I've met Alain. I know what he's like. And nothing actually happened. Forgive yourself or grow as a person or whatever you need to do. I'm fine and I understand you made a mistake. But I'm not your priest, your friend, or your therapist. So...yeah? Thank you for reaching out. I don't think we need to talk again."

"Thanks for"—Liv still sounded if not wrecked then at least dinged around the fenders—"for not hanging up on me. And yeah, I'll...I won't bother you again. Good luck with the show."

Skidding her phone across her bedside table, Rosaline flumped back against her pillows and exhaled.

As days went, it had been like the eggs, sugar, flour, butter, milk, and baking powder in a perfect Victoria sponge.

Mixed.

Week Eight

Finale

Tuesday

"YOU, SUNSHINE," JENNIFER Hallet was saying, "are the bane of my fucking life."

Telling Jennifer Hallett that she didn't want Cordelia and St. John involved in the "Very Special This Is What Our Adorable Finalists' Adorable Lives Are Like" episode was not something the Rosaline who had started this competition would have done. But a lot had changed since. "All I'm asking is that you do this without speaking to my parents. Don't think of it as losing footage. Think of it as saving a train fare to Kensington."

"Are you really going to pretend you're doing this for my convenience? I planned this shit months ago. You serving your nice middle-class family cakes at a nice middle-class table in a nice middle-class house. And then them sitting side by side on a sofa, saying, *We're so proud of her, she was always such a good girl, it's great she's finally doing something for herself.*"

"Excuse me"—Rosaline voice rose without her meaning it to—"I've done a lot of things for myself. For example, a thing I'm doing for myself is telling you I want you to leave my parents out of this. This show does not get to claim it empowered me."

Jennifer Hallet rose from Rosaline's one armchair like Poseidon from the depths. "Of course it fucking empowered you. When you first showed up here you were just a mouse with an apron and a pretty smile. And now you're a mouse with fucking ideas who won't shut the fuck up and let me do my fucking job."

"Right." Rosaline could do this. She wasn't scared of Jennifer Hallet. Well, not very scared. Okay, she was quite scared but she was also committed. "If my arc is that I've got more confident, because I'm a woman and not a grandmother and therefore that's the only arc I can have, why do you need my parents to validate that?"

"Context, sunshine, context. We need to know how diffident and shit you used to be, so everybody can think *Gosh, hasn't she come a long way.* We want sad little girls and stifled housewives up and down the country to look at you and think, *If she can do it, then so can I.* And if enough of them think it, you'll get a huge book deal at the end of this, which you can use to put your daughter through university or rehab, whichever she winds up needing."

Rosaline just stared at her. "You are the worst human being."

"Flattery'll get you nowhere. Smile, look relatable, and ride this train to Big Pile of Money Station."

If Jennifer Hallet had a superpower more subtle than shouting, it was her ability to make you question yourself. Because, ultimately, money mattered, especially with Amelie in the picture. And maybe the mature thing to do was to swallow her pride and leave everything to the professionals. After all, if Jennifer was right—and Rosaline thought she probably was—then she could be throwing away the very opportunity she came on the show to get.

"Look." One more try. Then she'd cave. "If that's the story you're telling, why can't I be the one to tell it? Because, yes, you're right. I've got things out of the show, and I'm a stronger, more confident person because of it. Which is why I'm pissing you off so much right now."

Jennifer Hallet's eyes had narrowed in a way that was either very good or very, very bad. "You've been pissing me off for a lot longer than that, but I'm listening."

"You've got a file on me. You know the deal. I got pregnant at nineteen and now I'm a single mum in a dead-end job. But my parents have never made me feel anything but shitty about myself. So I don't want them to be part of my story. Not when there are people in my life—like Amelie and my ex-girlfriend Lauren—who can say all of this, but the difference is that when they say they're proud of me, they'll fucking mean it."

"Fine. The moppet will probably play better anyway."

"On top of which— Wait. What?"

"You win, sunshine." It was hard to tell just then if Jennifer Hallet was secretly respecting Rosaline or hating her guts. "But if this isn't the most heartwarming bucket of oversweetened bull semen I've ever poured down the throat of the nation, I will come to you in the night and burn your pubes while you sleep."

Rosaline felt actually slightly dizzy with adrenaline, success, and several mental images she really hadn't wanted. "Okay. Deal."

And so, with Rosaline's tiny living room stuffed full of filming equipment and production crew, Lauren and Amelie sat on the sofa and tried to take Colin Thrimp seriously.

"What's it been like," he was asking, in the terminally misguided tone of somebody who thought he was good with children, "having Mummy on *Bake Expectations*?"

"It's been good. I've been staying with Auntie Lauren and she tells me things she's not supposed to and lets me get away with murder."

"I do not," Lauren protested.

"You bloody well do," said Rosaline from the doorway.

Colin Thrimp wrung his hands. "Um, ladies. Can we make

sure this is usable footage? Amelie, would you say that Mummy has, for example, made a lot of cakes?"

Amelie nodded emphatically. "Yes."

"Could you say that, please?"

"Why?"

"So I can film you saying it."

"But you've said it."

"I'm not going to be on the television. You're going to be on the television. So you need to say the things. And what I'd really like you to say is something nice about your mummy."

"Oh." Amelie seemed to be thinking about this for a moment. "I am very happy Mummy's on *Bake Expectations* because it means she's made loads of cakes and normally I have to eat healthily because she's a responsible parent. Which is why social services shouldn't come and take me away."

There was a moment while Colin Thrimp listened to his earpiece. "No, no—I think that's fine. We'll just cut the bit about social services."

"Don't cut that bit," said Amelie. "That's the important bit."

"Amelie darling." Despite it being fairly early in the afternoon and there being, Rosaline could have sworn, none left in the house, Lauren had somehow acquired a glass of wine. "I keep telling you social services wouldn't want you."

"Why not? I'm great. I'm obstreperous."

"That's not a good thing," Rosaline told her.

Amelie did a stubborn pointy thing with her chin that Rosaline hoped she hadn't picked up from her. "It means noisy and difficult to control. And I don't want to be easy to control because people being easy to control is how Hitler happened."

"So, Lauren." Colin Thrimp made a sort of clapping gesture to remind everybody he was still there. "You've known Rosaline for a long while. Would you say this is the first time Rosaline has really done something for *herself*?"

One of Lauren's many skills was that she could laugh in your face from the other side of the room. "God no. She does things for herself all the time. You should see her bedside drawer."

Amelie, too, took this poorly. "That's a mean thing to say. Mummy's very clever. She can do lots of things for herself. She can tie her shoes and she always remembers to brush her teeth in the morning *and* in the evening. She couldn't fix the boiler but that's because boilers are complicated. And she never learned to drive but that's because she had a baby instead of driving lessons."

"Oh, that's interesting," Colin Thrimp pounced. "Are there lots of things your mummy hasn't been able to do because of you?"

Rosaline pushed her away through the forest of cameras. "Colin, say anything like that again and I will go to broadcasting standards and the press and fuck what the contract says."

"Sorry. I...I...didn't mean it to come out like that. I just meant, well, you've obviously made a lot of sacrifices."

"Amelie's not a sacrifice."

"I'm a mammal," agreed Amelie. "We learned that in science. You're a mammal too."

This made Colin Thrimp retreat into his mic again. "Look, you promised Jennifer you'd behave. I need to make some kind of story out of this; otherwise, you're going to be the one without an arc and nobody will like you and that will be my fault and I'll get fired. And please ask your friend to put down the wineglass." He was sounding perilously close to tears. "The only people we ever show drinking are students out with their friends and it's never more than two friends and it's always a quiet pub."

"Fine." Lauren downed her wine and passed the glass to a production assistant. "The pissing thing about Rosaline—sorry, BBC audience. The thing about Rosaline is that she's one of the kindest, strongest, most amazing people you'll ever meet. But until she went on this show, I don't think she ever realised it. She's always been a fighter, she's always stood up for herself, and deep down she's always known what she wanted. Problem was, she used to worry far too much about what other people thought. But now she's done so well on the show and that's given her the confidence to realise everyone else can go fuck themselves."

"That was mostly lovely," said Colin Thrimp, "and exactly what we were looking for. But could we possibly have the last sentence again without the f-word."

Lauren cleared her throat. "But," she went on, "now she's done so well on the show and that's given her the confidence to realise that the people you want in your life are the people who love you no matter what."

"Auntie Lauren's right," added Amelie. "My mummy's the best mummy in the world and I will love her no matter what. Unless I'm dead or asleep or an anglerfish because I don't think anglerfish have human emotions."

Rosaline, however, was not an anglerfish.

And once Colin Thrimp had confirmed they had all they needed, she went and hugged them both, and definitely wasn't crying.

Wednesday

IT WAS ONE of those humid summer nights where stifling heat was giving way to torrential rain. Which meant Rosaline had to dash through the house trying to close all the windows that she'd previously had to dash through the house opening, and do it quietly enough that Amelie—who had insisted it was so hot that she would never fall asleep ever in a million years—wouldn't wake up. Returning to the kitchen, she found a combination of the weather and the various distractions, many of them Amelie-shaped, that had punctuated the evening and turned her practice mousses into a series of brightly coloured puddles.

She was just starting on the washing-up when the doorbell rang. And someday she was going to receive an unexpected communication without immediately assuming it was the police come to tell her that her daughter was either dead, in prison, or possibly both. But today was not that day. Although, given that it was already quite late, Amelie was already in her room, and the police thing was clearly paranoia, Rosaline had no idea who it could possibly be.

Opening the door, she found Cordelia Palmer outside, her suit rapidly soaking through and her hair plastered to her head like—well—like somebody who'd been caught in a sudden rainstorm and hadn't thought to go back for the umbrella that Rosaline knew for a fact she always kept in the boot of her Tesla.

"Mum?" It was an unoriginal opening but the best Rosaline could manage in the circumstances.

"I don't suppose I could come in? It's a little wet out."

Honestly, Rosaline had been hoping for a bit more breathing space between her last conversation with her parents and one of them showing up on her doorstep to guilt-trip her about it. "I mean, I guess so. But Amelie's in bed."

Standing aside, Rosaline let her mum into the hallway and—not really knowing what else to do, because Cordelia Palmer wasn't a guest on account of being a parent and uninvited—went back to the kitchen. A few moments later Cordelia joined her. She'd taken off her shoes and her jacket, which, even as a concession to the rain, was as informal as she ever got. It slightly weirded Rosaline out.

"I wasn't actually here for Amelie," said Cordelia Palmer eventually.

Rosaline scrubbed vigorously at a mixing bowl. "Then—don't take this the wrong way—why are you here?"

There was a long silence. It was the sort of silence you normally filled by offering someone a cup of tea. But Rosaline had made a lot of cups of tea for her parents down the years and wasn't entirely inclined to make another.

Cordelia didn't seem to know where to look or what to do. "Your father and I got a call yesterday from the BBC."

"Oh yes?"

"They told us we wouldn't be needed for the...the finalist thing."

This was going to be the cleanest bowl ever to have had things mixed in it. "I asked them not to bother you."

"Darling, you know it wouldn't have bothered us."

It would have. But for once, that wasn't the point. "Fine. I told them I didn't want them speaking to you. I told them I didn't want you to be part of my story."

There was another long silence. Rosaline put the mixing bowl on the drying rack and braced herself for a bollocking.

"That's what I thought," said Cordelia quietly. "Do you...do you really hate us that much?"

Fuck. *Come back, bollocking; all is forgiven.* "How do you expect me to answer that, Mum? Seriously? If I say yes, I'm basically the worst daughter in the world. And if I say no, then...then...it's like everything's okay. And it isn't. It hasn't been for a long time."

"It's my fault, isn't it? I should have been there for you."

"For fuck's sake." Rosaline stared into the washing bowl like she was looking for answers...or patience...or that one teaspoon because she could have sworn they used to have six. "It's not about you. And can you please not make it about you?"

"I'm not meaning to, but...you have all this anger, darling. And I know that I wasn't like your friends' mothers or like you are with Amelie. That I made different choices. But I really thought I was setting a good example."

Shaking her hands dry, Rosaline went to put the kettle on. It felt like a mercy for both of them at this point. "I didn't want you to be like other people's mums. I just wanted you—you and Dad—to listen to me sometimes. Instead of assuming that the best thing for me was to be you but shorter."

"We listened, darling."

"Do you not think"—Rosaline put a mug down very carefully—"the fact I this second told you that I never felt like you listened to me and you responded by flatly contradicting me indicates that maybe you don't listen as much as you think you do?"

Cordelia Palmer opened her mouth, then closed it again. Then said, "We've always supported you. You wanted to be a doctor so we did everything we could to make that happen for you. You wanted to keep Amelie and raise her yourself and so we stood by you in that as well and gave you money whenever you needed it. And even now, when you're doing this television thing, we've looked after your daughter every weekend."

"Mum..." Rosaline was tired from the competition, from the filming, from the job she still had to do, and was nowhere near close enough to figuring this out for herself to be able to explain it to somebody else. "If the plan is for us to have the same argument every two weeks for the rest of my life, I don't know if I can hack it."

"It feels like you've decided all these terrible things about us. About me. And we're not allowed to defend ourselves."

"You're not back at the Oxford Union. This isn't a debate. You can't use logic and evidence to prove to me that you didn't make me feel sad and worthless."

"Darling, that's unf—" All at once, Cordelia's face crumpled. "I made you feel *worthless*?"

"Yes, like I let you down. Like everything I did I let you down. Because I was supposed to have this amazing life that looked exactly like yours. And instead I wanted a home and a child and a kitchen that always smelled of something wonderful." Admittedly, Rosaline's kitchen currently smelled of Fairy Liquid and angst, but... details.

A glance confirmed that Cordelia was on the verge of tears. And not in her usual *I want you to feel bad so you'll put up with my bullshit* way. "Because I never gave you any of that when you were growing up?"

"No. I mean... no. These are the things I like. And I'm allowed to like them. Even if they're small or seem stupid to other people."

"But"—Cordelia blinked rapidly—"you could have so much more. You could have *anything*. I made sure that you could have anything."

"Listen to yourself." With Amelie asleep upstairs, Rosaline couldn't quite shout and didn't quite want to. "You've just said you wanted to make sure I could have anything. Why can't I have this?"

"Because...because it's what my mother had and what everybody I went to school with had and what I had to fight my whole life not to have. And I swore that would never happen to you, and now"—Cordelia covered her eyes with a hand—"it's like you're throwing it back in my face."

"Oh, Mum." Rosaline put two badly made mugs of Earl Grey down on the kitchen table and slumped down into one of the chairs. She didn't remember her grandparents on that side very well—just vague recollections of a perfect house, a slight, diminished woman, and a man in an armchair shouting "Mary, where's my tea?" "I'm sorry. I didn't mean to make you feel...face-thrown. It's...I'm not you. We want different things, and it should be okay that we want different things. Because...because..." Rosaline sucked in a breath so fast and deep it almost made her dizzy. "I'm so proud of you. You are literally brilliant and I'm lucky to have this brilliant, world-renowned, slightly absentee mother who's always stood up for what she believes in."

Cordelia was crying now in an open, ugly, very real kind of way.

"I don't want you to be anyone other than who you are," Rosaline told her. "I just need you to let me be who I am."

Rosaline went to retrieve a box of tissues so Cordelia could dry her eyes. Then they finished their tea in a silence filled with ambiguities.

"I'm going to try, darling," said Cordelia at last. "I really am going to try."

It wasn't exactly the fatted calf, but it would do. It was more than Rosaline had ever expected. "Thank you."

"Your father...your father is going to need some time."

"Fine with me."

Cordelia gazed at her half-imploringly. "You mustn't...He's a good man. He's just..."

"I know."

"He was the first person I ever knew who took me seriously. It's hard not to fall in love with someone who gives you that."

Rosaline liked to think she was an adult with a nuanced view of the world. But it still fucked with her head to realise her parents were human beings. People with flaws and histories and vulnerabilities and baggage. And some day, Amelie was going to have to learn the same thing about her.

And hopefully, if Rosaline hadn't made a complete hash of everything, still find a way to love her afterwards.

Saturday

SO THIS WAS IT. Well, half of it. Rosaline gazed round the oddly empty ballroom, marvelling that she was now, officially, one of the best bakers in the country, if you didn't count all the people who'd won previous seasons and everyone who was good enough to do it for actual money. Nora seemed about as relaxed as she usually did—and whether her secret was age and experience, wisdom and apathy, or a steady diet of books about Greek billionaires, Rosaline really hoped she could get in on it one day. By contrast, Alain looked ever so slightly like death. From the bags under his eyes, he'd either been studying his recipes or unable to sleep, and it felt bad to feel good about that. But not so bad that she didn't. After all, he'd been a complete cock to her.

The cameras circled them, catching their various expressions of pre-final anticipation, and then the doors opened with a touch more ceremony than they usually did, admitting Grace Forsythe and the judges.

"Welcome, my trio of talented tartlets," announced Grace Forsythe, "to the finale of *Bake Expectations*. You've proved both your worth and your bread, and while the other contestants have snapped like brandy or crumbled like rhubarb, you're standing before us today like a display of artisanal grissini, tall and proud and faintly knobbly. But there can be only one winner, and the first step in this final stage of the competition is our most challenging blind bake yet."

A pause to gather reaction shots of them, well, reacting. Rosaline gamely gave her best terrified face, which, honestly, involved very little acting.

"Your first grand final challenge," Grace Forsythe continued, making Rosaline wonder how many times they'd mention that it was the final, "is a traditional confection found all over the Spanish-speaking world, first introduced to the Iberian Peninsula in the eighth century. We'd like you to make fifty, yes *fifty*, identical, delicious alfajores. You have two hours, starting on three. Three, darlings."

Rosaline took a deep breath and looked at the first step in the instructions: "Make dulce de leche." Which was, on the one hand, good because she'd made it before. And, on the other hand, bad because she'd stood over a pan of it in this very ballroom, crying because she was ballsing it up.

Time, then, for a dulce-de reckoning. Because she was damned if she was going to be defeated by a milky pudding sauce.

Well...not twice anyway.

It was strange waiting for the judging when it was just the three of them— Alain, who was still looking shattered and sullen, went off for a walk; and Nora sat under a tree, contentedly reading *The Scandalous Spanish Magnate's Pregnant Mistress*.

"Well," Rosaline said to Colin Thrimp and his camera operator, "I wasn't crying so I think that went better than last time."

And as it turned out, she was right. In fact, she'd sort of smashed it, claiming the win, which made her feel great, except for the tiny detail that it was a lot easier to do a good job at something you'd already practised loads.

"I thought I did well, considering," remarked Alain pensively in his post-judging interview, "given that I've not made dulce de leche since before the competition started."

There were sufficiently few of them left that they couldn't not eat lunch together—which made for an awkward dining experience.

"Are you enjoying your book?" Alain asked Nora in what Rosaline now recognised as his "secretly mocking you" tone.

She shrugged. "Well, you know. There's a secret baby and a sexy Spaniard, what more can you want?"

"Literary merit, perhaps?" offered Alain.

Nora gave him a withering stare. "One of the best things about being seventy-three is that you can read whatever you like."

"The last thing I read all the way through"—Rosaline made a game attempt to smooth things over—"was a book for nine- to twelve-year-olds about a young witch who discovers last Tuesday is missing."

"How about you, Alain?"

Rosaline would not have trusted either the edge in Nora's voice or the look in her eyes, but Alain apparently had no qualms. "*Lincoln in the Bardo.*"

"And what happens in the end?" asked Nora, in the same voice, with the same look.

"Plot," returned Alain, "in the conventional sense is not the point of the novel."

"You haven't finished it, have you?"

"In case you haven't noticed, I'm in the final of a televised baking competition. I've had other things to do."

Folding her sandwich box into a neat square of cardboard, Nora smiled. "See, when I'm enjoying a book, I bring it with me."

"Not all books require the same degree of focus. I prefer—"

Suddenly unable to maintain even a facade of politeness, Rosaline laughed almost literally in Alain's face. "Oh my God.

Just admit you haven't read the fancy book that you're only reading anyway so people will be impressed that you're reading a fancy book, you gigantic hipster piece of shit."

This had clearly made Nora's day.

As for Alain, he flushed and then paled, and then raised an eyebrow. "Is 'piece of shit' really the wittiest insult you can come up with?"

"Probably." Rosaline shrugged. "Because unlike you, I don't spend my free time coming up with inventive ways to be cruel about people just to make myself feel less pathetic."

"Somebody who has made your life choices," he drawled out in his poshest, nastiest voice, "is in no position to call anybody else pathetic."

She rolled her eyes. "Oh, Alain, Alain, Alain. I'm sure that would have been devastating if I gave a crap about what you think."

"Well, you cared enough to turn Liv against me."

"No, you did that yourself. Because, funnily enough, women don't like it when you try to make them fuck your girlfriend. Now come on." She stood and helped Nora gather up the remains of her lunch. "We should be back on-set."

In the ballroom, Grace Forsythe and the judges were already assembled, and the three finalists hastened to their stations for the briefing.

"I hope you're ready, mes amis boulangers," began Grace Forsythe, "because for your final, final baketacular of the final, final episode of this series, which is to say the final, we have a doozy of a challenge for you. We want you to produce your finest, most elegant, most exquisite, most trophy-winning, series-ending entremets."

She put on her exposition face for the sake of viewers at home. "These are layered mousse cakes originally served between courses or *entre mets* as the French would have it. And because they often need to be frozen overnight, you'll be starting work now and finishing tomorrow just in time for the celebratory high tea. You have three hours from the count of three. Three, darlings."

Okay. This was it. Really it. The final it. Everything came down to this: Rosaline's ability to get mousse to set, biscuit to snap, and mirror glaze to, well, mirror.

It felt strange knowing this was the last time any of them would be in the ballroom, trying to make something ludicrous and extravagant in far too little time in an environment totally unsuited for it. Could it really only have been a couple of months since she'd stood here, forgetting how to blanch almonds, and terrified she'd never done anything except make bad decisions and disappoint people?

Because she'd finally worked out that life wasn't the blind bake. The aim wasn't to follow someone else's vague instructions in the hope you'd produce something they'd approve of to a set of standards they hadn't told you.

It was your ex-girlfriend coming through for you when nobody else did.

It was yelling at your kid's teacher for being casually biphobic.

It was having the same goddamn argument about brushing your teeth every night for four years.

It was maybe meeting someone who was like nothing you thought you were looking for.

It was winning a TV baking competition. Or not winning it.

Or getting chased by a goat you thought was a bull.

It didn't matter what it was. It just mattered that it was yours.

Sunday

"WHAT I'VE GOT for you today," said Nora, placing her bake, or technically her freeze, before the judges with a lot less ceremony than everybody else used, "is a tiramisu entremets. It's the flavours of a tiramisu, which I like, but it's an entremets, which I've never made before."

Nora's cake was a pristine disc of shiny dark chocolate, decorated with truffles and uncharacteristically delicate sugar work.

"I'm impressed with your presentation," said Marianne Wolvercote.

"Well"—Nora gave a slightly pleased-with-herself smile—"it *is* the final. I thought I'd push the boat out. First time I've done spun sugar. Won't lie: probably be the last."

Marianne Wolvercote gave a stately nod. "It was worth it."

Meanwhile, Wilfred Honey cut out a generous slice and angled the layers towards the camera. "Now what have we got here?"

"I think they've probably got fancier names," Nora said, "but as far as I'm concerned you've got the chocolate bit, the coffee bit, and the vanilla bit with the mascarpone."

"That's good enough for me." Wilfred Honey popped a generous forkful into his mouth. "By 'eck, it's gorgeous. Perhaps I just never got past the seventies, but the way I see it you can't go wrong wi' a tiramisu."

"You can definitely go wrong with a tiramisu," put in Marianne Wolvercote, "but I'm pleased to say you haven't in this context. Your layers are distinct, even, and well-defined, everything's perfectly set"—she took her own sample—"and the flavours come through clearly. I will say that I'm not the biggest fan of tiramisu—I think it's hard to interpret it in a modern way. But I think you've succeeded admirably here. Well done, Nora."

There was a pause, Nora blinking back a few tears. "Thank you. Thank you very much."

Rosaline gave her arm a squeeze as she sat back down. And then it was Alain's turn.

"This is a spiced apple entremets," he explained, with slightly less conviction than he normally did. "Oh, um, with saffron."

Shit. Rosaline had been so focused on her own work that she hadn't paid much attention to what everyone else was doing. And Alain, of course, was doing apple as well. At least she wasn't *only* doing apple. But the comparison was still...unhelpful.

And his bake did look rather special. It was sort of Alain all over: glazed in a delicate, almost honey tone and decorated with an elegant minimalism. Just an artfully placed cinnamon stick and a spiral of fresh apple that the fucker had probably picked from his private orchard.

"The apples," Alain continued, "have come from my garden."

"This is very you," said Marianne Wolvercote, in that ambiguous tone that was sometimes worse than criticism. "It's certainly chic, it's modern, it's understated. I could see this in the window of a number of patisseries."

Alain bobbed his head. "Thank you."

"But of course"—Wilfred had his knife at the ready—"it also has to taste good."

The judges took a moment to determine whether it tasted good and decided that it did.

"The apple gellee," said Wilfred Honey, with the air of

someone who didn't like having to say "gellee," "is tart but well-spiced and contrasts well with the white chocolate mousse. And the dacquoise is perfectly executed."

"But I'm not getting the saffron," added Marianne Wolvercote. "To be honest, I don't miss it—I think there's enough here already—but if you're going to the trouble of including a spice like saffron, it should bring something to the dish and I should be able to taste it."

Rosaline found herself wishing she could see Alain's expression. "Mmhm," he said. "Thanks."

"But overall"—Wilfred Honey quickly stepped in—"this is lovely. And you should be very proud of what you've achieved in the time."

As Alain walked back to his place, Rosaline avoided meeting his eye. He didn't look angry exactly. But there was definitely frustration tightening his jaw, and he'd gone a little red.

That just left her. She picked up the basket in which she had very carefully arranged her miniature entremets and brought them to the front.

"Oh my," exclaimed Wilfred Honey. "These look special."

Rosaline's heart was racing like it had the first time she'd stood here. "So these are a half-dozen fruit-themed entremets. The ones in the shape of an apple are . . . well . . . apple. And the ones in the shape of a peach are peach. And the ones in the shape of a cherry are, um, cherry."

Marianne Wolvercote stared at them so intensely it was a wonder they didn't melt. "A little gimmicky, Rosaline, but these are so beautiful that I can't complain."

"Well, I'm a simple man myself," added Wilfred Honey. "And I think an apple pudding in the shape of an apple is just fun." He carefully selected one from the basket and placed it in full view of the camera. "See. Doesn't that look fun? And the shine on it is gradely."

"As a matter of technique," agreed Marianne Wolvercote,

"the mirror glaze is excellent. Are those real apple leaves they're decorated with?"

"Yes." Rosaline nodded. "But not from my garden."

Wilfred Honey, seeming genuinely delighted, was fishing out a cherry and a peach. "It's so clever the way you've done a set. And I love that you've done a shiny finish on the apple and the cherry but a matte finish on the peaches so they look more like peaches. That's great attention to detail, that is."

"Would you like to actually taste them at any point, Wilfred?" asked Marianne Wolvercote.

"It almost seems a shame to cut into them."

Marianne Wolvercote had no such qualms. She picked up his knife and sliced all three of them in half like she was playing Fruit Ninja. "I was a bit concerned that with so much attention paid to the shape we wouldn't get proper layering, but so far so good." She took a judgemental forkful of each one. "My other concern had been that in working on three flavours you might have spread yourself too thin. But I don't think you did. These are all well-put-together, each one tastes like it's supposed to taste, and they're light and refreshing. Perfect for a summer day."

"I think"—Wilfred Honey had devoured most of the apple—"you should be very happy with what you've done here. I know I am."

And that was that.

It was over—or almost over.

Dazed...and, okay, mostly dazed...Rosaline returned dutifully to her place so Colin Thrimp could get the necessary footage of her returning dutifully to her place looking dazed.

She was still dazed as they were herded onto the lawn for the celebratory high tea that always ended the series. They were met by an idyllic scene of traditional English life: long tables piled with goodies, bunting everywhere, families happily mingling over tea and ginger beer, and, of course, the giant fucking camera crew filming it all.

"Well, I'm rooting for Rosaline," Anvita was telling Colin Thrimp, "because she's excellent and sexy."

He drooped despairingly. "You still can't say 'excellent and sexy.'"

"I think it's going to be Nora," offered Ricky, who was standing next to her, grinning and gorgeous as usual. "I mean, she's a gran. Grans know how to bake, don't they? Unlike me."

Anvita jumped back in front of the camera. "Okay, can I say my Rosaline line again? I promise I won't say I think she's sexy."

"Fine." Colin Thrimp surrendered as usual. "But please, nothing suggestive. This is a happy moment and we're going out before the watershed."

"Yes, yes." Anvita nodded impatiently. "I'm rooting for Rosaline because—oh my God, she's over there."

And Rosaline found herself nearly knocked off her feet by an overly enthusiastic optician in sparkly glasses.

"How did it go?" demanded Anvita, still hugging.

"Well, I think, but you're holding me very tightly."

"It's a sign of affection."

Anvita finally let her go—just in time for them to avoid being flattened by six grandchildren charging joyously towards Nora. It was only now Rosaline saw everyone again—most of them helping themselves to cake and chatting freely with the other contestants and their guests—that she realised how empty the last couple of weeks had been. How much she had missed the peculiar camaraderie that could spring up between strangers in a strange situation. And that was the thing about journeys, wasn't it? They weren't about where you started or where you ended. They were about who came with you.

"All right, mate?" said Harry, stepping out from the crowd.

And without thinking about it, Rosaline flung her arms around him and squeezed him Anvita-style. "I am, actually."

"It's nice catching up with everyone again." Blushing slightly, he disentangled. "I was just talking to your bloke, Anvita."

Rosaline spun round. "Your boyfriend's here?"

"Yeah, that's him." Anvita pointed to tall, well-dressed man eating a fairy cake and talking to Claudia. She cupped her hands around her mouth and called out to him. "Hey, Sanj. Look, it's Rosaline."

"Wow," said Rosaline. "You never mentioned he was a stone-cold hottie."

Anvita shrugged. "I mean, you've seen my taste in men. I thought you'd take it for granted. Besides, he's my boyfriend. We hang out all the time. I'm kinda used to it. Anyway, I have to go congratulate Nora as well. Partially because I like her but mainly so Alain knows I'm snubbing him."

And with that, she dashed off into the crowd like a bespectacled torpedo. Leaving just Rosaline and Harry surrounded by an anonymising mill of strangers.

"I can't believe it's only been a week since I last saw you," she said.

He smiled slowly at her, his eyes honeyed by the afternoon light. "Yeah, I wanted to text, but then I thought, *Don't be a ballsack, Harry, give her some space.*"

"Did you miss me then?" She was fishing shamelessly. And she didn't care.

"Course I did, mate. Like I'd be making a pie for my tea and then I'd be wondering how your practice bakes was going. Or I'd be thinking something and I'd wonder what weird thing you'd think about it. Or I'd be watching *Downton* on DVD with my nan and I'd be like, *That's what Rosaline's house looks like.*"

Laughing, she punched him lightly on the arm. Which,

admittedly, was mainly an excuse to touch him again. "Hey, that's my *parents'* house. And it's nowhere near as big as Downton Abbey."

"You got two drawing rooms is all I'm saying."

"So…" She didn't quite scuff her toe against the grass, but she moved her foot in a way that was definitely grass-related and scuff-adjacent. "You know…last week when I sort of…and you sort of?"

His smile deepened. "Yeah?"

"And how I wasn't in the right place to, well, anything really? And you didn't want to start anything with a slightly drunk person who'd just got out of a disastrous relationship with an arsehole and was in the middle of reevaluating her entire life."

"Yeah?"

"Well. I'm not drunk today. And the arsehole, like most arseholes, is behind me."

"Bloody hell." He gave her a look of affectionate bemusement. "I did miss you."

The words curled up inside her like a contented cat. "The life thing, I will admit, is a work in progress. But I've got a great kid, I look good in a pinny, and I'm a nationally recognised amateur baker. Which I think, frankly, makes me a catch."

"I reckon it does."

"Good." She gave a decisive nod. "I'm glad we're agreed."

"You was the only one weren't sure, mate."

"I'm sure now. I'm sure about a lot of things."

His gaze was half-challenging, half-teasing. "Like what?"

"This."

She kissed him. And it was exactly like she'd imagined it might be. And nothing like it at the same time. The way he met her, mouth to mouth, as familiar as home, and unfurling sweetly with all the promise of days to come and moments to share. And they and this and he could be hers. Simply for knowing she wanted them. That they were worth wanting.

Because how could she have doubted for a moment that she wanted him? This strong, kind, slightly awkward man. Her stone-cold hottie who'd always listened to her and had her back. Who made her laugh. And was kissing her now in a way she wasn't sure she'd been kissed since she was a teenager, when passion had been the easiest thing in the world to find. Except this carried with it an adult's certainty, strong hands and firm lips moving against hers and a slow, steady warmth building between them.

"Kiss," Anvita was shouting. "Kiss kiss kiss."

Rosaline de-Harryed herself. "Literally what we're doing."

"I'm encouraging you."

"Well, you failed. Because now I'm talking to you instead."

Anvita probably had a reply to that because she had a reply to most things, but it was lost to a sudden cry of "Mummy" as Amelie, trailing Lauren and Allison and Cordelia behind her, raced across the lawn. And Rosaline, caught by a moment that seemed to be everywhere and come from nowhere, and fizzed through her like lemonade in spring, broke free of the group and ran to catch her daughter in her arms.

"I love you," she whispered.

"We were in the car for ages," Amelie said. "And you're squashing me."

"I'm squashing you because I love you."

"That's not fair. I'm small and can't squash you back. But"—and here Amelie surrendered briefly to the squash—"I do love you. To the bottom of the Mariana Trench which is the deepest thing that there is and they've just found a new type of snailfish in it."

"Well," Rosaline told her, "I love you to the bottom of the Mariana Trench *and back*."

"Ummmm." There was a wavery static squeal. Someone had given Colin Thrimp a megaphone. "If we could, you know, have the finalists in front of the house and everybody else standing around being happy—remember to be happy—that would be perfect and also completely necessary. So if you could do that as in right now. Please. Thank you."

For a bunch of strangers being herded by a man with the gravitas of a whelk, they all organised themselves into appropriate positions with surprising efficiency. It turned out that if being on reality TV taught you anything, it was how to stand somewhere that looked good on-camera.

A few moments later, the host and the judges descended in state from the steps leading to the hotel.

"Contestants," began Grace Forsythe, who had no need of a megaphone, "friends, family, finalists. We've reached that moment again when *Bake Expectations* closes the ballroom doors for another year and we celebrate eight weeks of the finest baking Britain has to offer. And, of course, it's time to crown—although I say 'crown,' the budget wouldn't stretch to a crown, so it's more sort of a cake slice—our winner."

There was a pause, the timing of which spoke to her classical training.

"Much as we would love," she went on, "all of you to be victorious, there can only be one champion, and this year...and it has been a very difficult year for the judges because you're all so fabulous, so talented, so downright wonderful, but after lengthy deliberation, Wilfred and Marianne have decided that the winner..."

Pause. Another damn pause.

"Of this year's..."

Pause.

"*Bake*..."

Really? Another pause? Did that need a pause?

"*Expectations* is..."

A pause that put all other pauses to shame.

"Rosaline."

That evening's argument for why Amelie should be allowed to stay up past her bedtime was that Rosaline had won first place on a nationally televised baking competition something something so she didn't have to go to bed yet.

"It doesn't work that way," Rosaline insisted.

"Well it should. Because today is your special day and you should be allowed to celebrate it with me."

"I've been celebrating with you all day."

"It wasn't all day. I had to sit in the car with Grandma and Auntie Allison and Auntie Lauren for hours and hours and hours. And then I had to sit in the van for hours and hours and hours on the way back."

"Oi," said Harry, "don't be having a go at my van."

"Also, I was in the van as well," Rosaline pointed out.

Amelie folded her arms defiantly. "But we weren't celebrating. We were in a van."

"Amelie." It was time for Rosaline's parent voice. "Go to bed. You have school in the morning."

"But it's not fair," protested Amelie, with outraged sincerity.

"Yes, it is. You just don't like it."

"I'm not sleepy though. If I have to go to bed when I'm not sleepy it's like being in the van again except I live here so I can't leave."

Drawing back the covers, Rosaline tried to make Amelie's bed look as appealing as it could to an unsleepy eight-year-old. "This isn't a negotiation."

"Yes it is. You want me to do something and I don't want to do it."

"Technically, that's an impasse. But how about if I read you a bedtime story?"

There was a thoughtful pause. "Can Harry read it?"

Rosaline glanced over to where he was leaning in the doorway. "You don't have to."

"You will though, won't you?" said Amelie, hopping under her duvet. "You're nice."

Pushing himself upright, he took a few steps into the room. "Oh no you don't, Prime Minister. Me and my sisters used to play them games."

"Harry can read you a story"—it was still Rosaline's parent voice—"if he wants to and if you ask nicely."

As it turned out, he did want to, and she did ask nicely. And soon Rosaline and Harry were sitting by Amelie's bed, while Rosaline tried to talk them out of tackling *Twenty Thousand Leagues Under the Sea*. Amelie's copy had been a well-intentioned but, on this occasion, ill-judged gift from Cordelia and St. John. While it was certainly a very pretty edition, with art-deco sharks and submarines on the cover, the text itself remained resolutely Victorian, and despite Amelie's enthusiasm for the idea of the story, they'd never made it past the first chapter. Still, if they got lucky, the sheer density of the prose would bore Amelie to sleep.

"'The year 1886,'" Harry began valiantly, "'was signalised by a remarkable incident, a mysterious and puzzling phenomenon'— bloody hell, this is hard going, init?"

It was, indeed, hard going. And Rosaline's brain, full of entremets and victory, didn't even try to keep up.

"'Naval officers of all countries,'" Harry was saying, "'and Governments of several States were deeply interested in the matter.'"

"What matter?" asked Amelie.

"Well, we ain't been told yet. Some kind of mysterious and puzzling phenomenon."

"Maybe it's a hydrothermal vent. David Attenborough says they're mysterious and puzzling so they must have been very very puzzling in 1866."

Harry smoothed the page. "Hang on, we're getting to it. 'For some time past vessels had been met by "an enormous thing," a long object, spindle-shaped, occasionally phosphorescent and infinitely larger and more rapid in its movements than a whale.'"

"I know what phosphorescent means," offered Amelie. "It means it gives off light. Lots of things give off light in the sea because it's very dark. It could be a squid but squids aren't bigger than whales. And a blue whale is the biggest thing ever so it can't be anything. Unless it's one of those jellyfish with the fronds that go for miles and miles and miles."

"Tell you what. There's some more information here. 'The facts relating to this apparition (entered in various log-books) agreed in most respects as to the shape of the object or creature in question, the untiring rapidity of its movements, its surprising power of locomotion and the peculiar life with which it seemed endowed.'"

"That's the *same* information."

"Yeah." Harry sighed. "That's Victorians for you."

He returned to the book, back-and-forthing with Amelie about the identity of the strange monster and whether it might, in fact, be a small reef or a floating island.

"That would explain why it's bigger than a whale when nothing's bigger than a whale," said Amelie.

"Yeah, but how's it move so fast?"

"Maybe it's a rocket-powered island."

They reached the end of the chapter, with neither Amelie nor the seafaring folk of the 1860s much the wiser as to what was going on.

"Now," Harry concluded. "'It was the "monster" who justly or unjustly was accused of their disappearance and, thanks to it, communication between the different continents became more and more dangerous. The public demanded sharply that the seas should, at any price, be relieved from this formidable cetacean.'"

Amelie tucked Mary Shelley under the covers with her. "That means a whale. But they keep saying it's not a whale and it's a reef, which is stupid. This book is stupid. The Victorians were stupid."

"Yes," said Rosaline. "They were."

And kissing her daughter goodnight, she left Amelie to dream of spindle-shaped objects.

Probably the decorous thing to do would have been to go downstairs and put the kettle on. But Rosaline was a single mum who had won the nation's favourite baking competition and she wasn't in a decorous mood. Catching Harry by his T-shirt, she reeled him into her bedroom. No sooner were they over the threshold than he kissed her again.

"Is that all right?" he asked, already breathless. "Been wanting to since Anvita interrupted."

"More than all right."

She kissed him back—and it roared through her like a motorcycle. Because she'd been wanting this, too, and waiting for it. All the way through the congratulations and the well-wishes. All the way home. All the way through Jules fucking Verne. Because while her life was full of good things, friends and family and baking and a whole new future, this one was just for her.

Like before, they started sweetly enough—not-quite brushes of lips to lips—but it didn't stay that way for long, not once Rosaline discovered she was in no mood to be sweet. She was in a seeking mood. A taking mood. A hungry mood. And Harry was perfect, his mouth as eager as hers, and his body a solid weight that bore her to the bed, the strength of him a kind of liberation in those moments. An invitation, even, encouraging the rough clutch of her hands and the eager arch of her hips.

"I think," Rosaline said, tugging at his T-shirt, "I need this off. Right the fuck now."

Harry pushed himself to his knees between her legs—looking

flushed and tousled, his mouth slightly red from her kisses. "You sure?"

"Fuck yes, I'm sure. I want to tell Anvita all about it."

"I know you're joking but please don't. I'd be embarrassed."

Slipping her palms beneath the hem of his T-shirt, she inched them upwards, the ridges of his abs against her palms. "You are aware she says you're a stone-cold hottie and I really *really* agree?"

"Well, she has got pretty good taste. Sanj seems like a top bloke."

"And I'm glad to say my taste in blokes is definitely improving."

"Don't let it get too good. You might dump me."

He dragged off his T-shirt and Rosaline took a moment—okay, several moments—to appreciate it. He had a faint tan, of the "goes outdoors in summer" rather than "spray" or "bed" variety, and clearly got his money's worth from his gym membership, his body defined but not consciously built. A tattoo of an angel's wing covered one pec, and the words "Audere est Facere"—which she suspected was a football thing—followed the curve of his collarbone on the other side, the dark ink in perfect contrast to all that smooth skin and hard muscle. Anvita would have lost her shit.

"I think," Rosaline said, "dumping you is very unlikely."

He laughed. "You're proper shallow sometimes, mate. I feel very objectified."

"How about we objectify each other?" Rosaline de-bloused with a flourish.

Harry's eyes flicked down and then up again. "Sounds good to me. Fucking hell, you're fit." He drew her in for another deep kiss. "And like"—he was openly blushing now, his fingers curled gently in her hair—"really pretty. Like princess pretty."

"Very few brunette princesses."

"There's Belle. And she's the best one, ain't she?"

"I'll take it."

She settled back on her bed and drew Harry down with her. More kisses, hotter and deeper, rough with breath and the occasional moan, as they moved together. Beneath her hands, the muscles of his back rose and fell like waves—and she allowed herself simply to enjoy him. To want what she wanted. A man she could revel in and depend on and dig her nails into.

He teased her bra straps from her shoulders, his lips moving softly over the band of newly exposed skin. They made her shiver, those small, unexpected touches, soothing away a couple of tender spots where the elastic had rubbed. And slowly he worked his way downwards, his tongue exploring the ridges of her collarbone, and his mouth pressing kisses over the tops of her breasts. Sliding a hand behind her back he unhooked her bra, with a deftness that suggested practice, and she arched up to help him get her out of it. His thumbs brushed her nipples as his hands cupped her, and then he lowered his head to kiss her again.

"Not your thing then?" he asked, glancing up again a second or two later.

She froze, instantly self-conscious. "No, no, it's fine."

"Hoping for better than fine, mate."

"Well, I mean"—great, now she was blushing—"people like breasts."

"Yeah. And you've got great tits, but I like you enjoying yourself more."

"I'm not *not* enjoying myself."

He grinned and traced his tongue up the side of her neck—making her flash hot and cold and shuddery. "*That's* you enjoying yourself."

"Yes, but—"

"Look, I get it. Some birds don't get much out of having their boobs touched. It's all right. Everyone's different. I'm weird about my ears."

"So I shouldn't blow in them then?"

"Not if you want this to go well, no." He nipped at her shoulder, kissing into the hollows, until she was back to wriggling and clutching at him. "Though while we're at it, I should probably check how far you wanna take this."

"Um...what?"

"Well, you know. Don't wanna do anything you're not up for. But don't wanna leave you hanging either."

Somehow, Rosaline hadn't expected this kind of directness. She'd always secretly suspected there was a chunk missing from the middle of her sex life. When she was a teenager, she hadn't had a clue, but she and Lauren, and Tom for that matter, had been horny enough that it didn't matter. And then when Amelie was old enough that Rosaline could start dating again, everyone else seemed so confident they knew what they were doing, she hadn't quite had the courage to disagree.

Harry pushed himself onto an elbow, gazing down at her with a slightly bewildering combination of passion and consideration in his eyes. "You all right, mate? We can stop whenever you want. Doesn't mean I'm not into it. Just want to make really sure you're into it too."

"I'm definitely into it," she said hastily. "I'm just not used to talking about it."

"Neither's anyone else, but, I dunno, it helps. Like, how do I know what you like, if you don't tell me what you like?"

"Okay, but that's...that's...scary."

"Yeah, but it's better than crap sex, init?" He trailed a hand lightly up and down her side. "I mean, I'm not saying you have to give me a list up front. Just, y'know, talk to me. Tell me if you want more of something, or less of something, or if I'm going too far or not far enough."

"Right, but what do you want? This can't only be about me."

"Mate, I'm a bloke. It's not complicated. I'm half-naked with a girl I fancy who wants to be with me. I'm well made up."

"But that's not helpful either," protested Rosaline. "If you want me to tell you what I want, you have to tell me what you want."

Again, one of those searching, hopeful, slightly vulnerable looks. "As long as you don't think I'm trying to pressure you into nothing, I reckon I'd want to keep doing this. Figure out what gets you off. I reckon that'd get me off."

"ExceptIdonthaveanycondoms."

He laughed. "That's all right."

"It's bloody well not all right. I got pregnant thinking it was all right."

"I didn't mean that. I just mean, we can do other stuff."

"Oh." She fell back against the pillow, faintly embarrassed. "Although, actually, there's a twenty-four-hour Tesco's down the road if you want to."

"Not really, mate. I'd rather stay here."

"You won't feel...cheated or like you wasted your time?"

He looked mostly amused. But only mostly. "Fucking hell. How do you ever get any?"

"I do fine, thank you. But in my experience men like to...y'know. Have sex."

"We are having sex. Or we was. Now we're having a conversation. But come on, you've been with girls, you must know sex don't have to mean getting a cock up your muff."

"I do know that," she told him. "It's just most straight people haven't got the memo."

"Well, I've got three sisters, and one of them's married to a girl. So...I did. Now, how do you feel about me getting you off? Unless you'd rather carry on having a debate about it."

"I...I've killed the mood, haven't I?"

"Mate, I know I keep saying this, but I'm a bloke. You're hot and you've got your tits out. The mood's not going nowhere."

Rosaline reached up and ran her fingers over his tattoo,

following the detailing on the feathers, and then—on the other side—the letters as they flowed into each other. "I like these."

"Got 'em a while ago. Bit teenage really, aren't they? But me and Terry had 'em done for his eighteenth—he had a bunch of things he wanted, with like, meaning and shit, and I thought well, the wing was pretty and the club motto looks better in Latin."

"Honestly," Rosaline admitted, "I did something similar when I was sixteen." She rolled over to show him her back. "I went with one of my best friends at the time—this girl called Antonia, I haven't seen her in years—and we both decided to get butterflies. And she came out with this tiny little thing on her hip, and I was already one session deep into, well, these."

Leaning over her, Harry pressed a deep, warm kiss to her shoulder blade. "Go big or go home, init."

His hands meandered across her back, the calluses on his fingers slightly rough against her skin, and she sighed, lost in the simple sensuality of it. It was strange, because she couldn't see him now, but she never lost her awareness that it was him—there was something so *familiar* in his touch, something unmistakably Harry, that reminded her of eating fish fingers at her kitchen table and running away from a goat in the dark. It made her feel sort of safe and sort of tender and sort of like ripping the rest of his clothes off and claiming him: someone she almost hadn't let herself want.

She wriggled back round, reaching for his belt. "You know how I was going to tell you what I liked? I think I'd like you to be more naked."

"I think"—he grinned—"I'd like you to be more naked and all."

There followed a few clumsy moments of buttons and buckles and denim on denim, and the sudden realisation of being exposed in a fully lit room. Thankfully, Harry was very much worth it—and, by the best available evidence, seemed to think she was, too, for all she'd made no particular effort in that direction. He pressed her back onto the bed, kissing her hard, his hand between her legs, teasing and seeking.

"So…" His eyes held hers, full of intent. "You got anything in your bedside drawer you like?"

Oh God, she was blushing. "Aren't the contents of a girl's bedside drawer meant to be private?"

"Even to the bloke what's trying to get you off?"

"I…um. Isn't it cheating?"

And now he was laughing, his breath rippling against her neck. "Look, if you ask me to fix a plug, I'll borrow a screwdriver."

"I'm not a broken piece of electrical equipment," she protested.

"It's not about that. It's about using the best tool for the job."

"Haven't you already got a tool for the job?"

He gave her one of his slow smiles. "Got a bunch of tools for the job, mate. But nothing wrong with a bit of variety. You don't have to if you don't want to."

"No, it's fine," said Rosaline squeakily. "It's just I haven't got that much. I'm not the dodgy end of Etsy."

"I'm not leaving a review. I thought you might enjoy it is all."

Propping herself on her side, Rosaline nervously opened the drawer in her bedside table and peered inside as if she wasn't sure what she'd find. "I've got a couple of vibrators and a rose quartz dildo that Lauren got me for a joke."

"Pass us your favourite."

"I'm not sure I've got a favourite."

"Everyone's got a favourite."

And, actually, he was right. After a moment's hesitation, she handed him the slightly overdesigned bullet vibe she tended to fall back on. It looked totally different in Harry's hand—not, admittedly, that she'd spent that much time really looking at it. Using the very tip of it, he traced a line down her body, the coolness in notable contrast to the warmth of his fingers.

He let out a long breath. "Fuck me, mate. Can't believe we're here."

"Me neither," she admitted, lifting her leg to brush a knee gently along his side. "But I'm glad we are."

"Hold that thought."

And with that, he sprawled out on his stomach, and went down with a confidence that Rosaline was briefly, but only briefly, too startled to enjoy.

He started low-key—brushes of his lips against her thighs and over her hips, the teasing press of his tongue spreading her open, drawing little gasps from her—letting the anticipation gather slowly inside her, as rich and sweet and inevitable as sugar melting into caramel. Normally too much of this sort of thing left Rosaline self-conscious, not wanting to be greedy or selfish, or take too much of her allotted time in the unspoken negotiation of who got who off when. But it was hard to think about anything right then, except the heat of his mouth and the circling of his fingers and the occasional whirr of her vibrator. It was a little bit amazing how good it felt, all those sensations, layered together and coming together—this perfect alchemy of care, passion, and a certain expertise. And she quickly lost track of time, slipping almost effortlessly into the world of her body, where she was indulged and pleasured and cared for.

When she came it was a toe-curling rush that swept through her in endless waves, leaving her shaky and breathless and a little bit giggly on the sheer release of it.

"All right, mate?" Harry reappeared from between her legs, flushed and smiling.

"I'm very all right. Are you all right?"

"Couldn't be better. Got me girl off, didn't I?"

She settled limply against the pillows. "Oh, I'm your girl now, am I?"

"Sorry. I just mean, like, I like it when people like it. And I especially like you liking it 'cos I like you."

"Well," she told him, "I really, *really* liked it."

He crawled up the bed to lie beside her, and she turned to kiss him—tasting herself on his lips, which was an odd, possessive thrill. "Say when and we can do it again."

"What about you?"

"Got plenty of time for that."

"No, but"—she rolled onto her side to face him—"I want to."

Taking her wrist, he guided her between their bodies and to his very...*there*...erection. She gripped it slightly tentatively. This was the problem with men, you never knew if you were doing too much or too little, whether you should be passing the baton in a relay or trying to get ketchup out of the bottle.

"Bit harder," he murmured, covering her hand with this. "Yeah, like that. That's good."

She was surprised by the intimacy of it—his cock and their hands, the drag of skin against skin against skin as he helped her learn what he enjoyed. And lying as they were, facing each other, she got to see him react to her touch: the oddly vulnerable flutter of his lashes, the shapes his mouth made when he gasped or moaned or muttered her name, the tightening of his brow in that weird intensity of pleasure-pain as she brought him close to the edge. It still undid her a little, how willing Harry was to show himself to her and give himself to her, and it made her want to do the same. To put aside everything she'd once thought she should have been and build something else—something true— for herself. With him.

With everyone she loved.

Autumn

Tuesday

"DON'T HOLD HER like that," Anvita shouted. "She's the queen of France."

Rosaline hastily backed away from the Marie Antoinette cake that was currently occupying more of her hallway than any item of patisserie had a reasonable right to. "I'm sorry, but she's going to have to get round the corner somehow."

"I'm going to drop her. Seriously, I'm going to drop her." That was Sanjay from somewhere on the other side of Anvita's multitiered masterpiece.

"If you drop her," Anvita told him, "I am leaving you for Ricky."

"Do I get a say in that?" Ricky's voice drifted through the front room. "Because I'm sort of seeing someone."

"You should have brought him, her, or them." Lauren. Of course.

Ricky made a sheepish nineteen-year-old noise. "We're not really at the 'come watch me on TV with a bunch of strangers I met on TV' stage of our relationship."

"Is that a stage?" asked Rosaline.

"It is when you've been on TV."

"Guys"—Sanjay's voice had risen sharply—"Marie Antoinette is in genuine danger."

"It's all right." Terry emerged from the living room into a

hallway that was already struggling to contain its occupants and certainly couldn't cope with the addition of a six-foot-two gym bunny. "I've got it."

The immediate chorus of "Terry, don't" got as far as "Terry, do—" before Terry did. And to his credit, he managed to get Marie Antoinette all the way to the coffee table before stepping on one of Amelie's Legos, hopping in pain, and dumping the whole thing into Ricky's lap.

And for a moment, there was a reverent silence for the second demise of Marie Antoinette.

Then Harry called through from the kitchen. "Is what just happened what I think just happened?"

"That depends," said Amelie, who was on the floor with Allison, building a shark from what was left of the Lego, "on what you think just happened. If you think that a big jellyfish came out the ceiling and stung everybody then no. But if you think that Terry dropped a huge cake all over the place then yes."

Harry groaned. "Tel you total knobhead."

"I was trying to help," protested Terry, managing to look genuinely aggrieved. "It's fine. I'll—"

"No!" shouted everybody.

"Let me get some napkins," said Rosaline. "I'm pretty sure we can salvage most of it. Ricky, do you mind staying where you are for a second?"

Ricky blinked. "I've got a cake the size of a small Labrador in my lap. Where do you think I'm going?"

Ten minutes later, Ricky was mostly de-macaroned, and everyone was tucking into what remained of Marie Antoinette.

"You know"—Anvita chewed thoughtfully—"I think it still went better than it did on the show."

Terry was wearing an utterly unwarranted expression of vindication. "See, tastes all right. Not like I wrecked it or nothing."

"Mate." Harry appeared with a golden-brown filo pie that he

set down very carefully on a table already slightly overflowing with baked goods. "I'd say quit while you was ahead but you ain't ahead."

"Your pie looks beautiful, Harry," offered Allison, with the flawless social grace of—arguably—the only real grown-up in the room.

He blushed slightly. "Thanks. It's spinach and feta, so we can all have a bit."

"You didn't have to," said Sanjay. "Even with half of it on the floor, Anvita's cake is going to last for days."

"It's fine, mate. I've been trying to learn some veggie cooking anyway, but the old man complains if you try to feed it to him. He's all like, 'This ain't a pie, it's a salad in a crust.'"

Pushing herself off Sanjay's lap, Anvita prowled around Harry's blameless pie. "Good colour," she drawled, in her best Marianne Wolvercote. "Surprisingly sophisticated considering what a gargantuan hunkmuffin you are."

"You know," remarked Sanjay, "it's a good job I'm secure in my masculinity or I might be threatened by the amount of time you spend calling other men hunkmuffins."

"Are you not flattered?" asked Anvita. "That I have chosen you, and only you, above the vast array of hunkmuffins I see constantly around me?"

Lauren yanked the cork from a bottle of red and poured herself a Laurenly measure. "That's a refreshingly sensible attitude for a heterosexual."

"Yep." Anvita nodded emphatically. "Sensible is absolutely a thing that I am."

Allison was briefly distracted from whatever shark-related Lego conversation she'd been having with Amelie. "Please don't encourage my wife. And, Lauren darling, stop othering the straights."

Wiping a smear of Swiss meringue buttercream off the screen, Ricky checked his phone. "Guys. Show's starting."

With part of the advance for her first recipe book, Rosaline had defied years of her middle-class upbringing and bought a bigger television. An investment that had ambiguously paid off by allowing Amelie to watch squoogly fish in high-definition. Digging the remote from its habitual hiding place behind the sofa cushions, she flicked to iPlayer while Harry dimmed the lights. Her guests, who still didn't quite fit in her living room, did their best to huddle into what seating was available. Terry—true to his knobhead nature—had claimed the only armchair, though Lauren—never one to be out-knobheaded—had perched herself on the arm in as annoying a position as possible. Amelie and Allison were on the floor surrounded by Lego, and the two-seater sofa was already overfilled with Ricky, Sanjay, and Anvita. So Harry stood against the wall, and Rosaline stood against Harry, his arms folded gently around her.

"And now," said the announcer, for the benefit of the twelve people who were still watching live television, "it's a brand-new series of *Bake Expectations*."

The screen came alive in shades of green and blue and gold as the eye of the camera swooped across the British countryside, through the gates of Patchley House, up the long gravel drive, and finally alighted on the dapper figure of Grace Forsythe.

Harry's hands tightened over Rosaline's. "Hope I don't come across as too much of a ballsack," he whispered.

"You won't. And even if you do, who gives a fuck."

"Be honest with you, mate. I give a little bit of a fuck."

"Oh my God," shrieked Anvita. "It's me. And I look *fiiiiiine*."

Amelie had got close enough to the screen that it was both bad for her eyes and other people's viewing experience. "Where's Mummy? Where's Mummy?"

"There's Dave," said Ricky. "I really wanted to like him. But I think he might have been a prick."

"He's wearing a fedora, mate." That was Terry, craning awkwardly past Lauren. "Sure sign of a wanker."

Half turning, Lauren contrived to get in Terry's way to a frankly impressive extent. "Excuse me? I own several fedoras."

"It's okay, Loz." Rosaline nestled deeper into Harry's embrace. "There's different rules for lesbians."

"It's Mummy," cried Amelie, pointing helpfully. "Mummy, you look pretty."

"Excuse me," Rosaline told her, "I look like somebody who is going to win this whole damn thing."

Except…she didn't. She looked like somebody who'd missed her train, tried to impress an arsehole by lying to him, and had no idea what she wanted or what she was doing. But that was okay.

Because she was going to work it out.

Since Leaving the Competition

DAVE dropped out of university to travel round Nepal and has not been seen since.

FLORIAN and his partner Scott are still not married. They still do not care.

RICKY has completed his degree and now works for Procter & Gamble, a job he describes as "a bit of a laugh."

CLAUDIA returned to her legal practice, but still bakes at weekends.

JOSIE continues to bake for children and her husband's parishioners. Apparently they like her payne foundewe even if the judges didn't.

ANVITA has qualified as an optician and is finally engaged to her boyfriend. Her nan is very proud of her.

HARRY is still working as an electrician with his dad, but has started running hands-on cooking classes in primary schools on his days off. His nieces' friends continually ask him for mermaid cakes.

NORA turned down a six-figure book deal, saying, "It's just cakes; throw it in a bowl and see what happens."

ALAIN launched his own cooking-themed YouTube channel called The Cotswold Baker. It currently has 247 subscribers.

ROSALINE is now a full-time cookery writer. She and Amelie live in a house that no longer has aliens in the boiler. They are currently negotiating pet options between a very small dog that Amelie feels should be called Anglerfish or a tank of hissing cockroaches.

Grace Forsythe, Marianne Wolvercote,
Wilfred Honey, Colin Thrimp,
and Jennifer Hallett return next season on
Bake Expectations with a delightful
new group of bakers in
Paris Daillencourt Is About to Crumble!

Available Summer 2022

READING GROUP GUIDE

A LETTER FROM THE AUTHOR

Dear Reader,

I was asked to put something here for people who are reading *Rosaline Palmer Takes the Cake* as part of a book club. Which I thought was a lovely idea until I realised that what it meant in practice was that you probably only read the book because someone else in your club picked it. And, you know, good on them. Or, if it was you, good on you. And, hopefully, you're not currently feeling that they/you made a horrendous mistake.

As you might have noticed, I'm finding this section a little bit awkward, partly because I'm British and am therefore required by law to find everything awkward. But partly because it just seems a bit odd to be asking you questions about my own book. I've always been a big proponent of the Death of the Author—and I feel it's really important for readers to have as much space as possible to decide what's important to them about what they've read and to draw their own conclusions.

But discussion questions have been requested. So, discussion questions you shall have. Please do feel very much at liberty to ignore them and talk about whatever the hell you want. And thank you again for taking a chance on one of my books.

Lots of love,
Alexis Hall

QUESTIONS FOR DISCUSSION

1. Screw it. Let's start with the big one. Do you think Rosaline made the right choice, back when she was nineteen? Sure, by the end of the book she is in an unambiguously happy place where there is nothing she would change about her life. But she was *nineteen*. That is a hell of a young age to be committing to a set future.

2. Double screw it, let's dig deeper into that question. If you think Rosaline made the right choice, how far would you take that? Is it *only* the right choice because deep down she realised she didn't want to be a doctor? Or is getting pregnant at nineteen just as valid a choice? And, if so, what implications does that have for the way, we as a culture, approach teenage pregnancy?

   If you think Rosaline made the wrong choice, on the other hand, what does that mean in practice? It certainly seems harsh on Amelie, who has clearly had a very happy childhood. True, Rosaline has obviously suffered emotionally because of the choices she made, but isn't part of that *because* people keep telling her it was the wrong one?

3. Okay, how about a slightly lighter question. Would you rather be an anglerfish or a sarcastic fringehead? Why?

4. Back on the subject of Rosaline's choices, how do you feel about Harry? Superficially, it seems like Rosaline chooses quite a traditional life at the end of the book, settling down with a child and a romantic partner. But how conventional is it really? What do you expect Rosaline and Harry's relationship to *look* like after the show? Will Lauren still be such a big part of Rosaline's life? If so, is that a problem? If not is *that* a problem?

5. Did you know what ceps are? Be honest.

6. The British class system is a near-constant concern for many characters, especially the Palmers. What examples stood out to you? If you're British, what examples stood out to you that you *don't think would stand out to non-Brits*? If you're not British, was there anything that either reflected similar social concerns in your own country or struck you as genuinely foreign and weird?

7. At what point (I hope I don't have to say "if any" but just in case "if any") did you realise Alain was a total shit that nobody should touch with a barge pole? If you realised early, could you at least sympathize with Rosaline's reasons for taking longer?

8. The giant marble run with the magnets that the Palmers buy for Amelie is real. How much do you want one?

9. Let's talk about sex, baby. Sorry, that's an incredibly dated reference. The way Harry and Rosaline's relationship develops, they never actually have penetrative sex on-page. How did you feel about that? What do you think it says about her

relationship with Harry compared to her relationship with Alain? What do you think it says about sex in general?

10. Somehow I've got this far without asking any questions about baking or *Bake Expectations*. How does the way the book is structured as days and weeks on a TV show instead of chapters in a novel affect the flow of the story? How did it affect your experience of reading? How does the way the contestants bake express their character? If you want to go full high school English class, you can discuss a specific bake and what it tells you about a specific person. But I won't hold it against you if you don't.

11. When I decided to write a love triangle with a bisexual protagonist one of the things I had to think about was the gender identities of her two romantic interests. In the end I made both of them men because I thought it was really important to emphasize that Rosaline's bisexuality isn't invalidated just because she's never in an on-page relationship with a woman. But that wasn't the only call I could have made about the love triangle. What other choices could I have made? And what implications would they have had?

12. In an early draft of the book, Rosaline's parents didn't appear directly. How do you think this would have changed the story? Would you have felt differently about Rosaline if you hadn't met the people who raised her?

RECIPES

Harry's Cheesy Bites

Makes about 24

I got this recipe off my nan and she told me she got it off her nan, but I asked my granddad and he says she got it from some bloke what was on the telly in 1973.

½ cup water
½ cup milk
A big pinch of salt
1 cup butter (2 sticks)
1 cup flour
Four large eggs
3½ ounces cheese, grated
A bit of pepper
A bit of nutmeg

Preheat the oven to 400°F/200°C. Don't forget about this because you'll feel a right prat.

Line two baking trays with greaseproof paper.

Put the water, the milk, the salt, and the butter in a saucepan. Stir while bringing it to a boil. Add the flour and stir it for a couple of minutes until you got a smooth dough that pulls away from the side of the pan.

Put the dough in a bowl and let it cool down for a bit.

Beat the eggs into the dough one at a time. This takes a bit of welly and it don't half make your arms hurt if you're not used to it.

Mix most of the cheese. When we done it on the show they said to use Gruyère 'cause of how it's French but it works fine if you only got cheddar.

Add the pepper and the nutmeg. You'll have to guess how much is right until you're used to it and you know what you like.

Put all the dough in a piping bag. This gets well messy and if you've got a kid helping you they'll get covered but it's just dough, init?

Pipe out little blobs of dough onto the baking tray. They should be a couple of inches apart and about as big as a tablespoon. If you're doing it on TV make 'em all the same size but if it's for your family or your mates, don't bother. Also, my granddad said the bloke what did it on TV used spoons.

Sprinkle your leftover cheese over the top. If you ain't got any leftover cheese grate some more.

Stick them in the oven for twenty minutes or until they puff up and go all golden brown.

Give 'em to whoever you're making 'em for. Or stick 'em in the fridge for later.

Rosaline's Other Cream Liqueurs Are Available Shortbreads

These are my latest version of the biscuits I made on the show. They don't have much of a kick to them, but they're rich and buttery and go down well at viewing parties.

Makes about 15

Mummy said I could help write this recipe because I might want to be a baker when I grow up. My bits are in italics because italics are what you use to write things that are important.

For the shortbread:

1 cup butter
½ cup light brown sugar
2 cups flour
½ teaspoon baking powder
a pinch of salt

For the filling:

½ cup butter
1½ cups icing sugar
2 tablespoons Irish cream liqueur *(This is the bit that makes it not-for-Amelie biscuits, which is discrimination)*
1 teaspoon vanilla extract

Preheat the oven to 350°F/180°C (320°F/160°C for a fan oven) and prepare one or two baking trays lined with greaseproof paper.

I can do this bit because I can reach the knobs but once I put it on 220 to see if mummy would notice and she didn't and then the biscuits were burned.

Cream the butter and brown sugar together. You can do this in a bowl, a food processor, or a stand mixer depending on what you have in your kitchen.

Sometimes mummy does this by hand and I help but it's really hard because the butter is really thick and then we put it in the mixer and it does it for us.

Add the flour, baking powder, and pinch of salt to the mixture and mix until smooth. Then get your hands in and squeeze it into a ball.

This is the best bit because you get dough all over your hands but if you lick your fingers you have to wash your hands again because it's unhygienic, which means it can make you ill.

Roll the dough out to ¼ of an inch (or 1 centimetre) thick on a floured surface and cut out your biscuits using a small round cutter. Although, actually, I use a champagne flute, which probably says bad things about my lifestyle.

I can't help with this bit unless I stand on a stool.

Transfer the biscuits to the baking tray and bake until golden brown. This should take about 15 minutes, but it's worth checking after twelve. It's also worth checking your daughter hasn't changed the settings on the oven.

I only did that once.

Once the biscuits are ready, remove from the oven and leave to cool.

If you're very good you can eat one of the biscuits now before the not-for-Amelie filling goes in.

While you're waiting for the biscuits to cool, beat the butter and icing sugar together until smooth. Then add the other cream liqueurs are available and the vanilla extract and beat the whole thing together.

I tried a bit of this when mummy wasn't looking and it was okay but a bit funny tasting.

Spread a generous helping of the other cream liqueurs are available buttercream on half the shortbreads, and sandwich them with the other half. The filling can sometimes be a bit squishy, so you might want to pop them in the fridge to firm up. Alternatively, you might want to pop them on a high shelf so your daughter can't steal them.

And that's how you make the discrimination biscuits! I helped even though I'm not allowed to eat the biscuits because I have a generous hearty nature and a sympathy with all poor men, like the spirit of Christmas present.

Goodbye! Enjoy the biscuits!

Alain's Celebrated Chocolate Cake with Basil Buttercream

I've refined this recipe considerably since the version I debuted on the first episode, and so you may find that your results don't wholly match those you might remember from the series. I do, however, think that this version is strictly superior.

For the cake:

1¾ cups caster sugar
1¾ cups plain flour
1 cup cocoa powder (unsweetened)
1½ teaspoons bicarbonate of soda
1½ teaspoons baking soda
1½ teaspoons salt
Two large eggs
½ cup sunflower oil (you may substitute any other flavourless oil if you wish)
1 cup buttermilk (you can substitute whole milk)
1 tablespoon vanilla extract
¾ cup boiling water

For the buttercream:

½ cup unsalted butter
A handful of fresh basil leaves, torn (I use about ten, but you can vary this to taste)
½ cup mascarpone
3 cups icing sugar

A pinch of salt

Fresh basil leaves to decorate

Preheat the oven to 350°F/180°C (or around 330°F or 165°C if using a fan oven). Then grease and line two eight-inch cake tins.

In a large mixing bowl, whisk together the sugar, flour, cocoa powder, baking powder, bicarbonate of soda, and salt. In a second, smaller bowl, combine the eggs, sunflower oil, buttermilk, and vanilla extract (the oil will naturally separate itself, so you will need to mix these well and vigorously). Mix the wet ingredients into the dry ingredients and add the boiling water. Everything should combine to give a smooth, slightly runny batter that pours easily.

Divide the batter equally between the two cake tins and bake for between twenty-five and thirty minutes. You will, I am sure, already know how to tell when a cake is done and if you don't I direct you to some of my simpler recipes. When the cakes are cooked through, remove them from the oven and leave them to cool.

While the cakes are cooling, you may turn your attention to the icing.

Melt the butter in a small saucepan and add the basil leaves. Cook for fifteen minutes over a low heat, stirring intermittently. Then strain out the leaves, and transfer the butter to a small bowl. Leave it to cool in the freezer for five to ten minutes, until slightly thickened.

Once the basil-infused butter has thickened, beat it into the mascarpone, then gradually add the icing sugar and a pinch of salt.

When the cakes have fully cooled, level them as you will have seen me do several times on the show, and assemble the cake, separating the halves with a generous layer of the buttercream.

Ensure the icing on top of the cake is smooth (I recommend a palette knife or offset spatula for the purpose) and decorate *sparingly* with leaves of fresh basil.

Bon appétit.

YOUR
BOOK
CLUB
RESOURCE

VISIT
GCPClubCar.com

to sign up for the **GCP Club Car** newsletter, featuring exclusive promotions, info on other **Club Car** titles, and more.

 @grandcentralpub

 @grandcentralpub

 @grandcentralpub

About the Author

ALEXIS HALL lives in a little house in the South East of England, where he writes books about people who bake far better than he does. He can, however, whip up a passable brownie if pressed.